# THE COLLAR OF HONOUR

THE CHRONICLES OF VENARY

# THE
# COLLAR
## OF
# HONOUR

P. W. JACOB

Matador
9 Priory Business Park,
Wistow Road, Kibworth Beauchamp,
Leicestershire. LE8 0RX
Tel: 0116 279 2299
Email: books@troubador.co.uk
Web: www.troubador.co.uk/matador
Twitter: @matadorbooks

ISBN 978 1 8004 6535 0

British Library Cataloguing in Publication Data.
A catalogue record for this book is available from the British Library.

Printed and bound in Great Britain by 4edge Limited
Typeset in 11pt Adobe Garamond Pro by Troubador Publishing Ltd, Leicester, UK

Matador is an imprint of Troubador Publishing Ltd

For my nephew Harry.
I promised you a story.
Uncle Phil

# PROLOGUE

I F YOU HEAD towards our sun (preferably at night) and remember to turn left you will find a pocket universe where evolution took a different turn. When the only sun cooled it went too far, and no creature on the universe's sole planet without fur, wings or scales could possibly survive. So, without humans to mess things up the planet Venary threw up diverse animal life, and never developed an obsession with a chain of identical coffee shops or flashing rectangles.

The planet is in many ways similar to our own, except there are fewer oceans. Bad news for the fish but it does make travel between the realms so much simpler. The poles are cold like ours, although in a twist the animals there really don't like it. So much so that the Brundians (a species of flightless bird with oiled skin, beady eyes and a fierce intellect) are unique in that they were the first species of any universe to invent the four-bar electric fire before the wheel, and promptly drowned ninety per cent of the population within four months. The survivors huddle together on the floating ice land of Brundia, desperately trying to refreeze the oceans and repopulate the species. So successful have they been in the latter, and so hopeless have they been in the former, that they hold a ceremony every year where the oldest Brundians are thrown into the ocean to create space for the new generation. The ceremony is known amongst the young as "The Great Opportunity", and amongst the old as "Bugger This For a Laugh". Proof if proof were needed that as long as a species gets regular sex they'll put up with almost anything.

In another difference to our own planet Venary almost lazily floats through its' universe and its' rotation is best described as lackadaisical. Once cycle is the same as three days on Earth and one span would be three years.

In the old cycles there were no kings, no rulers, and the various tribes would war and trade amongst themselves. This was until the Family Mowser made a stand. At first glance there appeared to be nothing unique about the Mowsers, they were typical Rodentians. That is to say, they were small, furry, long of whisker and tail, and prey to pretty much every animal on the planet. Most Rodentians were resigned to their lot in life. If a species could have a motto theirs would be "Oh well, can't complain". Rodentians lived in huge communes in the mountains of the Western Isles. Most Rodentians rarely left the safety of the caves, the only exception being those brave souls who volunteered for raiding parties. Songs were sung in honour of the raiding parties who travelled unimaginable distances to bring back hearty fare for their people. Many foraging parties never returned. Those who did were often disfigured and missing body parts. Even so it was considered an honour to have a raider in your family.

Perix Mowser had tried for many cycles to get onto a raiding party, only to be refused on every occasion. It wasn't that he was too weak or slow (he was in fact large for a rodent and despite his size could run very quickly), he was distrusted because he was too intelligent. It was Perix who suggested an alliance with the Hedgeons and Molexs. He proposed that if all of the smaller animals got together then raiding parties could take place at all hours rather than waiting for pre-dawn when most predators were still asleep. He reasoned that the Hedgeons could offer protection to parties by marching on either side and using their long spikes to form a protective barrier over the rest and that the Molexs would allow access to their many tunnels. It was an excellent and popular suggestion which had full support until he suggested that the Hedgeons and Molexs should pay for the "privilege of joining the noble endeavour" and that "they should feel proud to lay down their lives for the greater cause". While many of his fellow Rodentians supported this suggestion, there were more who felt that he was a dangerous supremacist. Funnily enough, however, he did get a measure of support from some in the Hedgeon and Molex camps. During the arguments that followed his suggestions Perix realised that if he could create this much influence with raiding parties, what could he do if he had the ear of the leader?

Charex wasn't just big for a rodent, he was big for a mammal! He had been leader for many cycles now but the bloodstains of previous leader Scrix were still marking the walls and his skin adorned the throne room floor. Charex's coup had been the bloodiest in living memory and as a result nobody felt inclined to challenge him. Charex had led more raiding parties than any other Rodentian in existence. Stories were still told of his first excursion when he returned wearing a severed bird's head as a hat and mystic symbols painted on his chest in blood. He was a fearsome sight. As time wore on Charex's legend grew and Scrix became more and more paranoid. He would lock himself away and refused to welcome the raiding parties on their return, but still Charex's popularity grew. Eventually Scrix hit upon an idea. One early morning he sought out Charex in the weapons room. Charex was testing the weight of a huge club with spikes protruding from the top, pointing in every direction. He was rhythmically swinging the club over his head and slamming it into an old flour bag stuffed with straw. Scrix nervously noted that the club often became stuck in the sack. No matter how embedded the club appeared to be Charex would just wrench it free. There was a lot of straw littered all over the floor, indicating that Charex had been at this endeavour for quite some time and it hadn't seemed to tire him at all. Back and forth he swung the club, a feverish look in his eyes. He seemed to be in a world of his own.

"Ahem," muttered Scrix, disgusted that he was unable to prevent his nasally high voice going even higher out of nervousness. The massive warrior still swung his massive club back and forth. "Ahem," Scrix squeaked again, quickly followed by a muffled oath as he threw himself to the floor.

The reason for this sudden dive was that Charex had spun round at the sound of the squeak, still with the club in his mighty paws. The club passed quickly yet harmlessly through the air, which until recently had been occupied by the head of the leader.

"Grand Leader Scrix," Charex said, in a manner which he thought was soft and welcoming but could in fact splinter wood, "I did not see you there, I hope that I didn't hurt you."

Charex offered an oversized paw to Scrix who took it grudgingly.

"Not at all," Scrix muttered, trying to ignore the mud stain he had earned in his fall spreading across the back of his thin tunic. It was cold and he could feel his fur already starting to mat. *No matter*, he thought to himself. *Get this oaf out of my hair and I can celebrate with a lounge in the hot springs.*

He was just mentally choosing which of the Rodentian maidens he would request as "company" in the springs when he became aware of a terrible metallic smell suddenly all around him. Snapping back to reality he found that Charex had seemingly grown bored with the conversation and had made his way to an ancient wooden table at the other end of the room. There he had placed an open metal container and was dipping the tips of his paw into it. It was obvious that the container was the source of the foul odour but Scrix couldn't make out what was inside it. It wasn't until he saw what Charex did next that he realised he might have left this plan a bit late. Charex removed his paw from the container. It was stained with a reddish-brown mucus. Charex then proceeded to paint himself with this goop.

Scrix stood transfixed, his eyes wide and his tail pointing straight up. *Blood*, he thought to himself in horror. *This muscle-bound freak is painting himself in blood, why would he do that?* If only Scrix had thought to ask from where he got the blood he might have stood a chance, but the path of an individual's life so often hangs on "What ifs". (It is a fact that before the Dreaded Thaw the keenest intellects of Brundia had tried to work out a formula which would allow anyone to work out what they should think before they realise they need to. They had come close but decided at the last minute to switch their research into heating. The last Brundian to point out the irony of this had promptly been set alight. His ashes were decanted into an urn on which was written the legend, "Think before you try to be smart".)

Choking back the vomit which had accumulated in the back of his throat, Scrix drew himself up to his full (if meagre) height and in a voice he hoped carried the authority of his high office he exclaimed, "I did not dismiss you."

At this Charex merely looked mildly irritated but he had paused his exercise and was looking at Scrix with an unreadable expression on his face. Buoyed by what he thought was a bit of respect at last, Scrix walked closer to the giant rodent. He squared his thin shoulders and positioned himself as close to Charex as the smell would allow. If Scrix had hoped to present an intimidating presence over the other Rodentian it was completely undone by the fact that he barely came up to the giant's navel. To his credit he pressed on regardless.

"I'm changing the hunting rota."

He paused at this, expecting some sort of reaction. If only Charex would do something stupid like challenge him then he would have the ideal opportunity to have him removed. The silence stretched on for an uncomfortable length of time. *Come on*, Scrix thought to himself, *do something!*

Guards had been placed in the long corridor leading to the training room, all of them under orders to charge in when Scrix snapped his claws. The guards were all heavily armed and if they should regretfully kill Charex in the act of protecting their leader then it would be sad but death by treason should put a halt to this interloper's popularity. Indeed Scrix had already selected the very pole onto which he intended to display the severed head of Charex. But the hunter was spoiling this plan by being reasonable. Scrix thought for a second of clicking his claws anyway but without evidence he couldn't risk triggering a possible rebellion.

"Can you hear me?" he eventually asked.

"I hear you," was the booming reply he received.

*Damn this creature! Why won't he react?*

Scrix pressed on with the plan. Truth be told he wasn't convinced that the second part would work. He had banked on Charex reacting angrily to any change and giving him the excuse he needed. Part two of the plan meant that Scrix had to persuade him to lead the night raids. He had already tipped off the owls who would be waiting to rip the party into shreds before they could utter the word "retreat". Obviously Scrix would be overcome with the grief of losing a hunting party in general and the great Charex in particular. He might even commission some sort of statue in his honour and ride the resultant popularity right up until his comfortable death of advanced old age. Scrix swallowed hard. If he was to convince Charex that the changes were good there was still a chance he could get rid of a possible rival.

"You have done well with your audacious daytime raids, but I feel that you might do even better leading the night patrols. I have heard of a stash of stockpiled fruits and nuts, deep in the forest, that would set us up for the winter."

He moved behind Charex, momentarily alarmed at the sight of bulging muscles leading all the way down his back. Fighting every urge he had, Scrix reached and grasped the shoulders of the much bigger Rodentian in what he thought was a comradely gesture.

"Think of it," he cooed into Charex's ear, "the biggest haul in our history, our people safe all winter, and you…" suppressing the urge to audibly gag he leaned in even closer, his whiskers brushing Charex's thick right ear, "you will be the greatest hero in our history, songs will be sung in your honour."

There was still no response. Charex might as well be made of stone. With frustration Scrix climbed up on the ancient table and walked around until he was face to face with his rival. Charex was impassively staring forwards. Scrix waved his paws in front of the huge face.

"What is wrong with you? Can you hear… urggh."

The question was cut off suddenly when Charex, with a speed that shouldn't be possible in a being of that size, grabbed hold of both of the leader's paws in one of his and slammed his other paw over his face with such force that Scrix realised with horror that his nose was broken in several places. He went to scream but found his airways completely cut off. He struggled fruitlessly against his bonds but it was no good, Charex had him held in place and he would shortly run out of oxygen. At last the beast spoke.

"Do you think me a fool?"

At the word "fool" Scrix felt himself being lifted from the table and dragged by his painful nose to another darkened corner of the training room. Before he blacked out totally Charex released his grip on the leader's face but increased the pressure on his paws. Scrix could feel the small bones in his paw rub together. He was too terrified to make any sound, however, and allowed himself to be dragged to a curtained-off area he hadn't noticed previously. With only two giant steps they had arrived at their destination. With his spare hand Charex ripped down the curtain. If Scrix didn't appreciate the trouble he was in before he certainly did now. Before him were the remains of two of the biggest owls he had ever seen. They were clearly dead and their bodies had been arranged into a macabre tableau. Their wings had been stretched out and painted across them in blood was the word "TRAITOR!"

Scrix was so terrified that he lost control of his bowels. The disgusting smell seemed to not bother Charex at all. He grabbed Scrix by the ruin of his nose and pulled his head downwards. Scrix nearly passed out from the pain, but then he saw it. At the feet of the owl corpses was an open scroll. With a sense of dread, he recognised his signature at the bottom of it and any hope he had of surviving this vanished.

"Do you think me stupid?" Charex boomed. "Did you think I was unaware that you would betray us to the owls?"

All Scrix could do was mewl pathetically. Charex lifted the defeated leader above his head, and with a sickening ripping noise he tore Scrix in two and threw the bloodied pieces into the owls with such force that the owls shattered on impact and Scrix's bottom half stuck to the wall, which would be amusing if it wasn't so tragic. When the guards (who until now had put the smashing noises down to Charex's training regime) came charging into the room, they found Charex sitting on the floor, breathing heavily, surrounded by blood and viscera. Many of the younger guards vomited at the horrendous sight that greeted them, while their older comrades dropped immediately to one knee proclaiming, "Hail the new leader," which shows that while they may lack power Rodentians do not lack pragmatism.

Charex had been ruling for a few solar cycles now and while he may not have been a wise ruler he certainly inspired loyalty. Perix waited before his leader who was thinking over the idea he had been presented with. Eventually he spoke.

"Mowser," he said.

Perix's ears pricked up as Charex slurred the second syllable, his keen eyes spotting the many empty bottles of blackberry wine tucked behind the leader's chair. *Heavy is the head that wears the crown*, Perix thought to himself, suppressing a smirk. If Charex was struggling he could well use this to his advantage. Charex seemed to lose focus momentarily. He blinked a few times and shook his head as if to clear it. Perix pretended not to notice.

"Mowser," he said again, "are you proposing that I should share my crown?"

Mowser took a step back, theatrically placed his paws over his heart and dropped to one knee.

"My liege," he stated, affecting mock indignation at the very suggestion, "I was merely suggesting that you appoint an adviser, a loyal assistant if you will. Someone to look after the more mundane elements of your day, someone to relieve you of the tedium of day-to-day nonsense. Someone who could speak on your behalf, while you attend to those duties more suited to your unique and numerous skills."

For a moment he suspected that he might have overdone

it. Charex was many things but he wasn't a total idiot. Perix could only hope that the blackberry wine had sufficiently pickled his brain. Long, dangerous minutes ticked by. Perix was starting to wonder if his head would be placed next to Scrix's or if he wouldn't even be afforded that meagre honour. The silence was broken by Charex's deep laughter. He hauled himself from his chair and tottered unsteadily towards Perix. Perix braced himself for the pain he was sure was coming. Instead Charex patted him on the back so hard that he momentarily lost his footing, staggering forward, surprised yet relieved to still be alive.

"Mowser," Charex finally managed to say between deep belly laughs, "you are a smooth one. Very well, if you feel that you can deal with the rubbish that comes my way I appoint you executive leader."

The word executive came out as "eshecutive" but Perix understood well enough.

"My lord, you honour me. Perhaps we could meet every seven suns to discuss my duties to you?"

Charex waved him away and started rummaging amongst the empty wine bottles, picking up each one in turn and tipping it towards his mouth. Perex continued to bow as he backed out of the throne room. When he was alone in the corridor he allowed himself a sly smile. It was all falling into place.

As time progressed Perix assumed more and more control from the increasingly erratic Charex. He found that a charming smile and winning turn of phrase is all it took to charm the average Rodentian. For the more cynical members of the populace Perix found that if he was strict during punishment meetings they generally fell into line. Strictly speaking he shouldn't be leading punishment meetings at all, the justice of the colony being the responsibility of its leader. However, Charex had become increasingly indisposed lately. Advisers had noticed that the regular meetings between the leader and his executive had been going on later and later into the night and that Perix had been bringing more and more bottles to each one.

Eventually Perix restricted access to the leader to all but himself. When questioned about this he would flash a winning smile and simply say that "The leader is unwell and requires his rest. Don't worry about anything, I speak with his authority."

One adviser (a small Rodentian named Firex) joked that if Perix spoke with the leader's voice he "should at least slur". When word of this reached Perix he had Firex dragged outside and force-fed blackberry wine until he passed out. His unconscious body was left for the owls to find, and find it they did. Nobody ever joked about the leadership again.

Perix always referred to what happened next as "The Great Awakening" but he always was a shameless self-publicist. It was late at night when he called all the advisers together for an emergency meeting. The advisers all took their usual seats around the round wooden table. The leader's seat at the very head of the table was empty and there was no sign of Charex. The door to the chamber opened suddenly and Perix swept in flanked by heavily armed guardsmen. Silently he walked past the assembled advisers, pulled out the leader's seat and sat with two of the largest guards on other side of him. He surveyed each adviser in turn. Eventually he addressed them.

"It is my duty…" he announced, his voice flat and emotionless; he spoke so quietly that the advisers had to lean in closer so that they could hear him, "that our leader, the brave and strong Charex, has died."

At this word all of the advisers leapt to their feet and started shouting wildly. Perix nodded once and, as one, the guards took each one by the shoulders and placed them with great force back into their chairs. Each adviser was momentarily stunned into silence, which gave Perix the chance to carry on.

"My friends," he said, smiling wickedly, "I understand your distress. Sadly I was the one to find his body. It appears that he was practising a new fighting stance when he became tangled up in his own tail, slipped and fell on the rack of swords he kept nearby. A tragic accident but our late leader had become somewhat…" at this Perix waggled his paws up and down like scales, "unsteady on his paws of late…"

He would have liked to carry on his prepared speech but he was interrupted by an old and shaky voice from the other end of the table.

"Then our path is clear," the voice said. "We go into mourning for twelve solar cycles and begin the election of our new leader."

Perix squinted to make out who it was that had spoken. He found the voice's owner quickly. There was only one adviser who would be so bold.

"Adviser Birex," Perix stared the older Rodentian right in his eyes, his voice like honey, "I understand your concerns, but the old ways have prevented us from moving on. Besides, Charex was hardly elected, now was he?"

Birex returned shakily to his feet. At this the guard standing behind him moved to place him back in his seat. Perix shook his head and the guard stepped back. Birex pointed a long shaky claw at Perix.

"I suppose you plan to follow in this new tradition, my dear executive leader." His chin was splattered with spit and his whiskers dripped with foam as he became more enraged. Perix steepled his claws together and allowed him to continue. "Don't you see," Birex wheezed to the assembled advisers, "he planned this all along. I wouldn't be surprised if he killed Charex! Why are the guards here? Why are you sat in the leader's chair? Why…"

Whatever Birex intended to say next was drowned out by a coughing fit which wracked his entire body. The coughing fit was so violent that Birex went red in the face and was so short of breath that he clutched at his chest and with regret he was forced to retake his seat.

"Finished?" Perix asked, smiling for the first time. Birex glared at him from the other end of the table still unable to catch his breath. "As I was saying…"

Perix knew that he would enjoy this moment but even he didn't expect that he would enjoy it this much. He got up from his seat and walked to where Birex was sitting. He had managed to get his breathing back under control and some colour was returning to his face. Perix stood directly behind Birex and addressed the assembly. "Who amongst us can honestly say that they are happy living underground? Happy that they are hiding from animals that by rights we should dominate? I will lead us to our rightful place at the top of the food chain! All who oppose us shall meet the same fate!"

As he said the word "fate" he reached into his long robes and produced a jewel-encrusted knife. Without pausing he buried the knife into Birex's neck. The older mouse gargled slightly and clawed fruitlessly at his neck. He managed to turn around and grasp at Perix's robes. The younger mouse looked down at him and whispered into his ear, "And so begins the new dawn." Birex's corpse slipped out of his seat and thudded to the ground. Perix looked down at it with disgust.

"I do so hate litter," he said dramatically. "However shall I clear this up?"

He clicked his claws. At this cue ten foxes slipped into the room. The panic was immediate. Every Rodentian in attendance tried to leave but found their escape blocked by the foxes. They failed to notice that each fox was wearing a chest plate on which was embossed an image showing a lump of cheese being impaled by a thin sword. Eventually all of the advisers had huddled together on top of the table in a circle, all facing outwards, all visibly afraid.

"My friends, my friends," Perix said, insincerity clear in each word he spoke, "the foxes are our new allies. They have agreed to fight with us against the other races. With their help we are assured victory."

"H… How do you know w… we c… can trust them?" a nervous voice from the circle stammered.

"We?" Perix asked, arching his eyebrow. "WE can't trust them at all, they are loyal to me."

"Th… Then what d… do you need f… from us?" the voice asked again.

Perix didn't care to whom the voice belonged. He smiled again and headed towards the door. At his approach two of the foxes snapped to attention on either side of the door and saluted his approach. He turned and addressed the huddle. "An example."

He stepped outside and before the door closed he heard the snarl of ten foxes and a horrified squeak. He was disappointed that the squeak didn't stammer. *But you can't have everything*, he thought as the door closed. Perix was surprised to see that he was still holding the knife which had so recently dispatched Birex. The blood had dried on the blade and Perix was momentarily mesmerised by the patterns it made on the blade's edge. He replaced the knife inside his voluminous robes and went to address his new people.

"So it begins," he said to himself.

## CHAPTER ONE

# A HUNDRED SPANS LATER

IF THERE WAS one phrase that Brabbinger hated it was "as the crow flies". He had known many crows and while they made for largely competent wizards (although he personally felt that magic was something best left alone), they didn't move at any great speed. If a crow were to fly (although they had long since decided that physical flight was beneath them. Why fly when you can be carried by giant domesticated lizards? they rationalised) it would take them at least five solar cycles to cross the desert wastes of Aridier, which lay between their keep and the royal palace. They certainly wouldn't make the effort required even for the jubilee celebrations. He prepared himself mentally for the frankly annoying roar of the carrier lizards which would announce the arrival of the crows.

"Busy day," he muttered to himself as he got out of bed and limped across his room to the wooden dressing table.

Whenever he was asked about his room Brabbinger would always say that it was "adequate for my needs". In truth he considered himself lucky to have been housed in such splendour but he always found outward displays of enthusiasm distasteful.

The room was south-facing and the main window afforded him a glorious view of the land of Venary. On a clear day he could see as far as Silvestri Forest, the ancestral home of the cat knights, Felix Regalis. As a Rodentian, Brabbinger was naturally apprehensive around the cat knights but there was more to it than that. There was something about the way their eyes would linger on him for a fraction of a second too long, as if they were sizing up his weaknesses or (he suspected) more likely checking to see if he would fit in one of their giant cast iron cooking pots.

To the west lay Pacidermia. On this morning black smoke was coming from the docks. The war with the Giraxians was now entering its fifth span and Brabbinger realised that the Giraxian forces must have bombed the port.

"Such a waste," he muttered to himself.

Disgusted by what he saw he turned away from the window.

"Senseless," he muttered to himself as he shuffled slowly to the old dressing table.

It had been a very long time since the Cheese Wars but his left paw still ached on cold mornings. His old hand shook slightly as he grasped the ornate gold handle on the dresser and slid open the drawer. Inside (as always) was a small wooden comb and a jar of Gentlerodents whisker wax. He steadied himself and dipped the comb into the wax and proceeded to smooth each whisker into a perfect yet sharp point. As he did so Brabbinger stared into the mirror and regarded the old Rodentian that stared back at him.

"Still a noble bearing," he exclaimed.

As he continued to smooth out his whiskers he found his thoughts returning to his father. Deringer was the Royal Butler for many spans before his son and was an imposing figure. Legend told that Deringer could spot a speck of dust from across the room and once dismissed a parlour maid for arriving to work with her tail improperly tucked away. Brabbinger had tried for many spans to live up to his father's standards, and although he had seen King Hirax Mowser grow up and felt a certain pride in how he had turned out he still felt that he never quite measured up. As he placed the wax and comb back into the drawer he remembered the words his father had said as he lay dying: "You are the Royal Butler now, Brabbinger," he croaked, alternately coughing up blood and phlegm. "Never settle, never rest, and never forget your place."

Brabbinger always felt a glimmer of shame when he thought of his father but there was no time for that now.

"So much to do," he muttered to himself.

With the sound of creaking joints he lifted himself out of the seat. After fumbling with the buttons, he got his uniform on and headed for the door. Stopping only momentarily to pick up his much-loathed walking stick he headed out for another day's work. The stairs leading down from his room were steep and uneven, and it had been taking him longer and longer to navigate them. For a while the only sounds that could be heard from the tower were wheezy breaths and the tapping of walking stick on stone. It was a sound Brabbinger hated as it highlighted his weakness but was loved by the staff as it gave them warning that he was coming.

The staff had been busy. The main corridor leading from the head butler's tower to the main courtyard had been decorated with the purple and gold colours of House Mowser, and the royal crest displaying a lump of golden cheese being run through with a very fine blade had been hung over each door. Brabbinger started walking towards the kitchen and was immediately horrified by what he saw.

"Boy!" he screeched as loudly as he was able. "Here now."

The young footmouse being addressed was so shocked that he nearly dropped the boots he was in the process of cleaning, instead smearing the golden laces with boot polish.

"Y… Yes, Mr Brabbinger," the young Rodentian stuttered as he made his way quickly to his employer.

"What is that around your neck?" Brabbinger enquired, barely able to keep the disgust out of his voice.

"My cravat," the footmouse replied nervously.

*Surely the butler knew this*, he thought to himself. Perhaps the rumour that he was losing his mind wasn't as farfetched as he had previously assumed.

"I think not," Brabbinger replied. "A cravat is black, yours seems to be multicoloured. If this is some idea of a joke I am baffled at what you hope to achieve."

"They are the royal colours, Mr Brabbinger, I thought that today…"

He didn't get the chance to finish.

"You THOUGHT…" Brabbinger was clearly getting annoyed now. Experienced members of staff started looking for excuses to absent themselves. They had seen this sort of thing before and had no desire to be the next one to earn their employer's wrath. "You thought that on the day of His Majesty's tenth jubilee you would festoon yourself with the royal colours! Tell me, boy, are you a horse being ridden into battle?"

The footmouse couldn't reply, he was far too terrified.

"Perhaps you see yourself as a knight of the realm," Brabbinger continued, clearly warming to his theme. "Or perhaps you think we should display you from a flag post and salute as we pass!"

Brabbinger could feel himself getting hot and the chest pains he had been ignoring for months started to announce their return. He forced himself to calm down.

"In my employ," he stated calmly but with a voice like ice, "footrodents like yourself wear black. You are not to be noticed, you are not to be remarked upon. I expect you to return to your room and attire yourself correctly."

He internally criticised himself for calling the younger Rodentian a "footrodent". It was an old and offensive term and he had hated it when his father used it on him. The footmouse quickly retreated towards the door but was stopped by Brabbinger calling after him.

"On your next break, boy! Too much time has been wasted already, and those boots need to be polished again, they are a disgrace."

With a cursory glance around the room Brabbinger turned smartly on his heels and marched out of the room.

He passed by the kitchens where food from throughout the realm was being prepared. As a Rodentian and a butler Brabbinger's tastes were simple. He felt that even melted cheese was extravagant. When he entered the kitchens he was horrified to find dozens of dead birds spread across the

5

kitchen tables. *Surely these poor unfortunates have been found in the giant kitchen's chimneys*, he thought, as many had become trapped in them over the spans.

As he was trying to settle his stomach the sound of an axe hitting wood brought him back to reality. He slowly turned in the direction of the noise and was horrified by the sight that greeted him – a giant Rodentian in a blood-spattered chef's whites with an unshaven face was raising an axe above his head and bringing it down with force across the neck of one of the dead birds, neatly severing the head from its body.

"What are you doing?" the butler shouted around the unpleasant-tasting vomit in his mouth. "Have you gone mad?" Brabbinger was almost screaming by this point. He waved his arms around, dismayed that nobody else in the kitchen was as outraged as he was. "Have you all taken leave of your senses? Someone fetch the Chief of the King's Guard! Where is Scarex?"

The kitchen staff had surrounded Brabbinger by now and their sympathetic staring was more than he could stand.

"This creature is a killer! What possible reason could you have for butchering these poor innocents?"

As much as it made him sick to the very bottom of his stomach he gestured towards the gruesome scene across the multiple kitchen tables. The chef visibly relaxed at this point.

"Mr Brabbinger," he said in a surprisingly soft voice, "His Majesty ordered I make a large bird pie for the flea scratchers."

Brabbinger was so relieved he nearly smiled but spans of training meant that instead he merely smoothed down his waistcoat.

"If this is the case," he stated, "those tables must be thoroughly sterilised..." He paused for a second. "Actually you can throw those tables away." As he was about to leave a thought struck him. "Don't let His Majesty hear you refer to his guests as 'flea scratchers', it is disrespectful and if you wish to end up like those poor avians I would avoid the cat knights entirely if I were you."

As Brabbinger left the kitchen he couldn't help reflecting that he had had better cycles. He still felt rather nauseous and he couldn't shake the image of the many dead and headless birds.

"Fresh air, I think," he muttered to himself and decided to head towards the courtyard.

He would never admit it to anyone, least of all himself but he was tired and his left paw was throbbing inside his stiff lettuce leaf glove. If he could be said to have desires he desired a sit down and to soak his foot in his mother's special paw soak recipe. The courtyard was beautiful at this time of year. The sun shone down directly onto the ornate fountain and the reflected light made it look like the fountain was spilling gold into the oyster-shell-shaped bowl below. In honour of today's event banners were hung from the surrounding walls and towers, showing the house colours and sigils of the invited guests. Brabbinger glanced around at the banners, checking that they had been hung correctly and were free of creases. The Giraxian banner with its blue background stood out against the greys of the castle wall. This was the newest banner amongst the tribes of Venary.

The Giraxians were huge giraffes with opposable thumbs at the end of each of their four feet. For spans they had been considered a basic slave race with a low intelligence quota, which is why nobody was surprised when the Pacidermians had pressed them into service. Brabbinger had a certain level of respect for the Pacidermians, a large race of elephants who had realised that the ivory in their self-replicating tusks was the strongest material yet discovered in Venary. However, before it could be used to create walls, ships and bridges (amongst other things) it had to be removed from the host without severing the root and thus ensuring that it would grow back, then pickled in preservative fluid. The Pacidermians with their huge pads couldn't do either of these things very well and had tricked the Giraxians into working for them in return for protection from Flying Drexes. It still surprised Brabbinger that it took the Giraxians so many spans to discover that the Flying Drexes were a fabrication and that they had been working for free. The rebellion was bloody and even Brabbinger, a veteran of the Cheese Wars, shuddered at the memory. Every Giraxian tasked with removing the tusks from the Pacidermian hosts instead removed their trunks. Once the Pacidermians realised that their slaves were rebelling they hit back by attacking the Giraxian nursery in an attempt to wipe out the next generation. The war that had been raging between them ever since was now entering its fifth span. The Giraxian banner had a symbol of a snapped tusk on it, which Brabbinger considered bad taste in the extreme.

He found his way to the wooden bench he knew was placed underneath the old oak tree and slowly lowered himself into it. Luckily those idiots in planning hadn't put the Giraxian banner next to the brown and grey banner of the Pacidermians. Having delegates from both sides would be problematic enough. Not that the Pacidemians had deigned to reply to their invite of course, had he not been so well trained Brabbinger would have refused entry to any Pacidermian rude enough to turn up uninvited. However he had personally overseen the complicated restructuring the entire east wing which was necessary to house those massive beasts, should any of them arrive that is.

With great effort he levered himself out of his seat. Further reflections would have to wait, it was time to awaken the King. Putting more weight on his stick, Brabbinger limped off towards the royal tower. He passed through the gardens en route and, as he did every day, he snipped a red rose from its stem with a practised flick of his claw and gently placed the flower in the buttonhole on his lapel. He knew the gardens were the pride and joy of the young King, having been planted ten spans ago to mark the sad passing of King Tyrell and the ascension of his eleven-year-old heir, the new King of Venary, Hirax Mowser. Over the last decade the garden had grown in splendour and contained flowers and plants from all over Venary. His Majesty had been heard to say that it was ironic that so many plants could grow together and live in harmony but that his citizens could not. It had not been easy for Hirax coming to the throne as young as he did. His father was a great king who ruled over Venary justly and fairly.

*Such an improvement over his own father*, Brabbinger thought to himself as he hurried past the koi pond and hedge maze (whose recently painted sign boasted "World's Hardest Maze" in gold).

Tyrell's father, Faustus, was a tyrant, a king who was both cruel and unpredictable. Brabbinger was a very young Rodentian when he came to live at the palace, during

Faustus' rule, and he well remembered just how terrified he was of him. He remembered the way that King Faustus would stare into his young face and how he would regard him with that cruel squint.

Brabbinger remembered being woken up one night by the sound of a cart with a squeaky wheel stopping at the darkened north tower. The young Brabbinger stood on the very tips of his paws so that he could see out of his bedroom window. The cart had come to a complete stop as the driver pulled back on the reins securing one thin and clearly exhausted horse. The driver jumped down from his seat and made his way to the back of the cart. As he was sorting through the many keys on his belt Brabbinger saw a darkened figure head towards the cart driver. He was too far away to hear what they were saying but he knew that something was very wrong indeed. The driver held out a gloved hand and the mysterious figure placed a golden sovereign into it. As this transaction was completed the driver finally found the key he had been looking for. As he opened the door on the back of the cart Brabbinger held his breath. The driver banged on the side of the cart and a small set of steps unfolded and hit the flagstone ground with a bang. At this unexpected noise the mysterious figure jumped in surprise and his hood fell down, revealing his face. He struggled to pull the hood back up and Brabbinger gasped in shock as he recognised King Faustus. The King impatiently banged his staff on the ground. A small head poked out from behind the cart door followed by another and then another. Brabbinger watched in horror as two kittens and two Giraxian calves nervously stepped out in front of the King. They were filthy and the rags they were dressed in hung from their emaciated bodies. Brabbinger was surprised that they could stand. Was Faustus bringing these poor unfortunates inside for shelter? Had he changed his ways?

Faustus turned towards the north tower and opened the door. He ushered the youngsters inside and followed them in. Brabbinger never saw the younglins again but the following night he spotted some familiar rags being placed on a bonfire. They seemed to take a long while to burn due to some very damp and dark-looking stains which covered them.

The King's tower was (as should be expected) very ornate. Pure white stones made up the building. The stained-glass windows which were placed all around the tower showed all of the previous Rodentian kings leading all the way back to the very first, King Perix Mowser ("the Saviour of his Kind"). The last window was covered with a thick red cloth as it displayed King Hirax and was due to be unveiled later today as part of the jubilee celebrations. The top of the tower gleamed in the sunlight. Many of the junior staff believed the old rumour that it was fashioned out of solid gold. Of course this was impossible as it would be far too heavy and even the impressive number of stones underneath it would not be able to carry the fantastic weight a golden tower would produce. Even so, it was a very impressive sight.

The King's bedchamber was at the top and afforded His Majesty a clear view of the entirety of his kingdom. Brabbinger took a deep breath and pushed open the wooden door at the base of the tower. Being perfectly hung the door swung open easily and Brabbinger, with some degree of difficulty, ascended the winding staircase. When he reached the summit he made sure that his breathing had settled back down to normal and that his uniform was still smart. Once he made sure that he was presentable he rapped three times on the door of the bedchamber.

"Come," a deep voice from inside intoned.

Brabbinger pushed open the door and entered. King Hirax was standing with his back to the door hunched over an oak table carved into the shape of Venary. Dispensing with any niceties King Hirax looked up at his butler.

"I assume you've noted this morning's unpleasantness."

When the King spoke it was with a quiet voice, forcing everyone nearby to lean in closely and give their full attention to what he was saying. Brabbinger knew this was intentional and he admired the King for this habit. It was, in his humble opinion, most appropriate.

"Unpleasantness, Your Majesty?" he replied.

Hirax smiled a humourless smile.

"The Pacidermian port was attacked last night. It appears the Giraxian forces are not as disorganised as we all assumed."

Although there was no reproach in the King's voice Brabbinger felt that he was being blamed for this oversight.

"Information from Pacidermia is often unreliable, Your Majesty," he stammered.

"How am I meant to rule over a divided kingdom?" Hirax mused. He had turned away from Brabbinger at this point and was staring out of the large open window. "Are you sure we can't send a force into the battle zone and force them into peace?"

"I'm afraid not, Your Majesty, we must allow them to work this out for themselves. If we were to interfere, I fear

Your Majesty would be forced to solve every crisis in the kingdom."

"But what am I for?" Hirax muttered.

For a moment Brabbinger saw Hirax as a small child again, absolutely terrified of taking the crown. Brabbinger stepped as close to the King as he dared. He would never touch his ruler, the strictness of his upbringing would not allow it, but he wanted nothing more than to take him in his arms and tell him that everything would be okay. Instead he addressed the King's back.

"You are a symbol, Your Majesty. The people look to you for stability in times of difficulty. You cannot be a tyrant. At your coronation you promised a degree of autonomy to the lands of Venary. That is why you appointed a steward from each region to watch over their lands with only advice and warning from you, those same stewards who are arriving today to celebrate your jubilee."

At the mention of the jubilee Hirax spun around to face his butler for the first time. Brabbinger was shocked by just how old the King looked. There were thick black circles under his eyes, which made it clear that he hadn't slept all night, the fur on top of his head was tangled and greasy, and his tail flopped listlessly from left to right.

"Tell me how the preparations are progressing."

Brabbinger sighed, relieved that the King had moved on to a happier topic.

"Well, there are a few things for Your Majesty's attention… but first I think Your Majesty would benefit from a bath…"

Later that day a freshly bathed King Hirax walked confidently into his throne room. Privately he considered his throne room to be a bit excessive. It was by far the largest room in the palace. The only access point were the large doors at the entrance. The gates were wrought iron carved into swirling patterns which gave the illusion of delicacy. Further to this they had been painted gold. They always reminded Hirax of the illustrations in the Holy Book showing the gates of paradise. He wasn't a superstitious Rodentian but there were times when he would look at those gates and hope the almighty didn't think that he was mocking him. By the gates was a long red carpet with golden trim running the length of the throne room. It swept past numerous suits of armour and portraits of the Mowser family, coming to a stop at the foot of a wide staircase leading up to his throne.

The throne was placed so high up that everyone else in the throne room was forced to look up to it. A hangover from the cycles of his grandfather, Hirax knew, but he liked being sat far away from his audience so they couldn't see how nervous he often was. The throne was huge and golden, cushioned with red velvet-covered padding. It was a very comfortable throne and this too made the young King feel guilty. Carved into the throne, just above where Hirax's head would rest, was the image of a lump of cheese with a crown wrapped around it.

Above the throne was an ornate window on which were stained-glass images from the histories of Venary. One showed the wooden ships of the first mouse lords as they landed on the shores of Venary, another showed the victorious mouse troops of House Mowser returning from the Cheese Wars. The windows were arranged into a spiralling shape, forming a great dome over the throne. On a sunny day the sunlight was refracted into a kaleidoscope of colours which created a glow around anyone seated on the throne, "the Shine of Kings", Hirax once called it, and to his embarrassment the name stuck. The windows showing the ancient history of his family were arranged around the bottom of the dome and forced the viewer to follow them along to the later windows which showed more recent history. As Brabbinger once said, "The future of House Mowser reaches ever closer to the heavens." As a child Hirax used to enjoy lying on his back and following the story as it played out above him. He enjoyed the stories of war and wise kings who could do the impossible. He used to be inspired by them. Now with unrest in his kingdom dragging on he just felt inferior and overwhelmed.

Hirax was walking slowly along the long corridor. The ridiculous red velvet robe that Brabbinger insisted he wear today was twice as long as the King was, and he was finding it heavier than he would like to admit. If the robe was an annoyance it was as nothing compared with the ridiculous boots he was wearing. Oh, they were beautiful boots, made of the finest black leather and polished to such a shine that not only could Hirax see his face in them he could spot the individual lines etched into his forehead. Undoubtedly Brabbinger had spent much of the previous evening applying layer after layer of that foul-smelling polish onto them. It was the image of the old butler working late into the night to make sure that everything was just right that prevented Hirax from refusing to wear the uncomfortable things. Hirax hated himself for being so easily cowed. He remembered his ancient grandfather admonishing him.

"You are too soft, boy!" he would screech. "If you are ever to be King, and I pray nightly that your equally weak father should produce a more suitable heir than you, you must realise that the feelings of others are meaningless!"

Hirax blinked away this unpleasant memory. Even today, many spans after his death, he feared his grandfather and found that even the memory of him caused him to break into a cold sweat. Whenever he was asked about his ancestors Hirax would say that Faustus was a determined ruler who knew exactly what he wanted, however his closest servants had heard him remark that Faustus was proof that not only do the good die young, the truly evil go on forever. Faustus' reign had been a long one, in fact so long was it that Hirax's own father was well over fifty when he finally took the throne. Tyrell never got to celebrate his tenth jubilee, and at that moment Hirax envied him that. While Hirax had meekly accepted the boots he had argued bitterly against wearing the sword. Naturally Brabbinger had been horrified at this.

"Your Majesty," he had spluttered, "the sword of Mowser has been passed down from father to son for over a hundred spans from the cycles of Liberator Perix. It is a symbol of strength. Your subjects expect you to wear it, especially in these dark times."

Hirax had rolled his eyes at this. He was pleased to have provoked such an emotional response from the usually stoic Brabbinger but tried (again) to explain his position.

"I have never even been in a sword fight," he wearily explained. "It would make more sense if I wore a cheese knife! At least I've used one of those."

Brabbinger paused from his task of brushing Hirax's lapels to look the King in the eye.

"Your Majesty," he patiently began, "do I need to remind you of royal protocol?"

Hirax was suddenly reminded of the tedious hours he spent as a child in Brabbinger's pantry being lectured endlessly on how to walk, how to talk, even how to behave. He could swear that to this day he could still feel the books that Brabbinger would pile up on his head to teach him how to walk correctly.

Brabbinger coughed. Hirax blinked in surprise. The butler clearly expected an answer.

"Good lord no," he quickly replied. "One lifetime of lessons is quite enough."

If Brabbinger detected the sarcasm he made no reference to it. So, Hirax had reluctantly allowed him to fasten the hated weapon to his belt. *By the stars it is difficult to walk with this thing running down my leg*, Hirax thought as he shuffled towards the throne. *I only hope I don't trip.*

Hirax had his thoughts interrupted by the sound of heavy footsteps. The sound was regimented and metallic so he wasn't surprised when Scarex came marching into the throne room accompanied by six of the biggest mice the King had ever seen. They loomed over Hirax in the way that only a wall of solid muscle can. Each of the guards was dressed in a full suit of armour with a breastplate made of solid gold with the insignia of House Mowser etched upon it. The breastplate must have been of considerable weight but the guards gave no indication that it was any heavier than a silk shirt. Across their broad backs was a sword whose hilt was longer than Hirax was tall and sharpened to such a degree that Hirax feared they could slice the air itself in two. Standing in front of the six massive guards was the ugliest mouse Hirax had ever seen. Shorter than most with a nose which had been broken and poorly reset several times,

Scarex still managed to cut an imposing figure, even when surrounded by a wall of muscle and brightly polished metal.

"Your Majesty," he wheezed, every word accompanied by a whistling sound coming from the ruin of his nose, "may I introduce your new Royal Guard."

The last two words were accompanied by a grand sweeping gesture towards the monsters standing behind him. Scarex grinned at this, affording Hirax a front seat view of various smashed teeth. Only Scarex's front two teeth weren't smashed, and as he obviously felt that this spoiled the effect somewhat Scarex had sharpened both of them into razor-sharp points. Hirax raised an eyebrow. What was this ridiculous creature expecting? It seemed unlikely that he wouldn't notice the hulking guards standing directly in front of him. Presumably Scarex thought he was blocking the view somewhat. Perhaps his head of security really had lost all sense of reason this time. No, it was apparent that Scarex expected some sort of recognition.

"I still don't understand why I need a personal guard all of a sudden, my father and grandfather never needed one," he enquired.

Scarex grinned an infuriating grin.

"Your Majesty," he said, mock indignation heavy on each syllable, "these are worrisome times. Why, today alone you have two warring factions coming to a…" he struggled to find the appropriate word, "… party," he continued. "I'm sure that one or both of Your Majesty's honoured guests would consider kidnapping your royal person as an excellent bargaining chip."

He paused at this point, expecting a reaction to his reference to the King's jubilee as a "party". He was disappointed at the blank expression on the King's face. *Drat*, he thought to himself, *he's learning*.

"And besides," he pressed on, "your royal father did sadly vanish on that expedition ten spans ago. Perhaps if he had guards he might still be ruling over us."

Scarex was pleased to note that the King had no response to this. He pressed his advantage.

"And as for your grandfather, well…" to Hirax's horror Scarex winked at him, "it would have to be a very brave or foolish being to sneak up on King Faustus."

Hirax opened his mouth to protest but Scarex continued.

"I'm sure Your Majesty won't even notice them. Better to have them and not need them than… well, I don't want to disturb Your Majesty further on your special day."

At this he bowed low yet never broke eye contact. It appeared that the audience was at an end.

Hirax felt (as he often did after talking to Scarex for any length of time) that he'd agreed to something he didn't want. "Another compromise," he muttered to himself. For a moment he saw an image of his hated grandfather laughing at him. Hirax involuntarily shuddered at this thought.

"Is Your Majesty well?" enquired Scarex.

Hirax realised too late that the vile rodent was still there. He pulled himself up to his full height, which looked ridiculous compared to the hulking guards, but he felt that he needed to reassert himself somewhat.

"Perfectly well," he said, his voice icily cold. "I don't need to detain you any further, Chief of Security."

To further emphasise this point he continued walking towards the throne without looking back.

"As you wish, Your Majesty," Scarex contemptuously muttered under his breath.

With a great deal of effort Hirax got himself to the throne. Despite Scarex's assurances he did notice his Royal Guard, it was difficult not to. After spending an exhausting amount of time laying out his robe so he could at least sit with a certain degree of comfort he plopped into his throne and finally had a good look at his new bodyguards. He wasn't sure if it was due to the faceguard over the helmets but he was sure that every guard looked identical. He felt that there was no need to be rude to these men, after all, he rationalised, they didn't ask for this duty, they probably had no desire to be here babysitting a weakling king any more than he wanted them there.

He turned to talk to the group and was surprised to see that they had arranged themselves into two lines, three guards on either side of the throne. They had done this so quietly and swiftly that Hirax hadn't even noticed them move. Damn Scarex, he might be insubordinate and sly but his training methods were the best in the kingdom. The two guards at the front of both lines had drawn their massive swords and were holding them in front of them, arms extended with the hilt pointing skywards. Hirax noticed that the hilts were so well polished that the light coming in from the windows gleamed along the entire length. It gave the impression that the guards were holding two thin columns of light. Despite himself he was impressed.

"So," he began, feeling ridiculous, "did you volunteer for this duty?"

He had addressed this question to the guard on his right, deciding for no real reason that this one was the leader. All six guards answered at once, the noise of their collective voices echoing out over the throne room.

"No, sire," they boomed in perfect unison. "We were selected from the regular army, sire." Hirax felt that last "sire" echoing around his skull as the guards continued talking as one. "Chief Scarex wanted the best of the best, sire."

Hirax waited for the noise to subside before continuing.

"Well, sorry to call you away from active service, men, I'm sure you'd rather be out there with your fellows."

Internally he chastised himself for calling them "men" and using the word "fellows". What was it about talking to strong, capable males that turned him into such a pompous fool?

"The honour is to serve, sire," was the reply that returned, their combined voices reaching an even higher volume.

Hirax decided it would be best if he just stopped talking to them. *It might also be helpful to ask Brabbinger if earplugs could be added to my regalia,* he decided shortly after.

Brabbinger had been correct about one thing: Hirax had been up all night but he had not been studying the progress of the Giraxian/Pacidermian conflict, he had been in the royal library. Hirax had been spending a lot of time in the library of late. For one it was quiet in there. He had given orders to the chief librarian that he was not to be disturbed and that nobody, particularly Brabbinger, was to know that he was there, and for another he had become convinced that the answers to his problems were to be found in Venary's past. For many cycles he had pored over the various potted histories of his kingdom, from the war diaries of King Perix to the forgotten magical history of the crows. It was while reading through a chapter about mythical objects that he stumbled upon accounts of the fabled Collar of Honour. He had been about to move onto the next chapter when he saw a passage that captured his attention:

*Of all the mythical objects in Venary the Collar of Honour remains the most compelling. An object imbued with the power of the ancients to grant the heart's desire of whomever owns it. When granted the Collar would then disappear and reappear in a random area of the land to await its next owner. Legend states that the Collar even has power over life, death and time itself.*

Hirax was far from a supposititious ruler but something about this legend reminded him of something his grandfather had said on his death bed. Faustus had lived a long and bloody life. He had never inspired much love in his people but they feared him. When word of his increased frailty had reached the streets surrounding the palace the peasants would nervously smile at each other. Although still too scared to openly celebrate they felt hope for the first time in as long as any of them could remember. On the last day of Faustus' reign, Tyrell and a very young Hirax had been summoned to his bedside. The ancient King had been propped up on many pillows but he still presented an awful sight. His face was grey and his skin as thin as old parchment. His voice croaked but still carried its old authority especially when addressing his son and grandson. Tyrell positioned himself on the right side of his father's bed while Hirax had been nervously ushered by Brabbinger to the left. For a while nothing happened, Faustus coldly regarding both of them, not even bothering to hide his disgust.

"Well, here they are," he croaked, "the heir and the spare."

He found this remark so amusing that he broke into a huge coughing fit. With a shaking paw he reached into his pyjamas and pulled out a large silk handkerchief and coughed up a large amount of blood into it. When finished he tossed the blood-soaked rag casually at one of the nursemaids placed at the end of his bed. The nursemaid was too well trained to shriek but the look of horror on her face was plain for all to see. Faustus looked at her and winked, a lusty grin on his ruined face.

"Father! Really!" Tyrell said in shock.

"Be silent, boy," Faustus snapped back. "This is your lucky day after all. I'm dying and soon you shall take my throne. The only advantage left to me is that you'll be so inept at the role that there'll be no kingdom left for this little wretch to inherit."

At the word wretch he pointed a long, bony claw at Hirax who in fear buried his head in Brabbinger's tailcoat.

Faustus turned back to his son.

"Now listen, boy, I haven't got long. It is in the north tower." He stopped to catch his breath, his eyes were frantic. "It isn't meant to end like this, it promised me, promised me…" Another coughing fit took over. The old Rodentian's body racked violently back and forth, blood spewing from his mouth. "Heart's desire," he spluttered, "promised heart's desire." This last sentence was screeched and Faustus began to thrash wildly about. "Heart's desire!" he shouted again.

"Brabbinger!" Tyrell shouted. "Get my son out of here, he shouldn't see this."

Brabbinger nodded his head once and steered Hirax to the door as quickly as he could. Hirax was rooted to the floor, his terror so overwhelming him that he forgot how to move.

"This way, young master," Brabbinger said encouragingly and Hirax allowed himself to be led from the room but not before Faustus could yell at him one last time.

"Run away, young wimp, but you shall never escape me, we shall meet again…"

There was more but by this point Brabbinger had successfully navigated his charge out of the door.

Had his grandfather found the Collar of Honour? Hirax had thoroughly searched the north tower over the past few nights and while he had found disturbing artefacts there was no collar. If Faustus' greatest desire had been granted then it would have vanished but Faustus had died, that can't have been his greatest desire. Painful though it was he thought back to that day. He never saw his grandfather's body and the coffin had been left closed during the funeral, which Hirax later found out was a breach in tradition. Every royal funeral had an open casket so that the people could see their fallen ruler one last time. Why would Brabbinger of all people break tradition? What was his father searching for on the expedition that killed him? There were too many questions he needed answering. A few cycles ago he sent out letters to the stewards of the various realms of his kingdom inviting them to his jubilee and to bring with them any information they had about the Collar of Honour. He knew he was giving them information they could use against him, but if there was even a small chance that the Collar existed he must find it, before anyone else. All he could do now was wait.

SEVERAL SPANS AGO...

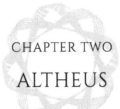

CHAPTER TWO

# ALTHEUS

S OME REVOLUTIONS START with inspiring words and phrases, many have banners and chants. The accepted theory is that a revolution is only successful if it ends with a pile of bodies and very full orphanages. Some, however, are different. Some happen so quickly that if a holidaying citizen came back from a weekend break they would be completely oblivious to any change... well, until they saw the old statues being destroyed and that the flag was a new shade of blue. If the crow revolution was an opera it would only have one song: "Smash It".

"I beg your pardon, Supreme Leader?" simpered Crasis.

It wasn't that he naturally simpered, he just felt that as Chief Adviser to the Supreme Leader it would be better if he did. Crasis trusted his instincts, they served him well, and he had a point: as adviser to the old regime for nearly twenty spans his head should have been amongst the first into the basket but despite external appearances Crasis was a wise old crow. As soon as he saw the way the winds were blowing he altered his flight path and pledged himself to the new order. Crasis had once read about loyalty in the city library and decided that it was all very nice but he preferred living in relative comfort thank you very much. However, as he surveyed the young female standing in front of him wearing the leader's robes and (horror) trousers he was starting to think that death might be a blessed release, he rather liked his ancestors after all.

"Did I stutter?" the new Supreme Leader (whose name was Altheus) asked sweetly.

Crasis shuddered. He'd heard Altheus use that tone only once before. She had asked previous supreme leader, Cragzac, if he would be very kind and sign the abdication papers. Cragzac was still laughing after Altheus used a combination of spells at a speed nobody thought possible to slice him into strands so thin the old women could have sewn him into a fine gown.

"I said smash this hideous chair."

To further emphasise her point Altheus extended a long and expansive wing towards the twisted wooden monstrosity in the corner of the room. The "hideous chair", or more correctly "The Nest of Almighty Authority", was BIG. It dominated the courtroom in a way that only a ginormous nest made of twisted wood collected from all over Venary could. For many spans the supreme leaders of the crow people had sat in this nest and dispensed justice and decrees. Even after the conquest of Venary by Perix Mowser, when the Supreme Leader was reduced to little more than a mouthpiece for the royal family, the nest was still seen as an emblem of power. There was a brief moment where Crasis considered arguing about tradition. He opened his mouth to begin but Altheus' eyes had started glowing a very faint red and the tip of her magic staff had started to make the same high-pitched whining sound it made before dissecting Cragzac.

"As you wish," was all he said.

Altheus simply nodded at him.

"It is obscene," Altheus said in a worryingly calm voice. "We are placed in the middle of a desert. The population have to import everything they need to survive so that even the price of kindling is beyond many of their means and our fat leaders have been sitting on this!" She was suddenly angry again. "Smash it! Take it apart! Distribute the remains to the people."

She spun on her heel and marched out of the courtroom. Crasis let out a breath he hadn't realised he was holding. *I wonder if I can get my old job as a flight instructor back*, he thought to himself.

As Altheus strode through her new home, the sound of her boots hitting stone cobbles echoed throughout the halls. She made her way to the stables but she wasn't in any particular hurry. As she walked she saw signs of the old regime being quickly removed. Some would be destroyed but more would be taken by the people and either hidden away as souvenirs or sold to the inevitable loyalists who would try to undermine her authority. She didn't mind, she found it fitting that they were desperate for her scraps. Altheus had grown up on the streets of this citidel, being ignored by those self-same crows. She thought back on those cycles bitterly. She was the youngest of her parents' hatchlings, and she vaguely remembered that her home was always full of noise and people. As the smallest in the family she would often be stepped on as she crawled under claw, but every time this happened her father would scoop her up in his wings and sing her favourite song to her. It was a song about brave heroes protecting the innocents and it always made her forget the pain in her wings and pretty soon she would be asleep. This all ended early one morning when the family's small front door was destroyed and amongst the explosion of splintered wood and dust the leader's guards came charging in. Her father stood in front of Altheus' mother and fellow hatchlings.

"What is the meaning of this?" he demanded. He had to shout to be heard over the sound of crying baby birds and the clomp, clomp of metal boots as guard after guard came charging into his home. "You can't do this," he shouted.

A cruel, thin voice replied from the ruined door frame, "Oh, but I can."

Every head turned towards the voice. There, framed by the destroyed entranceway to the family home, was Supreme Leader Cragzac. He stepped over the shattered wood which until recently had been the family's front door and surveyed the scene inside with a look of utter disgust on his face.

"You call this a home?" he enquired almost conversationally. "I would have thought that a man with your…" here he paused before an evil smile spread across his beak, "considerable talents would make himself more comfortable."

At this Cragzac paused to pick up a piece of parchment which had fallen from the hallway table. It wasn't much, a drawing done by one of Altheus' brothers. It showed the family standing outside a house. Everyone was smiling. Even the sun drawn in the top left corner of the picture had a big lopsided smile drawn across its face. Cragzac sneered down at it.

"Sweet," he said in mocking tones before using it to wipe a slick of mud from his boots.

He let the image fall to the floor and quite deliberately walked over it, pausing only to wipe his booted claws upon it. The sound of ripping parchment seemed to rouse Altheus' father from his shocked silence.

"You monster!" he screamed, launching himself at the Supreme Leader, claws drawn, ready to scratch the leader's sneering face off.

It was a futile gesture. As soon as he launched himself towards Cragzac one of the guards whacked him across the back of his head with his spike, bringing him to the floor in a pile of wings and blood. He lay there for a moment struggling to breathe, a look of loathing clear across his face. Cragzac stood over him.

"Violence? Really?" he questioned, contempt dripping from every syllable. "We both know you can do so much more."

"Leave him alone!" a shrill voice had shouted out, and as one every head turned to see who dared to interrupt the Supreme Leader. Surely more blood would soon be spilled.

It was Altheus, tears streaming down her face, who had shouted.

"Leave him alone, you bully," she screamed.

She attempted to rush forward to look after her father who had managed to lift himself into a seated position but was still very frail and coughing up blood. A guard went to strike Altheus to shut her up but was stopped when Cragzac lifted one of his wings and spoke.

"Bring the little children unto me," he exclaimed, a wicked idea forming in his mind.

He beckoned the guard to bring Altheus over with his outstretched wing. Altheus tried to struggle but it was no good, the guard was incredibly strong. In no time at all she had been brought over to Cragzac, who smiled down at her. The smile was cold and terrifying and all she wanted to do was to run to her daddy and hide in his big strong wings. Instead Cragzac knelt down so that his face was level with hers and placed his wings on her shoulders. He stared into her pale blue eyes and, as if he was telling her a bedtime story, he said, "How much do you know about your father, girl?"

Altheus was terrified but she met his gaze and said, "He is my daddy and he is stronger than you, you bully."

She whispered those last two words, scared by what might happen next. What did happen surprised her.

"Yes, he is," Cragzac admitted. "He is your daddy." In his beak the word sounded like an insult. "And he certainly is stronger than I, wizards often are."

When he said "wizards" he pointed one long black feather directly at the pitiful sight in front of him. The whole room gasped in horrified surprise. They all knew that wizards had existed but that was back in the old times. They were said to have been all powerful, capable of fantastic and horrifying acts. They were strong and mighty. The pitiful figure with the cracked beak they saw in front of them couldn't possibly be one of them surely? Especially since all of the wizards had wiped each other out in the Mage Wars…

Altheus' recollection was interrupted by the sound of snorting coming from the lizard pen. She turned her head just in time to see a young stablehand being flung into the air by a rearing lizard. Altheus flicked her wing and a red glow enveloped the

32

stablehand. His flight was immediately arrested and he was gently returned to the stable. A large fat crow – Altheus seemed to recall was named Grisof – ran to her. The sheer effort of moving across a short distance exhausted the large crow and it took him a long time to catch his breath. Eventually, after much wheezing, the red-faced crow was able to speak.

"Your Supremeness," he wheezed, "the beasts are unsettled."

Altheus stared at him hard over her beak with no obvious effect. Eventually she sighed.

"Any reason why?" she asked, exasperation heavy on every syllable.

Grisof blinked a few times. This was all very new and unsettling for him. Until now the only female he had had dealings with in the castle was the cook and most of their interactions involved her hitting him over the head with a heavy wooden ladle every time he tried to help himself to some little titbit from the kitchen. There was his wife, obviously, but she was a strong, silent woman who was more than capable of wrestling a lizard to the ground.

"They are… unsettled," was all he managed to croak out.

Altheus took pity on him.

"Well, I'm sure that if anyone can settle them down it's you, stable master."

Grisof felt pride warm up inside him. He stood up a bit straighter and brushed himself down, suddenly embarrassed by his scruffy appearance and the faint smell of lizard poo that seemed to follow him wherever he went.

"Well… well…" he spluttered, suddenly finding his voice, "they are tricky beasts, I think they can sense a change in the atmosphere."

"Yes," muttered Altheus as she wandered off. "There is certainly a lot of change in the air."

As if to empathise the point they was a loud snort from the lizard pen. Three young crows were frantically running around with ropes, desperately trying to rope the beast before it could cause any further damage. Altheus considered using magic to sort things out but knew that people were still afraid of mages. A lesson Cragzac had taught her all those spans ago...

The silence in the little house was unsettling. Since Cragzac's revelation every guard present pointed their weapon at the pitiful old crow in front of them. Cragzac must have noticed that many of his guard were shaking with fear as he swiftly moved behind them. Altheus watched as her father staggered to his feet. He shook out his wings and spat a bright red stream of blood at the feet of the closest guards. For their part the guards took a step backwards. For the first time since they charged into her house Altheus felt calm. They'd be sorry now. Her daddy would sort this out and everything would be okay again. Cragzac grinned from his place behind the guards.

"Go on, old bird," he goaded. "Show me what you can do, show me how you and your kind ruined our land, show me and your lively daughter here."

At this Cragzac pointed at Altheus.

"Show her why our land is now a desert, show her how you weakened us and allowed the Rodentians to rule over us." This last part was screeched right into the face of her father.

"That is why I am here," he explained. "It took a while but I tracked you down, the last of the wizards! Your people brought us down. My ancestor had to bend the knee to those dratted mice. You STOLE MY BIRTHRIGHT."

Altheus' father stretched out a wing, his eyes glowed green and the ground under foot started to tremble.

"Yes, yes," whispered Cragzac. "Show me your power."

The ground stopped shaking.

"No." The word was barely a whisper. "I swore, never again."

"Pathetic," sneered Cragzac. "What is the point of a wizard who refuses to use his power?"

"Bro... Broken my staff," wheezed the old wizard, leaning against a wall. It was clear that even that small example of his magic had drained him considerably. "War was a mistake. I'll not use magic again."

This claim sent Cragzac into a rage.

"MISTAKE?" he shouted. "MISTAKE! I'll have your power, if I have to bleed it from you."

At this he reached into the inside pocket of his velvet robes and brought out a curved dagger. The sunlight streaming through the hole in the wall reflected well against the polished hilt.

"No, not you!" Cragzac said, suddenly calm.

Altheus noticed that as he spoke he moved closer to her mother.

"Noooo," she screamed out, but it was too late.

In one swift movement Cragzac had dragged the sharp blade across her mother's throat. Her mother gurgled softly for a second before her lifeless body hit the floor. All eyes were fixed on the old wizard. The guards shuffled nervously, expecting any moment vengeance to appear in the form of blazing magic. Tense moments passed and nothing happened.

"Nothing," Cragzac taunted. "You really are a coward, perhaps you need further persuasion." Altheus did not like the grin he flashed towards her. "You're very quiet all of a sudden," he said to her. "What do you think of your daddy now?" he taunted. He was standing directly behind her now, whispering in her ear, gently tracing patterns in her back with the sharp point of his dagger. "Don't worry," he cooed, "I won't kill her, I'm sure we can put her to some use in the fortress. She seems small enough to fit in the drains. I'm sure someone with this much passion could clear them of the sludge build-up, at least before drowning."

As if on cue the guards laughed at this. They were getting braver. While Cragzac was distracted entertaining his guards, Altheus turned around and sunk her beak into his shoulder, hard. Despite her rage she managed to get her beak into the soft spot between neck and shoulder.

"Little bitch," screamed Cragzac, dropping the dagger in surprise and pain.

With a sickening sound he wrenched Altheus' beak out of his shoulder and held the struggling chick in both wings. With a grunt he lifted her high into the air and threw her with force out of the opening of the small house and into the hard brick wall outside. Before she blacked out she heard him say, "Let the streets teach her some manners, she is not who I came for in any case."

* * *

Altheus decided against checking on the lizards. The giant beasts were clearly being a problem today and she had no wish to further excite them. It suddenly occurred to her that she had no plans other than revenge and now she had it she wasn't sure what it was a Supreme Leader actually did. She could ask Crasis, she supposed, but she still wasn't sure where the old crow's loyalties really lay. Yes, he had been invaluable to her during the revolution. Without him she wouldn't have gained such easy access to the leader's fortress, but he had taken a long time deciding which side to back.

As she stood in a state of confusion she heard a soft squeaking at her feet. She glanced down to see a black rat sitting on her boots. Her first instinct was to kick the foul creature as hard as she could across the courtyard until she noticed that far from being a dirty street rat this rat had impeccably clean and well-brushed fur. Around its neck was a red satin collar in which was tucked a piece of parchment folded neatly in half and sealed with the wax stamp of House Mowser.

*A royal missive*, Altheus mused. *I wonder what His Majesty wants with us mere underlings now?*

The rat squeaked a few more times, clearly impatient. Altheus reached down and scooped up the rat in her wide wings.

"What? Do you want a tip or something?" she asked, plucking the parchment out from underneath the collar.

Altheus broke through the wax seal and unfolded the parchment. The message was written in a swirling script, which took Altheus a few minutes to decipher:

*My Lord Steward,*
*On my orders you are requested and commanded to share all information in your possession about the fabled object the Collar of Honour. All information*

*about this relic must be proffered when you arrive for*
*the jubilee celebrations to which your attendance has*
*already been summoned.*

*Yours*

*King Hirax the First*
*Ruler of Venary*

Altheus stared into the rat's expressionless black eyes.

"Return to your master," she ordered.

The rat hopped down and sped along the courtyard, disappearing through a crack in the stone wall. Altheus wasn't surprised that Crasis had failed to mention the jubilee celebrations. She accepted that the aide had been busy lately. She had no idea what this Collar of Honour relic was though, however if the King was interested in it she decided that it was worth looking into. With a new sense of purpose, she hurried towards the library.

# CHAPTER TWO

# LEX

For the third time that day Lex leaned his considerable bulk back in his wooden chair and for the third time that day he cursed the creaking noise this produced. He reached into his desk for an order form and made a request for a new office chair. He had in fact sent several such forms in the past but he remained optimistic that one of them would be approved. Feeling annoyed with the chair and his day in general he placed his enormous front two pads on his desk and hauled himself up. Once up, Lex attempted the tricky task of manoeuvring his way across the floor of his office without disturbing the many towering stacks of paper placed around at seemingly random intervals. After successfully navigating his way around a stack of yellowing telegrams (all labelled "Top Secret") he found what he was looking for. The drinks cabinet was decidedly battered and well used but it contained a green bottle half full of tree bark gin and that was all that concerned Lex. Greedily wrapping his trunk around the cap, he opened the bottle and poured a large measure straight into his open mouth.

"Arrrrrh," he sighed happily.

He lifted the bottle in a mocking toast to the piles of papers surrounding him.

"Here's to making a 'valued contribution'," he said mockingly.

He sighed, looked at the remaining liquid in the bottle and with regret resealed the cap and placed it back in the cabinet. Using his trunk Lex reached into the pocket of his green fatigues, produced a mint and popped it into his mouth. As he worked the mint around his mouth with his tongue he reflected bitterly that there really wasn't any point in his wearing the drab and ill-fitting fatigues in any case. He was so far behind the lines that he could safely wander around with a target painted on his back and the worst injury he could suffer would be a paper cut.

"Nobody ever got a medal for services to administration," Lex would often complain to his colleagues, yet even after eleven requests the Pacidermian High Command steadfastly refused to grant him a battlefield commission, stating time and time again that "Communications is a vital position" and that he was "the eyes and ears of the entire campaign".

Lex regarded these as mere platitudes and with every day that the war dragged on he became more and more bitter about the snub. Lex just knew that if he could be given a platoon he would overrun the Giraxian forces in short order. Many times he could be heard loudly stating that, "The Giraxian front line is not as strong as everyone thinks" and that "Your average Giraxian is basically a coward who would flee at the first sight of flashing ivory." His colleagues had pointed out to him that such a strategy would result in multiple Pacidermian casualties but Lex would shrug and say that, "The end result will justify the means" and that "Any true Pacidermian would willingly lay down their life to wipe away the filth that is the Giraxian race." If Lex noticed that his colleagues were making great efforts to avoid him he didn't notice.

Slowly and with no enthusiasm Lex made his way back to his desk to continue to plough his way through the seemingly endless pile of communications that had accumulated during the current solar cycle. They were mostly the usual collection of death notices and position reports. Lex noted with little surprise that the territories hadn't changed much since the previous cycle. The Pacidermians still controlled the major cities but the Giraxians had managed to block supplies from getting through. Lex did a quick bout of mental arithmetic and calculated that if this continued then food would run out in three cycles. Suddenly furious he started writing another suggestion to High Command bemoaning the siege mentality he blamed for the gridlock to this war and that a final decisive push would see the Girexian cowards scatter in fear. He was sure that this would be the suggestion which would earn him the battlefield commission he craved.

As thoughts of victory parades and medals danced in his imagination Lex failed to notice that a small rat had appeared on his desk and was frantically waving its tiny paws to attract his attention. Growing frustrated the rat tried to sink his teeth into Lex's arm. Unfortunately his skin was too tough and the rat's teeth just grazed him. Eventually the rat climbed to the top of the nearest stack of papers and launched himself at the daydreaming Pacidermian's face.

Lex felt the tiny impact the rat made when he landed. Lex had to cross his eyes to see what was happening and when he spotted the rat he went to flick him off. This was until he noticed that the rat was wearing a red satin collar, underneath which was placed a folded piece of parchment. Lex gently plucked the rat from the bridge of his trunk. He placed it on the table where it shook the parchment free from its collar. Lex glanced down at the parchment and with a wicked smile flicked the rat through his office window. Chuckling to himself Lex unfolded the parchment and read the contents:

*For the attention of the Pacidermian High Command, On my orders you are requested and commanded to share all information in your possession about the fabled object the Collar of Honour. All information about this relic must be proffered when you arrive for the jubilee celebrations to which your attendance has already been summoned.*

  *Yours*

> *King Hirax the First*
> *Ruler of Venary*

Lex refolded the parchment and placed it in his pocket. He didn't know what the Collar of Honour was but if the King was interested in it then it must be very powerful indeed.

*It must be a weapon*, he rationalised to himself, *a weapon which could vanquish the Giraxian*s.

He couldn't allow the High Command that had foolishly overlooked him for so long to take all the glory for this. Perhaps he could be his people's hero after all.

## CHAPTER FOUR

# YANI

D RIP, DRIP, DRIP. The foul-smelling water continued its relentless onslaught from a hole in the stone ceiling, which was too dark to see. It had been dripping for so long now that it had created a pool of viscous liquid on the cell floor large enough that the sole occupant had been forced to squeeze herself into one of its dark corners. As a Giraxian this was not easy. Yani had to fold her four long legs into an uncomfortable position and rest her long neck into the corner of the cell where two walls met. It was bitterly cold. Yani tried to wrap herself up in the tattered remains of her once-prized Science Corps uniform. When it had been new the uniform was a deep blue colour. The long coat reached down to her hooves. The single-breasted coat was always worn buttoned up. On the chest was pinned the Science Corps badge. The badge was shaped like a long neck and patterned with the familiar brown spots that marked every Giraxian. Written underneath the neck was the slogan of the Giraxian Science Corps, "Through Oppression Comes Will".

Suddenly the cell door swung open. Yani was aware of multiple arms hauling her to her feet and dragging her away. As the party stepped outside the bright sunlight stung her eyes so much that she had to screw them up tightly. The guards found this very funny. One of them leant down and whispered in her ear, "You'd do better to enjoy the sun while you can still see it, traitor."

The rough stone floor of the courtyard scraped her knees as she was dragged along. The guards dropped her a few times, their laughter making it evident that these incidents were not accidents. Eventually Yani was dragged into another building and was roughly pulled up a flight of winding stairs, her escorts making sure that her already injured knees were banged against the edge of every step on the way up the seemingly impossibly long staircase, until eventually she was dumped into a chair in a featureless room and left alone.

Yani looked around her. The room was large and sparsely decorated. Apart from the (deeply uncomfortable) chair in which she sat there was only a wooden table in front of her with another chair on the opposite side. Yani noticed bitterly that the other chair was clearly more comfortable. She contemplated switching seats but realised that she was probably in enough trouble as it was, besides all four of her knees were throbbing and she couldn't be sure that she could get up to move and if she could there was no guarantee that she could remain on her hooves for long.

After a long time, the door to the room opened and another Giraxian walked in. Yani noticed that his neck was short for a Giraxian and that the hairs behind his ears were white. Clearly the male was old. Yani felt a slight relief.

Old men usually have nothing to prove and he didn't look capable of performing any further acts of violence against her. He wore a plain brown suit which matched the colours of his neck patches, on his nose were perched a pair of thin spectacles. He paid her no attention as he crossed the room, he was engrossed in a report of some kind. He pulled out the second chair and sat down, still reading from the many sheets of paper that made up the report. Eventually he turned his head towards the door to address a guard that Yani hadn't even noticed.

"Warm leaf tea, if you would," he said.

His voice was thin and reedy. It croaked slightly from underuse. The guard merely nodded and headed off down the corridor, presumably in search of the requested beverage.

"How have you enjoyed your stay?" the stranger asked, looking at Yani for the first time since entering the room.

Yani said nothing, she hadn't spoken to anyone for a very long time and wasn't sure where this conversation was going.

"Yeeees," the stranger said, extending the vowel sounds. Yani already hated his voice. "The facilities really aren't up to much, are they?" He giggled at this, a high-pitched SNEE-SNEE sound that made Yani shudder in revulsion. "Your file makes for interesting reading," he continued, idly tapping a quill on the stack of papers in front of him. Yani briefly fantasised about stabbing him through the eye with it. "The brightest member of our Science Corps." He made a big show of reading from the report. "Part of the team that discovered faux tusks."

"Team leader," Yani croaked.

If the stranger was surprised at this he didn't show it.

"Team leader," he conceded. "Former holder of the Giraxian Medal of Honour."

"Former?" Yani questioned.

At this he finally looked at her and for a moment she saw genuine hatred in his eyes and Yani realised that she was dealing with a very dangerous male. The anger in his eyes died out quickly and he returned to that interminable tapping.

"You've been away for a long time, Doctor, aren't you interested in the progress of the war?" Yani still said nothing. "Really?" he enquired. "You were very vocal about it for quite some time, you and…" he returned to the papers, a wicked grin spreading across his face, "your late husband."

Yani fell out of her chair and hit the ground with a large thump. She wept, she wept and she screamed. So upset was she that she failed to notice the return of the guard. When she eventually looked up the stranger was sipping from a thin china cup with sweet-smelling green steam rising from it.

"Sorry," he said with no warmth in his voice, "didn't you know?"

Yani stayed on the ground. The stranger muttered something and Yani was lifted from the ground and placed back in her uncomfortable seat.

"Execution," continued the stranger calmly. "Quite an amusing method too, would you like to hear about it? Oh, what am I thinking, of course you would."

Yani felt absolutely devastated but knew that she would have to listen to this sadist. The stranger flicked through a few sheets.

"Ah, yes," he began. "Yaxil Greenleaf, arrested with you trying to pass on secrets to the Pacidermian High Command. It was decided that an example needed to be set, so he was tied to a wall in the capital and stabbed a hundred times with some sharpened faux tusks. Took him three cycles to bleed out, most undignified."

At this the stranger shuddered.

"Is that what you have planned for me?" Yani asked, her voice flat and emotionless.

The stranger gave her one of his thin smiles.

"Oh, we have plans for you, don't worry about that. Don't you want to help your people? Don't you think you owe them that?"

So Yani listened to the stranger as he outlined his plans. When he finished Yani decided that he wasn't just a dangerous sadist he was possibly insane, but it wasn't like she had much choice.

A long time had passed since she had agreed to the proposal that had been put before her. In truth she didn't have much choice. She either did what she was told or she'd be executed in the same way her husband had. The death of her husband was just too big for her to take in fully. Intellectually she had known for some time that it was unlikely that he had survived but she had held on to that hope. Now it was taken from her she made herself a promise. If she survived this foolhardy mission she would kill the stranger with her bare hooves.

After the briefing she had been taken to another part of the castle. A bath had been run for her and despite her misgivings she lowered herself into it. The bath was much needed. She had spent an uncountable amount of time locked in a dingy cell and was offending herself with the various odours that came off her whenever she moved. She allowed herself to relax into the hot water. The bath was long enough to allow Yani to stretch out her large body and deep enough that she was able to float.

While she was dozing in the warm bath various uniformed Giraxians, whom she assumed must be serving staff, brought in golden plates of apricot leaves and acacia twigs. Usually she would refuse anything served to her by the government but it had been so long since she'd eaten anything that wasn't growing out of a cell floor that she cleared all of the plates brought to her.

*Besides which*, she rationalised, *I am working for the government now, might as well sell out completely.*

After her bath she found an ornate outfit laid out for her. After putting it on she found that she missed her old science uniform. This outfit was made of much softer fabric, the neckline was lower. Yani speculated that this must be intentional, a way to show off whatever necklace or jewellery the occupant of the dress was wearing. Yani had never owned that much jewellery (in the lab it was considered a bad idea to wear anything that dangled) and any riches she had ever possessed had been seized the night her home had been raided by the Giraxian People's Democratic Police Force (the dreaded CPDPF). At least the supplied shoes were flat. Even as a Giraxian Yani was self-conscious about her height. Begrudgingly she forced herself into the unfamiliar outfit and stepped out of her room.

She was disgusted but not surprised to see the stranger (who in a moment of smug pomposity insisted that she call him

"Number One") waiting for her. He had changed his outfit but Yani did wonder why he bothered. The new suit was black but that was the only difference. The cut and style were exactly the same as the brown suit he had worn during that first interview. Yani realised with a surge of hope that she was dealing with a pencil-pushing bureaucrat. Perhaps his lack of imagination could be something she might be able to exploit.

He looked her up and down. She seemed to pass some sort of inspection as he nodded and simply said, "You remember your role?" She nodded. "Well then, smile," he cooed. "You're a very lucky girl, after all, it's not every traitor who gets to go to a party."

They walked through the long sparsely decorated corridors. Number One finally broke the silence.

"The war has gone on longer than we first predicted," he stated simply.

Yani noted that he said this with no emotion in his voice at all. He wasn't upset or pleased about this news, it was just news.

"I never wanted war," was the only thing she could think to say.

"Really?" he replied. "You'd rather we remain slaves to the Pacidermians?"

"I didn't want this much death and destruction," she replied, suddenly annoyed.

"Much of it caused by you, Doctor," he countered.

There was something about the way he said "Doctor" that made it sound like an insult. Yani decided that it was best not to antagonise this man any further so she started counting internally to ten to calm herself. If he was annoyed at her lack of response he didn't let it show.

By now they had reached the main doors to the fortress. There were two Giraxians in pages' uniforms standing on either side of the heavy oak doors, and as Yani and her escort approached they heaved the two doors open. It was clearly an extreme effort on the part of the two stewards but Yani noticed that they steadily refused to meet Number One's eyes. They were terrified of him. Before long the doors were open and with only a cursory glance at the pages Number One stepped through. Taking a deep breath Yani followed him out.

The sun was only just starting to set. Orange skies surrounded her and there was still heat in the air. For the first time Yani was grateful for the thinness of her new outfit. The heat combined with the company would be uncomfortable enough. Within seconds a large carriage pulled up in front of them. Yani was disappointed to note that the carriage was very plain-looking. It was coloured green and the wheels were thick and coated with tar. The carriage was pulled by two pitch-black horses. Although the horses had been groomed and cleaned it was obvious that they were war horses, more used to riding into a smoke-covered battle ground than being pressed into domestic service. Yani was surprised and delighted to see that the coach driver was female, young and beautiful despite the mud on her face and the scowl that seemed to be a permanent feature on her lips. Perhaps Yani had found a potential ally. She reached up to shake the driver's hand.

"Good eve…" she began, only to be cut off by the plume of spit the driver aimed at her, landing squarely at her feet.

Yani stepped back in horror. The look of hatred on the driver's face was chilling. The carriage door swung open. In her horror at the driver's reaction she hadn't noticed that Number One had already entered the carriage. He was holding the door open and was giving her a superior smirk.

"Well, what did you expect?" he asked. "Your reputation certainly precedes you."

He held out a hoof, clearly expecting her to take it. Instead she walked around the coach and climbed in the other side. The inside of the carriage was even sparser than the outside. Two wooden benches faced each other and the floor was bare. Yani pointedly sat opposite Number One, determined that he wouldn't see the look of sorrow on her face. Was this how all of her people viewed her? she wondered.

"Do you understand now?" he asked, clearly exasperated. "You are not a hero to your people." Yani opened her mouth to argue but he raised his hoof to stop her. "You were once," he conceded. "The creation of faux tusks allowed us to undercut the Pacidermians in EVERY market they controlled, YOUR invention allowed us to financially cripple our enemy. Coupled with the discovery that they had used a fabricated predator to placate us and we were riding high for the first time in our history."

Yani looked out of the window of the carriage at the landscape and immediately wished she hadn't. Where once her land had been lush and green with fields and trees stretching out in all directions all Yani could see was churned-up mud.

"We were free," he continued. "The Pacidermians couldn't control us anymore. They had nobody to remove their tusks for them and if even they did, your invention was cheaper and stronger so they had nobody to sell them to in any case. We won."

At this he leaned back in his seat. Placing his long arms behind his head he closed his eyes as if lost in the memory.

"I didn't butcher them," Yani stated. "My invention was meant to help both of our species. I never meant for us to attack the Pacidermians in that way."

She shuddered again. The attack on the Pacidermians had been brutal. A strike team of Giraxians had reported to the Pacidermian tusk-trimming plant as normal. The Pacidermians were at this stage unaware of the twin discovery of faux tusks and the non-existence of the Flying Drexes. They allowed the Giraxians to strap them into the padded chairs as they had done so many times before. Then the order was given and every Giraxian took the trimming blade and in a display of unexpected brutality hacked away at the very roots of the trunks of each Pacidermian, only stopping when each trunk hit the floor in a combination of ivory, nerve endings and blood. In a further insult the Girexians sliced off the trunks of their former opressors. It was said that the screams of the Pacidermians could be heard right across Venary.

Number One suddenly slapped Yani hard across the face.

"That wasn't your decision," he snarled at her. Yani was stunned, she knew that he was a dangerous man but hadn't thought that he had a temper like that. "They treated us like cattle," he continued. "Twenty spans we worked for them, trimming their tusks, processing them, choking on ivory fumes every day!"

He was getting angry again. Yani instinctively raised her own hooves in preparation for another painful slap across her face, which was already stinging from the last one. The predicted hit never came, instead he continued with his rant.

"Did you ever stop to think about how many of our people died in those processing plants? Yet we continued to serve them, because they convinced us that they were the only beings who could protect us from the Flying Drexes." He leaned forward in his seat and stared at her directly in both eyes. "Tell me," he asked, his voice quavering with barely suppressed fury, "when you discovered that the Flying Drexes didn't exist, how did you feel?"

Yani let out the breath she had been holding.

"I was angry," she admitted.

Yani closed her eyes at the memory of that day. She had been angry, very angry. Like all of her people she felt foolish and used.

"Did you imagine what the other species in Venary thought of us?" he asked, his face still mere inches away from hers. "Did you hear their laughter, I wonder?"

Yani could only nod, afraid to speak, afraid to admit that yes, she did hear the laughter of others whether real or imagined. It had spurned her on. After revealing this she worked night and day to develop faux tusks. She had never admitted this to anyone but she created faux tusks purely to ruin the Pacidermians. She fondly imagined the Pacidermians finding themselves desperate enough to have to work for the Giraxians. She felt that was poetic judgment.

Number One asked again, "Did you?"

"YES I DID!" she screamed back at him. "WHY DO YOU THINK I MADE THOSE BLOODY FAKE TUSKS! I WANTED TO DESTROY THEM! I WANTED TO BRING THEM TO THEIR KNEES!"

Number One grinned and leaned back.

"There she is," he said proudly. "I thought they might have broken you, but no." There was definitely admiration in his voice as he continued, "So, you lived high for a while. What was it the media called you? 'The Bringer of Truth', wasn't it?"

Yani nodded. Her throat was sore after all the shouting.

"Then you betrayed us. Tell me, why did you take the recipe for faux tusks to the enemy? That was ours! We had them on their knees."

"You went too far," was her reply. "You butchered them! Financial revenge is one thing but you carved them up while they were helpless. They might have used us but we were meant to be better."

This time Number One didn't interrupt, he clearly wanted to hear more from her.

"So I took them the recipe, I just wanted to make us even, I just wanted things to be fair. I didn't know what they would do."

"And now you know." He asked, "Do you still want to make things even?" Yani shrugged. "Well," he said, "if we find out what this Collar of Honour is that the King wants perhaps you'll get your chance."

CHAPTER FIVE

# GREETA

THE SILENCE OF the night was interrupted by the almost imperceptible noise of pressurised air being released and the sound of metal scraping across stone and then clattering to the cobbled streets.

"Bugger," a soft yet clearly annoyed voice whispered. "Cheap bloody metal," the voice continued to hiss to nobody in particular. "Should know not to trust badger labour," the voice continued, clearly warming to its theme.

As it spoke, the body to which the voice belonged dragged the "cheap metal" towards itself slowly so as to not make a noise. Occasionally light from the flickering street lamps fell upon it, revealing it to be a four-pronged hook attached to a long rope. Slowly and deliberately the hook inched its way towards a short leather-clad figure wearing goggles. When it reached the desired location, the figure reached down and with tiny paws manipulated the hook back into its launcher.

"Right then," the voice whispered, still tense but noticeably calmer than earlier, "let's try this again."

It hefted the launcher up to its shoulder and pulled the trigger once more. "*Pffft*" was the pathetic noise made by the launcher. At this the figure made no effort to remain silent, throwing the launcher, complete with hook, to the floor with an almighty crash.

"Bloody badgers!" the voice shouted into the night.

There followed a string of muttered curses which gradually faded as the figure walked away from the town square, heading towards Silvestri Forest which dotted the edges of the capital city.

The forest was dark but this didn't bother the would-be thief. She was nocturnal and her goggles had been fitted with night-vision capabilities, which enhanced her already very keen night vision. She reached her location, a large tree with a distinctive carving of two crossed keys on it. She reached up and tapped three times on the carving. After a short while a small window opened just above her head and a squirrel popped its head out. The squirrel had clearly been woken up by her knocking as it was bleary-eyed and its fur was pointing in all directions. As tired as the squirrel obviously was he didn't forget to ask the required question.

"Who demands entrance to this noble establishment?" he asked, the obvious solemnity of the question somewhat ruined by the enormous yawn which punctuated it.

"Squireal! Stop pissing about and open the door! It's bloody freezing out here," the figure said testily.

Squireal clearly felt that if he was going to be woken up at all hours then his question demanded an answer.

"I repeat," he said, trying to keep his malicious smile from showing in the moonlight, "who demands entrance to this noble establish…?"

The end of this question was cut short by the unprintable level abuse he received. He waited for the tirade to end before theatrically looking back into the tree.

"I know nobody by that name," he called back over his shoulder, "but if you leave a message I'll make sure he gets it."

"SQUIREAL!" the voice screeched in return. "When I get in there I'll make damn sure that you have no nuts for winter! Or spring or summer or autumn for that matter! Now open the door!"

Squireal couldn't contain the laughter anymore.

"That's as maybe," he replied, "but that doesn't answer my question."

"Fine," came the defeated reply. "It is I, Greeta, daughter of Heeta, sneak thief and house breaker of this guild and I demand admission."

There was a long pause.

"Pardon?" came the reply.

Greeta ripped off her gloves and started silently climbing the tree. She waited by the window for Squireal to poke his head out again. She waited patiently and after a while her patience was rewarded. Squireal, who was having far too much fun to let this stop, leaned out of the window, hoping to see where Greeta had gone. Quick as a flash Greeta reached out and grabbed Squireal's neck with her paw. She dug her sharp claws into the soft part of his throat and hissed, "Hello, Squireal, let's play a game. It's called open the door or open the throat. I feel generous tonight so I'll let you go first. What are you going to open?"

Squireal tried to swallow but Greeta had his throat in a vice-like grip. Eventually he managed to splutter, "I pick the door."

"Good boy," Greeta said with a smile. "You win."

With the sound of bolts slipping back and keys being turned, a door in the base of the tree swung open. Greeta stomped through, her bad mood unabated by the warmth that greeted her. Squireal appeared at her side, gently rubbing his throat. He was slightly alarmed when he pulled his paw away to see that she had drawn a small amount of blood. He wasn't about to let her see any discomfort though.

"Hestor demands you report directly to her," he said, being wary to keep his distance.

"But of course she does," Greeta sighed. "Any chance I can get out of this outfit first? My spikes are being forced into my back and I'd hate to curtsy too low in case I stab myself."

Before Squireal could reply a loud female voice boomed through the caverns, "NOW!"

"Well, I guess that answers that," was all Greeta could think of to say.

The underground caverns of the Thieves' Guild were heated by numerous fires placed inside the hollowed-out roots of the tree in which the guild was located. Heat would travel through the root network, resulting in a permanently warm hideout with surprisingly very few fires. Holes had been carved into the wooden trunks so that orange light from the fires could spill out, illuminating the maze-like corridors with a warming orange glow. Greeta walked along the longest of these corridors leading to the main office of Hestor, leader of the Thieves' Guild. It was a long walk and Greeta was in no mood to hurry. She had returned empty-handed again and this couldn't end well for her. On and on she trekked, the heat and closeness of the ever-shrinking corridors adding to her sense of discomfort and dread. Eventually she arrived at the archway to Hestor's office. Hestor had designed the archway in such a way that anyone who used it had to crawl through on their knees. This way she would always have the upper hand on any visitor or possible assassin.

Greeta crawled through the small opening into Hestor's dimly lit office. Despite her excellent night vision Greeta needed to blink a few times to reaccustom her eyes to near darkness after an extended time in the brightly lit corridors. Eventually she started to notice dim shapes. The shapes started to take form, the office furniture came into focus, but Greeta couldn't see Hestor anywhere. This wasn't unusual. Hestor (as leader of the Thieves' Guild) could move very fast and remain unnoticed.

Greeta chose to remain totally still, relying on Hestor to make her presence known when she chose to. Greeta became aware of hot breath on the back of her neck. She turned around slowly to find Hestor standing uncomfortably close. For a hedgehog Hestor was very tall and thin. Her spikes were long and slicked back so that they ran like a prickly waterfall down her back. Greeta, being short and scruffy, always felt somewhat inferior to Hestor. She realised that this was Hestor's intent but it still made her feel inadequate when she compared herself to her glamorous senior.

Hestor didn't make any attempt to move so, cursing herself inwardly, Greeta took two steps backwards.

"You wanted to see me?" Greeta eventually said.

Hestor raised one eyebrow and audibly sighed.

"Cold night," she said eventually. There was no emotion in her voice at all, it seemed like she was merely stating a fact. "Still too," she added, her eyes locked on Greeta's.

The calmness was maddening. Hestor stepped off on her left foot and walked towards her wooden desk in the far corner of the room. Her heeled boots made a clicking noise on the floor as she walked. Upon reaching her desk she picked up a cup with hot steam rising from it.

"On a cold and still night like this I always enjoy a hot cup of moss tea."

Greeta could take this no longer. "If I might explain…" she started to say.

At the sound of her voice, Hestor looked up sharply from the cup of moss tea she was sniffing at and raised one long claw to silence her. Greeta stopped talking immediately. Hestor took a sip from her cup and smiled. The previous fury in her eyes had dimmed.

"It was a very still morning when we first found you," Hestor continued. "Do you remember?" Greeta went to reply but Hestor cut across her. "Of course you don't," she continued. "A fair few spans ago now, and you were so very young! Even as a cub you tried to pick my pocket, such impudence, although I admired your form and rather than immediately remove your head from your body I took you in and trained you in our art." Hestor went silent and sipped her tea, seemingly lost in the memory. "I taught you to be stealthy, to come and go like a shadow. Under my tutelage you were taught to break into the palaces of the rich and greedy and…" at this she waved her paw in an expansive fashion, "redistribute their wealth." Hestor sighed again.

"Have I been wasting my time?" she asked, suddenly seeming very tired. "You haven't brought back anything in over thirty cycles." Greeta went to protest but was silenced once again by a raised claw. "I am discounting the purple gem you found in the street, partly because other than being very shiny it is worthless but largely because a drunken feline threw it at you in the mistaken belief that you were a demon intent on snatching his immortal soul."

Greeta stifled a snort of laughter at this, unsuccessfully trying to turn it into a cough. It was a funny memory though. She'd just been chased away from the Felixian bank by a platoon of cat guards who had taken her by surprise. After losing them she had to lean against a nearby wall to catch her breath. She had been running hard in an unforgiving leather suit so was out of breath and was very red in the face, when a door directly opposite her opened and a very drunk Felixian was thrown through it, landing at her claws. The cat eventually staggered to his paws, shook his head gently, blinked twice, and was then violently sick right at her feet. He was a pitiful sight, his whiskers all matted with the now rapidly drying vomit. His eyes were bloodshot and his fur (usually well maintained by the famously vain Felixians) had patches missing from it.

He stood unsteadily on his feet and Greeta thought he was the most wretched thing she had ever seen. She felt moved to help this creature. Despite him being a dangerous carnivore, she moved closer to him, a movement somewhat hampered by her need to navigate her way around a large pool of red and green sick.

"Excuse me," she had said upon reaching his paws.

She had meant to say more but was suddenly hit by the foul smell emanating from the Felixian. So vile was it that Greeta nearly added her own meagre contribution to the lagoon of sick now behind her. As she was retching the drunk Felixian looked down and noticed her for the first time.

"DEMON!" he shouted. "Get away, get away."

He swung his fists violently and tried to stamp on Greeta, who managed to dodge away at the last minute.

"Be gone!" the Felixian continued, eventually becoming entangled in his own feet and falling face first into his own pile of sick.

Fearing for her life, Greeta couldn't help but look back as she ran away. The Felixian had managed to get back to his feet and was drunkenly fumbling at his belt. Greeta paused at this. It looked like the Felixian was reaching for a sword but only the Knights of Felicius Regalis carried swords and they lived by a strict code of sobriety. Eventually the Felixian's paws closed around something in his jerkin pocket and he threw it at Greeta.

"The wages of sin," he shouted after her. "Take your wages, demon."

And that was how she had returned to the guild with a funny story and a shiny purple gem which turned out to be worthless and had picked up the scent of its previous owner. She kept it on her person as a souvenir of a night that to this day made her laugh to herself.

"Catnip wine is a terrible thing," said Hestor, ruefully bringing Greeta back into the present, "but taking advantage of the poor and unfortunate is not our way," she admonished. "By rights I should expel you from our order and I am sorely tempted to do just that."

Greeta's eyes went wide with fear. She had been with the guild for most of her life and couldn't imagine life on the outside. Her fear must have shown on her face, as Hestor smiled a wicked smile at her.

"But I might have a use for you yet," she said.

Reaching into a desk drawer, she withdrew a parchment which had been sealed with the royal sigel of King Hirax Mowser. Hestor tossed the document to Greeta and said, "What do you know of the Collar of Honour?"

Greeta remained frozen to the spot for a moment. It was only when Hestor raised one perfect eyebrow that Greeta was able to find her voice. She coughed quietly to give herself some thinking time. She wracked her brains desperately trying to remember if she'd heard anything about a collar of honour. She had heard talk about an enchanted goblet that never emptied and the sparrows were forever twittering about a magic tree which produced wood as comfortable as silk but nothing about a collar came to mind.

Hestor had started tapping her claw on her sleeve. She was becoming impatient. Greeta had only seconds to come up with something believable. Feigning a confidence that she certainly didn't feel Greeta went for broke.

"Ah, yes," she flustered, "the Collar of Honour, made by the first animals to control the larger predators. I believe they made several in an attempt to create an army of willing slaves. The Collar of Honour is the last one left."

Greeta beamed.

"Impressive," Hestor said, clearly impressed.

"Thank you, Hestor," Greeta replied smoothly. "But it's all thanks to your guidance and our extensive library."

"No," Hestor said sharply, "I mean it's impressive how you can lie to me so smoothly."

"Oh," was the only thing Greeta could think of to say, starting to think that perhaps being expelled from the guild might not be that bad. She could go freelance she supposed.

"Nobody knows anything about the Collar of Honour," Hestor explained patiently. "However, the King is clearly very interested. We have been invited to his tenth jubilee and he expects us to bring everything we know about this Collar."

"Whoever goes will be travelling light," Greeta said before thinking.

To her surprise Hestor chuckled at that. *There might be hope for me yet*, Greeta thought, feeling confident for the first time since entering Hestor's quarters.

Still chuckling, Hestor walked over to the open fireplace built into the largest wall in her quarters. She picked up a metal poker and began to idly poke at the simmering embers.

"Do you know why I moved the leader's quarters to the fire room when I took over?" she asked without looking up.

"I'm guessing it wasn't for the view," Greeta replied, hoping her sense of humour would continue to keep her safe.

It didn't. Hestor threw the poker back to the floor, but not so hard to risk scorching anything, Greeta noticed, so Hestor hadn't completely lost her fierce temper yet.

"I moved here because it reminds me how fragile our existence is. Imagine if this fire ever went out."

In all honesty Greeta hadn't given it much thought. She supposed someone would just light it again. Wisely she chose not to voice this opinion.

"Within seconds," Hestor said solemnly, "the heat tubes would stop distributing heat all through the guild. In turn the earth surrounding us would stop being dried and the weight of several hundred tons of mud would engulf us. If we could escape every predator around us – including the Felixians, who usually can't find their nose with their paws – will know where we are and descend upon us. It would be the end."

Greeta thought this all very unlikely but hoped that her expression didn't show this.

"So," Hestor continued, "being here reminds me that even the smallest detail, if overlooked, could doom us all. Am I making my point?" she asked Greeta, both eyebrows raised in enquiry.

"You want me to look after the fire?" Greeta offered hopefully, sure the job wouldn't bring excitement but she wouldn't be homeless.

Hestor slowly counted to ten under her breath and tried again.

"You might think that you are a small part of the guild," she said slowly, "but everything you do has an effect on us. Do you, for example, think that Squireal will be so thorough in his examination of visitors in future after your performance?"

Greeta couldn't believe she was hearing this.

"Oh come on," she blurted out suddenly, "he knew it was me, he was just playing about. He deserved far more than the little scratch I gave him."

Hestor appeared to ignore this outburst.

"Have you eaten tonight?" she asked instead.

"Y... Y... Yes," Greeta stammered, unsure of where this was going.

"Nice meal was it?" Hestor asked sweetly.

"Very nice, thank you," Greeta replied, now completely confused.

"And how did you pay for it?" Hestor enquired, her voice still dripping honey.

"We don't pay for it," Greeta said, "it's given to us."

"From where do you think it comes?" Hestor asked, a note of impatience creeping into her voice. "It doesn't fall from the sky," she added, before Greeta could say anything.

"Our hunting parties bring it back or we bargain with the shrews with the trinkets thieves like you acquire. Or should be every thief EXCEPT you acquire."

Greeta started panicking again. This was it, Hestor was building up to her expulsion. She braced waiting for the final judgement.

"At present you are to our guild what a sudden flood would be like to the great fire. Destructive and wasteful."

Greeta considered running. She knew it wouldn't be long before she said something she'd regret, but Hestor was really milking this moment. How could she be so cruel?

"However," Hestor said, her voice returning to its normal tone, "you might yet be useful to us. I cannot go to the jubilee, there's far too much to do here. So, I've decided to send you. Find out what you can about the King's new obsession and get this information back to me. This is your last chance, Greeta, don't mess it up."

BACK TO THE PRESENT

## CHAPTER SIX

# SCRATCH SNIFFSUNN

S CRATCH STARED AT the pews in the cathedral. They seemed to go on forever. Sighing deeply, he placed the bucket of soapy water he had been carrying down on the rough stone floor, dipped his scrubbing brush into the water and began the laborious task of deep cleaning each and every one of them. It was early, most of the knights were still sleeping, but Scratch and the other serfs had been awake for hours. He had already polished the many breastplates stacked in the armoury and sharpened the pike staffs which lined the walls. In truth there hadn't been a campaign in many spans so the armour didn't require that much work. Scratch did it because he had been ordered to. Likewise, the pews he was presently scrubbing probably wouldn't be used until the next ceremony, which could be many more cycles away. He once asked the General (a fearsome cat with one eye named Oscar) why he had to polish unused weapons and scrub unused pews. The question had not been received well.

"We all have our duties," Oscar replied, staring intently at Scratch with his one good eye. "Perhaps you consider your duties beneath you?" he enquired. Before Scratch could answer Oscar continued. "What if we all abandoned our duties?" he asked. Scratch stayed silent, realising that Oscar was being rhetorical. "What if the patrol hadn't been on guard duty the night you were found? What if they decided that as they'd already marched the previous night there was no need to march again?"

Scratch sighed inwardly. He was growing tired of this. It wasn't his fault that he had been left on their doorstep in a small wicker basket. He was just a kitten back then, it wasn't as if he had a lot of choice in the matter. He hated Oscar for this. Every time he asked anything this one-eyed bastard would start with the guilt trip.

"Cold night, as I recall," Oscar continued, no longer really caring if Scratch was listening or not. "The fur gods only know how long you'd been out there but you certainly required lots of our hot milk to bring you round. Still a fan of our milk, I believe?" he said accusingly.

Scratch flashed hot under the stiff collar of his work smock.

"If life here is so arduous," Oscar said, sarcasm dripping from every word, "why are you still here?"

"I want to be a knight," Scratch said quietly. He had never admitted this to anyone before.

SMACK! Scratch felt the back of Oscar's paw as it connected with great force to the side of his face. The smack had been so fast that Scratch had no chance to defend himself against it and with such force that it brought him to his knees.

"You ungrateful little gutter snipe," Oscar roared at him. "After all we have done for you! We should have left you outside like the trash you are!"

Oscar was furious now, he hauled Scratch to his feet, dragging him to an open window, and forcing Scratch's head out of it he made him look at the square many, many feet below them.

"Do you see that?" he hissed, somewhat redundantly into Scratch's ear. "Our passing-out square! Where hundreds of noble cat knights have received their honours and their birthright, and you..." Oscar said "you" as if the word rhymed with scum, "you think yourself noble enough to stand with them? My knights all come from noble families. Honour and chivalry run through their veins! Whereas I suspect sewer water runs through yours! Tell me, boy," he spat, "who was your father?"

Despite being terrified that Oscar might throw him out of the open window Scratch forced himself to answer, "I don't know! My father is dead! I came here an orphan."

Scratch braced himself for the long descent he was convinced was coming but nothing happened. Nothing continued to happen for a long time. Eventually he felt himself being pulled back into the room. When he looked back at Oscar he was confused (and annoyed) to see that he was grinning.

"Yes, yes, you did," Oscar agreed quietly. "Perhaps I have been a bit tough on you." Oscar continued to smile at him but there was no warmth behind that smile. "Clearly I haven't treated you with the respect you deserve. Your tasks are obviously not suited to a cat of your undoubted stature. I really must find something more in keeping with your knightly persona." At this his smile became even broader. "Arise Scratch Sniffsunn," he intoned with mock solemnity, "Lord Protector of the Latrines and Knight Emptier of the Bed Pans."

Scratch wanted to cry but he held it together, not wanting to give Oscar the satisfaction. He straightened up, saluted Oscar and thanked him for the opportunity before fleeing as fast as he could to his cold and damp quarters.

That had been a few cycles ago and it had quickly become apparent that Oscar had not been joking, as Scratch found out the very next day when a group of trainee knights broke into his quarters pre-dawn and threw the contents of their bed pans at his sleeping form. Scratch woke in horror as the cold, fetid liquid soaked his fur and bedclothes. When he asked them what they were doing their leader, the impossibly attractive Mittens, said that as he had been so derelict in his new duty, Grand Officer Oscar had suggested that they take their complaints directly to the new Lord Protector of the Latrines and Knight Emptier of the Bed Pans." Scratch could hear their mocking laughter even now and from then on made sure that their bed pans were never that full again. This meant that Scratch was forced to rise even earlier each morning but the alternative was far worse.

Scratch's memories were interrupted by a sudden clang followed by a splash. He looked out from under the pew seat he had been cleaning to find Mittens and some of his friends standing there. Two of them were kicking his metal bucket up and down the church aisles, making sure to spread the water as far as it would go.

Scratch was horrified when he realised that they had been at jousting practice and were all very muddy. Mittens was laughing loudly as the muddiest of his colleagues rolled around in the water and then chased each other around the church, leaving streaks of mud all over the pews and church floor.

"My Lord Latrine," Mittens said, offering him a mocking salute, "I think you missed a spot."

On cue the others all fell about laughing. Incensed, Scratch launched himself at Mittens with his claws out. Mittens quickly sidestepped and Scratch flew through the air he had occupied moments ago, landing with force on the stone floor, chipping three of his claws as he landed. Howling with pain Scratch tried to stand upright but Mittens had caught up with him and kicked him hard with his booted foot. Winded, Scratch fell to the floor again. Lying there trying to catch his breath, Scratch felt himself being lifted up by both arms by two cats on either side of him. They held him so tightly that Scratch couldn't turn around. Slowly Mittens proceeded to walk around him, seemingly inspecting him. Eventually Mittens stopped in front of him, folded his arms and stared him right in the eye.

"You will never be one of us," he said quietly. "Why don't you just leave?"

Scratch stared at Mittens defiantly.

"I... will... be... a... knight," he wheezed between painful breaths.

Mittens held up his right paw. Dutifully one of the others (a ginger cat with long whiskers and a tail which twitched with pleasure at the pain its owner was witnessing) placed a metal gauntlet onto it. Mittens admired the gauntlet as it reflected the sunlight pouring through the many stained-glass windows which surrounded the church hall.

"I have to say, my Knight of the Turds..." this provoked yet more laughter from the assembled throng and Mittens stopped talking momentarily to savour his moment, "you have cleaned this gauntlet so very well, why it almost sparkles."

He raised his hands and struck Scratch across the face with it. Once, twice, thrice he continued striking Scratch, peppering each strike with a word.

"How... many... times... must... I... strike... you... to... dull... the... shine?"

Scratch was struggling to see with the blood pouring into his eyes but he could hear the laughter.

"Fifteen times," Mittens eventually said, disappointed. He ripped off the gauntlet and threw it into Scratch's bloodied face. "Do better next time," he sneered. He picked up Scratch's lolling and puffy face. Gripping his throat tightly he spat into his ear, "You'll never be one of us! Now clean this place up."

At this he let go of Scratch. He nodded at the two cats who, up to now, had been holding Scratch upright and they threw him to the floor. Pausing only to adjust his scarlet tunic he turned to his friends.

"Well, time for lunch I think, boys, sorting out rubbish always makes me hungry," and laughing they exited the church hall, leaving Scratch curled up in a small, sobbing, blood-covered ball.

Much later a limping and dishevelled Scratch painfully shuffled out of the freshly cleaned church hall. He'd had to work through both lunch and dinner and knew that a pile of washing-up was waiting for him in the kitchens. As he staggered through the corridors, trying to keep to the shadows, he wondered if this was worth it. Oscar would never admit him to knight training and Mittens would continue to make his life unbearable, but what else could he do? Scratch had wanted to be a knight for as long as he could remember. As a kitten he would watch them perform drills in the courtyard, their swords flashing in the sunlight as the knights swung them in perfect unity. He would listen to them sing the anthem of the Knights of Felix Regalis so many times that he knew it by heart but wouldn't dare to sing it out loud. He often fantasised about riding the giant fox cubs into battle, which he reasoned had to be preferable to shovelling their dung every night.

Despite everything he decided to stay. Oscar couldn't live forever and Mittens would grow bored of him eventually. Filled with a new resolve Scratch continued to limp his way to the kitchens. Turning a corner, Scratch was disheartened to meet Oscar coming the other way.

"Ah, where have you been hiding?" Oscar said accusingly. As Scratch moved closer to him Oscar spotted the many wounds on Scratch's still puffy face. "My God!" Oscar exclaimed. "What have you done to yourself?"

Scratch looked up at Oscar and sighed deeply.

"I tripped, sir," Scratch said, his voice muffled by his swollen face and broken teeth.

"Oh dear," Oscar said with mock concern, "how careless of you." He chuckled at this. "Well, obviously your mind isn't on your job. Luckily I have another opportunity for you."

Scratch wanted to refuse. He wanted to state he had still to wash up after the meals he had been forced to miss, but what would be the point?

"I'm looking forward to it, sir," he said eventually.

"Excellent," Oscar replied. "Now, as you know all of our knights are honourable gentlecats but occasionally we have some who are a bit eccentric and require looking after."

As he spoke Oscar placed his hands on Scratch's shoulders, roughly turned him on the spot and, continuing to talk, he navigated Scratch towards the sleeping quarters.

When they reached a long and ornate corridor with low-hanging golden candleholders dangling from the wooden roof beams, Oscar asked, "Now do you understand your new opportunity?"

Scratch was a bit shocked but nodded his head.

"I'm to look after an old knight, cook for him, clean him and take responsibility for everything he does."

Oscar nodded.

"Good, you can follow simple instructions. Now, your charge is behind this door, I'll leave you to get acquainted." Oscar walked back the way they came. He stopped, turned around slowly and shouted back, "Oh, and by the way, the kitchen will need those plates cleaned by the morning, don't forget."

And without looking back he walked away.

Scratch reached up to the gold doorknocker and knocked smartly three times on the door. He jumped back in surprise as he heard something made of glass smash against the other side of the door and a slurred voice shouting, "Bugger off." Scratch wanted to go but he realised that this was probably exactly what Oscar was hoping he would do, so instead he took a deep breath, opened the door and stepped inside.

The smell hit him first. It was like nothing he had ever encountered before. Scratch doubled over in horror and began dry retching, his eyes were streaming and he couldn't stop coughing. After a while Scratch got his breathing under control and wiped the tears from his eyes. He peered into the darkness and could make out a large shape at the end of the room.

"H… Hello," he called into the darkness.

The shape moved slightly, accompanied by the sound of glass bottles falling over.

"If you're going to be sick," a cultured yet slurry voice replied, "do it outside, we do have standards, you know." This was followed by a raucous laugh. Clearly the shape thought it was hilarious. "Are you still there?" the shape called again. "If you've died I may not find you for weeks."

This provoked yet more laughter. Scratch rolled his eyes. He knew that Oscar hated him but not enough to send him into a room to be killed by a mentally unstable former knight. Eventually it occurred to Scratch that all of the knights he had encountered liked it when anyone they considered beneath them grovelled a bit. Emboldened by this realisation he strode towards the shape, removed his leather serf's cap and performed the most elaborate bow ever seen amongst the Knights of Felix Regalis.

"My lord knight…" he began.

"Oh, don't do that or I'll be sick! My name is Zakk, just that," the shape said, suddenly sounding very weary. "Walk closer to me, let me see what I've been sent."

Scratch edged forward across the cluttered floor. As his eyes became accustomed to the darkness he saw his new charge. He was slumped in a high-backed chair dressed in a dirty and ill-fitting knight's tunic. Once the tunic had been beautiful, Scratch knew, but now it was coated in many stains and had been stretched across the old knight's stomach so far that it had started to tear.

"My God," he said suddenly as Scratch came into view, "someone definitely doesn't like you! That must have been quite a fight."

Scratch looked at his feet. "I tripped," he muttered.

"Oh, please," was the reply he received to this, "I've been in enough fights to know the signs, and those signs suggest to me that you lost." Scratch remained silent, staring at his feet. "Hmm, looks like we've got our work cut out for us, doesn't it? Well, let's have your name."

"I am Scratch Sniffsunn, my lor… owww," Scratch moaned in pain as Zakk, with surprising speed, hit him across the back of his head.

"I told you, my name is Zakk! If you can't remember that what sort of page are you going to be for me?"

"My lor… Zakk," Scratch quickly corrected himself, "I'm your personal servant not a page. I'm here to clean and look after you."

"You're here," Zakk said, suddenly exhausted, "because you've annoyed someone high up. But that is of no matter. I do not require a nursemaid, I need a page, and you," he said, pointing at the nastiest of Scratch's wounds, "need all the help you can get."

"I don't think Oscar will like that," Scratch countered.

"Well, I don't much like Oscar," Zakk replied. "So that's settled," he continued, "I'll train you as my page and you can tidy up in here. But first," he continued, "let's see what we can do about those wounds, can't have you getting infected."

With the creaking sound of protesting furniture Zakk hauled himself out his chair and made his way to the back of his quarters. Left alone Scratch looked around the squalid living area. As a cat he had excellent night vision but the gloom was almost all consuming. Eventually he spotted an oil lamp attached to the wall. It was flickering pathetically. Walking over to it Scratch discovered that rather than being empty of oil the lamp had been turned down. He reached out and turned the rusty dial clockwise and the flame responded by getting brighter and brighter. Scratch was shocked. Obviously Zakk had lived alone for a long time. It would take him forever to clean this place up.

Zakk returned shortly, dragging an old wooden crate behind him. He winced slightly as he entered the now brightly lit living quarters. He beckoned Scratch over. Scratch looked at the top of the wooden crate. Painted across the top in beautiful italics were the words:

*Zakk Morrison K.F.E.*

Zakk fiddled with the locks holding the lid down. Scratch noticed that his paws shook and that it had taken Zakk two attempts to grasp hold of the catches. With a click the trunk unlocked and Zakk lifted the lid. Scratch was surprised to see that the contents of the crate had been laid out very neatly. After taking in the state of his quarters Scratch half expected the contents of the case to come pouring out. He glanced in. The case was deep and Scratch could only see what was on the top. There was a pile of fresh tunics, slightly faded through age, a scabbard with no sword, and a neatly tied-up pile of postcards. Zakk rummaged in the case for a while, producing a glass vial of green liquid and a cloth. He motioned for Scratch to sit in his recently vacated chair.

After Scratch had settled himself Zakk pulled the stopper out of the vial. Scratch could smell a distinctly earthy aroma as Zakk poured a generous measure of the green liquid onto the cloth.

"Look up and close your eyes," he advised Scratch. Reaching out with the cloth he stopped only to say, "Oh, and I'd grab the armrests if I were you."

Scratch tightly gripped the arms of the chair in barely enough time as Zakk quickly pressed the cloth against the wounds on his face. Scratch howled and hissed as the cloth touched his wounds.

"Oh, do calm down," Zakk shouted over the howling, coating Scratch's face with more of the green liquid.

When he decided that he was finished Zakk stepped back and admired his work. Scratch was about to leap out of the seat and run away when he felt his wounds starting to pull back together and the pain started to ease. Suddenly he felt a sharp pain in the ruin of his teeth. Instinctively he raised his paws to his mouth and was amazed when he discovered that his broken teeth were starting to grow back.

He gaped at Zakk in amazement. "How did you do that?" he asked.

Zakk grinned at him. "Oh, Scratch," he sighed, "we have to get you out in the world, there is so much for you to see. In the meantime, however, this place needs a good clean."

## CHAPTER SEVEN

# THE RECEPTION

D URING THE SHORT reign of King Tyrell, the dungeons in the basement of the castle had been converted into workrooms and store houses. Tyrell believed that a criminal could be more profitably employed ploughing the fields that provided food to the kingdom or by serving in the royal army. It was a policy that had largely been successful, apart from the time the Southside Slasher had accidentally been assigned to work on a family farm, while Percivex, a small-time finance clerk who had been found guilty of minor fraud, had been sent to mine the cheese caves with the most dangerous criminals. Luckily the mix-up was discovered in time and the family had only been tied up for a few hours. Besides, as Tyrell said at the time, the Southside Slasher was recaptured after only a cycle and as he hadn't "slashed" the family he was obviously responding well to the rehabilitation techniques. After this, every work order was checked and double-checked.

It was in a dark cell, at the end of the corridor on the very bottom floor, where Stirex had set up his lab. Stirex was a tall, awkward mouse whose six whiskers all pointed in different directions. This coupled with the unfortunate tendency his eyes had of wandering to the side of his head at totally random intervals meant that he was given a wide berth by others in the castle. If anybody gave any thought to Stirex they might have asked him exactly what his function in the royal court was, to which he would have replied, "I am the Chief Necromancer, Conduit of Restless Spirits and Warden of the Darkest Acts."

Luckily nobody ever asked him. Stirex kept himself to himself and went unnoticed by the rest of the staff. It was doubtful that even Hirax knew of his existence. If Stirex was aware of this it wouldn't have concerned him in the slightest. "The living should rot" was the phrase Stirex was most keen on saying. He found the dead far more fascinating. Or at least he would if only they would communicate with him! He had tried everything to open a portal to the other side but to no avail. He had come close once a few solar spans ago. He was waving his hands over a pile of "Enchanted Bones TM" he had purchased only that morning from the more disreputable end of Cheeseton Town market when a massive flash of green light shot out of the bones and blasted him across the room and into the cold stone cell wall. When he regained consciousness a few hours later the "Enchanted Bones" (Slogan: "You'll Never Get Boned with Us") had been reduced to a pile of blackened dust and a small card was found poking out of the pile on which was written:

*The number you have called is presently banned in this dimensional plane of existence. Please hang up and*

*never try again, as being violently separated into your*
*component atoms sometimes offends.*

Stirex chose not to question why he hadn't been killed, nor did he question what else in addition to the anonymous card might have made it through from the other side.

While Stirex was lying unconscious on the cell floor the jubilee preparations continued until every tower was bedecked with flags and banners. Walking out into the courtyard Brabbinger reached into his waistcoat pocket and produced a small gold-plated whistle attached to a chain. Pausing only to look at the clock tower he brought the whistle up to his lips and gave three sharp blasts. On cue the surrounding doors opened and all of the staff marched out in unison and arranged themselves into several rows.

"Maids to the front, footstaff to the back," Brabbinger called out. "The guests will be arriving soon and we will not let His Majesty down." The staff moved quickly and efficiently, terrified at the prospect of displeasing Brabbinger. "The first of our honoured guests has arrived," Brabbinger proclaimed loudly.

Many of the younger staff gaped in surprise that such an old mouse could shout so loudly. The older staff kept their faces carefully neutral, only too aware of what Brabbinger was still capable of. The old oak gates to the courtyard swung open smoothly. Brabbinger nodded his approval at the maintenance staff who had been collectively holding their breath after oiling the gates. Trumpets sounded from the outside and two ginormous lizards strode into the courtyard. The staff were terrified at this sight but in testament to their training remained rooted to their assigned spots. They glanced up and saw that on the back of each of the lizards was an ornate red saddle, each with a high back.

On the largest of the two lizards they could see a female crow leaning back comfortably against the back of her saddle. She was dressed head to claw in form-fitting black robes. She spotted the crowd staring up at her in amazement and with a sly smile on her face produced a staff with a glowing red orb at the tip and fired three golden rockets up into the sky. The rockets exploded into streamers so bright that even against the bright blue summer sky they were clearly visible. The female crow stood up in her seat and bowed low to the assembled throng. Her companion, riding the smaller lizard, buried his head in his wings so that only the tip of his beak could be seen. Brabbinger wasn't sure but he could swear that he heard the male crow mutter, "Subtle, I begged her to be subtle." Rather than calm it down the female crow spun her staff in a wide circle in front her. Faster and faster it went until it became a blur. Red sparks started to appear in the arc of the staff's journey, getting larger and larger until they joined together, forming a huge circle. She then took a small step forward into the circle which expanded outwards into a translucent bubble, which in turn gently lifted her from the back of her reptilian steed and carried her smoothly to the stone floor. With a barely audible pop the bubble burst and Brabbinger found himself staring into the emerald green eyes of Altheus. For her part she slyly grinned at him and declared, "Greetings from Aridier."

Despite being rather shaken by this display, Brabbinger was too well trained to let any hint of surprise show on his face.

"My good lady," he exclaimed, inclining his head forward in a small court bow, "may I assume that His Lordship Cragzac has met with an unfortunate accident?"

Altheus winked at Brabbinger, who momentarily turned a deep shade of crimson before his training took over and he regained control.

"My lady…?"

"Altheus," she replied. "Is there anywhere we can stable our mounts? They are most exhausted from their journey."

"Of course," Brabbinger replied, "however, should we not assist your companion?"

On the word "companion" Brabbinger pointed a long thin claw up to the top of the second lizard. Altheus followed his claw and sighed with frustration as she spotted Crasis who was still atop his lizard waving frantically to her. As she looked at Brabbinger again she tried to regain her smile but couldn't be sure that the butler wasn't actually smirking at her.

"You just can't get the help."

At this she flipped the tip of her left wing idly and Crasis found himself lifted from his seat, and at a speed he wasn't comfortable with, and was roughly deposited at the claws of his leader. Quickly he stood up and brushed the dust from the front of his tunic. Not to be outdone Brabbinger produced his whistle and with four sharp blasts summoned every stablehand in the palace, who led the surprisingly docile lizards to the stables. With a further two blasts a younger Rodentian appeared at his side. Brabbinger turned to him.

"His Majesty is in the throne room. You will escort his honoured guests to him directly."

The younger mouse nodded, and after waiting to ensure that Altheus and Crasis were just behind him, turned and led them slowly to His Majesty. Altheus turned to Crasis, and although Brabbinger couldn't make out what was being said it was clear that Altheus was instructing her underling to assist the stablehands with the lizards. He obviously wanted to protest but clearly he knew better. Turning slowly on his heel he sloped off to the stables.

Brabbinger turned back to the gates, and just as he was wondering if all of the guests would insist on making such ostentatious entrances his nose was assaulted by a terrible odour. He produced an immaculately clean silken handkerchief from his top jacket pocket and placed it against his long snout. Walking carefully towards the courtyard gates where the smell was at its strongest he discovered a large steaming pile of green poo. Turning back to the staff, many of whom were steadfastly trying to avoid his gaze, he found two young footmice who realised too late that they were smirking and tried quickly to straighten their faces. Brabbinger limped over to them both and standing between them he smiled frostily back at them.

"Fetch a shovel," was all he needed to say and the two mice slunk off dejectedly to carry out their task. "Quickly," Brabbinger called after them and with a half-smile returned to his position to await the next guests.

He didn't need to wait for long. Just as the two unfortunate and now very green-looking footmice had completed their task a rather battered-looking carriage pulled by two exhausted black horses limped into the courtyard. One of the carriages' back wheels had worked itself loose and was wobbling alarmingly as the carriage pulled to a halt.

Brabbinger nodded at two more footmice in a wordless command to open the carriage doors. Before they could get there the door on the right side swung open and a female Giraxian fell out and threw up over the cobblestones. The two luckless footmice turned back towards the rapidly growing pile with their shovel and bucket. Clearly this was not their day.

As Brabbinger was about to rush to her aid the left-hand door slowly opened and a male stepped out. Brabbinger prided himself that he could read people and in one glance had decided that this "gentleman" was not to be trusted. The male Giraxian looked sharply at Brabbinger.

"Leave her," he commanded. Perhaps realising that he had sounded a bit curt he forced a smile with very little warmth behind it. "My sister has a delicate constitution," he said smoothly, walking towards her still waving away all proffered assistance. Leaning over the prone figure of Yani he whispered into her ear, "Sort yourself out, must you bring more shame to our people?" Yani merely glared at him with hatred. Ignoring her, Number One turned back to Brabbinger. "Where is His Majesty? We have much to discuss."

"His Majesty is naturally in his throne room," Brabbinger said smoothly. "I shall summon an escort."

"No need," Number One called back, already heading towards the palace. "I shall find him myself." He paused momentarily and without looking back said, "Sister dear, perhaps when you have regained some composure you will join me, I'd hate to have to come looking for you."

Brabbinger scowled at the back of the Giraxian as he galloped up the stone steps leading to the throne room. *He'll run right into Altheus if he's not careful*, he thought ruefully to himself.

Whilst the resultant chaos might well teach him a lesson Brabbinger thought it prudent to send another footmouse after him, instructing the servant to stay out of sight but be ready to intercede if necessary. After arranging this he turned back to the female Giraxian, gratified and – he admitted to himself – proud to see that some of his staff had gone to her aid. It had taken ten footmice to lift her and although she looked unsteady she was at least back on her feet and being led to a nearby bench.

Brabbinger wandered over. As he got closer he could swear that he recognised her. She looked older than she should be and her arms and legs looked so thin that he wasn't surprised they didn't hold her up very well but it was unmistakable. At his approach all but two of the servants left her to return to their allotted positions. The two that remained were alternately fanning her with their tails and trying to provide some shade for her.

"Get our guest some water," Brabbinger said softly to the staff. "I'll look after her now."

Yani muttered her thanks to Brabbinger, who sat next to her. The bench had of course been built for the slight frame of the Rodentian and Yani from necessity had taken most of the available space. Brabbinger perched on the end and, placing his cane across his lap, he turned to address her.

"Madam Yani, His Majesty believes you dead. Is this by design or do I need to find him some new advisers?"

He spoke quietly, ensuring that nobody could overhear their conversation. At the mention of her name a look of terror momentarily flashed across her face. She quickly composed herself but not so quickly that Brabbinger didn't notice.

"You are mistaken," she said at last, "I am Yunei and I'm just accompanying my brother to the jubilee. I'm sorry to have caused so much trouble."

As she spoke she tried to rise, however her thin legs started to shake so alarmingly that Brabbinger feared that she would collapse again. Returning to her seat Yani tried to avoid Brabbinger's seeking gaze.

"I see," he said eventually. "Well, your 'brother' will be busy for some time yet and the festivities aren't scheduled to begin for quite some time. I suggest you retire to the guest quarters and I'll make sure that you are not disturbed."

"Thank you," Yani whispered.

"Perhaps, when you feel better," Brabbinger continued, "you might want to have a look at our science quarters? They're not as good as you are used to but you might find something there to interest you."

Yani snapped back at him.

"I told you," she hissed, "you are mistaking me for someone else. I don't know anything about science."

"As you say," Brabbinger said conciliatorily, "should you change your mind about anything His Majesty would be happy to talk." Before Yani could reply the servants returned with the ordered water. "I shall leave you now, Madam Yunei, I have other guests to attend to."

Yani wasn't sure but she could have sworn that Brabbinger winked as he said "Yunei". As she let the servants lead her to the offered room she thought that she should keep an eye on the wily old butler, however he might turn out to be an ally. If only she knew who to trust.

Brabbinger was getting tired and there were more guests still to arrive. He would love nothing more than a quick lie down. His left paw ached and he was sure the day was getting hotter. He hooked his right paw into his stiff collar and tugged it loose, hoping for a moment of relief.

"Mr Brabbinger! Mr Brabbinger!" an excited voice called to him. "The cat knights are coming, we've seen them!"

Brabbinger pulled his paw out of his collar as quick as he could, nearly dislocating his shoulder in the process. He looked up to shout at whatever ill-trained servant had the nerve to break formation without his permission when he saw Tommu, the young stable lad, hopping his way. Tommu was small even for a Rodentian but he seemed to possess almost limitless energy. Brabbinger smiled at the sight of the boy.

"Ah, young stable lad," he said, trying not to smile too much, "the cats have come, have they?"

"Yes, Mr Brabbinger, they are riding big red foxes, and they have flags and armour and kittens playing drums."

Tommu was jumping up and down by this point. Brabbinger placed a hand on his shoulder to calm him down a bit.

"If they have mounts," he said calmly, "you had better get back to the stables, your father will need your help."

Tommu stopped his bouncing and stuck out his bottom lip.

"But I wanted to see the cats," he said clearly disappointed.

"Now, Tommu," Brabbinger explained, "we all have a duty, it is the King's special day after all."

"I suppose so," Tommu said with disappointment.

"Besides," Brabbinger whispered, "you'll get a better view from the top of the stables."

Tommu's smile was so wide his face looked like it would split in half.

"Yes, Mr Brabbinger." He sped off towards the stables. Stopping suddenly he turned back. "Will you visit us later, Mr Brabbinger?"

Brabbinger went to say that he had a lot of work to do but the young Rodentian looked so hopeful all he could say was, "Perhaps, young mouse, perhaps."

Making sure to regain his fierce composure Brabbinger once again made his way back to the courtyard to welcome the cats. Of all the guests invited to the jubilee the cat knights were the ones who worried him the most. So far both the cats and Rodentians had obeyed the terms of the truce after the devastation of the Cheese Wars. However, Brabbinger remembered the wars all too well. He remembered being ambushed by a platoon of knights as he and his regiment stalked through the thickest parts of Silvestri Forest. It had all happened so quickly. As a young private Brabbinger had been dawdling on the outskirts of the regiment when suddenly more cats than he could count leapt from the trees and set about his mates with such savagery that blood was sprayed across great distances. Being so far behind the others gave Brabbinger time to act. He threw himself into the roots of a nearby tree and squeezed his diminutive frame between narrow gaps until he was completely buried out of sight. From his hiding place he could see the cats playing with the bodies of his fallen comrades. Two cats were throwing the decapitated head of his former commander between them, another was rolling around in a puddle of blood until its fur was matted with it. This ghoulish show went on until the sun set when the cats curled up and purred contentedly all night. Brabbinger was so scared he could barely breathe. Eventually the sun came out and, pausing only to kick the remains about a bit more, the cats packed up and moved on. Much later Brabbinger pulled himself out his hiding spot then he ran back to Rodentian HQ where he was thoroughly questioned and sent back into the field indecently quickly. Brabbinger always considered himself lucky to have survived the war but he never felt comfortable around cats ever again and now he had to welcome them into the palace he called home.

Brabbinger heard the drumbeats before he made it to the gates but refused to hurry. *Better late than flustered*, he thought to himself. By the time he arrived the drumming had thankfully come to a stop and the impossibly young kittens who had been making the din had formed themselves into two lines facing each other. Eventually a well-groomed russet-coloured fox was ridden between them. On its back sat a large one-eyed cat who was staring at the lines of kittens almost daring them to make a mistake so that he could demean them. Brabbinger immediately hated him but tried to keep his face neutral. Behind the lead fox was a long line of fully dressed knights sitting atop their own foxes being led by their pages. The pages were dressed in silk with feathers protruding from huge floppy hats. Brabbinger rolled his eyes, he couldn't help it. Trust the cats to overdo it on the ceremony.

Lazily, Oscar raised a paw to bring the procession to a halt and sat staring down at Brabbinger. Brabbinger for his part leaned a little more heavily on his cane and stared back up at Oscar. Brabbinger could see beads of sweat on Oscar's brow but still said nothing. *Serves you right for wearing full armour*, he thought to himself. "Where do you think you are? This is a jubilee not a jousting tournament," he wanted to say but kept it to himself. It was protocol for a guest to introduce himself first and Brabbinger certainly wasn't going to be the first royal butler in a generation to break protocol, so the two adversaries continued to stare at each other. Eventually the silence was broken by a loud voice from the very back of the procession.

"In the name of sanity, Oscar," it boomed, sounding slightly slurred to Brabbinger, "introduce yourself. If I have to sit on this bloody mongrel any longer my bum will give out."

At the word bum two of the kittens started to giggle nervously. Oscar was too embarrassed to deal with this. With his face scarlet he dismounted his fox, walked over to Brabbinger and after proffering the smallest court bow ever given announced, "Greetings from Silvestri Forest and the Knights of Felix Regalis. My name is Oscar and I am the officer in charge of training."

"But of course you are," Brabbinger replied. "His Majesty is in the throne room and our stables are at your disposal."

As he spoke he waved his paws to show them where to go. Oscar merely nodded at this.

"Squad, forward!" he shouted.

Brabbinger had to suppress a laugh as at his command the kittens all turned and, while attempting to reform their line, nearly knocked Oscar off his feet. Enraged, Oscar swiped at the nearest kitten, catching him a stinging blow on the back of his head.

"Wait for me to move first, you little fools!"

He then dragged his fox through the remaining kittens, alternately kicking them if they didn't move fast enough and hissing at those he couldn't reach.

After a while the chaos subsided and the procession made its way slowly to the stables. Brabbinger counted ten mounted cat knights and their pages as they marched past. The knights were all sitting primly on their horses and the pages all stared straight ahead, no doubt being warned what would happen if they dared do anything else. This was until the last knight rode by. He was possibly the fattest cat Brabbinger had ever seen. His tunic had many faded stains on it. Clearly his page had done what he could to clean it but some of those stains looked like they dated back to the cycles of Perix the First. If the knight was bothered by this he clearly didn't show it. He smiled broadly and kept taking generous swigs from a hip flask. As he passed Brabbinger he looked down and said, "Only the grub cart to go past and then you can take that rod out of your bum."

Brabbinger recognised the voice as the one that had heckled Oscar earlier so couldn't be too mortified by him. The knight's page on the other hand turned to him.

"Zakk, you can't say things like that," he hissed.

Brabbinger winced, expecting the knight to chastise his page either verbally or physically. Instead Zakk chuckled.

"Young Scratch," he said down to his page, "I thought you knew by now that I can say whatever I want, a benefit of growing old disgracefully."

Scratch looked to Brabbinger and mouthed "Sorry" to him. *Clearly the cats aren't going to be as pompous as I expected*, thought Brabbinger. Zakk was correct, however there was only the rations wagon left to go and he might be able to relax for a little while at least.

As the wagon rolled past, Brabbinger was surprised to see a hedgehog in a blue evening gown sitting on the back steps whistling a tuneless song to herself. Across the hedgehog's lap was a small crossbow. Obviously the representative of the Thieves' Guild had sneakily arranged a lift for herself as the cats went through Silvestri Forest. When Greeta saw Brabbinger staring at her she cheekily saluted him. Brabbinger decided he was just too tired to go through another welcome so he half saluted her in return and pointed towards the white tower. Greeta for her part nodded, leapt down from the wagon and, with her weapon casually swung across her shoulder, sauntered off towards the throne room.

Brabbinger was now faced with a problem. The Pacidermians had still not replied to the invite, however they often didn't and would just turn up regardless. For how long was he supposed to keep the staff waiting? He was getting nervous about what the other guests were discussing with the King, he had to get back in there. The sun continued to beat down. Two maids had fainted in the heat and had been taken inside to recover and yet the Pacidermians had still not graced him with their presence.

Eventually he had enough. Turning to the rows of hot and flustered servants he went to dismiss them, when he was distracted by a noise which sounded like a trumpet being played by an angry goose. He turned as quickly as he could to see a lone Pacidermian marching through the courtyard doors, his trunk stuck out in front of him braying that awful noise. As he got closer and the noise became almost unbearable Brabbinger realised that he was attempting to play the Pacidermian national anthem and, judging by the quality, had been playing it since setting off and was running out of puff. To Brabbinger's mind turning any anthem into a noise like that was tantamount to treason but he kept his face neutral as the Pacidermian approached him. He was dressed in the full military uniform of the Pacidermian defence force. Brabbinger noted the red tabs attached to the uniform lapels which denoted the wearer as office staff.

Eventually the noise ended. The Pacidermian, despite being clearly exhausted, came to attention. Smartly clicking his heels together loudly, he turned his already raised trunk to his enormous forehead and gave the traditional Pacidermian salute. Once given he let his trunk drop back down.

"Lieutenant Lexican Tuskforth," he announced, his throat rasping from clear dehydration, "I bring greetings from Pacidermian High Command."

Brabbinger made a big show of looking behind Lex.

"And little else, it appears," Brabbinger replied dryly.

Lex bristled at this.

"As I'm sure you are aware," he said curtly, "those cowardly long necks attacked our port last night. We are a bit too busy for a tea party."

Brabbinger was annoyed now. It was hot, he had been standing for far too long, and now this pompous buffoon was attempting to lecture him! Pausing only to mentally count to ten he looked up at the enormous figure of Lex and when he was sure he had the giant's full attention he said, "Firstly, this is neutral space." As he spoke he opened his arms to indicate that he was talking about the entire area occupied by the royal tower and surrounding building. "The war is to be left outside these lands, that includes any colourful names you may have for your enemies!"

Lex went to speak, outraged that this common servant should speak to him in such a way, but Brabbinger cut him off before he could begin.

"Secondly," the old Rodentian continued, "this tea party is the tenth jubilee of your King and I must demand that you show it the adequate respect."

Lex just gasped at this. He could step on this annoying creature and grind him into the dirt with minimal fuss but instead he found himself embarrassed by what he was saying.

"Thirdly," Brabbinger hissed, "we received no notice of your attendance at all and so have set aside an entire wing for, as it turns out, one Pacidermian! In any case, you are of course welcome. His Majesty and the other honoured guests are in the throne room."

Still in a state of shock Lex walked towards the tower of the King, squeezed himself through the doors and set off to find out who else had attended.

The servants, who had been flagging somewhat, had snapped back into tight formation when listening to Brabbinger berate the Pacidermian soldier for fear that their employer might well turn on them too. Brabbinger regarded them coldly.

"Good," he said at last. "You all did well. Don't rest now though," he warned them. "This is when the hard work begins." He looked up at the rows of assembled staff. "Dismissed!" he cried. As the servants returned to their stations he called after them. "Remember," he threatened, "I see and hear everything."

## CHAPTER EIGHT

# A MEETING OF MINDS

THE NOISE WAS deafening. Brabbinger was staggered by it before he even reached the throne room. Loud voices were echoing through the corridors, bouncing from ceiling to floor, the bare stone amplifying the noise. Brabbinger took a deep breath and stepped into the throne room. He wasn't surprised to see Lex loudly shouting at the sinister Giraxian who sat casually on the stone steps barely regarding the furious Pacidermian at all. There was a party of cat knights loudly trying to goad the royal bodyguards into a fight. Nobody was listening to anybody else and King Hirax was sitting with his head in his paws clearly wishing he was anywhere else.

Brabbinger scanned the room looking for Altheus. He eventually spotted the tall crow leaning against a wall watching the chaos unfold, an amused smirk on her beak. Brabbinger limped over to her and tapped her gently on the wing. If she was surprised or offended by the action she didn't show it. Instead she leaned down so that Brabbinger could talk directly into her ear. When he finished talking, a wicked smile split Altheus' beak and she angled her staff so that it was pointing directly over the throne. She muttered a few words under her breath and with a loud bang, long coloured streamers fired out of the end of the staff, coating the throne in red and gold. So loud had the bang been that the guards had broken away from the cat knights and had surrounded King Hirax with their spears pointing outwards in a vicious circle. Silently every head turned towards Altheus, their mouths open in shock.

"I'm always popular at parties," she said wickedly.

The silence was broken by Lex who at the first sign of trouble had attempted to dive under a nearby table. Being too big to fit he had instead bashed his forehead on the tabletop and knocked a wooden jug of water straight onto his head. He stood now dripping wet with a nasty red welt developing on his enormous forehead.

"What in the name of the old kings did you do that for?" he bellowed, clearly embarrassed to have been shown up in such a way.

Before Altheus could say something cutting the King took advantage of the situation. Quickly climbing up the back of the throne he stood on the top of it so that he could be seen over the heads of his guard.

"Please, honoured guests," he shouted, "all this noise is getting us nowhere, this is a day of peace."

Unfortunately at the word "peace" Greeta's crossbow went off. She had been fiddling with it throughout the arguments and with an unfortunate sense of timing the catch had released. The deadly projectile fired into the air, luckily nowhere near any of the guests. Unluckily it went straight through a stained-glass window depicting "Perix the

Strong fighting off a very large – and Hirax secretly suspected fictional – badger". The glass shattered into many tiny pieces which rained down like a fine rain onto the throne room below.

"Sorry," the tiny hedgehog called, "my bad. Never buy crossbows from ferrets, they have longer fingers you see and…"

Her voice trailed off as the assembled guests glared at her with undisguised menace.

"I would have thought," began the refined tones of the Giraxian, "that weapons would have been banned in the throne room. At least for the safety of those unable to use them correctly."

Greeta blushed a deep red.

"It's okay," Hirax said quickly, trying desperately to prevent another argument before it happened. "I never liked that window much anyway." He ignored the pained noise which emanated from Brabbinger at this admission and continued to push his advantage. "I called you all here to discuss the Collar of Honour."

"Yes" Altheus replied, "I appreciate that I haven't been in charge for very long but I have been unable to find anything in our libraries relating to this object, mind you…" she added thoughtfully "My predecessor wasn't keen on knowledge".

"Understood" Hirax added thoughtfully, "The Collar of Honour is said to grant the deepest wish of whoever owns it. My own studies lead me to believe that it exists but I don't know where it is" he paused for dramtic effect.

"A children's fairy story," Lex snorted contemptuously.

"Perhaps," Hirax conceded, "but surely one worthy of investigation. After all," he continued, "I believe your ancestors…" he pointed at Lex as he spoke, "refused to believe in the existence of magic but at the start of your war you sent a delegation to the crows asking for an alliance."

"It is not OUR war," Lex stated. "It was a cowardly attack. We have the right to defend ourselves."

There followed an awkward silence as every head turned to the Giraxian. The Giraxian for his part leaned casually up against a wall, breathing on his front two hooves in turn and rubbing them on his coat. When he was happy with the shine he looked up and smiled. There was no warmth to it.

"I think we all know the truth," he said simply.

Hirax, quickly spotting that Lex was building up to another tirade, spoke, staring directly at Lex.

"My investigations lead me to believe that far from being a children's fairy story, the Collar of Honour does in fact exist. Its powers might have been exaggerated over time but in everything I've read it does grant certain wishes."

"Exaggerated how?" Altheus asked.

She was trying to give the illusion of intellectual scepticism but inside she was almost excited. Could she restore her father and the other mages wiped out during Crasis' purge? It was too good to be true but there was something about the serious tone Hirax had adopted that was convincing her.

"As far as I can tell, any wish given to the Collar MUST be worded precisely. There are stories of previous owners wishing for great wealth, only to be haunted by the noise of a laughing child as they once flippantly said there was no greater treasure than a child's laughter."

"It seems," the Giraxian said laconically, "that the Collar, should it exist, has a sense of humour."

"So it's useless?" a quiet voice piped up from amongst the cats.

Hirax was surprised by the reaction this question provoked. The cats all turned inwards and Hirax could hear shushing noises, and he wasn't sure but he thought he heard the sound of punching and kicking.

"Let my page speak, he has that right," a refined voice rang out from the chaotic clowder of cats and the tight ball opened to reveal three cats all glaring at each other.

Brabbinger recognised them immediately. The young page who had been so embarrassed by the behaviour of his sponsor was kneeling on the stone floor. He was clearly winded as he was clutching his stomach with both paws and breathing heavily. Standing over him, his paw still clenched, was Oscar. He stared down at the page with such hatred Brabbinger feared for the young cat's continued existence. Standing just behind him was the knight identified as Zakk. To Hirax's eye he seemed very unsteady on his feet. The three cats glared at each other.

"He has no right to even be here," Oscar hissed at Zakk.

Hirax could hear a low growl coming from Zakk. His paw was reaching towards the handle of his sword. Hirax regretted allowing weapons at this meeting. He thought it would be a show of good faith and trust but the Giraxian was correct, he should have banned weapons in the throne room. Things were getting tense again, he had to do something.

"Young cat," he called out, "approach the throne."

Zakk immediately removed his paw from the sword handle and helped Scratch to his feet. Making sure that his tunic was unruffled and that he could breathe comfortably Zakk assisted Scratch to the throne, pausing only once to throw a sour look at Oscar who, for his part, was turning purple with repressed rage. Sensing that the atmosphere had become calmer the royal bodyguard moved back into position on either side of the throne, allowing Scratch and Zakk to approach the King. They still pointed the sharp end of their weapons at the approaching cats almost casually but the implication was clear: they would not tolerate anything out of the ordinary. Zakk and Scratch reached the bottom step of the raised dais on which the throne was placed.

"Kneel," Zakk whispered into Scratch's ear.

Somewhat awkwardly Scratch dropped to one knee, wobbled slightly and stared open-mouthed at the King as he walked down the steps towards him. Close up Scratch thought that Hirax looked old but was fascinated by the light shining off the jewels in his crown. He tried to focus on the face of the King but his eyes followed the reflected light as Hirax looked down at him, his eyes darting left and right. Like most kittens Scratch liked to play hunt. One of his only happy memories was chasing a firefly through Silvestri Forest one summer evening. Of course, he had been punished by Oscar for leaving the fort at night but he still remembered his first hunting trip fondly. If Hirax noticed Scratch's darting eyes he didn't mention it.

"What is your name?" he asked softly.

"My name is Scratch Sniffsunn," Scratch whispered, too scared to say it out loud.

"Sire," Zakk whispered into his ear.

Scratch looked up at Zakk, confused.

"You address a king as sire," Zakk whispered back to him.

"Sire," Scratch quickly added.

Hirax smiled with kindness at Scratch.

"Tell me, Scratch Sniffsunn, are you a cat knight?" There was a sudden snort from Oscar at this question, which he unsuccessfully tried to cover with a cough when Hirax looked over at him. "I'll assume not," he added coldly. "You are a page though. I thought pages were knights in training?"

Scratch stammered for a bit. Zakk went to answer but was beaten to it by Oscar.

"My liege," Oscar said, obsequiousness dripping from both words; Zakk sneered at the very sound of it, "young Sniffsunn is not of noble birth, he is an orphan. We give him food and shelter but he is not eligible for knighthood."

Hirax raised an eyebrow.

"Yet he is page for this honoured knight?" he asked, pointing towards a clearly furious Zakk with a long claw.

Oscar put on his most indulgent tone.

"Sire, Knight Zakk is indeed one of our more senior knights and is of course entitled to his whims. He has taken a shine to Sniffsunn but this is little more than a…" he paused, thinking of the right word to use, "hobby for him. I've allowed it as it hasn't yet interfered with his duties but he will never be a knight. Quite impossible," he added empathetically.

Hirax nodded at Oscar and turned his attention back to Scratch.

"Imagine though," he said conspiratorially, and for that moment Scratch felt that he was the only person in the throne room, "that there was a magical device that could make you a knight. A device which could do the impossible but only if being a knight was your true desire."

Scratch gaped at him. In his head he could already see himself dressed in the claret robes of a knight. He could see Oscar giving him the salute he gave to all cat knights and he knew that he wanted the Collar of Honour more than he had wanted anything before.

"However," Hirax continued, "if you just wish to be a knight, the Collar could make you a knight in a different army or at a different time. You need to be exact in your wish." He patted Scratch on the head. "Don't stop wishing, Scratch, the impossible happens every day."

Hirax then turned around and walked back up to the throne. He felt that he had regained control of a tense situation, right up until the refined tones of the Giraxian punctuated the silence.

"I hate to interrupt such a deeply motivational moment," he drawled, holding up a hoof, "but we've yet to establish if the Collar actually exists or where it is."

Hirax regarded him coldly.

"And that is why I have called you all here. I think I know where it was last." Collective gasps ran through the hall at the news. "I believe that my grandfather owned it," Hirax said, once everyone had calmed down. Many of the older guests crossed themselves at the memory of King Faustus. "I do not know what he wished for but he cannot have been clear as he died slowly and in pain and I can't imagine he'd wish for that."

"Maybe for others," an unknown voice said quietly. Hirax chose to ignore the comment, partly because he didn't know who said it but mostly because it was quite true. "However, he must have used it because an extensive search of the palace has failed to discover it."

"So, there is an object that grants wishes once owned by your grandfather but it's not here? You'll forgive my scepticism, sire, but are you sure it even exists if it isn't here?"

"Did you fail to look into it like I instructed?" Hirax asked.

For the first time there was a slight edge to his voice. The Giraxian noticed the change in his King's mood and changed his tone smoothly.

"Forgive me, sire, but the war rages ever on and our former…" he glared at Lex as he continued, his voice for once deviating from its smooth, slightly mocking tone to anger, "masters denied us any books or writing materials, something about it displeasing the Flying Drexes."

Instead of looking ashamed, or even trying to avoid his gaze at all, Lex just chuckled to himself. Hirax could feel the mood in the room changing once again. He realised that this Giraxian (who had still managed to avoid giving his name to anyone) was very dangerous indeed. Hirax had sent the invite out to Giraxian High Command and wasn't surprised that they had sent representation but this was no mere functionary, this Giraxian was used to being obeyed.

"Fair enough," Hirax said quietly, encouraging everyone else in the room to quieten down so they could hear him. "It is written, that on granting the wish of its previous owner, the Collar of Honour vanishes and reappears somewhere else in the kingdom, hidden, where it lies in wait of its next owner."

The assembled guests were like children listening to a bedtime story, each one thinking about what they would wish for. Hirax continued, never once raising his voice above a whisper. Everyone leaned in further.

"Reading the journals of my father I believe that the expedition which cost him his life was an attempt to seek out the Collar. Clearly this is a task for more than one. SO…" he leapt to his feet and shouted the last word so loudly that everyone jumped back suddenly. Every cat landed on their feet with their backs arched, Greeta instinctively curled herself into a ball, even the Giraxian jumped slightly. Hirax was definitely in control. "ON THE OCCASION OF MY TENTH JUBILEE I GIVE YOU, THE ASSEMBLED BEINGS OF VENARY, A ROYAL QUEST. YOU ARE TO SEND YOUR VERY BEST ON A QUEST THROUGHOUT THE LAND TO FIND AND RETURN TO ME THE COLLAR OF HONOUR."

In the silence Lex coughed softly and raised his trunk. Hirax held up a paw imperiously to stop the obvious question.

"The one who finds it and returns it to me will win independence for their region. I will surrender the control my royal house has on your lands in perpetuity. You and your future offspring could be kings again…" he caught Altheus' eye, "or queens, obviously," he added. "However, if you betray me and keep the Collar for yourself…" he paused, looking at each person in turn, "you had better be prepared to use it quickly as I will send my Royal Guard down upon you to put your region and its people to flame and drag you back to be tortured for the rest of your life." A gentle murmur started amongst the assembled groups which Hirax silenced by clapping his paws together. "However," he said almost jovially, "that is for tomorrow, today we have a jubilee to celebrate. I believe my staff have allocated you rooms. Please, leave and prepare yourselves. Today should be a joyous day for us all."

Hirax remained standing while the assembled guests all shuffled out of the throne room. As the last one left he collapsed back onto his throne breathing heavily. He could feel his paws shaking and suddenly desired a glass of sweet wine. Before he could order it though, Brabbinger had hopped up each step towards him, the usual pain in his paw quite forgotten.

"Your Majesty," he spluttered, "have you taken leave of your senses?"

Hirax glared at him but if anyone could get away with talking to him like this it was Brabbinger, besides Hirax was exhausted from hiding the nerves he had felt throughout the previous meeting. He hated acting so imperiously, he just wanted a normal, quiet life like so many of his subjects, but if he could get the Collar he could bring peace, he could make everyone get along and while he could never escape his royal duties he could for the first time enjoy them.

"Why didn't you tell me about this fool's errand?"

"You wouldn't understand," Hirax said quietly.

"I understand this," Brabbinger countered. "If you think you can trust any of them to return the Collar to you then you are the fool your grandfather thought you were." Brabbinger was almost breathless with fury. "You have no idea the power the Collar wields."

Hirax looked up quickly.

"It WAS here, wasn't it?" he exclaimed. "Why didn't you tell me about it?" He was angry now, properly angry for the first time ever, his depression and despair finally cast aside. "Spans of pointless sword-fighting lessons, horse riding, tedious etiquette rules. The one thing that would have actually helped me in this hateful role and YOU kept it from me."

"I did what I thought was best, I saw the power of it consume your grandfather and lead your royal father to march to his death. I wanted more for you."

Brabbinger was talking calmly but privately he was glad to see Hirax finally show a bit of passion. He was at last acting like a king.

"That wasn't your decision to make," Hirax roared. "I've had nursemaids all my life when what I needed was the means to bring peace! You must tell me what my grandfather wished for, quickly."

"It is of no consequence," Brabbinger sighed. "It didn't work, it must have gone wrong, terribly wrong. You were too young to understand the illness that took him."

"I remember him dying," Hirax replied. "You told me it was consumption," he said accusingly.

"That was the easiest thing to call it," Brabbinger said defeated. "It came on so quickly and brought a madness with it."

"That shouldn't be news," Hirax said. "My grandfather often ranted like a madman, why should his illness be any different?"

"With respect," Brabbinger began, "we've gone past respect." Hirax snapped back, "I'll settle for honesty now."

"Very well, but be warned, you might not thank me for telling you this tale…"

## Brabbinger's Tale

Brabbinger stared at his belongings as they were laid out on his bunk. It wasn't much to show for the last five spans of his life: fatigues, his old civilian suit, a pocket watch and his long thin sword. He picked up the sword and slid it into the scabbard slung over his left shoulder, and turned to the cracked mirror positioned at the end of the barracks and stared at his reflection. He couldn't deny that the dress uniform was very flattering, the deep yellow colour of it complimenting his sharp black eyes beautifully. He ran a paw along the crease in the trouser legs and was pleased to see that on both they were perfectly straight. His campaign medals stood out well against his chest and Brabbinger was glad that he had decided to use that extra coat of polish last night. He sighed with frustration when he spotted that his yellow beret had slipped forward again. He had never really had the head for hats with his scalp rising to a peak, resulting in every piece of headwear he had ever tried looking like a thimble placed precariously on a pencil.

Brabbinger removed the offending article and proceeded to stuff the edges with old newspaper in the hope that he could build a wall around the peak of his head. As he worked he looked at the beret pin. It showed the insignia of his battalion, a Rodentian head wearing an eye patch. The motto of the battalion, "*Morditi Sempre La Coda*", was inscribed underneath the image. With a slight rustling noise Brabbinger reaffixed the beret on top of his head and looked once more at his reflection. *Yes*, he thought to himself, *as long as I don't need to move too much I should get through the discharge ceremony with this still on.*

He still had trouble believing that the war was over. The war had been a bloody one, costly on both sides, and had achieved very little. The cat knights had been slowly expanding their territory, claiming that they had an ancestral claim on the lands surrounding Silvestri Forest. The lands in question were mostly deserted fields and nobody was entirely sure why, after so many spans of peace, the cats sent a fully armed battalion into the area, but advance they did and immediately started to build a new village there. Brabbinger couldn't see the harm but King Faustus had been apoplectic with rage. He demanded that the entire royal army go and "teach those upstart fur walkers some manners". Many advisers had tried to talk him out of immediate military action, after all, the fields had lain unused for spans and perhaps the cats could be convinced to pay a yearly sum to the Crown.

"The royal treasury could always use topping up," one adviser had claimed hopefully.

Instead of taking this advice Faustus had the adviser stuffed with gold coins until he choked to death. He did this in full view of his royal council and never once did he break eye contact with the luckless adviser, smiling throughout. When the body of the now dead adviser hit the floor with a sickening jangling noise Faustus giggled softly and said, "Cut him open and get my money back. After all," he added with a grin, "the treasury could use topping up."

After this display there were no further objections and with much pomp and circumstance the army was formed. Every male Rodentian of mature age was automatically signed up for a full tour of duty. The newly formed army was assembled in rows in the palace courtyard ready to be addressed by the King. Faustus stepped out on the balcony in his newly designed and created officer's uniform. It was brilliantly white with real gold braiding and many medals glinting in the sunlight. He surveyed his army and began his address.

"Simpering wretches," he called into the crowd, "today your life begins! For too long you have suckled at the freedom and prosperity provided for you by my family."

Many of the assembled crowd felt that this was a bit rich given the increased taxes they had been forced to pay to fund this army but Faustus was rumoured to have "powers" and everyone was too scared to speak up.

"Now is the time to repay your debt to me," Faustus continued. "Like you, those heathen cats have shown nothing but disrespect and have invaded MY sovereign land! You will finally prove your loyalty to me and butcher EVERY SINGLE ONE OF THEM!" Faustus had worked himself up into quite a fervour. Foam had started to coat his chin and he had balled his two claws into fists and was waving both of them in the air. "Our enemy are cowards and traitors and will roll over and present their soft bellies as soon as they see you coming, but you must show them no mercy. Now go and return to me what has been stolen."

As one the columns all turned and marched towards the fields. Far from rolling over the cat knights met force with force and after the loss of many lives the cat knights eventually retreated back to Silvestri Forest, claiming that the conflict had rendered the fields uninhabitable and that there was nothing left to fight for. Of course Faustus claimed a glorious victory and ordered that the force storm the forest and annihilate the cat knights once and for all, that is until he visited the site and saw how devastated his army had become. He realised that to raise another army would put his own kingdom at risk from others so decided to offer clemency to the cat knights. Surprisingly this tactic worked. He was regarded as a magnanimous victor by the other species of Venary and the cat knights had to live with the fact that they had "run away". Neither side was happy but neither side could continue the war so an uneasy peace had broken out. Brabbinger's battalion had been disbanded and he was allowed to return home, home being the royal castle where his father had served as Royal Butler for many spans.

Brabbinger reached into his pocket and retrieved the brown envelope containing the telegram he had received a few cycles ago and reread it for the umpteenth time:

*To Sgt Brabbinger\*\*\*STOP\*\*\*Regret to inform you of your father's ailing health\*\*\*STOP\*\*\*Please return to Castle Mowser following your discharge to take over your father's duties\*\*\*STOP\*\*\*Don't delay in returning\*\*\*STOP\*\*\*His Majesty awaits your return\*\*\*STOP\*\*\**

Brabbinger always knew that one day he would return to the castle to take over from his father but he had hoped to travel the world of Venary before this. Just once he would have liked to put himself first even. His childhood had been spent as a footmouse polishing a seemingly endless pile of shoes and shovelling horse manure in the stables, forever being told that these tasks were "character building" and "good training for when he became butler". Then the war came and although he had no choice he was almost happy to be out from that castle and away from the disapproving comments of his father. Like many young Rodentians he sang songs of the victory they would have over the cats. He made many friends during his service. All too quickly the good times had ended. The war had been long and brutal and as he stared at his reflection he realised that this was the first time he'd seen himself not covered in mud and it felt somewhat disloyal to all of the friends he lost. Stuffing the telegram back into his pocket he snapped to attention.

"Life is duty," he said to his reflection.

Stopping only long enough to jam the paper-filled beret onto his head Brabbinger headed towards the discharge ceremony, the only member of his battalion left to attend.

By late afternoon the next day Brabbinger was standing outside Castle Mowser. He had hitched a ride from a travelling caravan of performing stoats. They had been delighted to pick him up as they had had so little chance to perform for an audience. Throughout the long journey back home the stoats leapt and tumbled around him. They juggled and capered, leaping from wagon to wagon. Brabbinger clapped politely but he was too preoccupied with thoughts of returning home. He tried to be worried about his father's condition but he just felt empty. His father had always been more like an employer to him. Brabbinger's mother had died bearing him and he remembered hearing some of the kitchen staff saying that a part of his father died on the same day.

Eventually pulling up at the imposing castle Brabbinger said his goodbyes to the stoats, squaring his shoulders he approached the entrance. Knocking on the large oak door he felt a rising annoyance as he was left waiting on the doorstep. Knocking again, louder this time, Brabbinger began to sigh heavily. His left paw was starting to throb painfully.

"Bloody field surgeon," Brabbinger muttered to himself. "Said it should be healed by now."

After a yet longer interval the door opened to reveal a young Rodentian who had been stuffed into a butler's uniform at least three sizes too big for him. Brabbinger looked him up and down. The shirt hadn't been ironed and there was a large stain (Brabbinger suspected it was egg) on the right lapel. The "butler" slouched against the door and with an unsuppressed yawn started to close the door again.

"We don't give 'andouts to broken-down soldiers. Get a job."

With a fury he didn't know he possessed Brabbinger pushed the door back open, knocking the butler down as he did so.

"HOW DARE YOU!" he bellowed at the cowering Rodentian. "You are a disgrace to that uniform. Now take me to my father, the REAL butler, or I'll show you exactly what this broken-down soldier is capable of."

The smaller Rodentian scrabbled to his feet and for a moment Brabbinger thought he was going to make a fight of it. Instead he mumbled an apology and beckoned Brabbinger to follow him. As they walked, Brabbinger replayed the incident in his head. He had been annoyed, truly annoyed, by the sight he saw but couldn't explain to himself why he felt that way. He tried to rationalise it to himself. He was annoyed at having his plans to travel changed so drastically but that didn't feel right. He realised with a sinking feeling of inevitable dread that he was annoyed at the lack of respect the young idiot had shown towards the position to which he had been entrusted. He was the Royal Butler and should be ashamed.

"What is your name?" he asked curtly.

"Maximal," he replied with a surly tone.

"What training has my father provided you with, Maximal?"

Maximal snorted at this.

"When were you last 'ere?" Maximal sneered. "Your old dad is at death's door and if it were up to me I'd kick 'im through it." Before Brabbinger could react to this latest insult they arrived at a closed door. "'is 'oliness is in 'ere."

Maximal indicated the door by poking his thumb over his shoulder and slouched off down the corridor without looking back. Brabbinger considered following him but realised that dealing with Maximal could wait but if he was correct, seeing his father couldn't. Bracing himself for an unpleasant reunion Brabbinger entered his father's room.

Mercifully the reunion had been brief. Deringer hadn't asked his son anything about his life or experiences during the war, preferring to lecture him on the many tasks and obligations that his new life required of him, and reminded him many times of his duty and warned him not to let him down. Deringer fell asleep soon after this. Brabbinger remained at his bedside all night, either through love or duty he was never sure. As dawn arrived Deringer passed away and Brabbinger sobbed. He sobbed for a long time. He cried over the death of a father he had never been close to, a mother he had never known, and, more deeply, he sobbed for a life he knew he could never lead. Eventually he dried his eyes, hardened his heart and went to begin his new life.

It didn't take Brabbinger long to realise that King Faustus either didn't care about his staff or (more likely) he didn't notice their existence. The King would attend council meetings and make the occasional proclamation but he spent most of his time in the newly built north tower, often spending cycles at a time up there. Brabbinger would bring meals up to him but would often bring them back untouched. The staff had taken full advantage of their employer's disinterest and the incapacity of Deringer. Brabbinger had found them all as surly and uncooperative as Maximal had been. For the first time Brabbinger found himself grateful for his army experience. After a few cycles of watching his staff at "work" he called them all into the kitchen and lined them up. He berated them for their attitude, their laziness and the state of their uniform.

As he was outlining what he expected from them going forward he heard an exaggerated yawn. Turning he found Maximal (who else?) pretending to be asleep as he slouched against a wall. Without saying a word Brabbinger lifted Maximal by the scruff of his footmouse uniform (better fitting but dirtier than the butler's outfit he had worn previously) and slapped him across his face, hard. The other servants gasped in shock as Brabbinger, still gripping Maximal, propelled him with violent force along the corridor. At one point the struggling Maximal lost his footing but this didn't slow Brabbinger down. Instead he dragged the protesting footmouse across the stone floor, making sure to swing him into a wall at every opportunity. Maximal screamed for help but his fellow servants remained rooted to the spot, watching with fascinated horror as Brabbinger, having reached the front door, hauled the cowering Maximal to his feet and without a word kicked him down the stone steps into the rain and slammed the door.

Brabbinger was breathing heavily and his left paw was throbbing. He paused to straighten his uniform and, trying his best to hide his limp, he walked back into the kitchen. He was pleased to see that the staff had not only remained in place but they had straightened up considerably.

"We'll need to recruit a new footmouse," he said almost conversationally to the petrified staff. "Better get a new uniform too," he added. "Blood is a difficult stain to remove."

The staff just nodded at this. After Brabbinger dismissed them he allowed himself a seat but not before getting a cold damp cloth for his aching paw.

Brabbinger never had a problem with the staff again. In fact, under his direction more staff were hired and each one heard the tale of the unfortunate Maximal. As the King's son Prince Tyrell grew older his father paid less and less attention to him, so Brabbinger took it upon himself to tutor him in the ways of royalty. When he reached school age, Tyrell had been sent to Strig Academy for the Children of Nobility, where the owls would take over his training.

The castle seemed empty with the young prince absent, but Brabbinger was kept busy by the increasingly erratic demands from King Faustus. The King had developed a mania for folklore, and Brabbinger had been required to find every written report about ancient and mythical artefacts. One memorable summer, the King sent him to find an old academic from the badger community and bring him straight to the north tower. It had been a long journey there and back, and throughout the journey Brabbinger received many telegrams from the King demanding that he hurry. The telegrams had become more frequent and the threats contained within them more vivid so that when

Brabbinger finally returned with the academic (a somewhat befuddled old badger named Brockstein) he feared he would be executed. Instead, the King barely acknowledged his return, preferring to usher Brockstein up the many stairs of the north tower.

Time passed as it always does. Prince Tyrell returned from the academy with a fiancée, a striking female Rodentian who went by the name Perdita. Brabbinger had been struck by her piercing blue eyes and down-to-earth attitude. Brabbinger loved Tyrell like a son but he was always a bit of a dreamer. *She'll straighten him out*, Brabbinger had thought to himself after their first introduction. Brabbinger had been sitting in the servants' kitchen enjoying a nettle tea when the young prince bounded into the room, obviously delighted to see the old butler still in residence. Although he had been taken by surprise by the arrival, Brabbinger had become too well seasoned in his role to let it show. He was glad to see Tyrell return to the palace, not least because he would be expected to take over many of his father's duties.

During his absence the King's obsession had become all consuming. He had levied many high taxes on his people to fund his experiments and Brabbinger knew that the cells had been emptied. He didn't know what had happened to the prisoners but there had been reports from the night maids that the sounds of agonised screaming could be heard coming from the tower. The local town was rife with rumours that a black carriage with no livery had been seen slowly cruising through the streets picking up the homeless and the insensible and taking them away. Whispers in the streets were turning against the King but rumours of his dark powers scared most people into submission. Mothers would tell their children not to go out at night and the local tavern, the Whisker and Claw, found that only the bold or desperate would stay there late into the night. Brabbinger wasn't one for rumours but even he had to wonder if there was any truth to them. Perhaps the return of Tyrell could turn the anti-royalist feelings growing in the town and beyond but secretly he feared he might be too late.

Fortunately, Tyrell did seem to have a relatively calming effect on his father. Brabbinger never knew what the two had said to each other during their reunion but Faustus could often be seen outside of the tower. He was a fearsome sight. His fur was ragged and missing in places; he was so thin that his robes practically enveloped him. He was often spotted walking through the gardens alternately muttering and shouting to himself at all hours of the day and night. The younger staff were terrified of him and even the more experienced amongst them would avoid him when they could.

Tyrell and Perdita married the year after they arrived at Castle Mowser in a simple ceremony. Brabbinger had tried to persuade them to have an elaborate ceremony, reasoning that everyone likes a party. Tyrell had proved to be very shrewd, however. By making the ceremony simple and intimate he endeared himself to the populace. They thought he understood their hardship and, in some quarters, many Rodentians were hoping for the death of Faustus and the accession of Tyrell. For the first time in a while there was hope amongst the villagers. This hope grew further when the happy couple announced the birth of their son, Hirax. When word of this reached King Faustus he flew into a rage that even Tyrell couldn't calm. The King was furious. Despite his emaciated frame he flew back up his tower shouting that "If those ingrates think they've had it tough before they should prepare for an eternity of servitude."

That night more black carriages had been reported prowling the village. Tyrell tried multiple times to speak to his father but he was ignored. Things became worse when Hirax was born. Faustus openly hated his grandson and daughter-in-law, believing that they were trying to replace him. He ignored Hirax and insulted Perdita, often to her face. So vicious had he been to her that one night, fearing for her life, she fled the castle with the young prince. Tyrell was frantic with worry and practically tore the kingdom apart looking for her and Hirax. Then one night an elderly mouse from the village knocked on the doors of Castle Mowser. She was holding a blanket which Brabbinger recognised as Perdita's cloak. There wrapped up inside, sound asleep, was the infant Hirax. Perdita was never seen again and Tyrell fell into a dark depression which culminated in him locking himself in the wine cellar trying to drink himself to death. With Tyrell indisposed, things continued to get worse. Brabbinger found that many members of his staff had been arrested by the King under the belief that they had been plotting against him. There was no trial and he couldn't find out what had happened to them.

Things came to head shortly before Hirax's tenth birthday. There had been mutterings from the village that they weren't going to put up with things any longer, and fearing a rebellion a broken and depressed Tyrell came to Brabbinger and asked him to help him overthrow his father. Brabbinger found this difficult. While he believed that Tyrell would be a better king he had sworn an oath to serve the legitimate king. Long into the night Tyrell would debate and attempt to persuade Brabbinger that it was for the best.

Eventually when Tyrell explained that his father would be looked after and would be allowed to live in comfort, Brabbinger grudgingly agreed. In the early hours of the morning the two conspirators walked up the long staircase to the King's tower, Tyrell leading the way and Brabbinger following closely behind, wooden cuffs in hand (he had been assured by Tyrell that they would only be used to prevent the King from hurting himself and others but he still felt disloyal and shuddered at the thought of what his own father would make of this). Upon arriving at the door to the King's room Tyrell hesitated. Holding up his paw palm outwards to stop Brabbinger, he placed his ear against the door and listened intently. Brabbinger noticed the colour drain from Tyrell's face and instead of feeling disloyal he felt very afraid. Whatever Tyrell could hear must be dreadful indeed. Tyrell jerked his ear away from the door suddenly and nodded at Brabbinger.

"Get ready," he whispered urgently.

Brabbinger felt his paws tighten around the cuffs. Tyrell reached down and grasped the ornate golden door handle and turned it quickly, flinging open the door, allowing him and Brabbinger enough space to charge in.

As he entered the room Brabbinger realised that he should have done something much earlier. Brabbinger had seen many horrific sights in the war but nothing could prepare him for the tableau in front of him. Faustus was standing at a worktable wearing a blood-soaked apron and holding a viciously sharp hacksaw in his paws. On the table was a thankfully unconscious female Rodentian. She had been stripped of her clothing but far from being naked Brabbinger and Tyrell noticed that patches of metal had been crudely welded all over her body. Wires snaked from each piece of metal to a skull cap bolted to her head. Her legs had been removed indelicately and replaced with metal stumps which were thin at the top where they had been melted to her hips but flared out as they went down. The poor female must have been in agony and Brabbinger hoped that she had died quickly. With a mixture of horror and revulsion Brabbinger noticed that her chest was rising up and down. She wasn't dead. Disgustedly he turned away, only to see that five more Rodentians were lined up against the wall. Clearly Faustus had finished working on them. The five Rodentians stared glassy-eyed at the intruders. Tyrell rushed towards them to offer help but as he approached they all raised their arms defensively, and both Tyrell and Brabbinger noticed that long sharp blades had been welded to their wrists.

For his part Faustus acted as though nothing had happened. He continued to saw away at the arms of his latest victim.

"Father!" Tyrell asked eventually. He received no response. "What are you doing?" he asked louder.

Faustus eventually looked up from his work, finally acknowledging Brabbinger and Tyrell.

"Working," he answered shortly.

"FATHER, WHAT HAVE YOU DONE TO THESE INNOCENTS?"

Tyrell was angry now. Faustus sighed, put the hacksaw down and rolled his eyes at his son.

"Innocents?" he scoffed. "Ingrates more like," he added. "But to answer your question, I'm improving them." There was no pride in his voice. Faustus could have been discussing the weather. Tyrell stared open-mouthed at him. "Close your mouth, boy," Faustus admonished. "I don't know what they taught you at that school."

Brabbinger had started to move behind the King, taking each step as slowly as he could. The floor was covered in blood and innards, and Brabbinger was trying not to step in anything or to throw up anywhere (although he felt that he might not have much choice in the latter if they stayed there any longer).

"Imp… Imp… IMPROVING THEM?!" Tyrell spluttered.

Faustus sighed again, more deeply this time.

"Try to wrap your head around this simple concept. It is vitally important that our family continue to rule Venary. To do this we need soldiers. Our subjects are fat and lazy. They also slow down and die far too quickly. Take Brabbinger here…" at this he turned to indicate the butler, "the only survivor of a cowardly cat attack, but now he can't even sneak up on an elderly Rodentian." He turned to address Brabbinger directly. "Really, Brabbinger?" he asked mockingly. "What would your father say?"

"He wouldn't approve of this," Brabbinger said eventually, his natural respect for protocol quite forgotten. "It's monstrous."

"MONSTROUS?!" Faustus yelled at him, and with this Brabbinger realised that Faustus had finally lost all grip on his sanity. "Who are you to question a king?" he screeched.

"These citizens are mine! I own them, I can do whatever I like to them. I am their King."

"NOT ANYMORE!" Tyrell added forcefully. "Father, for your actions against these six innocents I relieve you of your duties, you will be King in name only. I shall rule as Regent until you either recover or die."

Brabbinger stepped forward, opening the cuffs as he did so, but was frozen with shock when he realised that Faustus was laughing. It came out as a high-pitched whine and there was certainly no merriment behind it but it was unmistakably a laugh.

"Six?" Faustus said mockingly. "You think I've worked this long and hard to create merely six loyal soldiers? Tell me," he sneered, "have you been to the stables recently?"

Tyrell felt sick.

"Father? Please tell me you haven't…" He couldn't finish the sentence, the very thought of it was repellent.

"Oh, but I have," Faustus said victoriously. "My army grows larger every day! Even that fool badger has been put to use."

Tyrell felt dizzy. He grabbed at the wall behind him but lost his footing and hit the floor. There was a sickening thud as he landed in a visceral-looking pile. Faustus merely giggled at his plight.

"But how will you control them?" This question came from Brabbinger.

Faustus turned slowly to answer him, rummaging in the large front pocket of his blood-spattered tunic. Eventually he found what he was looking for and dangled it in front of Brabbinger's face. Brabbinger didn't know what he expected but was surprised by what he saw.

Faustus was holding a collar. Brabbinger had only seen officers during the war on both sides wearing collars and none had worn one as beautiful as this. Rather than cloth the collar was made of interlinked metals which shone so brightly that Brabbinger suspected (quite correctly as it happens) that it was made of solid gold. The collar was studded with bright blue sapphires. Brabbinger was shocked into silence.

"THIS…" Faustus shouted, his head leaning back so that he was shouting to the skies, "THIS COLLAR WILL GRANT MY FONDEST WISH!"

He was breathing heavily now. He looked down just in time to see Tyrell jumping towards him. In an action that surprised both Tyrell and Brabbinger, the frail and old Faustus jumped up onto his operating table, paws astride its unfortunate occupant. He held the collar out in front of him like a shield.

"I had hoped to have more time, to increase my ranks," he panted, "but you leave me no choice." He held the collar above his head and called, "I have my wish." As he spoke the sapphires started to glow, getting brighter and brighter as Faustus spoke. "Oh Collar of Honour," he intoned and Brabbinger was sure he could hear the collar humming in response, "I wish for me and my army to survive death and protect my lands from dangers." He looked down at Tyrell and winked. "Long live the King," he spat at his son.

There was a blinding bright flash from the collar and the humming had reached a pitch so loud that all three Rodentians had to cover their ears. There was a sudden explosion of blue light and Faustus was thrown violently off the operating table and into a wall. He slid down the wall unconscious, blood pouring from his nose and eyes. Brabbinger ran to him but was stopped by the sound of screaming coming from outside. He and Tyrell dashed to a window and looked out. The screaming was coming from the stables. A familiar blue light had engulfed the stables and the servants were running around in a panic. The blue light had become so bright that the stables could no longer be seen. The light condensed into a line which shot up into the sky, burning through the clouds as it went. As soon as it had come the light disappeared. Brabbinger turned to see Tyrell leaning over the prone body of his father.

"Is he...?" Brabbinger started to ask.

"No, he's alive, although barely," Tyrell replied, not looking over. "Take him to his bed and summon the royal physician."

Brabbinger nodded.

"What about the others?"

As he spoke he went to point at the six victims of Faustus' experiments and was shocked to see that they had vanished.

Back in the present day King Hirax just stared as Brabbinger finished his story.

"The rest of the story you already know, Your Majesty." Brabbinger's voice was hoarse from the retelling. "Your grandfather struggled on for a few cycles but his illness took him in the end and we buried him in the royal graveyard. Your father ascended to the throne but became obsessed with tracking down the collar that had killed his father and hasn't been seen since. I chose not to tell you as I feared you would go the same way."

Hirax stared at his butler, his face blank. Eventually he spoke.

"Butler, you are dismissed. We have a jubilee to celebrate."

## CHAPTER NINE

# PLANNING

W HEN YANI WOKE up it took her a while to remember where she was. She sat up and discovered that she had been put to sleep in a giant bed. After a long time sleeping on a cold cell floor she took a moment to luxuriate in her new-found comfort. Even in the spans when she had been a respected member of the scientific elite the best she could hope for was a cot. After marrying Yaxil they had been assigned married quarters on the base but all this entailed was a room large enough to push two single cots together. Even this was better than the slave quarters she had been forced to sleep in during the occupation. The Pacidermians used to pack ten Giraxians to what amounted to little more than a stable. She better than to complain about her new quarters for fear of being accused of disloyalty to the glorious Giraxian rebellion, a crime punishable by flogging under the new order. Like everything on the Giraxian base the pillows had been designed with function being considered more important than comfort.

With a start she remembered where she was. Sitting bolt upright in the large bed Yani was somewhat disturbed to find that whomever had put her to bed had dressed her in a silken nightgown. Like many Giraxians Yani didn't embarrass easily but even she drew the line at being undressed while unconscious. She looked around the room. By the standards she was used to the room seemed needlessly opulent. There was a dresser *and* a cupboard, neither of which were required as she only had the two outfits (travelling and formal). She turned around and sat on the edge of her mattress. Her hooves settled on the deep carpet and despite herself she let out a contented sigh. She was used to solid stone floors and her hooves had become tough and calloused as a result. To rest them on such a deep carpet was a treat she wouldn't soon forget.

She surveyed the room again from this new angle. The pictures on the wall confused her. She wasn't sure what purpose they served. In their quarters she and Yaxil used to pin their work shifts on the walls. Sometimes if she'd had a new idea she would stick it to the walls just to have somewhere to keep it. During the occupation the only things ever stuck to the walls were ever-growing list of rules and infractions the Pacidermians enforced on them, the breaking of any of them severely punished.

She got up and walked towards the nearest of these pictures. It showed a long field in the summer. As she squinted at the picture she saw that dotted about in the field where many small white crucifixes. Yani knew that some species used crucifixes as instruments of torture and shuddered inwardly. Did the Rodentians practise torture? That old butler had been so sweet to her earlier but she resolved to keep her mouth closed from now on. There was a small plaque at the bottom of the picture on which the words "Never Forget" were carved. Yani didn't think that she would. Walking back to the bed she discovered a thicker coat with a frilly lace pattern running down the whole length on the lapels right down the hem. It was thicker than her nightdress so she gratefully wrapped herself up in it.

Just as she had fastened the cloth belt she found wrapped around the coat, the door to her room flew open. Without knocking or asking permission to enter, her hated travelling companion casually sauntered into the room.

"Dear 'sister'," he drawled, taking her by the shoulders and pulling her into an embrace.

Yani shuddered with revulsion and made to push him away. Rather than let her go he pulled her in closer and with his mouth right by her ear whispered nastily, "Keep up the pretence or I'll cheerfully throw you out of an open window and claim you tripped." Yani froze and he continued whispering, "Is there a sink in this room?"

Still unable to talk Yani merely shrugged her shoulders as best she could. With an undisguised sneer on his face he disengaged from the embrace and started to hunt through the room. As he walked he made what seemed like small talk.

"Oh, dear sister," he said brightly while looking under the bed, "you should see His Majesty's throne room! Such splendour."

He moved on to the cupboard, opening the doors and running his hooves gently along the sides and across the horizontal wooden pole from which strange metal implements were hanging, on one of which was her evening dress.

"So many people here," he continued breezily, not bothering to look at her as he spoke.

Seemingly happy with the cupboard he walked across the room and opened another door. This one opened up into the most beautiful bathroom Yani had ever seen. All the fixtures looked like they had been coated with gold and, remembering whose castle she was in, she reasoned that they probably were. She was finally waking up and her old cognitive abilities were returning to her. She wondered what he was doing as he turned all the taps on at once and left the room with them still running. He re-entered the room and all trace of his previous jollity had left. He surveyed her with cold eyes.

"Riiiight," he said eventually, making sure to draw out the i's as he spoke, "that should make it difficult for anyone to overhear us."

"Have you gone totally mad?" she asked eventually. "Who would want to overhear us?"

The look he shot her made it clear that she had gone too far.

"We are two doors down from a damned Pacidermian!" he hissed. "I have already resisted the urge to smack the smug bastard in our earlier meeting, a meeting at which you should have been in attendance! If you weren't so feeble."

"I tried to tell you, I'm not used to travelling. I hadn't done it before," she protested.

"You hadn't tried treason before either," he hissed back at her, "but you made a success out of that, didn't you?"

Yani went to speak but after three cycles travelling with this male she realised that it would have been pointless. Every time she had tried to engage him in conversation or ask questions throughout their journey he had either ignored her completely or told her he wasn't "in the business of giving information to traitors". He stared at her.

"Nothing to say?" he asked nastily. "Good, keep it that way."

Suddenly there was a knock at the door. He rolled his eyes in frustration.

"WHAT?" he bellowed at the already open door.

Standing in the doorway was a small female Rodentian dressed in an impossibly clean and sharply ironed maid's outfit. She was carrying a tray which was covered by a thick piece of cloth. Yani could see a small white teapot underneath the cloth with green steam coming from the spout. Suddenly she realised just how hungry she was. If the maid had heard anything she made no show of it.

"Begging your pardon, ma'am," she said in a voice louder than her diminutive frame should have allowed.

She ignored the scoffing laughter her use of the word "ma'am" had provoked in the male. As Brabbinger said, "It is not your job to judge our visitors, just get there before the tea gets cold."

She continued to address Yani.

"Mr Brabbinger sends his regards and hopes that you are feeling better. He has sent me up with some of his homemade eucalyptus tea. Just the thing for settling a rumbly tum."

As she spoke she walked towards the edge of the bed where Yani was sitting and, pausing only slightly to stand on her tiptoes, she passed the tray up to her. The maid pulled off the cloth and Yani could see some light brown toast on which was spread a thick green paste. The maid followed her gaze.

"Oh yes, Mr Brabbinger thinks of everything. Took him two cycles to track down some the ingredients just in case anyone fancied a bit. I don't know how he does it." She continued talking as she poured some of the sweet-smelling liquid into a pristine and delicate-looking cup. "We've been so worried about you, poor thing, collapsing like that. It wasn't right, begging your pardon. Lucky you had your brother there," she said, looking up at him and smiling warmly.

"Yes, well," he replied testily, "thank your Mr Brabbinger for his kindness, but my sister and I have much to discuss so if you would…"

He continued pointing to the door.

"Of course, sir," the maid replied primly. "Just a reminder that His Majesty expects you both at the jubilee by mid sun."

Yani had enough experience over the previous cycles to know when her "brother" was about to lose his fierce temper and this was one of those times. Placing the tea tray to one side for now, Yani ushered the maid through the door, alternately thanking her and promising her that both she and her brother would be at the jubilee in time. Breathing heavily, she closed the door.

Pulling herself together Yani turned around and wasn't surprised to see that he was now lying back on the bed. He had one of his long front legs tucked behind his head and he had helped himself to a cup of tea. He was taking long sips and looking directly at her, seeming to dare her to challenge him. She decided not to rise to the obvious bait. He would only say something cruel, like traitors like her don't deserve things. Seeming disappointed he moved on to the toast. He held it up to the light, brought it up to his nose and took an exaggerated smell. A smile broke across his thin lips and he bit into the toast. He made a show of moving the toast around his mouth with his tongue.

"Hmm," he cooed. "I'll say for the King, his staff have good taste."

Yani sighed. Walking over to the dresser she pulled out a stool and sat down, waiting for him to finish making whatever point he was building up to. She knew that she wouldn't have to wait for long.

"I don't know about you," he said around the final piece of toast in his mouth, "but sometimes I find our own eucalyptus spread rather bitty. This is smooth though. I could get used to this. I wonder what's on the menu for the jubilee banquet."

Disappointed that Yani wasn't responding he sat up and scowled at her. Hoping to move things along Yani asked him, "Did you find out what the Collar of Honour is? You said that the King was looking for information about it."

"Hmm," he replied. "Yes, His Majesty said much. Tell me," he asked suddenly, "do you remember why I brought you here? Or did you vomit this out of you along with everything else?"

Yani blushed a deep scarlet. She hated appearing weak in front of this creature. During the high points of her scientific career she had led whole teams and nobody intimidated her quite like he did. Perhaps it was the casual way he told her about the execution of her husband, Yaxil. She thought back to her briefing.

"I am to search the castle and find the Collar. You said that as the King is so desperate for information about it he must already have and will pay a lot to get it back."

"Yes," he conceded. "That would have been a good plan." He seemed lost in thought for a second. "However," he said quickly, snapping back to reality, "he hasn't got it and has no idea where it is."

"So why are we here then?" she asked.

"Oh, do keep up," he snapped back at her. "Officially we're here for the jubilee. No, His Majesty," he practically spat out the word, "has decreed that we are to find it. He will grant independence to whatever species finds it."

"So what's the problem?" she asked and immediately regretted it.

He leapt off the bed and paced around the room waving his long limbs around.

"The problem is, Doctor…" and at this he stared directly at her, "imagine if your friends amongst the Pacidermians get independence. They'll have a much stronger claim on our lands and I'm sure that even you don't want to go back to the work camps. That's the best-case scenario by the way. If the King is right and the Collar grants wishes they could wipe us all out totally. It's imperative we find it before they do."

Yani's head was spinning. *The Collar grants wishes*, she thought to herself. She could bring Yaxil back, she could find a peaceful outcome to their war. Obviously, Number One saw the look on her face.

"Making plans, are you?" he sneered at her. "Thinking of all the things you'd like to do to me, I suppose."

Yani kept quiet. The advantage with him being so self-obsessed was that he couldn't imagine any situation which didn't involve him directly. Suddenly she realised that she had an advantage.

"Well, you can stop thinking that right now," he warned her. "We need that Collar for our people. I expect you to put that alleged intelligence of yours to work and find out where we can start looking. According to that be-crowned idiot it could be anywhere in the kingdom."

With this he looked inside the teapot and, clearly disappointed that it was empty, he made to leave. As he got to the door he called back over his shoulder.

"I'll expect to see you at the jubilee. Don't get any ideas, there's nowhere you can hide that I won't find you."

Feeling that he had got his point across he marched out of the room.

* * *

"Stand up straight," Zakk admonished Scratch. "You took a nasty punch to your stomach earlier and I need to check that you are okay."

"I'm fine," Scratch whined.

"Well, you'll do I suppose," Zakk admitted. "Now on to the important issues."

Scratch could barely stop himself from jumping up and down with excitement.

"We've got a quest," he started to sing in an excited fashion. "We've got a quest," he continued, dancing around their palacious quarters. He stopped when he realised that Zakk meant something else.

"Now where did I put you, you little beauty?" Zakk muttered, his voice muffled by the fact that he had jammed his whole head into the bag and was rummaging about. "Ah ha!" he cried with triumph, emerging from the bag, clutching a bottle of deep red liquid. "Thought you could get away from me, did you?" he cooed almost lovingly at the bottle. With a contented sigh he sat straight down on the floor and began to worry the bottle stop loose with his paws.

"Err, Zakk..." Scratch began.

Zakk ignored him but Scratch knew from a familiar twitching of his ears that he could hear him and that he knew he was being spoken to.

"Isn't it too early for that? We have a noble quest to prepare for after all."

The end of this sentence was cut off suddenly by the popping noise of a cork leaving its bottle and a delighted cheer coming from Zakk. He took a long pull from the bottle before addressing Scratch.

"You prepare in your way and I'll prepare in mine," he intoned solemnly. "If I had prepared this way for the Battle of Towering Wood I wouldn't have felt it quite as much when that damned rodent sunk his sharpened teeth into my arse."

He rubbed his large backside for emphasis and took yet another swig.

"But if we get the Collar of Honour," Scratch stated, ignoring Zakk who rolled his eyes when Scratch said "Collar of Honour" in an artificially deep voice, "we'll be royal heroes! And Oscar will have to make me a knight!"

"Is that what you think?" Zakk asked him sadly, slowly shaking his head.

"B... But the King said..." stammered Scratch.

"The King offered independence for the state who finds and returns the Collar," Zakk explained. "He will no longer be in charge of that state. Felines like Oscar would be. Do you think giving him even more power would be a good idea?"

"It might make him happy," Scratch countered, although he didn't think that anything other than torturing him would make Oscar happy. "Besides," he said, brightening at the thought he'd just had, "if I present it to him I might get a knighthood as a reward. Come on, Zakk, we have to try, we have to…"

He trailed off when he looked at Zakk. The old cat looked sad and old. His chin had sunk into his enormous chest and he was shaking his head sadly.

"I used to think like that," he said quietly. "I thought that our code meant something. I was a fool. I've fought in every battle they sent me to, laid siege to towns just because I was given an order. I've travelled over most of this land and what rewards did I ever get?"

Scratch looked down at the left breast pocket of Zakk's tunic where the medals he had spent hours the previous evening polishing shone brightly. Zakk followed his gaze and chuckled mirthlessly.

"These?" he asked, pointing at the shiny medals. "Trinkets and baubles. After every mission fewer and fewer of us returned. I wanted to be remembered as a bold explorer but how did I end up? A broken-down soak with more blood on his paws than even you could scrub off. Nobody will reward you. Oscar will take the credit and, who knows, might end up being appointed King and where do you think that will leave the likes of you and me?" Scratch shuddered at the thought. "We'd be better off finding and using that Collar for ourselves."

"But the King said," Scratch interrupted, horrified

at the suggestion, "he would burn down the forest and torture us."

"Only if we get caught, and as I see it we have nothing to lose. If we give the Collar to Oscar I'll be kicked out of the castle and you'll most likely be given to his favourite student Mittens for hunting practice. If any of the other champions get it they'll probably use it to either suck up to Hirax or if they have any sense at all use it to give themselves more power. I think it's best we get to it first, don't you? Then you can be a knight and I can get a life of comfort." He stopped to stare wistfully into space and drain the rest of the bottle. "Perhaps I could get a nicer quality wine too," he added.

"But we only get one wish," Scratch argued.

"Who said one wish?" Zakk answered. "The King said it will grant our heart's desire. I'm big enough to admit that my heart holds many desires, it's just a matter of being careful how we word our requests." He held the empty bottle upside down over his mouth optimistically but growled with frustration when this proved fruitless. "I suggest you leave the heavy thinking to me for now, we'd better prepare for the jubilee."

\* \* \*

Lex looked at himself in the mirror, that is to say he tried to look at himself in the mirror. As the largest species on Venary, Pacidermians often struggled outside of their lands (and as far as Lex was concerned all the lands were Pacidermian by right, granted some needed clearing of upstart Giraxians but they were still Pacidermian by right of conquest). While the mirror was tall enough it wasn't wide enough to accommodate his considerable frame. Lex had to place the mirror at one end of the room and stand right at the other end to be able to see half of himself reflected in it. A minor academic from Strig Academy once put forward the theory that it was these constant annoyances that made the Pacidermians so angry and opposed to all of the other races. This theory had been debunked as being needlessly speciesist but if anybody had heard the language Lex directed at the mirror as he dragged it across the carpeted floor they might have rethought the theory.

"My fellow Pacidermians," Lex intoned under his breath, "I come to you with the means to ensure our victory." With a flourish Lex reached into the breast pocket of his fatigues. His pad came away empty. "The Collar of Honour." He grinned at his reflection. *Perhaps I should drop to one knee when I present the Collar*, he thought to himself. *No*, he decided after some more thought, *I'll be the saviour of my people. No need to bow before others, they'll be bowing before me.*

From the very second that Hirax issued his decree Lex was making plans. In actuality he had been making plans since he received the royal telegram back in his hated office. He knew that he should have taken the telegram to High Command but they would have sent some stuffed-shirt dignitary who had every achievement handed to him. *Besides*, he had reasoned to himself, *I have paid my dues*. It had only taken a quick scan of his hated office for him to make up his mind. Keeping the telegram out of view he told his commanding officer that he was suffering from a severe stomach upset and had to return to his quarters. Then, under the cover of darkness he snuck out of the compound and made his way to Castle Mowser. Technically he was now AWOL but he was banking on the hope that nobody would discover his absence as no one wants to disturb the sick. Besides, if somebody did discover him missing he was sure all would be forgiven when returned victoriously with the means of their salvation.

Lex returned to rehearsing his speech for when he was inevitably awarded the coveted Legion of Trunk medal. He could see it now: all of those fools who denied him a commission would have to eat their words when he got what was coming to him. He did admit (but only to himself) that the King's warning was concerning. He had no problem with the moral aspects, he had long been of the opinion that Venary would be better off by far with a military leader in charge. He had little time for a ranting rodent who was foolish enough to trust anybody else with a weapon of such power but he did worry about getting the Collar back home. If the King was right (and he darkly suspected that in this case the King probably was) the Collar could be anywhere in the world and trying to smuggle it back across great distances would be a challenge. Even in his youth Lex hadn't been particularly swift and the issues with the mirror reminded him that his size would leave him with a disadvantage. When faced with a problem of size Lex would traditionally bulldozer his way through it. This usually worked (although it didn't so much solve the problem as remove it completely). Even he would have to admit that this solution would draw even more attention to himself.

*Well, worse case I could use the Collar to make myself invincible*, he thought. More to convince himself he quickly added, *But only as a last resort obviously. My first duty is to High Command.* If anyone could hear him at this point they might have believed him, until they saw the wry smile that had broken across his face.

\* \* \*

The crossbow bounced slightly as it landed on the bed. Greeta hadn't expected that. She was more used to sleeping on the floor of Silvestri Forest and much preferred it. Castle Mowser was very large and she'd had to resist the impulse to help herself to the many treasures she had seen dotted around the place. Honestly, the lack of security was absolutely criminal. However, Hestor's instructions had been clear: this was a reconnaissance trip. She had to find out what the King wanted and report back to Hestor as soon as she could. Greeta double-checked that she had firmly closed the doors to her quarters and when she was absolutely sure nobody could see she untied a small cloth pouch which had been tied around her waist and slowly and with great care opened it out.

"SCREEECH!" The noise echoed around the room far louder than Greeta had expected. "SCREEECH!" the noise repeated.

"SHHHHHHH," Greeta said urgently to the small pygmy shrew which until now had been wrapped up tightly in the cloth pouch. "Will you shut up?" she hissed urgently at the shrew, smothering the tiny creature with a paw as it petulantly took a deep breath and went to scream again. She had just been in time. Even muffled by her paw the screech was loud. "I swear I will see how many times I can make you bounce from wall to wall in here if you don't shut up." The muffled screeching stopped suddenly. "Good choice," she hissed into her paw. "I'm going to let go now but I have two quills in my other paw ready to drive into you at the slightest sound."

She didn't of course. She'd had to grab him so quickly that there wasn't time to rip out any quills from her back. In any case it was very painful and she would rather not go through that. Ever so slowly she lifted her paw. Fortunately the shrew didn't move or make a sound. Instead it sat on its hind legs and glared at her reproachfully. It was very smartly dressed, although the tweed three-piece suit he had chosen looked very rumpled after being wrapped up in the cloth pouch for so long. He continued to glare at her.

"Don't look at me like that," Greeta said. "I left plenty of berries in there with you. You didn't have to walk most of the way either, so if either of us has the right to complain it's me." The shrew just glared at her. "Do you think you'll be executed if you're found? Oh no, that'll be me too," Greeta complained. "Nobody ever suspects the little shrew. Besides, you'd do better to save your breath. You have work to do."

The shrew rolled his eyes and folded his arms, the very picture of defiance. Greeta resisted the urge to shake the attitude out of him.

"Okay," she admitted calmly, "I'm sorry I smothered you."

The shrew nodded at her and unfolded his arms. He still scowled slightly at her but it was clear that he was now prepared to be more co-operative.

"What did you hear?" Greeta asked.

The shrew jumped to his feet and mimed using a bow and arrow. As he let go of the imaginary bow he threw his arms out wide to indicate an explosion and started waving them around in an exaggerated impersonation of panic. He couldn't do any more because he was laughing so hard he had to hold his sides, tears were streaming down his face and he couldn't stop the high-pitched giggling. Greeta flushed red with embarrassment.

"That was an accident," she muttered.

The shrew laughed louder and louder. Eventually he ran out of breath and was left doubled up, his tiny paws on his knees, gasping for breath. Greeta waited impatiently for the shrew to finish. Eventually, breathing heavily, the shrew pulled himself together. He produced a tiny pad and quill from his waistcoat pocket. Quickly yet neatly he scribbled away at the parchment. Eventually he filled the pad and handed it over to Greeta. She held the tiny pad between two claws and read the report. She had to squint, and halfway through the pad she started to get a headache, whether from squinting or the stress of the day she couldn't tell. However, she finished reading and handed the pad back to the shrew.

"Get this back to Hestor as quick as you can," she told the shrew. "Make sure that you don't get caught."

The shrew flashed her a sarcastic salute and disappeared through a crack in the wall.

Greeta began dismantling her crossbow. It was a long task but she found it easier to think if her hands were busy and she wanted to reposition that bloody trigger. The accident in the throne room had bothered her more than she showed. She was used to being looked down on, and as a thief she often used this to her advantage, but that damned Giraxian had really got under her quills. As she worked she thought about everything she had been told. Somewhere in the kingdom there was a magical collar which could give her anything she wanted and she would be expected to hand it over to the King! As a thief this went against everything she stood for. Removing the trigger mechanism she discovered that it had worked its way loose. She'd been lucky to have not shot herself in the foot earlier. Rummaging through her pockets she found her trusted multitool and began retightening the trigger. Greeta thought about the others who knew of the quest. She identified the Giraxian as her most immediate threat. There was no way he would willingly hand over the Collar. Greeta decided that no matter what Hestor said she'd have to get to the Collar before him. Perhaps she could make an ally out of the crow leader?

* * *

"Supreme Leader, I must protest," Crasis blustered, puffing out his miniscule chest as far as it could go.

"But of course you must," Altheus replied playfully, idly twirling her staff between the longest of her wing feathers.

She knew that this was dangerous. The staff contained powerful magic and there was no telling what would happen if she dropped it with enough force to shatter the globe tied to the top. However, this action always made Crasis nervous and Altheus considered that worth the risk on its own. Crasis wasn't nervous this time, however he was far too annoyed.

"I am your vizier," he reminded her hotly, "I am not a stable boy! How could you send me to deal with those low beasts?" he whined.

"That's no way to talk about our hosts," Altheus scolded, allowing the twirling globe to brush past his chest feathers, singeing them as it touched. Crasis jumped back in horror, patting out his smouldering feathers as he went.

"Supreme Leader," he said, hurt, "I was referring to those dratted reptiles. I should have been by your side in the throne room."

"It's not like you missed anything important," she teased, "just His Majesty offering to make me a queen."

"Q... Queen," Crasis spluttered in shock. "I know the Queen died a few spans ago and like most I assumed that he would marry again. But interspecies marriage?" he questioned, shuddering at the thought. "Has such a thing ever been done before?"

"Surely congratulations are a more traditional response?" she said icily.

"Of course, Supreme Leader," Crasis said, panicking, "there's just so much to arrange. Should you wish to live here with your new husband I can assure you that Aridier would be in good wings."

Suddenly he could see a bright future for himself. With this unstable female happily stashed away here in married bliss he could get on with running Aridier properly! He was just wondering if the Nest of Almighty Authority could be rebuilt when he felt a burning sensation in his claws. He looked down. Altheus had placed the staff with its gently humming orb across both of his claws and they were starting to burn. He jumped so high Altheus thought he might become the first crow to fly in a millennium. Despite the comical sight she wasn't amused.

"Of course that's where your devious mind would go," she spat. "Did I say anything about marriage? I've worked too long and hard to hand my domain over to another stupid male."

"B… But you said Queen," Crasis wailed, still hopping from claw to claw, lifting them up alternately to ineffectually blow on them.

"I've been set a task," Altheus explained. "The reward is independence for Aridier. If you put your ambition to one side I'll tell you what it is…"

… "That's incredible," was all Crasis could think of to say after Altheus had told him of the meeting. "Does the King really believe that this thing exists?" he asked, slack-jawed with surprise.

"If he doesn't then he is a brilliant actor and I don't think pantomime is amongst his skills," Altheus replied dryly.

"But it's too incredible to believe," Crasis said under his breath, just in case saying it out loud might make it all disappear, "that sort of power would set you up amongst the gods. Does he expect anybody to actually give it to him?"

"This is why I keep you around," Altheus said brightly, clapping him on his shoulders. Crasis tensed, waiting for flames to engulf him. "You're sneaky and devious," Altheus said conspiratorially, "but in answer to your question…" she made a big show of thinking it over, "no, I don't think he does. Hirax is no fool, he knows that very few will give up power. That fool Pacidermian was practically rubbing his hands together and drooling at the very thought! Hirax is bound to have agents ready to pounce as soon as anyone finds the Collar."

"So what do we do?" Crasis asked.

Altheus shrugged her thin shoulders.

"I don't know yet. Hirax could be a powerful ally so it might be best to play along for now and wait for our opportunity."

## CHAPTER TEN

# JUBILEE

THE SOUND OF trumpeting echoed through the halls of Castle Mowser. From every door pretty young Rodentians emerged, throwing petals all around until each hallway was carpeted with colour. Yani stuck her long neck out of her quarters' window and could see that a circus act had started in the courtyard. Brightly coloured ferrets were swinging from a hastily constructed trapeze. She was slightly confused to see the butler in conversation with an elderly ferret dressed in a faded red tailcoat.

At first, she assumed that Brabbinger was giving instructions but she noticed that he was standing very close to the ferret and had a claw resting gently on the other's shoulder. Could they be friends? The thought of the clearly starchy and straight-laced Brabbinger being friends with a circus performer was so ridiculous that she almost smiled. She tried to make out what Brabbinger was saying but despite her impressive lip-reading skills she couldn't quite decipher it. It looked like Brabbinger was saying, "Yes, I loved her too," but that was clearly ridiculous.

Suddenly he turned and looked directly up at her. She was too surprised to move. If he was annoyed he didn't show it. Instead he nodded at her and returned to his conversation. Yani noticed that he had moved ever so slightly, however, so that she could now only see his back. Embarrassed she pulled her head back into her quarters and continued to pore over the map of Venary she had been studying before the trumpeting started.

She had surprised the young maid who had returned to collect the tea things with her request for a map. No doubt word of this request had made it to Brabbinger, maybe even the King himself! She had felt a little anxious about this but rationalised that she and the others had been tasked with finding the Collar of Honour, and with luck King Hirax would think that she was hard at work. This wasn't a lie. She had studied the map diligently since its arrival. She believed that she could rule out the war zones. Both the Giraxian and Pacidermian forces had churned up the land so much during the hostilities that nothing could remain hidden there for long. Silvestri Forest too seemed unlikely. Anything shiny would have been spotted by the Felixians or the Thieves' Guild rumoured to live deep in the forest. This left Aridier, the Jungles of Lac and the wastelands to the north. She shuddered when she thought of the North. There had been many expeditions there and none had been successful. Only a handful of explorers had ever returned from these lands and they had been driven insensible by who knows what?

The Jungles of Lac were less mysterious but still very dangerous. Yani thought that it was unlikely the Felixians would venture there. Rumours told of a flowing river of milk which no cat could resist. There was also talk of a tribe of savage big cats who hated other felines with a murderous rage. The only decision she had to make really was should she go where she thought the Collar was and try to get it away from Number One, or should she lead him on a fool's errand and risk someone like the Pacidermians getting it?

As she thought, an immaculately dressed footmouse arrived at her open door.

"Begging your pardon, ma'am," he said crisply but with warmth, "Mr Brabbinger presents his compliments but reminds you that all guests are expected in the throne room for the jubilee celebration."

"The others are there already," he added encouragingly when she made no effort to move.

She was disappointed. She had hoped that as she hadn't been in the meeting she might have been forgotten about so she could continue with her work. Suppressing a groan, she smiled at the footmouse.

"Just coming," she said brightly, and when the footmouse still refused to move she was forced to walk past him and proceeded towards where the noise was loudest.

Before the sounds could drown everything else out she heard the door to her quarters being closed and locked.

\* \* \*

Greeta entered the throne room and her eyes very nearly shot out on stalks. She had never seen so much gold in her life! She had once been privileged enough to be invited into Hestor's private stash and had promised herself there and then that her own stash would be even more impressive. However, she had to admit that King Hirax's wealth far outstripped Hestor's. Even the plates and cutlery sparkled. Greeta suspected that they were only gold-plated but would still fetch a small fortune, assuming she could find a fence brave or stupid enough to sell it through.

The throne room was filling up quickly. Greeta was quick and could avoid most of the larger animals but didn't want to spend the entire celebration dodging their big and clumsy feet, besides, she didn't want her view of this once-in-a-lifetime ceremony to be obscured by ankles. She was just curling up into a spiky ball and was calculating how many of the other guests she would need to fly through to get to the front when she spotted the curtains just in front of her. They were a deep red and when she gave them an experimental tug to test their strength she realised they were velvet. She followed the curtains and saw that they travelled above the heads of even the two Giraxians right to the other end of the hall. Greeta stuck her claws into the velvet, feeling slightly guilty at the many small holes she would soon be leaving, and climbed to the very top. She then scrambled halfway across and snuggled down into the velvet when she found a spot that directly faced the throne. She was sure of a good view and judging by the sounds of arguing coming from the entranceway the entertainment had arrived early.

\* \* \*

"You'll get it back after the ceremony," a portly Rodentian explained with exasperation evident in his voice.

"That's terribly sweet of you," Altheus replied icily, "but I am not handing it over."

She was trying to remain calm. The last thing she wanted was to antagonise the King – at least not while she was trying to convince him that she could be trusted – but she was sorely tempted to set fire to this idiot Rodentian's tail.

"This staff has the potential to blast you into many tiny pieces if you so much as knock it! So for your own safety it stays with me."

Calmness radiated out of every pore but the Rodentian, whose name coincidentally was Pompex, could see in her eyes that this wouldn't last long. However, with the spirit of so many functionaries before him he had a job to do and nothing was going to stop him from doing it.

"I'm afraid, madam," he said pompously, "no weapons are allowed in the throne room. If you could just hand it over I'll make sure it is looked after."

He pointed towards a large oak table on which were piled numerous swords, shields and something Altheus couldn't identify brimming with more spikes than any reasonable individual could possibly need. She rolled her eyes.

"The very second you place my staff on that pile," she said slowly, making sure that each word was clear, "there will be an explosion of metal so fast that you'll need to crown a new king, never mind celebrating the current. Not that you'll be able to do this," she added, her voice getting gradually louder, "because this entire region will be reduced to little more than a bloodstained hole in the ground."

Pompex swallowed hard, determined to continue, but Altheus hadn't finished.

"For the safety of everyone here," she intoned, allowing the staff to throb ominously in time with her words, "the staff stays with me."

Pompex looked around urgently, desperate to find someone senior to help or someone junior he could dump this on. The other members of staff were wisely not meeting his gaze and all had suddenly found something vitally important to do. However, he could feel their gaze on him, he couldn't back down now. Pompex swallowed hard and ploughed on.

"For safety's sake I must insist."

The last word came out as a strangled squeak as Pompex suddenly thought that perhaps he had gone too far. Altheus just stared down at him. Pompex wasn't sure but he could swear she was getting larger by the second.

"For safety's sake," she repeated quietly. "Very well, for safety's sake."

She went to hand Pompex the staff. He nervously reached out for it. At the last second, however, Altheus threw the staff into the air, muttering some indecipherable words under her breath. Pompex stayed glued to the floor in utter terror, watching transfixed as the staff spun through the air until eventually it disappeared with an almost comical popping noise. Pompex gaped at Altheus.

"Safety," was all she said as she walked confidently into the crowd.

Pompex looked up to the heavens as if searching for divine assistance. He didn't see any of the Rodentian gods but he could have sworn that he saw a small hedgehog laughing uproariously at him.

* * *

"ATTENTION!"

Oscar's voice echoed through the crowded hall and every head turned to see the Felixians march into the hall in perfect unison... well, in nearly perfect unison. Zakk was having too much fun deliberately marching out of time with the others and trying to get them to do the same. Oscar had tried to ignore this but the giggling coming from other guests was starting to embarrass him. He looked through the marching Felixians and when he spotted Scratch he shot him a poisonous look and nodded meaningfully at Zakk who had now progressed to some form of tap dancing. Scratch moaned inwardly and tried to attract Zakk's attention.

"Zakk," he hissed. "ZAKK," he hissed louder.

As if coming round from a trance Zakk turned to look at Scratch and waved merrily.

"What ho, young squire?" he slurred happily.

"Zakk," Scratch pleaded, "you must march properly," he insisted.

"Nonsense!" was the only reply he got to this.

"Oscar is really angry," Scratch said eventually.

"Good," Zakk said, laughing.

"What does he think he looks like?" Zakk added dismissively.

Oscar did indeed present an arresting sight. On his head he had perched a wide-brimmed hat which was completely black save for one long lily hanging from the front of it. Oscar thought nobody noticed that it was frequently swinging back, and the bulb would regularly brush against his nose, leaving behind traces of pollen that Oscar was unsuccessfully trying to remove by screwing his face up and shaking it slightly. His tunic was made up of many different-coloured square patches all stitched together with a golden thread. The tunic went all the way down to his knees where the hem brushed against the top of his long black boots. It was very clear that he hadn't worn these particular boots before and they were starting to hurt. Every few steps he'd utter a pained "meow" under his breath.

"Why are you listening to that buffoon?" Zakk asked merrily. "Once you've got the Collar of Honour, you can get him to polish your boots."

Scratch waved his paws frantically.

"Shhhh," he hissed urgently, "we can't let anybody know."

He looked about frantically, hoping that nobody had heard their exchange. Everything looked clear but he was increasingly worried about the plan he and Zakk had agreed upon. He wanted to be a knight more than anything in the world but he remembered the warning King Hirax had given them. Fortunately, the troop of Felixians reached their assigned seats. The knights were all guided to seats on the front row and their squires were directed to the row of seats directly behind them. Scratch made sure that Zakk was settled in his seat before taking his own. This took a while as Zakk was still a bit unsteady on his feet.

Eventually Zakk was settled and Scratch made his way to his seat. So flustered had Scratch become, being the last squire to take his seat, he didn't look at the seat before lowering himself onto it. He yelped with pain as he sat on a viciously sharp point. He shot out of his seat only to feel heavy paws on his right shoulder pulling him back down. As he returned to the seat the pain moved from his bum to his tail. Instinctively he tried to jump up again but found to his horror that he had been skewered to his chair. Frantically he looked to his right and found himself eye to eye with Mittens. For his part Mittens displayed no emotion on his face but he held steady eye contact with the terrified Scratch. The pain was unbearable.

Scratch tried to reach forward to alert Zakk to his predicament. Mittens was too quick for him though. As soon as he saw Scratch reaching forward he buried his claws deeper into Scratch's tail and whispered calmly and with menace at him, "If you so much as move I will rip it off."

Scratch paused, paralysed by fear. Mittens continued, occasionally twisting his claws to illicit the most pain.

"I know what you have planned," he hissed. "If you think that either you or that drunken old sot you call a knight think you have what it takes to get that Collar you must be more delusional than I thought!" He spat in Scratch's face, "I've told you before, YOU ARE NOTHING. Clearly you need a further lesson and when we are in possession of the Collar…" At this he pointed to the knight sitting in front of him. Scratch had never seen a Felixian that big before. He knew of rumours that said that giant cats lived in the dreaded Jungles of Lac but even if they existed they couldn't be as big as Mittens' mentor. He looked like he could fight a battalion on his own. His ears twitched as Mittens spoke, so he clearly knew what was going on but sat staring forwards. Clearly Mittens had found a mentor as cruel as he was. "you'll think your previous life as bedpan cleaner was a paradise compared with what will happen when Moglox…" as he said Moglox he pointed at the giant black cat in front of him, "makes me King. You will wish you were dead! Back away now and just nursemaid that old drunk and I might let you keep your old life. If not…" on the word "not" he fully extended his claws right into Scratch's tail. "I think I'm understood."

He let Scratch go and turned back to the jubilee celebrations, giving no evidence that anything had happened between them. After a while Scratch painfully flipped his tail onto his lap and used his tunic to soak up the blood. Cold terror gripped him. If Mittens and Moglox were also looking for the Collar then the King was the least of his worries.

\* \* \*

"Honoured guests!" Brabbinger's voice boomed through the throne room. "Please be upstanding for His Majesty King Hirax Mowser, the first of his name, ruler of all Venary and all the species therein."

There was a scraping noise as hundreds of chairs moved as one as their occupants all got to their feet. So transfixed on the entrance of the King were they that nobody noticed a mysterious green-lit smoke seeping through the marble floor.

Hirax felt ridiculous. He was dressed in a scarlet robe with white fur lining which was so long he feared that when he reached his throne the end of the robe would still be in the connecting corridor. Underneath the robe he was wearing the dress uniform of a field mouse in the Rodentian army. He had tried in vain to explain that as he had never served in the army he shouldn't wear a uniform but Brabbinger explained that as King he was head of the armed forces and besides it was a very nice uniform. Hirax thought that the niceness of the uniform was immaterial, he didn't feel that he had earned it. Privately he didn't think it was a nice uniform at all. It was made of a very stiff fabric and had far too much gold braid on it. *Clearly camouflage isn't a key concern for the officers*, he thought darkly to himself. The real embarrassment, though, was the royal sceptre. It had been forged out of solid gold and was therefore so heavy that Hirax had to be trained how to carry it without injury to himself or others. The sceptre was shaped like an oversized sword and Hirax had to grip the handle tightly with his right claw and place the tip of the hilt gently into his left claw. Sadly it was top heavy because the designer had decided that there should be a lump of gold shaped like a block of cheese stuck on the very end of the top half of the sceptre. Hirax had been told that this represented the ancient sigel of his family, but to him it always looked like something you'd find the morning after a boring cocktail party. He once voiced this opinion to Brabbinger and immediately wished he hadn't. The one saving grace was that as the robe was so long he had managed to get away with not wearing the ridiculous court shoes that had been laid out for him. *Better bare-clawed than wear something with that many buckles*, Hirax thought to himself as his claws sunk into the deep carpet leading to his throne. He reflected that at least one part of his body was comfortable.

Hirax walked past the crowds on either side of the carpet, being sure to nod and smile benevolently at the Rodentian citizens who had been rounded up from the village to have first-claw experience of the jubilee. Apparently it was a great honour but most of the younger Rodentians were yawning and looking longingly up at the sunshine as it streamed through the stained-glass window (and the one broken panel). Hirax wanted to tell them that he felt exactly the same. He'd like to go outside and play too. However, he kept walking slowly forward, dragging that heavy and needlessly long robe behind him as he went.

When Hirax reached the foot of the stairs leading up to his throne he was even more relieved that he had left the shoes in his royal quarters. He had walked up and down these steps many times and never once fallen but he had never had this big an audience before. As a young Rodentian Hirax liked to see how many steps he could jump up at once. His record had been five but this required a long run up. Sometimes when he knew he was alone he would smuggle in a tea tray and spend some time sledging down the stairs before someone would come looking for him to perform some duty or another.

He remembered a time when he flew down the stairs with no thought to his physical safety. It had been shortly after the death of his grandfather. His father was proving to be a popular king and Hirax had finally felt free to explore the palace without the fear that his hated grandfather would appear at any moment. It couldn't last. Shortly after this his father went missing and his fun times would come to an end. Hirax blinked back hot tears at the memory and began to slowly mount the stairs. Reaching the top, he turned (awkwardly in that dratted robe) and sat down on the cushioned throne. As he sat so did the guests. The silence in the throne room was almost deafening. He cleared his throat.

"Ten spans ago…" he began.

Lex was bored. He didn't see the point in all this ceremony. Somewhere out there was a trinket which would allow him to reshape the world into something far more pleasing, and yet he was stuck here watching a rodent walk up a flight of stairs! He had tried to gain some entertainment by staring at the Giraxians in a clearly intimidating manner but that weak female seemed not to notice and the male had merely smiled maddeningly back at him. He'd be smiling on the other side of his pompous face when Lex got that Collar!

He was just thinking of how sweet it would be when he would personally throw that smirking jackass into the dingiest work camp he could find. His nice suit wouldn't stay clean for long when Lex was through with him. In an attempt to stay awake he looked through the crowds but found nothing of interest – all weak and weedy pacifists! The Felixians had tried to field an army but in Lex's opinion they should be forever ashamed that they couldn't handle a group of upstart rodents.

Eventually his powerful trunk picked up a smell. It was slight at first so Lex wasn't surprised that no one else could detect it. It was foul though. A smell of blood and decay was assaulting both enormous nostrils. *Where in hell is that coming from?* he thought urgently. He started looking around but it wasn't until he looked down that he finally spotted the green smoke rising through the floor. Others had picked up the smell now, and whispered complaints started to ripple through the crowd. The green smoke was getting higher and thicker. Lex was startled when he began to see faces form in the smoke. He might be office staff but he knew trouble when he saw it! He took a deep breath but before he could trumpet out a warning there was a massive cracking noise and a jagged line appeared in the floor. As the crack widened more and more of the thick green smoke poured out and began to take shape. They looked like Rodentians but were insubstantial.

The King had stopped during his speech and was frantically working at the catch to his robes. Eventually he freed himself but before he could run down the stairs the biggest shape yet floated through the crack in the floor. It became larger and larger as more of it poured into the room. A giant face appeared at the top of the smoke and Lex thought that it was very familiar and, judging by the look on the King's face, he recognised him too.

"Grandfather?" Hirax said, completely amazed.

At this question the figure turned and looked directly at the King.

"I RETURN!" the figure boomed, flinging out his ginormous arms and turning on the spot as if to investigate his surroundings. "ALL HAIL THE KING!" he boomed, his voice echoing.

Chaos gripped the hall as more and more shapes began to take shape from out of the smoke.

"COME, MY CHILDREN," the giant green shape called.

Hirax's guards leapt into position, forming a circle around the King. They drew their long spears and started thrusting at the shapes as they flew by, the spears passing harmlessly through them, but the guards continued, determined to find something physical and real they could take down. Many of the guests were falling over each other in their scramble to get away. Knocked from his seat in the confusion Scratch hit the ground hard, but thanks to his Felixian reflexes he managed to jump back to his feet instantaneously. He surveyed the panic in the hall and with a look of disgust he spotted Oscar running through the door towards the safety of the courtyard.

"KNIGHTS OF FELIX REGALIS," Zakk's voice thundered over the panicked screams, "TAKE POSITION."

As one the previously fleeing knights stood to attention and thanks to their training had their swords in paw and had formed three lines between the exit and the many green shapes.

"STAND FIRM," Zakk ordered. "COVER THE EXITS."

As one the knights moved to create two straight lines on either side of the exit, neatly allowing the fleeing citizens and guests to funnel out quickly. Overhead the green shapes swooped and dived, wailing terribly at the already terrified guests.

"SUPPORT THE GUESTS," Zakk boomed again. "IGNORE THE PHANTOMS, THEY CAN'T TOUCH YOU."

Zakk didn't know if this was true but he was gambling that they were as insubstantial as they looked. Zakk was slightly ashamed to admit that he was enjoying this. With one final glance at the knights he nodded at Scratch and they both charged to the throne to assist the hopelessly outnumbered King's Guard.

* * *

Altheus spread her wings and clicked her two long feathers three times. With a flash of light her staff was once again in her claws. She spun it around and the orb lit up with a dazzling red glow.

"FIRESTORM!" she called, once, twice, three times.

At each command a large red fireball would shoot from the orb and hit one of the green figures square in the chest. The figure would blast apart but with a groan of frustration. Altheus noticed that the smoke was already starting to re-form the figure. She glanced towards the throne and spotted the fattest cat she had ever seen running alongside another knight who looked little older than a kitten. Despite their size and ages they were streaking towards the throne at an impressive speed. She turned her fire on the figures in their way and started to clear a path for them.

\* \* \*

Zakk didn't know where the help was coming from but he was grateful for it. His legs were aching and his lungs burned as he tried to keep up with Scratch. There was no point telling the youngster to slow down. He knew that every second counted but saw darkness creeping into the corners of his vision and feared he was about to black out at any moment.

\* \* \*

"Time to go, I think," Number One muttered, pausing only long enough to grab Yani's arm.

"We can't go," she protested. "We have to help."

"What do you propose?" he sneered. "Harsh words? Or perhaps you could throw your doctorate at them?"

"We have to help," she repeated.

"We don't have time for this. We all remember your last attempt at diplomacy and one war is quite enough! We need the Collar of Honour!"

"NO!" she shouted. "I'm going to help."

With a speed that surprised her he struck out with his two front hooves and hit her with resounding force to both sides of her head. Everything went dark as she slumped to the floor.

"Oh no!" he exclaimed in fake sincerity. "My sister has fainted with the shock. Will someone please help?" He grabbed the collars of two fleeing delegates from Aridier. "Help me, please!" he cried, forcing tears from his eyes. "You must help, my sister has fainted and we must get away."

The crows went to walk around him but stopped suddenly when from under his robes he produced a handheld crossbow.

"I repeat," he said slowly, "you MUST help."

One of the crows went to make a grab for the crossbow but Number One swung it upwards and struck the crow under his chin with such force he cracked his beak.

"I assure you flyboys," Number One said almost conversationally, "I can drop one of you and reload before the other has blinked. Now…" he said, pointing to the still standing crow, "take my sister's back two legs. While you…" he said, motioning with the crossbow for the fallen crow to get up, "take the front. Those fool cats have cleared a path to the exit so it shouldn't be too long.

"Oh," he added as an afterthought, "lift from your knees."

\* \* \*

Hirax couldn't believe what he was seeing. The giant smoke beast looked exactly like his grandfather but it couldn't be him, Faustus died spans ago. He remembered seeing him on his death bed and that broken old rodent couldn't be here now, but it was hard to deny the evidence of his own eyes. He climbed to the top of the throne and yelled at the spectre.

"WHO ARE YOU? WHAT DO YOU WANT?"

To his surprise the figure started laughing, not a deep booming laugh he expected from a creature of that size but a high-pitched, almost nasal whine, the same laugh he remembered from spans ago and which still haunted his nightmares even now. With lightning speed, the ghost pushed through the King's Guard as if they weren't even there and stared face to ghostly face at Hirax.

"Don't you recognise me, boy?" he hissed into the King's face. "Give your grandfather a kiss."

At this he broke off into yet more high-pitched giggling.

"It can't be you," Hirax countered, "you're dead!" The last two words were whispered.

"My last wish," the figure who looked like Faustus intoned with solemnity, "was for me and my army to survive death. The Collar clearly decided that I didn't need to survive it here! For an untold age we have lived between life and the great hereafter, unable to enter either, until a voice from this very palace pulled us through."

As he spoke he pointed to the now solid army of augmented Rodentians who stood emotionless around the room. They had overpowered the Felixian guards and were rounding up the remaining guests.

"What do you want?" Hirax repeated.

"WANT?" Faustus replied. "WANT! I WANT WHAT IS MINE! I WANT MY THRONE AND I WANT MY KINGDOM! BUT THIS TIME I SHALL RULE ALL OF VENARY FOREVER. IN THIS FORM I AM INDESTRUCTIBLE."

"Your Majesty," a voice called from the door. Every head spun in its direction. "Your Majesty," Brabbinger repeated, "I implore you not to do this! He is your grandson, your blood."

"Brabbinger?" Faustus questioned, clearly confused. "What happened? You are old! For how long have I been away?"

"For many spans," Brabbinger answered, limping towards the throne. "Your son Tyrell has passed and now your grandson Hirax rules and rules well."

"THIS PIECE OF EXCREMENT?" Faustus asked in disbelief.

"Your time has passed," Brabbinger said pleadingly. "Return to death. Can't you see the pain you have already caused?"

"You BETRAYED me," Faustus shrieked at Brabbinger. "After all I gave you and you betrayed me."

"I wanted to help you," Brabbinger said clearly, still limping towards the throne. "You were sick, you needed help."

"SICK!" Faustus repeated. "I was your King and will be again." With this he turned his back on the slowly approaching butler. "Once I remove you," Faustus said, reaching out for Hirax.

\* \* \*

"We're not going to make it in time," Scratch panted.

"Keep… going…" Zakk replied breathlessly. "We have to try."

Both of them had heard the conversation between Faustus and Brabbinger, and while they couldn't believe what they were seeing they couldn't deny that something big was happening. Scratch didn't know what they were going to do if they got to the King in time but he had absolute faith in Zakk.

\* \* \*

"ONCE YOU HAVE BEEN REMOVED I'LL RULE AGAIN," Faustus shouted at Hirax. "EVERYONE HERE SHALL WITNESS MY SECOND CORONATION! THEN BECOME EITHER SLAVES OR MEMBERS OF MY GLORIOUS ARMY!"

Brabbinger had a horrible flashback of that day in the north tower, of all those kidnapped Rodentians who had been so abused by Faustus. He couldn't let that happen. A sudden crashing sound came from the west wall, distracting everyone. Lex had managed to shake off the dozen or so members of Faustus' army and had charged the wall with his enormous head down. Luckily on the first charge he managed to smash through. Sunlight poured into the throne room and, sensing their opportunity, the remaining guests fled through this new exit. Rubble fell from the ceiling. A huge lump came crashing into the throne, causing Hirax to slide down the wreckage that had once been the stairway to his throne. Faustus howled in frustration.

"MY CHILDREN," he called, "ROUND UP THE COWARDS WHO FLED, MAKE THEM PAY FOR DEFYING THEIR KING."

As one the Rodentian army marched out of the hole in the wall, slaying those retreating guests who were too slow to get away and giving chase to the others.

\* \* \*

Hirax fell for what seemed like ages. He braced himself for what he was sure would be a very painful landing on the marble floor. He was surprised when he landed on something furry. The sound of a high-pitched grunt made him open his eyes. He was in the arms of that young Felixian squire he had taken a shine to in the meeting that now felt like it took place spans ago.

"Scratch?" he asked, confused.

"Yes, Your Majesty," Scratch panted.

"Apologies, Your Majesty," Zakk added, his voice sounding close to exhaustion, "but we had better get you to safety."

Hirax went to reply but was cut off by Zakk suddenly shouting, "LEFT!"

Hirax felt himself being violently thrown to the left as Scratch dived in between two fallen rocks. The space was narrow and the three escapees were pressed together.

"Now what?" hissed Scratch.

"Well… for… a… start," Zakk puffed, trying to catch his breath, "you can put the King down."

Suddenly startled Scratch dropped Hirax, who thumped to the ground.

"A bit gentler than that though," Zakk added under his breath.

"No matter," Hirax added from the floor, "I am indebted to you both."

"I wouldn't speak too soon, Your Majesty," Zakk replied, "we are not out of danger yet."

"HIRAAAAAXXXXX," Faustus cooed, flying around the throne room, a long green trail pouring out behind him. "COME OUT, COME OUT, WHEREVER YOU ARE!" He broke off to laugh maniacally. "COME ON, BOY," he snapped, suddenly angry, "COME OUT AND FACE ME."

"I have to go out there," Hirax said softly. "This is my kingdom and I must defend it."

Zakk threw a long arm out in front of the King.

"I cannot allow that, Your Majesty," he said firmly. "We don't know what we're up against."

"It's my grandfather," Hirax countered. "You are old enough to have fought against him during the war."

"With respect, Your Majesty, was your grandfather a giant made up of green smoke before?"

Before Hirax could answer the whole ground shook.

"Scratch!" Zakk yelled. "You're closest to the opening, find out what the hell is going on! Just be careful."

Before Scratch could move a long, thin and undeniably solid claw started to poke through the opening.

"Never mind," added Zakk, "I think we know."

"I KNOW YOU'RE IN THERE!" Faustaus boomed in a sing-song voice. "COME OUT AND TALK, I HAVE BRABBINGER."

"That's enough!" Hirax said, and pushing past Zakk and Scratch he stepped outside to face his grandfather.

Faustus was no longer green, which Hirax silently admitted was something of a relief. Less helpful, however, was the fact that the now entirely solid Faustus was easily as tall as the throne room. He held the struggling Brabbinger in one hand and smiled as he spotted his grandson emerging from a pile of rocks, closely followed by two pathetic-looking cat knights.

"Grandfather," Hirax called up, hoping that the giant didn't notice the crack in his voice as he spoke, "I must request that you cease what you are doing and return to wherever you came." There was silence and Hirax really thought that his grandfather was listening to him. "Your reign was glorious," Hirax continued, pushing his luck.

"AND IT WILL BE AGAIN," Faustus roared as he reached down and scooped up Hirax. Triumphantly the giant Faustus held Hirax and Brabbinger aloft in both hands.

"THE TRAITOR AND THE WIMP," he boomed. "SO END ALL WHO FAIL ME!"

Opening his mouth wide he slowly lifted the struggling Brabbinger and Hirax to his open mouth. Zakk and Scratch both drew their swords and prepared to charge but before they could run a loud voice yelled out:

"DESTRUCTOR!"

Every head in the throne room spun to where the voice had come from. Altheus stood on the ruins of a srow of seats. Blood was pouring from a head wound yet she was standing and had pointed her staff directly at Faustus and yelled out the most powerful spell she knew. Exhausted by the effort she dropped to her knees but not before a huge sparkling purple ball shot towards the giant Faustus. Faustus saw the ball coming his way. He dropped Brabbinger who fell awkwardly on a lump of rubble with a sickening crunch, his back clearly broken. Keeping hold of Hirax in his other hand he reached out to catch the incoming ball of energy with his free hand. He had to stretch but he plucked it out of the air and held it victoriously over his head. The ball exploded in his hand. Faustus screamed in agony and went to drop it but as he opened his hand purple sparks shot out, coating him and Hirax in a glowing purple light. The pair of them screamed in agony, their screams becoming so loud they became one. Still the purple energy surged through them until bright purple lights shot out of their mouths and eyes. A sudden rictus of pain shot through Faustus' body and in agony he let go of Hirax.

Instead of falling Hirax hovered in mid-air, as if suspended by the light pouring from him. The force radiating from Faustus and Hirax was so powerful that Scratch and Zakk struggled to stand upright. Dropping to all fours the Felixians tried futilely to use their claws for extra purchase as they dragged themselves across the floor. Scratch tried to make his way to where Brabbinger landed, although he knew it would be futile. Zakk was trying to get to Altheus. He could see that she was leaning on her staff and the colour was draining from her face, as if the staff were draining her as the orb continued to glow a brilliant purple.

Both cats looked up as one and were amazed at the sight that greeted them. It looked like Faustus was shrinking! It happened gradually at first but he was definitely getting smaller. Faustus continued to thrash about wildly as if trying to escape the purple energy that encased him. After a short while he had shrunk down to a more average size. At this point, as if coming out of a trance, Hirax (with a tremendous effort) threw himself towards his grandfather, his arms outstretched. With a scream of pain Hirax gripped Faustus by the throat and started to squeeze. Faustus' eyes began to bulge and he reached out with his own claws and gripped Hirax by his throat. Locked together the outcome would be decided by whomever could hold out the longest. While this was going on Zakk had made it to Altheus.

"RELEASE THEM!" he shouted over the noise. "WE CAN HANDLE HIM NOW."

Altheus nodded at him, exhaustion etched across her features.

"RE... RELEASE!" She stuttered the word out.

Immediately the light in the orb went out and Altheus fell forward, luckily into Zakk's arms.

The purple light surrounding the battling Faustus and Hirax went out in a huge explosion of light, so bright the surviving combatants had to shield their eyes. With a final scream Faustus and Hirax fell together and although the light was hurting his eyes Scratch could see that rather than bumping into each other it looked like Faustus fell into Hirax and disappeared, leaving Hirax to hit the floor alone and unconscious. Suddenly free of the powerful spell Scratch bounded over to where Brabbinger lay unmoving. Zakk led the weak but still conscious Altheus over to where Hirax had landed. Finally reaching Hirax, Altheus waved Zakk's assistance away and they both kneeled on either side of their fallen King. Zakk placed the side of his head on Hirax's chest and looked up in amazement.

"I can detect two distinct heartbeats," he said urgently.

"Impossible," whispered the still exhausted Altheus.

"Definitely two heartbeats," Zakk confirmed. "One beating far faster than the other."

Altheus shooed him away.

"Let me look," she snapped.

Carefully cradling Hirax's neck, Altheus gently pulled his eyes open and gasped in horror. Staring back at her were two glowing purple orbs. Hirax's mouth started to move. He was mumbling something. Altheus moved her ear closer to his moving mouth and promptly dropped him in shock.

"What is he saying?" Zakk asked.

Altheus was momentarily shocked into silence.

"God save the King!" she said eventually.

Their shared silence was suddenly broken by the sound of a large piece of masonry falling from the ceiling and crashing to the ground.

"We need to get out of here," Zakk said eventually. He looked over to Scratch. "How's the butler?" he called over.

He didn't need to wait for an answer, the ashen look on Scratch's tear-stained face was enough. Zakk closed his eyes. He had seen lots of death in his time but a death with no purpose still tore at him.

"Leave him," he called over. "It's not safe in here, we have to go."

Mechanically Scratch stood up and began to walk towards the hole in the wall. Zakk turned to Altheus.

"Can you walk?" he asked.

She nodded and then suddenly an idea came to her.

"We should try the stables. Our mounts are there, it will be the quickest way to get out."

Zakk nodded and the two of them followed Scratch through the hole.

All was quiet in the ruined throne room. The body of Brabbinger lay unmoving where it had fallen. The only sounds were high-pitched giggling from the being that looked like Hirax and the sounds of a small hedgehog trying to slip away unnoticed.

## CHAPTER ELEVEN

# ON THE RUN

WHEN YANI CAME to she was surprised to discover that she was outside and that it was night. She sat up with a start and regretted it as her head began to swim with nausea. She forced herself to focus on one thing, hoping the feeling would pass. As her surroundings eventually came into view she realised that she was sitting by a fire. It crackled away nicely and she was aware of the warmth it gave off. There was a smell in the air she recognised but couldn't quite place. A voice spoke from the other side of the fire.

"Welcome back."

Yani groaned when she recognised the superior tone of Number One.

"You've been out cold for quite some time," he added. "To be honest I was starting to enjoy the peace."

His voice was muffled. He clearly had something in his mouth. Suddenly Yani was ravenous. She hadn't eaten since her first meeting with Number One and she decided there and then that she was having whatever he had and damn the consequences. She looked over at him gnawing on a thin white stick. At first glance she thought he had stripped a long thin branch of all its bark, then with horror she recognised the smell. It was burning meat! Like all Giraxians Yani followed a strictly vegetarian diet.

In her time with the rebellion Yani once had to escape advancing Pacidermian forces by dashing across a recent battlefield. The Pacidermians had rounded up a battalion of Giraxian troops and rather than make them prisoners of war and march them back to the work camps made them dig a deep ditch which they then had to climb into. Once every captured Giraxian was in the trench the laughing Pacidermian troops poured a sweet-smelling liquid all over them and while their captors screamed for mercy each Pacidermian threw in a flaming torch. By the time the rebellion chanced upon the trench they found nothing but charred remains and a terrible smell in the air. It was that smell she could detect now. It wasn't as strong but it's not a smell that is easy to forget.

Yani forced herself to look at the fire. A sharpened stick had been used to skewer lumps of raw meat which had then been placed just over the flames. Next to the fire pit Yani spotted a pile of bones and she wasn't sure but there looked like there were two long black beaks poking almost comically out of the top of the pile. Finally, she looked at Number One. His formally immaculate suit was covered in dust and a worrying amount of damp stains. He was picking his teeth with the end of a long black feather. Yani was immediately and copiously sick.

"You monster!" she said eventually, between bouts of dry heaving.

Number One rolled his eyes.

"I saved you some," he said lightly. "Remarkable thing your average crow," he continued as if giving a lecture. "The only species in Venary with the ability to fly and yet they choose not to."

"Monster," Yani spat again.

Number One continued as if he hadn't noticed her comment.

"You'd think that after a few aeons the wing muscle would start to atrophy. Quite the opposite in fact. By using them as arms your average crow is capable of carrying great weight. Which is lucky for you." Yani looked at him with a mixture of confusion and revulsion on her face. "Oh come on!" Number One said impatiently. "I couldn't have carried you here on my own, luckily these two fellows were only too happy to help. Obviously, I had to show my gratitude by…" at this a cruel smile split his thin beak, "inviting them to dinner."

"How could you?" Yani asked quietly, hoping that what she was seeing must be a lie. Even Number One couldn't be that cruel.

"Hmm," he replied lazily, pretending to give the matter some thought. "I know, I should have paired the meat with a nice ale but we did have to leave the castle rather rapidly. There is a fresh stream running just behind you though, assuming water isn't too plain for you."

"You know what I mean," Yani said hotly. "Our species are vegetabalists, we couldn't murder another being just for food, that's what savages like the Felixians do."

"SAVAGE!" Number One bellowed at her, suddenly VERY angry. "Perhaps it escaped your attention but while you were running with the rebellion and playing at soldiers some of us were in the slave camps. Do you think an entire camp can survive on a bucket of leaves thrown at them by those Pacidermian bastards? It was hell, you ate whatever you could just to stay alive."

Yani stared at him in amazement. He had never discussed what he had done during the early days of the war. Yani had just assumed he worked in an office sending others off to their deaths without a second's thought. It hadn't occurred to her that he might have been in the thick of it.

"We were locked together, you know," he said quietly. "Males and females, even children. Dignity was forgotten, privacy a luxury none of us thought we'd ever see again. Every morning they'd line us up and order us all to strip."

He seemed lost in thought for a moment. Idly he pulled the stick of meat out of the fire pit, blew on the charred lumps a few times and then took a bite. Yani felt more bile rise up from her stomach but fought to keep it down. Number One had never spoken like this before, could he be about to break down? Could she get away if he did?

"If anyone refused to obey," he added, lost in the memory, "the guards would beat them to death. So naked and cold the guards would throw bucket after bucket of cold fetid water at us. We'd then have to re-dress in our stinking rags and get to work. Oh, we had been told that the Flying Drexes were a lie but the Pacidermians were still stronger than us and they meted out revenge tenfold for the attack on their processing plant. YOU…" he pointed the bloody stick with lumps of meat still swinging on it at Yani, "thought it was a war. You thought both sides were meeting up for nice organised battles that you and the rest of the intellectual elite…" he sneered as he spoke and Yani feared that the old Number One was coming back, "you all thought you were stopping squabbling tribes when you developed faux tusks AND gave the recipe to our enemy. You had no idea. It was a living nightmare. Many died in the camps. We used to keep records, trying to convince ourselves that we could remain civilised. We believed that we would be set free and that we could then hold remembrance services for our fallen." He laughed bitterly at this. "Time moved on and the bodies piled up. A deputation was sent to the Pacidermian commandant, a civil request to remove the dead. Disease was already rampant and we feared an epidemic. Do you know what the commandant said?" Yani shook her head, too horrified to speak. "He said, 'deal with it yourself,' so we did. Oh, we were all as disgusted as you are now when the idea was first suggested. I can't remember who came up with it…"

At this point his eyes locked on Yani's.

"And no it wasn't me," he said accusingly, carrying on before Yani could protest. "It was the longest night I can remember. At one point we went outside and walked amongst the dead. Our people were just dropping and those that remained were too weak to do anything. By dawn we had decided. The Pacidermians had turned us into savages and like all savages we knew we had to do whatever it took to survive. Before I took my first bite I promised that I would see the enemy destroyed. After time we were rescued by Giraxian forces but I never forgot what they turned me into so I felt no emotion at all as we locked our former masters in the camp and burned it to the ground."

Even the crackling fire seemed silent as Yani hung on every word Number One spoke.

"They did teach me a very important lesson, however," he added, the old and familiar cruel tone returning to his voice. "If I am to see them obliterated I must do whatever it takes to survive."

"But murder?" Yani asked before she could think.

Number One jumped to his feet.

"I don't need your moralising. You had a cushy job in packaging and fell into your discovery about the Flying Drexes."

"I… I…" Yani stammered but Number One was in full flow.

"I know you! I know your life probably far better than you in fact," he screamed. "You overheard two Pacidermians laughing about their lie and went public. Oh, our new leaders loved you for it, didn't they? Right little poster child for the revolution. But while some of us were fighting and dying you were elevated to the new Science Corps. Tell me, was it a nice view from the top?"

"I served my people," Yani replied.

"You believed your own image, you mean. You did have a chance to end the bloodshed though," he mused. "Faux tusks were meant to be our salvation. Instead you betrayed us, and the war ground on."

Yani fell silent. What was there to say that she hadn't already said?

"But once again you have the chance to redeem yourself." Number One sighed. "Find the Collar of Honour and we can undo every mistake you made."

"But the King…" Yani protested.

"Trust me, he is in no state to do anything, he is most likely dead along with everyone else who didn't have the sense to leave when they had the chance. So what's it going to be?" he asked, picking up the recently cooked meat from where it had landed. "Will you do whatever it takes to survive or die forever a failure and traitor to your people?"

With disgusted resignation Yani reached forward and plucked one of the lumps of crow meat from the stick and, disgusted to find that her mouth was watering, she popped it in whole. Almost immediately she wanted to spit it out but she forced herself to chew and deliberately swallowed. Covering her retch with an unconvincing cough she looked straight at the expressionless face of Number One and said, "Where should we start?"

She hated to admit it but as Number One laid out his plan she agreed that it made a lot of sense. If the story he told of ghosts attacking the King were correct (and she didn't think even his imagination could stretch that far) then the King's threat was now irrelevant. She didn't know what the "ghosts" (and as a scientist she shuddered at using the word) wanted but she was willing to gamble that they had no need of a collar. Number One suggested that as the Collar had remained undiscovered for a long time it must be in an area with a small or less sophisticated (he'd used the term stupid but Yani found this needlessly cruel) populace. She had suggested the Jungles of Lac but he dismissed this, stating that recent intelligence reports suggested that the Pacidermians had sent a long-range force out there recently and he didn't want to run into them unless he had (in his own words) "the Collar or a heavily armed force of my own". This left the wastelands to the north. So, with a sense of her own impending doom they packed up their meagre supplies, put out the fire, and headed towards the unknown.

CHAPTER TWELVE

# PRAISE HIM

GREETA'S LUNGS FELT as though they were on fire. Her paws were sore and starting to blister but she knew that she had to keep on running. She was only little and it would take her far longer than the other survivors to put a safe distance between her and the terrible events currently unfurling at Castle Mowser. As she ran she couldn't help replaying what she had seen. Even from her vantage point above the action Greeta couldn't believe what she had been witness to. She was too young to have been around during the reign of King Faustus but she had heard enough stories from older members of the guild to convince her that his return was disastrous. Had he returned though? Hirax had put up a fight she hadn't thought him capable of and Altheus had hit the creature full force with her magic, so maybe she was running from nothing?

Half convinced by this she began to slow down and take in her surroundings. She had set off with no particular direction in mind, just a desire to get as far from danger as she could. She was in a ginormous and overgrown field. The grass towered above her and jagged roots jutted from the earth, which meant that Greeta had to pick her way through carefully. It was as she jumped off a high root that her paws landed in something wet and warm.

"By the fates…" Greeta cursed.

Throwing her head back in frustration she went to scream into the sky in anger when she saw a sight that made the scream die in her throat. Impaled on the high thistles were numerous Rodentians. Judging by the smartness of the now ruined outfits the bodies were dressed in, Greeta guessed that they must have been the jubilee guests that fled after that cowardly Pacidermian smashed his way through the wall. Each of the Rodentian bodies had been put on the thistles face down and, judging by the twisted expressions on their bloodless faces, they had been alive when they had been put there. She didn't want to look but couldn't tear her eyes away from the graphic scene.

It was while she was transfixed by the sights above her that Greeta stopped paying attention to where she was walking. Suddenly and without warning Greeta felt the ground give way underneath her as a large hole opened up. Greeta fell into the darkness, too surprised to make a sound.

She landed with a thump on a hard dirt covered floor.

"Typical," she groaned after a while.

Greeta had managed to roll up into a spiked ball as she fell, so the landing, although painful, hadn't knocked the wind out of her. As she unrolled herself Greeta took inventory of her situation: she was lost, Faustus had returned in predictably bloody fashion *and* he seemed to command a ghost army, the Collar of Honour was missing and Greeta hadn't heard back from Hestor yet. At this point she wondered if the shrew had been captured. It was unlikely. Shrews are slippery characters at the best of times and they do possess an almost supernatural ability to find their way back to their handler wherever they are and Greeta hadn't heard an irritating squeal in ages.

*Well, that's the situation*, Greeta reflected bitterly and turned her attention to herself. The sharp pains in her back made it clear that she had snapped quite a few quills in the landing. They would grow back painfully over time. *So that's something to look forward to!* she thought bitterly. Luckily she had avoided major injury, although she had no food or water and no idea where to get them from. She would have to move soon but she had run so far and so fast, and this coupled with her recent fall had exhausted her. Greeta's body was alternately crying out for rest and water, and knowing that she couldn't have both Greeta sat up to survey her new surroundings.

It was dark. Like many woodland creatures Greeta had excellent night vision but she'd been outside for cycles and it would take a while for her eyes to adjust. She was sure that she could hear scuffling noises all around her. Painfully rising to her feet, she fumbled her way through the darkness. Waving her short arms in front of her Greeta had barely made two steps forward when her claws found a wall. It was perfectly smooth and even with her sharpened claws Greeta doubted her ability to scale it.

Feeling her way across the wall Greeta took small side steps. After a short while she realised that she was walking in a circle. Clearly she had landed in some sort of circular room. She panicked slightly when she wondered if she had landed in an old well. There would be no way out if she had. Eventually the smooth feeling of the wall changed to a rougher, more wooden feeling. With a feeling of great relief Greeta realised that she had found a door. After much fumbling she discovered what felt like a door handle. She gripped it with both paws and pulled. The door refused to budge. Determined to try every possibility Greeta placed her shoulder up against the door and began to push. The door continued to refuse to budge.

Greeta had had enough! So far today she'd embarrassed herself in front of the King, been forced to apologise to a shrew (who still hadn't made a reappearance), witnessed the return of the tyrant Faustus, and been left behind by those bloody cats and Altheus as they sped from the wreckage without a backwards glance. She'd fallen down a hole, been left in darkness, and was really hungry now. Balling up her tiny fists she started banging on the door.

"Oi," she squeaked at the top of her voice. "Is anybody there?" Silence. "OI!" she shouted louder still. "I've had a very bad day and if I have to kick this door down I assure you that I will seek out every one of you and…"

She faltered slightly here. She knew that she couldn't kick the door down and really wasn't sure what she would do to anyone, if anyone was there to begin with. Greeta took a deep breath and prepared a list of imaginative punishments she would perform on her captors if they failed to open the door. However, before she could speak a slow and simple voice replied from the other side of the door.

"Patience, sister," it intoned. "All barriers to light will be removed and all obstacles overcome."

Greeta waited in stunned silence but clearly the voice had finished.

"Well, what in the name of the old kings does that mean?" she hissed at the door. "Are you going to open this door or not?"

Greeta felt a flash of anger as the voice chuckled gently at this request.

"Patience, sister," it said again.

It sounded more distant this time. Clearly the owner of the voice was walking away from the door. Greeta flew at the door and banged and hollered as loud as she could but there was no further response. Eventually tired and exhausted Greeta curled up and waited for the inevitable.

Greeta must have fallen asleep because she was woken by the sound of a key turning in a lock. The sound of rusted metal scraping as the lock mechanism turned stopped suddenly with a disappointing "clunk".

"Damn it," a voice said from the other side of the door.

There followed much muttering and Greeta had to press her ear up against the door to hear what was going on.

"What do you mean wrong key?" a slightly panicked voice asked. This question was followed by a deep sigh.

"I don't know what to tell you, brother, but THIS key will not open THIS door."

The first voice piped again after some thought, "Are you sure?"

There was a sudden scuffling sound and Greeta jumped back as something thudded into the door.

"I mean," the other voice said calmly, "that this key, much like your head, will not open this door." He continued, "Would you like another demonstration? Or would you go and get me the correct key?"

"Can't you go?" the other voice replied quietly and in

obvious pain. "She'll go spare if we mess this up and you are the Key Master after all."

There followed another thump.

"And you are the Key Keeper, now go and ask Her Holiness for another key."

As an afterthought the Key Master clearly addressed the door.

"Apologies, sister," he shouted to Greeta, "there's been a slight delay."

He paused, clearly expecting a response from her. Greeta decided not to give him the privilege. Instead she removed a file from the inside pocket of her tunic and began to sharpen her claws in preparation. The Key Master continued, obviously feeling that he should fill the awkward gap.

"You can't get the staff these cycles, you see," he explained. "It wasn't like this in the before times." His voice suddenly sounded wistful. "No, in those times you had true acolytes. When I was Key Keeper I knew where everything was."

Greeta continued filing her claws into vicious points.

"It's not that I blame the High Priestess, you understand. It was so much more organised in her mother's reign, obviously. Regular as clockwork every third son was given to the order and it was an honour. But the quality in recent times, well, it speaks for itself it really does."

Greeta rolled her eyes and moved on to the claws on her left paw.

"Here he comes," the Key Master exclaimed dramatically. "Let us hope that he has brought the correct key this time."

There followed a brief exchange which Greeta couldn't hear and the sound of an ancient lock turning once again filled the air. This time the lock caught and the door started to open slowly. Clearly the door hadn't been opened for a long time as Greeta could hear laboured breathing from the other side as they pushed it open. She popped the file back into her tunic pocket and with a final check to see if her claws were sharp enough she braced herself in the pounce position and waited. Her eyes had adjusted to the darkness and she could see that she was in some sort of cell. As she had suspected, the room was circular and the only way in or out seemed to be through the door the Key Master and Keeper were presently struggling to open.

Looking up Greeta could see that in an attempt to create a high ceiling her captors had dug out much of the earth above her but had not supported the ceiling in any way. Frankly she was amazed that no one else had fallen through the ground before she had. Tucked up against what Greeta had dubbed the back wall was a cot. Closer examination showed that the sheets were ancient and filthy. Clearly this room hadn't been used for a long time.

With a final loud scraping sound the door swung open. Greeta took her opportunity and leapt at the newly created space claws first. She was surprised when the figures on the other side of the door deftly moved to one side and she flew past all of them. She had expected to land on a body so wasn't prepared for a ground landing. She skidded across loose shale and by the time she righted herself and spun back to face her enemy they had closed in around her. Clearly the Key Master hadn't been alone and Greeta found herself outnumbered.

Scowling she held up her paws in surrender. Her captors were circling around her and now she could see who they were.

"Are you… are you moles?" she asked eventually, the rasping in her throat reminding her that she hadn't had anything to drink since before the jubilee (which now seemed a lifetime ago).

All of the figures nodded as one. There were six of them all standing around Greeta. Each one wore a red robe which fell down to their feet. Four of them had their hoods up so that their faces were covered. In their claws they held simple but heavy-looking clubs. They were clearly the guards. The other two had removed their hoods and on their robes little keys had been embroidered. One was clearly older than the other, the tufts of hair on the top of his head having turned grey with age. The younger mole was much taller than his fellow and wore a confused look on his face (Greeta suspected this was his permanent expression). Those two were clearly the Key Master and the Key Keeper.

Greeta glared at the Key Master and for good measure glared at the Key Keeper too. The Key Master smiled beatifically back at her while the Key Keeper just grinned vacantly. He went to wave but the Key Master slapped his claw back down as he lifted it. For a while nobody spoke. Greeta refused to look away first so stared hard at the Key Master. As she did so she noticed that the robe he wore was clearly faded, stitching had come away from the embroidered keys and the bottom of the robe was very worn from an untold amount of time dragging on the floor as its owner walked around. Casting her eyes at the Key Keeper she could see that his robes were if anything in even worse condition. It was evident that he wasn't the original owner as it was far too small for him. The hem which was – Greeta supposed – meant to pool on the floor at his claws was instead hanging just above his thighs revealing long, thin, hairy legs. Greeta offered a quick prayer to the God of Thieves that he was wearing something underneath the robe, as she really felt that she had suffered enough.

Eventually the Key Master brought his front two paws together, interlocking his claws.

"Welcome, sister," he intoned quietly. "Welcome to the Church of the One Who Hops No More."

Greeta blinked.

"Hops No More," she repeated, gobsmacked.

As she said this every mole in the room solemnly chanted, "Praise Him, Praise Him."

She spun round on the spot but none of the moles had moved and it looked like this particular ritual had been completed.

"Is there any chance I could have some water?" she asked eventually.

It was a short while later that Greeta found herself walking through a series of underground tunnels. She didn't know where she was being taken. None of the moles had told her that she was a captive but all of her questions had been brushed off and she couldn't help noticing that the guards had arranged it so that the four of them surrounded her as they walked. They weren't crowding her but she was very aware that they were around her. Everything seemed deliberately casual. The guards went out of their way to give Greeta space but it was very noticeable that they were matching her pace. When she stopped they stopped, if she tried to speed up the guards closed in a little closer. They gave the impression of ignoring her utterly but they were clearly poorly trained. Greeta wondered if she could use that to her advantage.

The tunnels seemed to go on forever and were uniformly drab and featureless. Greeta expected to find roots along the walls or through the floors but the entire warren had been smoothed out so that each corridor looked alike. Occasionally they passed other moles. It was noticeable that none of these new moles wore red robes. Theirs were white, or at least at some point in the past they had been white. These robes were clearly as old and worn as the ones worn by the Key Master and Keeper. Many of them were closer in colour to grey and the hems all showed fraying to varying degrees.

When Greeta first spotted these other moles, she had tried to wave a greeting to them but every time she tried they looked right through her as if she wasn't there. It was unsettling but each mole she encountered had a slightly vacant smile and a glassy expression. Greeta felt someone staring at her and upon looking to her left she found that it was the Key Master, a bemused look on his face.

"Why is nobody speaking to me?" she asked him.

"Why would they?" he replied.

"Politeness, mostly," was all Greeta could think of to say.

The Key Master sighed.

"They are novices," he explained eventually. "Until they obtain enlightenment they are not permitted to speak."

"You ban them from speaking?" Greeta said, horrified.

"We consider our spiritual enlightenment far more important than idle chatter," he replied, condescension dripping from each word.

"Have you received enlightenment?" she asked.

"Naturally," he said proudly.

"And in what form does this enlightenment take?"

"Sister," he sighed again, "I truly hope you find out but your fate is not in my hands."

Greeta stopped suddenly, causing her guard escorts to crash into each other. Ordinarily this would have made her laugh but she was worried now.

"What do you mean?" she asked, the unbroken quivers in her back starting to rise.

"You trespassed on holy ground," the Key Master said conversationally. "Normally you would have been left to starve in the cell but the High Priestess wants to speak with you. You are very fortunate," he added.

Greeta looked around trying to find a way out. Even if she could get away she wasn't sure she could find a way out amongst all these identical tunnels. The Key Master spotted the look on her face and chuckled.

"Sister," he said, smiling, "be not afraid, for today you take a step into a larger world."

As if he had timed it the Key Master said "world" just as they reached a large carved entranceway leading into another room lit solely by flickering candlelight. (It wasn't timed, the Key Master for all his pomposity was just a low-level intermediary. If he ever had an original thought it would most likely die of loneliness.)

He nodded towards the opening. Greeta froze.

"Fear not, sister," he said. "In fact you need never fear anything again. One way or another."

He gently placed a paw on Greeta's back (not without stabbing himself quite badly on a quill, much to Greeta's delight it must be noted) and propelled her through the doorway and into the candlelight.

The room was HUGE. Greeta couldn't see where it

ended or how high its ceiling was. It must have taken the moles an untold age to complete. She was somewhat calmed to see that this room at least had several thick wooden pillars supporting the ceiling. *At least I'm safe from cave-ins*, Greeta thought to herself, trying against all odds to be positive.

She walked to the nearest pillar and when she got up close to it she was surprised to see that it was adorned with intricate carvings. The carvings had clearly been done in an earlier age, as water damage had split the wood in several places rendering some of it illegible. The parts that Greeta could see had faded over time but it looked like it told a story. One image in particular was repeated several times. It showed a being with what looked like enormous ears jumping up and down on what could only be an army of badgers. The story appeared to run from the top of the pillar to the bottom. Greeta seemed to be alone so she sunk her claws (grateful to have a chance to use them after sharpening them so well) into the wood and quickly clambered up to the top where she attempted to read the story it told.

As far as she could tell an army of badgers had attacked various mole settlements. The images showed crudely drawn badgers stabbing small moles with unrealistic-sized swords. (Greeta rolled her eyes. She knew badgers were big but they had such great strength that they preferred to not use weapons at all. In Hedgehogian the word for badger was the same as the word for dismemberment.) The next image she could make out showed a collection of moles wearing some very familiar-looking robes. They were all standing in a circle around a small hill, holding paws. The image didn't show any chanting but after what she had seen so far Greeta would have bet everything she owned that they were all chanting, and loudly too. Age and water damage had rendered the next few images unreadable but she managed to pick up the story further down. Clearly the moles had found a champion in the long-eared being, as the majority of readable carvings showed it tearing through badgers and other assorted creatures with apparent ease. Closer and closer to the bottom she climbed and the images became increasingly violent until she saw one which depicted the creature being thrown into what looked like the sea by smaller animals.

"Possibly Rodentians," Greeta thought out loud.

"Indeed," a voice replied from directly behind her.

Greeta had become so engrossed in the story being told by the column that she had forgotten to stay aware of her surroundings. Perhaps Hestor had been right all along, perhaps she wasn't a real thief. Determined not to show that she had been taken by surprise Greeta forced herself not to jump but instead turned around slowly to see who had addressed her. On turning she found that she was face to face with a female mole (the first she'd seen since falling into their stronghold). The mole was tall for her species and was dressed from head to toe in a flowing white gown which, unlike the others she had seen, was so clean it practically glowed. The gown came with a hood but the female wore it down. Her head was uncovered and she stood so close that Greeta could see into her eyes. Greeta wasn't an expert but after seeing the look in the eyes of the ghost Faustus she was sure that she could recognise crazy, and the mole's eyes looked calm, almost unnervingly so. The mole wore a long gold chain around her neck which had been polished to a dazzling shine. Greeta's thieving instincts kicked in and she found herself mentally pricing up how many gold pieces she could get for the chain. It was a shame, Greeta thought to herself, that appended to the collar was a mouldy carrot! She couldn't believe this was the original jewel but even with the vegetable attached she could clear a tasty profit.

"The Rodentian hordes led by Perix the Vile ambushed our lord in a cowardly attack."

Her voice was steady. If she was angered by what she had said she made no show of it. She might have been discussing the weather.

"Are you the High Priestess?" Greeta asked eventually.

A smile broke out across her face and Greeta could have sworn that even though they were underground the sun came out at that moment.

"I have that honour," the High Priestess replied serenely. "I assume our illustrious Key Master has been bemoaning my lamentable rule."

It was all Greeta could do to nod. The High Priestess was simply the most beautiful thing Greeta had ever seen. So captivated was she that she remained rooted to the spot as the High Priestess walked elegantly around the column, allowing her long claws to brush against the carvings as she spoke.

"I see that you are admiring our carvings," she said eventually.

Greeta merely gaped. *Damn it*, she thought to herself, *what is happening to me?*

"I can assure you all of these drawings show the truth. We used to keep an oral history but the males do so like to exaggerate, don't you agree?" she said, fixing Greeta with a playful smile.

Greeta turned a deep scarlet and felt her face grow hot but yet still couldn't turn away.

"So," the High Priestess continued, "a group of females established this…" she swung her arms out wide, the brilliant white gown becoming like a cape behind her, "the Church of the One Who Hops No More."

She paused, clearly expecting a better reaction to this from Greeta. When none was forthcoming a look of anger flashed across her face. It was quickly wiped away but Greeta saw it and something told her that someone was in a lot of trouble. She hoped with all of her heart that it wasn't her. She didn't want to do anything to upset this vision before her. The High Priestess laughed a melodic laugh and raised her paws in exaggerated fashion. Greeta felt her heart leap at this shift in mood.

"Of course, someone told you," she trilled. "Why wouldn't they? Everyone is so happy to be here. Like all families we love to share."

As she spoke she made an expansive circle with her paws, bringing them back to rest in front of her. She turned her head in playful fashion towards Greeta and winked at her.

"What they may not have told you," she continued, Greeta was hanging on every word, "is that we are entering a new age. Soon we will be 'the Church of the One Who Hops Once More'!" Greeta felt a surge of hope. "Yes," the High Priestess continued, clearly delighted to have someone new to tell this story to, "you being a surface dweller must have noticed a change in the air?"

Greeta chuckled nervously.

"You might say that," she said, "what with ghosts of former kings destroying castles and their descendants sending us all off on a quest."

She was babbling now, grateful for the chance to order her thoughts (it had been a trying cycle). The High Priestess listened with a look of confusion and concern growing ever deeper on her face. There was a voice in the back of Greeta's thoughts asking her what she thought she was doing. Her training at the guild hadn't been exhaustive but one thing her instructors had tried to drill into her was that she should never voluntarily share information with a stranger. Hestor always said that "Information is wealth. The more of it you give out the poorer you will become."

Eventually Greeta finished recounting the recent events (leaving out the part where she remained out of sight during the battle in the throne room). The High Priestess was trying very hard to remain calm but even underneath her flowing robes Greeta could see that her right paw was tapping at considerable speed. Eventually she spoke, only the merest trace of panic in her voice.

"We must have that Collar," she said eventually. "It's the final key to the Prophecy."

With this the High Priestess moved as quickly as her robes would allow across the room to a wooden structure Greeta hadn't noticed before. It was shaped like an inverted L and had a medium-sized bell hanging from the end. The High Priestess rang it three times. After a very short wait three younger females appeared. They wore versions of the same robe worn by the High Priestess only slightly shorter (their robes came down to their knees) and they didn't wear any golden chains. Turning to them one at a time the High Priestess issued her instructions. To the first she instructed, "Go to our Saviour's quarters and purify the body," to the second, "Fetch initiate robes for our guest," and to the third and youngest she said, "Bring us a platter of fruit." Without a single word each of them nodded once and headed off in various directions.

"Your Saviour has quarters?" Greeta asked, confused.

The High Priestess turned her radiant smile on her.

"Our story took place a long time ago and is perhaps best told over food."

## The High Priestess's Tale

"This is not good," Maxhel said eventually. He had been silent for a while, his face buried in his paws. "Not good at all," he continued.

As if to further underline his point his voice echoed around the empty barn he and his staff stood in.

"Err."

A high-pitched voice tried to speak but was silenced when Maxhel raised a paw and made a cutting gesture. The silence continued for an uncountable amount of time until eventually Maxhel spoke again.

"What happened to our food supplies?"

When Maxhel and team had locked the barn the previous day it was packed from ceiling to floor with various wheats and grains. The cold period was fast approaching and they had been given the task of finding and looking after grain supplies for the entire mole community. It had been a task that Maxhel had taken very seriously indeed. He was one of five team leaders tasked with ensuring the continued survival of the moles. The other four were in charge of: tending the worm farm so that there would always be a supply of fresh juicy worms; the fur store, ensuring blankets and fur-lined coats would be available throughout the cold time; the hospital wing, making sure that a bountiful supply of healing herbs and plant-based balms were in stock and ready to be used in emergencies; and finally (and secretly the team Maxhel had really wanted to lead) the treasure store – often while digging the moles would unearth various treasures which, while useless to them, they knew they could trade with the other species for more supplies.

It had been a tough season and they had lost many moles to exhaustion and accidents, not to mention those who had been picked off by the various birds of prey who seemed to swoop down from out of nowhere. It had been worth it, though, when all five barns were finally filled and the doors locked and bolted. Now, however, Maxhel was surrounded by emptiness. He felt a hot prickly sensation run down his neck as he realised that he would have to explain why there was no longer any grain. He was just mentally calculating how long he would survive if he ran away when he was distracted by a member of his team (whose name he had never bothered to learn) shouting for attention.

Rationalising that his day couldn't possibly get any worse Maxhel dragged himself towards his anonymous team member. The young mole was very excited, jumping up and down, waving his paws around. As Maxhel approached he spotted the cause of the younger mole's agitation. There was a deep hole in the far corner of the barn. Maxhel started to run towards it, eventually dropping to all fours so that he could cover the distance more quickly. As he approached the hole he spotted a line of grain leading from where the large pile had once stood right up to the newly formed hole. By the time he arrived he knew what had happened and judging by the screams of dismay coming from outside it had happened in all of the barns.

A short while later an emergency meeting was called. All five team leaders had been called to the Council of Elders to give testimony. As they all shuffled in Maxhel realised that he had never actually met the elders. They preferred to pass their orders on through their management team. For them all to be here now the situation must be even worse than Maxhel thought. There were three of them, all male and all unbelievably old. Like all moles Maxhel knew that what with their many predators and poor defensive skills very few of them made it to old age, and judging by the state of the three wizened figures in front of him old age might not be a good thing.

"SAVAGES!" a voice as dry as parchment tried to shout across the long oak table built into the floor of the meeting room.

Elder Radill tried twice to rise to his paws and was somewhat successful on his third attempt. He wobbled alarmingly and it took him a while to catch his breath but a charitable being would say that he was indeed standing.

"Thieves and savages," he opined after catching his breath.

He was very red in the face and Maxhel couldn't tell if it was through age or anger. As far as Maxhel was able to ascertain the other two elders (Elders Jary and Ulter respectively) might well have been dead. Elder Jary sat with his head bowed so far forward it looked like an extension to his chest and Elder Ulter at least sat upright but his one good eye was whizzing about so randomly nobody could tell if he was looking at them or keeping a lookout for predators.

High Manager Calh stood up smoothly and stood next to Elder Radill, subtly placing his arm behind the elder to better support the older mole.

"Elder Radill is justly angry," Calh said softly. "Indeed each of the elders feels much the same."

With an unfortunate sense of timing Elder Ulter farted. It wasn't particularly loud but the acoustics in the large meeting room amplified the squeak so that it was impossible to miss. Maxhel knew the situation was deadly serious but it was for precisely this reason that a laugh burst from his mouth. He tried to cover it with a cough but the glare he received from Calh made it clear that this hadn't been successful. Calh narrowed his eyes at Maxhel but decided it might be best to move on swiftly.

"All five of your barns were tunnelled into last night," he stated calmly. There was no hint of accusation in his voice but Maxhel felt concerned nevertheless. "We are satisfied…" Calh looked at each team leader in turn as he spoke, "that adequate security measures were carried out by you all."

As one, all five of the assembled team leaders let out a sigh of relief. Elder Radill, who had regained a measure of composure, snorted loudly.

"How long do you think we can survive on your relief?" he asked contemptuously.

He was right of course. Without supplies the colony simply wouldn't survive the cold season. It was eminently possible that the moles would become extinct.

Calh assisted the now exhausted elder back into his seat before proceeding to take his own. There were no seats for the team leaders. There was a rigid protocol amongst the moles and even at this dire time it was still strictly enforced.

Once the higher-ups were seated Calh continued to address the team leaders.

"From the evidence gathered we can say that one or more of the bigger species deliberately tunnelled into each barn and stole all of our supplies for the cold season. We don't know who did it and we have no idea where our supplies are now. We have to assume that they are gone."

In the silence that followed everyone in the room reflected on the dreadful impact of this news. Elder Jary then surprised everyone by having something to say.

"Dire times…" he wheezed into his chest. Everyone else in the room had to lean in close to hear what he was saying. "To ensure our survival…" he said between laboured breaths, "we must consider all of our options."

There followed another contemptuous snort from Elder Radill.

"What options, you old fool?" he sneered. "We can't refill the barns in time and we can't track down the thieves. Not that we'd stand a chance getting our supplies back if we could," he added bitterly. "No," he said, his anger turning to sadness, "our only choice is to split up. Each mole goes in his own direction, that way at least some of us might survive."

This suggestion provoked much panicked murmuring. Moles do not survive well on their own. Their limited stature and poor above-ground vision make them easy targets. The murmurings started to rise in volume as each mole realised exactly what was being proposed. Three very loud taps cut through the panic. Everyone turned to see from where the noise had come. Elder Ulter, still seated, had banged his heavy walking stick on the table and clearly had something to say.

"Has anybody considered," he asked, his voice surprisingly deep and clear, "seeking help from a higher power?"

Calh thought for a moment. His dull features screwed up as he tried to process what he had just heard. A horrified look crossed his face as he realised what was being suggested.

"You can't mean…" he said, so horror-struck his voice lost its usual simpering tone, "those cranks at the Church of the Hopping Saviour?"

Elder Ulter merely spread out his paws as if to suggest that they were truly out of options so had nothing to lose.

"But they are cranks," Calh sputtered out.

Maxhel coughed politely and every head turned towards him. It was clear that the team leaders had been quite forgotten.

"What?" Calh snapped testily.

"We were wondering," Maxhel said, trying to keep a nervous tremor out of his voice, "who or what this church thing is."

Calh sighed but the elders were silent so he realised that the explanations were best left to him.

"The Church of the Hopping Saviour," he began, contempt dripping from every syllable. "An organisation of females who believe in the coming of a saviour." At this he rolled his eyes theatrically. "A giant, hopping saviour if you believe such a thing. They say that this saviour will arrive during our greatest struggle and deliver us from our enemies."

As he finished speaking he threw himself into a nearby chair, clearly disgusted by what he had just said and scowling at everyone present.

"Yet…" Elder Ulter exclaimed calmly, as if talking to a pup, "this does qualify as our greatest struggle and it never hurts to ask."

This is why, after much arguing Calh found himself trudging through the undergrowth on his way to the small and scruffy mole hill that constituted the Church of the Hopping Saviour. He had dragged Maxhel along with him, saying, "You wanted to know more about these looneys and if I have to go on this fool's errand I'm not carrying my own bag."

It was scant comfort to Calh that their journey passed largely without incident. The only danger they encountered was a young hawk who attempted to swoop down on them. Fortunately being so young the hawk hadn't learnt how to attack silently so they had plenty of time to get underground before it could carry them off. The relative ease of their journey hadn't improved Calh's mood at all. He hadn't spoken to Maxhel since hurling his bag at him as they left. As he walked he muttered to himself about the many ingratitudes he had received. Every now and then Maxhel would hear phrases like "best spans of my life" and "sucked up to those old fools and THIS is my reward".

By nightfall the two moles arrived at the Church of the Hopping Saviour. Maxhel was distinctly underwhelmed.

"Well, here we are," Calh exclaimed, addressing Maxhel for the first time. "Remember this is a religious order so try not to be surprised by any of the nonsense you see or hear. The elders think they can help us and it's our job to get something out of this."

At this Calh strode towards the small brown door

Maxhel had only just spotted built into the side of the hill. Calh reached up but before he could grasp the knocker (which was coated in rust and hung alarmingly to the left where it had come off the right screw) the door began to open. It was a slow process. Clearly this door hadn't been opened in a while and Calh found himself impatiently tapping his foot and sighing heavily. Eventually something had worked itself free and the door suddenly swung open the full way, revealing a young female dressed all in white. Her blonde hair was a mass of uncombed tangles and her face was steaked with mud. She looked up at her visitors and her face broke into a massive (if slightly vacant) smile.

"Welcome…" she whispered so quietly that the two males had to lean in close in order to hear her, "TO THE CHURCH OF THE HOPPING SAVIOUR!" she suddenly shouted, throwing out her arms in welcome.

Sadly Maxhel had leaned in so close that she slapped him hard around the face. In surprise he fell backwards, landing in a muddy puddle. He looked up in pain and embarrassment and saw Calh shaking his head and blinking. Evidently he had leaned in further and got the effect of the welcome right in one ear. Maxhel picked himself up and resigned himself to the fact that for the rest of the day he would feel damp and uncomfortable. He turned to voice his objections to the young female but the look of distracted amusement on her face made him realise that any complaint would be largely pointless, besides which they were on a mission and needed something from these lunatics.

The young female extended a long, dirty claw in the direction of the corridor in front of them.

"Her Holiness is expecting you."

Calh rolled his eyes and stomped off in the indicated direction. Maxhel had to trot to keep up with him.

"How did they know we were coming?" he asked Calh, unable to keep the anxiety out of his voice.

Calh looked at him piteously.

"Well," he began, "they are either magic orrrrr…" he extended the r in "or" for exaggerated length, which Maxhel found needlessly patronising, "they have agents keeping an eye on all approaching entrances. It's not like they've got much else to do."

Maxhel wanted to ask where the church got its food from but didn't want to be made to feel like an idiot again so mentally stored the question away for another time. After a short while they reached a huge chamber which was completely empty save for a small golden chair. Seated on the chair was an old female in a brilliantly white gown. She observed the two males as they entered the chamber with barely disguised amusement. When he saw her Maxhel gasped with surprise. He had never seen anyone so ancient! Her face looked like old parchment. She was almost completely bald apart from three long strands of perfectly white hair, all of which protruded in different directions. She was so thin that her robes engulfed her and when she rose to greet them Maxhel found himself concerned that she might break in two. Her voice rasped but when Maxhel caught her eyes he realised that this was no frail elderly female. There was a sharpness to her stare that made him feel that she was staring directly into his soul.

Calh strode forward, cleared his throat, and opened his mouth to speak. Before he could get a word out, the elderly mole held up one of her wizened paws to silence him. With shock writ large on his face Calh closed his mouth suddenly.

"I know why you are here," she said suddenly, a surprisingly deep voice coming from her diminutive frame, "and I believe…" she added, a deep smile creasing her face further, "that we can reach an agreement…"

\* \* \*

"Would you like some more fruit?" the High Priestess asked Greeta suddenly.

"Wha…?" was the only thing Greeta was able to say. She had become so engrossed in the story being told that she had almost forgotten where she was.

"More fruit," the High Priestess repeated sweetly. "Would you like some?"

Greeta nodded slowly. The High Priestess picked up her bell again and within a very short time Greeta's plate was heaving with fresh juicy fruits, many of which she didn't recognise. She reached out and picked up a round, pink, spiky fruit. It was difficult to hold but eventually she was able to bring it up to her mouth without stabbing herself. With a certain amount of satisfaction she took a big bite out of the fruit and regretted her decision immediately. The fruit was extremely tart and she shuddered involuntarily. Blinking back the tears that had welled up behind her eyes she turned to the High Priestess, who quickly looked away when their eyes locked. Greeta's heart leapt when she saw that the High Priestess was blushing.

"So, what happened next?" Greeta asked to cover their mutual embarrassment.

Grateful for the distraction the High Priestess led Greeta

to the closest column. She pointed at a drawing which showed two figures (Maxhel and Calh, Greeta guessed) standing in front of what looked like a lot of flames.

"The High Priestess of that time was the smartest and wiliest of us all," the current High Priestess explained. "She knew that membership of our order had been dropping and had been waiting for just such an opportunity. She led the two males into the Sacred Sanctum of the Eternal Fire."

As she spoke she pointed to the far end of the chamber they were in. Greeta squinted, her keen night vision unable to detect anything.

"I can't see any fire," she said eventually.

"It… err… it went out," the High Priestess admitted quietly.

Greeta shrugged with sympathy and the High Priestess carried on.

"The three figures stood around the – at that time – Eternal Fire and made a deal. The High Priestess would use her magic to bring forth a champion for the moles and in return they would send every third-born male pup to the church where they would live and work forever. In their desperation the males agreed and 'The One Who Hops' was summoned."

"Then what happened?" Greeta asked.

She had absently-mindedly brought the spiky fruit back up to her mouth but at the mention of 'The One Who Hops' her paw froze.

"The moles had their champion of course," the High Priestess explained patiently. "And for a while all was glorious."

As she spoke she walked around the column pointing to images that illustrated the story she was telling.

"They reclaimed their supplies from the foxes who had stolen them and more besides. Of course, being males, they abused the power and used their saviour to steal from others. Soon they had land and servants of their own but this wasn't good enough for them. They looked across the fields at the power that the Rodentians were acquiring and decided it should be theirs. So, they sent their saviour to attack the Rodentian stronghold."

The High Priestess paused at the second to last panel on the column she stood at. It was at the bottom and she was required to wipe a thick layer of dust from it. The panel showed a large figure with two enormous ears. Its body was full of arrows and a crude drawing of the figure's mouth showed that it was screaming.

"As you can see," the High Priestess explained bitterly, "it didn't go how they hoped. Perix the First long suspected that this might happen, so laid a trap. He dug out a deep trench around Fort Rodentia and covered it with grass. It was a simple trap which the moles should have noticed but they were so blinded by ambition and corrupted by power that they led their saviour into it. Once in the trench the Rodentians set about him with their arrows until he died. The battle was over before it had begun. Once he knew it was safe, Perix ordered his forces to round up the moles. As soon as he had all of them he stripped them of their seized lands and properties and sent them back to be farmers. He made two further pronouncements: firstly, as penance the moles would be forced to pay restitution to them forever, and secondly, in a rare moment of compassion he ordered that the saviour's body be returned and that the males fulfil their promise to us."

At this the High Priestess folded her arms and walked slowly back to her chair. With an elaborate flourish she dropped into it, unfolding her arms long enough to wave in an expansive gesture before continuing.

"And so this is how you find us," she said sadly. "A church with no saviour staffed by the third-born children of inbred farmers still working off an infinite debt to the Rodentian royal family. But now," she said, her eyes alight, "you are delivered to us on a quest for our latest oppressors. As my ancestor once said, 'Perhaps we can reach an agreement'."

## CHAPTER THIRTEEN

# FALLOUT

"WHERE ARE YOU going?"

Scratch had to yell to be heard over the sounds of chaos around him. During his retreat Lex had not been gentle. In his panic he had charged through the royal gardens and dismembered the ornamental hedges. Rose bushes were strewn across the courtyard, their spikes catching the fleeing Rodentians as they tried to run across them. The sound of Lex's trumpeting could still be heard on the wind. This coupled with the terrified screams of those Rodentians who had been captured by the ghosts unleashed by Faustus made conversation almost impossible.

"Never mind me," Zakk yelled back, "you go with Altheus and get the mounts, I'll meet you outside."

For emphasis he waved towards the now missing courtyard doors and without looking back dived into the living quarters. Scratch watched him go in disbelief until he felt something pulling at his arm.

"Where's he going?" Altheus yelled into his ear. "He must be insane."

Scratch wheeled on her and shot her his best glare. Despite the seriousness of the situation Altheus couldn't prevent herself from laughing at him. His scowl deepened, which didn't help at all.

"Come on, kitty," Altheus said between chuckles, "we'd better get to the mounts."

Altheus then shot off at speed towards the stables and Scratch struggled to keep up with her.

As he entered the castle Zakk knew he had to be quick. That dratted Pacidermian had taken out a main wall and it wouldn't be long before the whole palace came crashing down! He picked his way carefully through the devastated halls, cursing himself for his lack of exercise as he very quickly became breathless with the exertion. He eventually found himself in a familiar corridor. All he had to do was make it to his assigned quarters.

"And make it out again," he muttered to himself.

The corridor shuddered meaningfully, dislodging ancient dust and plasterwork from the ceiling. Zakk coughed until his eyes streamed as the dust entered his nose and throat. He waved his paws around in a fruitless attempt to clear a path through the dust. Manically he started patting his pockets, looking for something to cover his mouth. Ordinarily his pockets would be overflowing with old napkins and silk handkerchiefs but Scratch had insisted he wear a new tunic for the celebrations and he hadn't had the chance to fill these pockets up yet. When he thought of Scratch he suddenly remembered something else the young cat had insisted he wear. Scrabbling at his neck Zakk hoped that the silk scarf he had been browbeaten into wearing hadn't fallen off. As his paws took a grip of the long, silken piece of neckwear he offered a silent thanks to the fates and wrapped it around his face, leaving only a slit to enable him to see where he was going.

During his thrashings Zakk had managed to turn himself around. It took him a few precious minutes to reorient himself. Despite it being considered primitive Zakk dropped to all fours to escape the rapidly rising heat. Clearly the kitchens on the lower levels were on fire, which meant he had even less time than he thought to get his bag back. Inching as quickly as he dared Zakk eventually made it to his quarters. The door was open and hanging dangerously from one hinge. Crawling around the debris Zakk began to crawl into his room. To his surprise he felt a pair of enormous paws grab him by the scruff of his neck and haul him all the way into the room.

Meanwhile, outside Scratch had caught up with Altheus and they were both sprinting towards the stables. The exertions of their running made speech quite impossible but every now and then Scratch would glance over to Altheus. There was something about her that he didn't trust. Some primal instinct deep inside of him was telling him to jump her and bite her head off. He ignored this instinct, partly because it was unworthy of a knight but mostly because she was quite a bit taller than him and he had seen what she could do with that staff. Altheus saw him staring at her and grinned at him. Instantly embarrassed Scratch turned his attention back to the stables.

They both skidded to a halt when they reached their destination. Crasis was already there, frantically trying to climb up the side of his lizard. He only made it a quarter of the way up before sliding back down into an undignified heap on the floor. Despite the urgency of their situation Scratch and Altheus stopped to watch this display. Crasis was so focused on his task that he hadn't noticed their arrival. Sweat was pouring from underneath the thinning feathers on his head, he was breathing heavily, but despite being clearly exhausted he kept trying to clamber up the lizard's back, his claws failing to find a purchase on the scales of his mount.

"Crasis," Altheus enquired politely, trying to mask her amusement, "what are you doing?"

Crasis jumped higher than Altheus thought him capable of. His wings unfolded and started to flap frantically, his eyes bulged in surprise, but once again he crashed unceremoniously to the ground. This time he stayed there, only moving to roll onto his back.

"Su… Su… Supreme Leader," he panted, "I was just getting the mounts ready for us," he explained too quickly.

"You seem to be struggling, Crasis," Altheus added slyly.

Pausing to tuck her staff into her belt, she turned to Scratch.

"Hey, kitty, will your mentor be much longer?" Scratch opened his mouth to answer but Altheus held up her wing to stop him. "Because if he takes much longer those ghosts will be back and I don't think they will be pleased to see us." Scratch tried to speak again but Altheus continued, "Plus we don't know if the King is alive or dead. We do know that Faustus is back and if he is in charge there may be nowhere far enough for us to regroup but hanging around here is not an option."

She was silent for a second, switching her gaze from Scratch to Crasis.

"Well?" she asked, clearly annoyed. "Where is he?"

Zakk winced in discomfort as his stomach scraped across the stone floor. He felt himself being lifted into the air and to his surprise found himself staring into the huge grinning face of Moglox.

"Ah, Moglox my dear fellow..." Zakk spluttered. "Fancy meeting you here. You haven't seen a bag, have you? Deep red in colour, a few patches on the... owww!"

Zakk felt the pain blossom out from his already delicate stomach following the punch Moglox had landed there. Zakk knew that he had pulled his punch somewhat but it still hurt a lot.

"I knew there had to be some way to shut you up," a voice from the shadows exclaimed.

Moglox was still holding Zakk upright so he was unable to turn but he was sure he recognised that voice. He knew that struggling was pointless but he felt ridiculous suspended in mid-air as he was, so he swung both of his hind legs backwards and with claws extended kicked Moglox square in his stomach. It was a good kick. It found its target and Zakk could swear that his claws broke the skin, however Moglox only staggered slightly and held Zakk more tightly.

"Finished?" the voice from the shadows asked with amusement.

"I might need a moment to regroup," Zakk replied, trying to keep the fear from his voice.

"Where's Sniffsunn?" the voice asked.

"Well..." Zakk thought for a minute, "if he has any sense he'll be leaving with the crows."

Mirthless laughter followed this answer and from the

shadows emerged Mittens. He tried to affect a swagger but he couldn't quite carry it off.

"Is that a limp, young Mittens?" Zakk smirked. "What have you done to yourself, boy?"

In response Mittens nodded at Moglox who once again punched Zakk in the stomach.

"Oof, come on, Moglox, vary your attack pattern! I don't know what has happened to basic training but in my day… owww!…" Zakk broke off mid-sentence as Moglox slapped him hard across the face.

"Varied enough?" Mittens asked.

Zakk decided he had best not antagonise these two any further. It had been fun but Moglox was dangerous and he didn't how much longer before the building collapsed or the fires reached this level. The stone floors would continue to hold it off but Zakk knew he couldn't have much longer left.

"Sniffsunn has no sense," Mittens exclaimed. "No doubt he'll come looking for you soon." At this he faced Moglox. "We'll have to arrange a special reunion for him."

* * *

"Supreme Leader," Crasis simpered, "we need to get out of here."

"Not without Zakk," Scratch countered.

"I don't take orders from you, pussy cat," Crasis sneered.

Scratch drew his claws and leapt at Crasis in response to this insult. Crasis hefted himself into the air, his sharp talons glinting in the now setting sunlight facing the approaching Scratch. The connection was never made. As the combatants flew towards each other they both found themselves slowing down rapidly. Soon they both came to a complete stop and were left hanging in mid-air glaring at each. Scratch made frantic swiping gestures, trying against all logic to reach Crasis who, for his part, had started cawing at Scratch in what he thought was a menacing fashion. So, they hung there impotently, hissing and swiping at each other until they felt themselves turn upside down and crash to the floor head first with a resounding clonk.

Scratch recovered first. Hauling himself to his feet he rubbed at the lump which was starting to rise on his head. Crasis had huddled himself into a ball of feathers from which pitiful chirping noises could be heard. Altheus stepped between them, her staff raised and her eyes flashing red.

"Have you quite finished?" she boomed, her voice magically enhanced so that despite being outside it echoed. "I could try knocking some more sense into you," she said, alternately pointing the staff at the furious Scratch and the huddled heap that was Crasis.

"I yield," Scratch said eventually.

Altheus nodded and they both turned to address Crasis who to their surprise was nowhere to be seen.

"Where..." Scratch began but he had no chance to finish this thought as he was drowned out by the bellowing howl of the biggest of the lizards.

Both Scratch and Altheus spun round and in horror saw that the lizards had been released from their pens and that something had clearly spooked them. With mere seconds to spare they both leapt out of the way of the charging reptiles. Scratch, remembering the training he had received from Zakk, turned his dive into a roll and was back on his feet as the last lizard thundered past. He looked around for Altheus and was horrified to see her lying face down in the corner of the barn. She wasn't moving and her staff lay abandoned some distance from her.

Without any thought he dashed towards her. Suddenly he felt a sharp pain in the back of his head and everything went black. Standing above Scratch's unconscious form Crasis smirked and threw the club he had fashioned from the destroyed pens.

"Lights out, Tiddles," he spat.

Without checking if Scratch was still alive he made his way over to Altheus. Crasis didn't rush, he knew that whatever the outcome his life would now be very different. As he passed the staff he reached down and scooped it up. It was warm and throbbed invitingly as he held it between his wings.

"Finally," he whispered, his attention fixed on the orb as it gently flashed between white and red. He pointed it towards Altheus and a bright white light shot from the orb, surrounding her prone form. As he lifted the staff Altheus' body raised itself from the ground.

"Hail, Cragzac," he exclaimed with dark amusement.

He strode from the stable with Altheus encased in the shining white light flowing behind like a balloon. Crasis paused to kick the unmoving form of Scratch and walked slowly towards the last of the giant lizards who had stopped charging as it passed through the ruined gates of Castle Mowser. Sweat stood out on its flanks and it had a deranged look in its eyes. As Crasis approached, the lizard lowered its head and started charging towards him. Crasis didn't break his stride. Instead he raised his free wing and in a clear and calm voice (his usual stammer and weak voice suddenly absent) called, "Stop!"

The lizard immediately ceased its charge and lowered its head in supplication. When the lizard's head touched the ground, it straightened its long neck, creating a smooth passage for Crasis and the floating Altheus to walk up with ease. Settling into the seat on the beast's back he glanced up at Altheus.

"Now we'll see who is in charge when I hold the Collar of Honour."

The lizard then plodded slowly away, leaving Scratch far behind.

\* \* \*

"I do hate to be a pain," Zakk said calmly, "but is there any chance I could have a drink?" He smiled at Moglox. "You must have one too, my dear fellow, it must be thirsty work following your page's orders."

Moglox growled at this insult and Zakk braced as best he could for the punch he expected. When it didn't come he whispered to the giant cat.

"You do realise," he said, feeling confident for the first time since he was dragged into the room, "that it really should be the other way around." Moglox glared at Zakk, his growl getting deeper, but still the punch didn't come. "I'll be happy to explain the page/knight relationship if you'd like... Perhaps over a drink."

"I think you've had enough to drink, you old soak," Mittens said from behind him. "You smell like a broken-down still."

"Ah, young Mittens," Zakk exclaimed in mock surprise, "growing a bit impatient, are you?" Mittens and Moglox exchanged glances. "If it helps," Zakk interjected, "we shouldn't be waiting much longer."

"And why might that be?" Mittens enquired, trying (and failing) to keep the impatience out of his voice. "Is Sniffsunn coming?" he asked with triumph.

"Good lord, no," Zakk chuckled. "It won't be long before the tower collapses and takes us with it… Shame really."

Mittens raised an eyebrow at this.

"A shame?" he asked.

"Yes," Zakk replied wistfully. "I have been saving a rather nice bottle of cat nip whisky for a special occasion. I do so hate waste, don't you?"

"Oh, for the love of fur!" Mittens wailed. "If it shuts you up…"

At this Mittens went behind the large sofa in the middle of the room. After a while he dragged out Zakk's bag and with effort carried it to him. He fiddled with the catch for a while before looking up at the smirking Zakk.

"Fitting that you should have a broken-down bag," Mittens said with bad grace.

"There is a knack to it," Zakk admitted. "I could open it for you… but… well, you know my present condition."

Mittens sighed.

"Put him down," he instructed Moglox. As Moglox slowly lowered the now grinning Zakk to the ground Mittens said to him, "Don't try anything."

"Wouldn't dream of it, young Mittens," Zakk said happily.

As his paws touched down on the floor Zakk noticed that it had become a bit warmer. Obviously the fires were burning out of control below them. He didn't have much longer left to get out. Feigning nonchalance he straightened his tunic and made a show of brushing dust from his shoulders. Mittens clucked with impatience and Moglox cracked his enormous knuckles. Partly through nerves and partly because he knew it would annoy them both, Zakk whistled as he strode towards his bag. He made a show of unfastening the straps with one paw. As the bag opened Zakk turned to Mittens.

"It's all in the claws."

Before the furious Mittens could respond Zakk reached into the bag and with a triumphant meow produced a bottle of dark brown liquid and three glasses.

"Ah, nectar," he exclaimed, grinning.

As he removed the stopper a sweet-smelling aroma filled the air. Zakk was pleased to see that both Mittens and Moglox had begun to drool. He quickly filled the glasses. Picking up one of them he inhaled the scent and sighed happily. Mittens and Moglox were staring intently at the other glasses.

"Well," Zakk said generously, "I do so hate to drink alone…"

* * *

In the ruined stables all was chaos. The pens had been utterly destroyed when Crasis released the lizards and wood lay splintered all over the straw-covered floor. The fox mounts had begun to howl in panic as their pens had remained untouched and they couldn't get out. Off in the distance light streamed from the remains of the throne room.

Inside the body of Hirax started to twitch gently. It

started with his tail. At first it slowly flicked itself from side to side. Gradually the rest of the body started to convulse until it was violently throwing itself across the floor. Eventually it came to a stop in a standing position. The eyes flew open and a look of wonderment spread across his face. Raising both paws in front of his face, turning them over alternately, he began to laugh. Surrounded by the dead and dying a long, high-pitched and mirthless laughter erupted from Hirax. It carried on for a while until he started walking, or rather, until he tried to start walking. The steps were clumsy and the legs seemed to be locked at the knees but he continued to pilot his way around the throne room until the steps became more natural. After a while the figure of Hirax could be seen running through the collapsed masonry. Occasionally he would attempt a jump. Sometimes he landed neatly on both paws, other times he would slam face first onto the hard floor. On these occasions he would get up and touch the grazes and cuts on his face. Each time he would wince with pain and then laugh that high-pitched laugh again.

"AT LAST!" he shouted.

Had anyone been there they would have recognised the voice as that of the King but it was wrong, there was a harder edge to it now.

"Time to reclaim that which is mine," he said, walking slowly towards the throne which, despite crashing down the collapsing staircase, had miraculously avoided any damage.

As he walked the remaining ghosts swarmed around him and like a pack of dogs floated ahead of him as he walked, that is all except one who had held back from his fellows and slipped unnoticed out of the room. Floating through the burning corridors the ghostly figure frantically searched each room he came across. Floating uninjured through flames and walls he found himself outside. Still he couldn't find what he was looking for, until that is he reached the stables. He saw the prone figure of Scratch laid out on the floor and with a final kick of speed floated towards him. To his great relief he discovered that the young Felixian was still breathing. Without a second's thought he flew into Scratch.

He wasn't sure what he expected but as soon as he penetrated Scratch's head the ghost felt as though his entire "body" was being stretched to its breaking point. He no longer had any control of where he was going. He was assailed by memories that were not his own. He saw a big castle which, to his horror, he was cleaning! This changed without warning to him receiving a savage beating. He knew these memories must belong to the Felixian he was inhabiting, and were therefore nothing to do with him, but he felt the emotions his host must have felt. He felt abandoned, and angry. If he had been able to, the ghost would have screamed in anguish. He saw another Felixian, this time far older and much bigger than his host. His emotions changed to hope and respect and the pain he was feeling abated, allowing him to explore Scratch's memories.

"Scratch... SCRATCH!" The strange voice echoed through his head as Scratch stirred. "SCRATCH SNIFFSUNN," the voice bellowed. "Get to your feet, Sir Knight!" it boomed through his skull.

At this Scratch sat up suddenly and pressed his paws against his head. The pain wasn't too bad. He had suffered far worse at the paws of both Oscar and Mittens but he could hear a voice and had no idea from where it was coming.

"Urrgh," he said eventually, shaking his head.

"To your feet," the voice commanded again.

"Bloody crow," Scratch muttered to himself.

"This is no time to feel sorry for yourself..." the voice stated. "TO... YOUR... FEET."

"Must have hit me harder than I thought," Scratch exclaimed. "I'm hearing things now."

"Yes, you are hearing things! ME for one and I'm not accustomed to being ignored."

Frantically Scratch tried to back away from where the voice was coming from but to his horror he discovered that it was coming from inside his own head.

"What... what... are you?" he stammered.

A deep sigh reverberated around Scratch's skull.

"We really don't have time for this."

"What are you doing inside my head?"

"Pay attention, Scratch, we don't have long."

"How do you know my name?" Scratch interrupted, and received another weary sigh to this question.

"I am all that is left of King Tyrell Mowser, Ruler of Venary." The voice, at this point expecting a response, became disappointed when Scratch said nothing. He continued, a trace of irritation becoming apparent in his posh accent. "I died on a quest for the Collar of Honour. I'm sure you haven't heard of it but needless to say it is a very powerful artefact."

At this, Scratch at last felt that he could regain some sort of control of the situation.

"The Collar of Honour has the power to grant wishes," Scratch said smugly. "King Hirax has sent many of us on a quest to find it."

"Hirax..." the voice said sadly. "My dear son, it pains

me to imagine the pain he must be in now. To have that evil infest him."

"What evil?" Scratch asked, but as he asked he remembered the sight of the ghost going into Hirax's body. "Are you telling me the King is possessed? That's impossible."

"I only had time for a quick look through your brains," Tyrell said impatiently, "but I thought even a novice knight would believe the evidence of his own experiences. You are possessed by a king, why not my son?"

"If you're possessing me then that means King Faustus must be possessing King Hirax," Scratch exclaimed with horror. "But if I'm in control of my body then King Hirax must be in control of his, so apart from being talked to death I don't understand the problem."

Choosing to ignore that last comment Tyrell interjected, "My father is far more experienced in the dark arts than I am, hence why while he is taking control of the ruler of this land I'm left trying to fill this vast expanse you call a brain."

"You don't know everything," Scratch said, pouting. "You keep calling me a knight for one! And I'm just a cleaner."

"A cleaner," Tyrell repeated. "But knighthood is all your thoughts are filled with, I just assumed that… No matter, we have to get away and find the Collar before my father does. The consequences will not bear thinking about. Scratch, you may not be a knight but you will have to do. Now get to your feet and let's get out of here."

"We must rescue Zakk first," Scratch said in a tone that brokered no arguments.

"Scratch, you cannot let your affections for your aged mentor get in the way of saving the kingdom, there are more important things to consider."

"NO!" Scratch yelled. "I'm sick of you old people telling me what to do! I'm in charge of my own body and we're going to find Zakk, whether you like it or not."

"I. AM. YOUR. KING!" Tyrell shouted.

Scratch winced at the pain of the aural assault but he was determined.

"NO!" he shouted back. "No, you are not! You're dead and my king is being haunted. I'm going to get Zakk... So there," he added when silence greeted his demand.

Tyrell continued to say nothing as Scratch picked himself up and started running towards the tower but Scratch was sure he heard yet another deep sigh.

* * *

Lounging back in the throne Faustus searched through the memories of his despised grandson and grew ever more furious. He hadn't been surprised with the ease with which he had taken full control over Hirax's body. Even as a child he had always been a weakling but to inform others of the Collar? Faustus couldn't believe it, in fact so angry did it make him that lightning had shot from his eyes and the remains of Hirax's consciousness which Faustus had locked away literally at the back on his mind screamed out in pain. *Clearly*, Faustus thought to himself, *I'll need some allies too*. At this thought he walked across to the lifeless body of Brabbinger. The butler was on his back, his long snout broken and his legs at unnatural angles. Faustus stood over Brabbinger's lifeless form.

"You betrayed me," he said quietly to the corpse. "However, I'm feeling charitable today."

With this he beckoned over the smallest of his ghosts and pointed at Brabbinger. Without a second's thought the ghost flew into Brabbinger's body. For a while there was no movement. Faustus began to wonder if Brabbinger's remaining consciousness was resisting. This had happened before. In the early cycles of his experiments Faustus discovered that the ghosts of the great beyond sometimes struggled to fully inhabit a body if it was still alive. Often the original inhabitant put up a struggle and drove the invading ghost out but this was rare. (Faustus had only really experimented on peasants and he put their surrender down to their natural and preferred state of servility. The truth was that the victims were so terrified of what was happening and had been so weakened by his experiments that they had no energy left to fight and gave up quickly.) Sometimes the ghost and their host developed a symbiotic relationship wherein they worked together. Faustus destroyed these creatures immediately, fearful of them turning on him. Dead bodies were usually easier, it was like filling an empty glass – the original inhabitant had moved out and the new occupant was able to put up residence. On occasions like this where Faustus wanted the original occupant dragged from the afterlife but still to be totally subservient he had limited success. Oftentimes the victim didn't want to return to the land of the living and the strain could be so great as to split the body in two. Faustus wanted Brabbinger back but he was not to be trusted. He would be allowed access to his memories and intellect but in all other respects the body would be under ghost control.

At first Faustus wasn't sure that the possession had taken hold. There was no sign of strain and the ghost hadn't been forcefully expelled but by the same token nothing seemed to be happening until Brabbinger stood up. He did it so suddenly that Faustus instinctively backed away.

"Good evening, Your Majesty," Brabbinger said calmly. "How may I serve you today?"

Faustus' triumphant laugh echoed through every corridor.

* * *

"What was that?" Scratch said, flattening himself against the wall.

"Hmm," Tyrell replied. "That laughter? Well, it means my father is awake. Told you we should have left when we could."

"Not without Zakk," Scratch growled.

They carried on in silence. A number of times Scratch had to abandon his chosen routes owing either to fallen debris or flames. Each time Tyrell would "tut" in annoyance but he had given up trying to dissuade Scratch from his chosen mission.

Eventually Scratch found himself in a familiar corridor. He straightened his shoulders and mentally prepared himself for any hidden enemies (Knight Code #1 Be Prepared Always) and stepped towards the quarters he shared with Zakk. He heard a noise and immediately drew his sword but as he inched ever closer he realised that it was Zakk's voice he could hear.

"… And we camped for a fortnight next to the long stream…"

Scratch groaned inwardly, prompting a chuckle from

Tyrell. After all he had gone through to get here and Zakk was singing!

"The maiden came down and offered surprise…" Zakk continued caterwauling, slurring each word. "She lifted her bloomers and gave us the eye."

Zakk bellowed this part. Scratch recognised the song as it was a particular favourite of Zakk's.

"Your mentor has an interesting baritone," Tyrell mused. "Somewhat spoiled by the slurring and mumbling though. Were you so determined to rescue him purely to preserve such a unique talent?"

Scratch wanted to explain that Zakk was an old and venerable knight who followed a strict code of honour, part of which was that you never left a fellow behind. This was somewhat undermined, however, when Zakk got to the second verse which involved the "fair maiden" performing acts Scratch had never heard of and was too embarrassed to ask about.

"Imaginative girl, this fair maiden," Tyrell said after an awkward pause. "However, I would suggest that several of her actions are a biological impossibility. Even for the most pliant of Felixians… Although I'm no expert," he added after failing to illicit a response from Scratch.

Upon entering the room Scratch couldn't help but smile at the scene that greeted him. Zakk sat in the middle of the room cradling an empty bottle. To either side of him Scratch was bemused to see the unconscious forms of Mittens and Moglox. Mittens had clearly vomited something sticky up all over himself. His fur looked tacky and stuck out at strange angles. Moglox on the other hand was clean but no less unconscious. He was laid out on his back, an empty glass held in one of his massive paws, a dopey smile across his sleeping face. Zakk grinned widely when he saw Scratch.

"Ah, dear boy," he exclaimed, pausing only to unsteadily rise to his feet.

This action seemed to disorient him somewhat. He shook his head, which was clearly a mistake judging by the pained expression that crossed his face.

"What kept you?" he asked eventually. "I had to waste a whole bottle of the good stuff on these savages," he said, crestfallen. "I mean, look at them," he added. "Took me ages to strip them of their weapons." With this he passed two ornate daggers to his young charge. "There you go," he said happily. "Better you have them than Mittens."

As an afterthought he snatched the dark crimson hat from Mittens' head and tried it on. Despite the danger Scratch couldn't help sniggering. The hat was clearly two sizes too small and perched on Zakk's head in a ridiculous fashion. Zakk grinned wonkily at Scratch.

"Not really my thing, eh?"

He removed the hat and with a dexterity he had no business possessing deftly threw the hat onto Scratch's head. It was slightly too large for the kitten and as he went to remove it Zakk shook his head at him.

"We need to head south," Zakk explained. "That hat will keep the sun off your head and might well save your life."

Scratch pushed the hat back on his head to stop it falling over his eyes and turned back to Mittens and Moglox. He couldn't stop looking at them. Comical as the sight was it did present a problem.

"How," he asked, exasperated, "are we supposed to get

these two out now?" *Not to mention you two*, he thought to himself.

Tyrell was being oddly quiet at this point.

"Them?" Zakk asked absently. "There's always the window."

At this he pointed towards the hole in the wall where Scratch recalled a stained-glass window had once been. He was sure it showed some sort of battle scene but then he thought to himself every one of the windows in this palace showed a battle of some sort. Dashing over to the window he saw that a large bush was just beneath them.

"How do we know it's safe?" he asked Zakk, stepping away from the window just in time to see Zakk hauling the unconscious form of Moglox up onto the sill and with effort push him out.

It must have taken a great deal of effort to drag Moglox across the floor, as Zakk was breathless and sweating profusely.

"One way to find out," Zakk giggled eventually.

"I can't believe..." Scratch said, stunned.

"Oh, look at the size of him," Zakk said, clearly talking about Moglox. "It would take more than a little tumble to injure him." Zakk then pointed at Mittens. "Your turn," he said, grinning.

Scratch eagerly made his way over to his old enemy. It took him a while to find a section of Mittens to grab that wasn't covered in vomit. Eventually he took hold of Mittens' scruff and soon they were at the window.

"Aim for Moglox," Zakk advised. "He'll break Mittens' fall."

With no small amount of pleasure Scratch roughly launched Mittens through the window.

"Now what?"

He turned to see Zakk standing at the doorway to the room, which was now framed in flames.

"No way out this way," Zakk exclaimed. "I guess we're taking the direct route."

With this he hoisted his bag onto his back and without pausing followed the paths of Moglox and Mittens.

"He's drunk!" Tyrell protested suddenly from inside Scratch's mind. "No, worse than that. He's insane. You can't seriously be thinking of…"

His complaints were cut short as Scratch took a deep breath and dropped into nothingness.

## CHAPTER FOURTEEN

# THE PESCAR SOLUTION

L EX LOOKED AROUND and took in his location. He had no idea where he was or how far he had run. He was exhausted though, more exhausted than he had ever been. A stream was running quickly next to him. With relief he stuck his trunk deep into the icy cold water and inhaled gallons of water. When he had slaked his thirst, he lowered his massive frame into a seated position and began to take stock of his present situation. Ordinarily a few sips of tree bark gin would help him to arrange his thoughts more clearly but he had left Castle Mowser with nothing but his dress uniform. His mouth watered at the thought of that sharp green gin delicately sliding down his throat, spreading warmth throughout his entire body. In an attempt to distract himself Lex put his trunk back into the icy stream and inhaled yet more water. It was refreshing but not in the same way.

Lex knew that he had done the right thing by retreating. The information he now carried was of vital importance to the Pacidermian High Command. They would need to know about the events of Hirax's jubilee. In fact, he reasoned to himself, they would most likely be so grateful for his covert actions that they would overlook the tiny matter of his going AWOL. He might even get a medal out of this. Lex felt his breathing calm as he fondly imagined the High Commander pinning the Pacidermian Medal of Valour to his chest. Of course, with that honour they couldn't very well send him back to that cramped office. They'd have to make him an officer (at last). Lex could see it now. The officers' bar had long been an unobtainable dream but they couldn't turn him away now, not with his inevitable commission. Lex allowed himself to imagine what it would be like when he walked through those heavy oak doors, undoubtedly greeted by the applause of his fellow officers. He'd be magnanimous of course, holding up his pads to fend off their grateful adulation.

"No, no," he'd say, "just doing my duty."

He could see the serving staff all bustling to be the one given the honour to wait on him. Lex wondered if he could get a Giraxian to serve him, in particular that slimy one from the jubilee. Yes, Lex would enjoy breaking that one! To bring him down a peg or two, teach him how to behave in the presence of a member of a clearly superior race. However, Lex realised, for him to finally get what he deserved he would have to make it back to his people.

He proceeded to empty his pockets to see what rations he had to survive on. This did not take long. After checking each pocket twice he found one small pack of mints, the book of regulations for all serving Pacidermians (any Pacidermian found without it would be executed without trial), a few coins (Lex cursed himself for leaving his purse in his quarters back at Castle Mowser but how was he to know that he would be forced to lead a valiant retreat? Couldn't rely on those furry bastards and he had spotted that the Giraxian cowards had already made their escape, which was just typical.), and the usual pocket fluff. Not much to survive on, he realised glumly. It was just so unfair. He had been promised a banquet so had been starving himself in preparation. After what seemed like a lifetime surviving on war rations Lex had been looking forward to a proper banquet and damn it he had fully intended to enjoy it. A long, low groan from his stomach underlined his annoyance nicely.

The next thing he needed to do was to work out where he was and how far from home he was. He looked up to see if he could work out the location of the sun. Again he cursed the short-sighted nature of High Command. If he had been given the commission he deserved from the start then naturally he would have studied his compass. As it was, as office clerk the best he could tell was that the sun was in the sky and that it was still daytime.

Lex racked his memory to see if he could recall any of the training he had received during his mandatory posting to the Pacidermian Youth Corps. Even back then the powers that be, their minds undoubtedly dulled from continuous marching, completely missed his genius. Vainly he explained to them that marching and drill exercises were a waste of his talents and that if they would just let him take charge of his battalion then they would see his natural ability. It must have been pure jealousy on their part that he spent his national service scrubbing floors and cleaning latrines, skills that wouldn't help him here.

"Well," he muttered to himself, "sitting here isn't getting me anywhere."

And with that he got up and looked around. He was surrounded by flat green space which spread as far as the eye could see. The horizon was flat and so with no landmarks to direct him Lex chose to follow the flow of the nearby river. Whistling an old Pacidermian marching song he had heard before, he strode briskly downstream towards the unknown.

It was growing dark by the time Lex reached anything approaching civilisation. During his long march he had become increasingly concerned that there was no sign of life anywhere. Lex had never really noticed birdsong before but the lack of it now was eerie. The only sound he could hear was the babbling of the river as it ran next him. Lex noticed that the flow of the river had quickened quite considerably and he was sure that it had taken on a slight green glow.

Before he could investigate this further he arrived at what at one time must have been a nice little village. Wooden buildings stood on either side of a dirt track road but they had clearly fallen into disrepair. Rotten slats of wood had been haphazardly nailed across doors and windows.

Feigning a nonchalance he certainly didn't feel, Lex walked along the dirt track road fighting the uncomfortable sensation that he was being watched. He made his way to a wooden jetty which had clearly rotted over time. Tied to this jetty were several small boats, which to Lex's surprise had not fallen into the same state of disrepair as everything else in this village. They looked seaworthy, and gently floating along a river appealed to the now exhausted and dirty Pacidermian. Gingerly Lex placed one foot on the jetty which gave an alarming creak in reply. Obviously it wouldn't support his weight. Walking towards the edge of the river to assess its depth Lex realised that if he waded out he could make it to the closest boat without any risk. Looking around one last time Lex began to strip out of his dress uniform. Now down to his greying britches he made sure to fold his clothes neatly and carrying them above his head made to walk into the river.

Suddenly and frighteningly several figures all screaming "NOOOOOOO" in twisted high-pitched voices leapt out and pinned Lex to the floor. It happened so quickly that Lex didn't have the chance to react and was quickly swamped by an uncountable number of writhing bodies. Managing only to give a strangled trumpeting of fear Lex was knocked unconscious.

"Owww."

It was quite some time later that a stinging slap brought Lex back into the world of the living. He went to rub his cheek but found that his hands were bound behind his back and that his legs had been tied together. He strained against his bonds, attempting to use his mighty strength to free himself, but it was no good, the ropes were thick and the knots felt like they had been tied by a professional. He had been tied to a wooden pillar and could feel straw underneath him. Clearly he was in some sort of barn. He wondered briefly about how his attackers had been able move him but then he remembered the sheer number that had leapt out at him and wondered no more.

"It'ssss no usssse you ssstruggling, intruder," a voice said from the darkness. "We knowssss how to tie knotsssss round thessssse parts, oh yessss we do."

In response to this statement other voices called out, "Yessss, Yesssssss," each one extending the final sibilant of their answer.

"Who are you?" Lex called into the darkness. "In the name of the glorious Pacidermian empire I command that you show yourselves and that you untie me."

"Sssshow oursssselves?" the first voice (whom Lex had designated the leader) hissed.

The other voices repeated, "Glorioussss empire," over and over again.

Lex was suddenly surprised to see a black shape jump down from the rafters.

"Ssssshow oursssselves?" the shape repeated.

Lex could see the figure more clearly now. He was covered from head to foot in a grubby cloak which he had wrapped around himself. The hood of the cloak had been pulled right down, obscuring his face. The figure was short. If Lex had to guess he would say that he would only come up to his knees but they were clearly quick and nimble. Lex wondered how long they would last in a fight with a Felixian.

As the figure continued to move towards him Lex noticed that he didn't so much walk as float. It wasn't a fluid movement. The figure bobbed up and down as if clinging to driftwood floating on an unsteady sea, his feet only occasionally brushing the floor as he moved in any direction.

Lex stared transfixed as the figure reached up and took hold of the hem of his hood. As he did so Lex noticed that the sleeves fell away. He wasn't sure what he expected the stranger's hands to look like but he wasn't expecting the sight that greeted him. They were webbed. This in itself wasn't unusual. Venary had an abundance of different life forms and while Lex didn't hold with most of them he had seen fur, feathers and scales aplenty. A webbed hand wasn't, in the scheme of things, remarkable. What did grab his attention was that they glowed. A dull throbbing green light pulsated on each webbed hand. They were also hideously scabbed and strips of skin hung from them like ragged bandages. Lex wondered if the green glow was some sort of infection and then immediately wondered if he could catch it. Instinctively he backed away from the advancing figure.

"What are you?" he whispered.

The figure quickly pulled the hood down and every voice in the barn yelled simultaneously, "PESSSSCAR!"

Lex was greeted with a nightmarish vision. The Pescarian's face was both familiar and like nothing he had ever seen before. It was largely fish-like except for the shock of wiry brown hair sticking out of its' head at random angles. Rotten scales ran down each side of the hideous head which rose from the neck into a peak. The eyes were bloodshot and spaced unevenly on either side. A strong odour of rotten fish came off him in waves and Lex had to fight not to gag.

The Pescarian formed the twisted mess of his mouth into something approaching a smile, revealing two large canine incisors. A thought occurred to Lex despite his fear and revulsion.

"You can't be, you're just a legend," the barn echoed with the sound of high-pitched hissing and Lex realised they were laughing. *Damn them*, he thought, *I won't be laughed at.*

Summoning all of his strength he strained with all of his might against the ropes that held him. For a time, nothing happened. Lex groaned and sweat was soon running down his forehead and into his eyes. Still he continued to strain against his bonds, the pain in his shoulders becoming almost unbearable. The Pescarians all laughed louder than before until the pillar Lex was tied to let out a huge creak.

"NNNRRRRGGGGH," Lex cried out as the pillar began to splinter.

The Pescarians had stopped laughing and were falling over each other in their attempts to get out of the barn before it collapsed around them.

"Sssstop thissss," the lead Pescarian cried, reaching out his arms in an attempt to stop Lex.

"CRACK!"

The pillar finally snapped, freeing Lex but bringing the roof down on him and the Pescarian.

Lex didn't know why he did it, but as the roof fell he threw himself on top of the lead Pescarian, using his mighty bulk to shield him from the falling debris. The dust was still settling as the remaining Pescarians hovered near the remains of the barn. One hovered higher than the rest and started singing in a high-pitched voice. The song had no words but the pitch went up and down several times in quick succession. Presently another Pescarian joined in and soon each one was hovering over the wreck of the barn, their voices joining together to create one very loud song. Many of them were crying and others had joined hands to create a ring in the space above the area where the barn had once stood.

The song seemed to be reaching its climax. Every Pescarian now had their hands raised over their head when suddenly "CRASH". From the wreckage a large grey head appeared. This was quickly followed by the rest of Lex as he struggled to free himself from the wreckage.

The Pescarians had been surprised by the sudden loud noise and had scattered throughout the town. The bravest of their number tentatively made their way to the clearly very angry Pacidermian. They quickened their pace when they noticed the lead Pescarian struggling to his feet next to him. The leader held up his hands.

"Be ssssstill," he said weakly, "and bow in the pressssence of my ssssssaviour."

He then passed out, falling gracefully to the floor where he was gently picked up and carried to a nearby shack. The remaining Pescarians dropped to the floor and fell to their knees in front of Lex who thought to himself, *Ssssssaviour, how interessssting.* Stifling a chuckle he walked amongst his new followers.

In a very short order Lex had the Pescarians turn their dilapidated village into a large training ground. He had them dig out two long deep trenches running parallel to each other. Being as close to water as they were the trenches quickly began to run with streams of mud so deep that even two floating Pescarians had been swept away. To solve this, he had them strip the wooden boards from the windows in the town and use them as walkways through the trenches. After he had discovered the Pescarian nursery he set the children to work sharpening stick after stick until multiple large piles of spears lay dotted around the village in what Lex believed were strategic locations.

The Pescarian leader was still unconscious in what passed for a hospital. Lex hadn't bothered to check on him. The ladyfolk were tending to his wounds and, besides, he was far too busy with his work. If he could return to his people with his own army then forget the Medal of Honour, they'd probably make him the new Supreme Military Leader. Perhaps he wouldn't return home. He'd lead his forces into battle against Faustus and single-handedly bring peace to

Venary. With this power he'd be as a god! With an army of this size he could easily track down the Collar of Honour and with it he would bring the Giraxian filth to their knees! He'd make them slaves again and this time they would know that this was their rightful station and there'd be no pesky rebellions ever again.

"Ssssaviour."

An exhausted voice brought Lex out of his fantasy.

"What?" he snapped unpleasantly at the small Pescarian who had floated up to his left side.

"Your people are exhaussssted," he wheezed. "We crave resssst."

"Nonsense," Lex boomed, affecting a jovial tone. "They just need to focus on their new future… No more will you hide! Soon you will rise up."

He turned to look at the Pescarian. He was slightly larger than the others and for this reason Lex had cut lieutenant strips into his ragged shirt.

"You are an officer, remember," he added, a harder edge entering his voice. "You know what is coming."

"Ghosssstssss," the lieutenant whispered in horror.

Lex placed his arm around the young officer's shoulders in what he thought was a fatherly gesture but was in fact extremely painful for the smaller Pescarian, and turned him towards the training grounds. Two battalions of Pescarians were advancing on each other with spears in one hand and shields in the other. Lex shook his head at the scene. No matter how many times he drilled them they just weren't prepared to hurt each other. They'd get close but would drop their weapons every time.

"Do they look ready to you?" he asked his lieutenant.

He felt the young officer's shoulders slump and wrongly assumed that was out of shame. It was just that the Pescarian could no longer stand the weight. Despite his discomfort he tried to reason with Lex.

"But, Sssssaviour, no Pessssscarian has ever hurt another," he pleaded.

Lex thumped him on the shoulder in a playful manner that shot the startled lieutenant several feet forwards. Slowly he floated back, trying to avoid those gigantic arms.

"Do you think the enemy will be so thoughtful?" Lex enquired with a mocking tone. Slowly the Pescarian shook his head. "Exactly!" Lex boomed happily. "Now set them up and we'll try this again."

With this he turned sharply and marched towards the newly created officers' mess to see what the females had prepared for his dinner.

"So help them if it's cooked seaweed again," he muttered darkly to himself.

It was well into the night when Lex gave three sharp blows on his whistle and the exhausted Pescarians returned their weapons to the rack and floated slowly towards their barracks.

"LIEUTENANT!" Lex bellowed across the field and the young officer floated slowly towards him.

"Yessss, Ssssaviour," he replied.

"What is my number one command?" Lex demanded of him.

The lieutenant wracked his brain frantically. Lex had so many commands! Was it to always keep his boots clean? Show no mercy? Wait until you see the whites of their eyes?

He could see that Lex was growing impatient so in desperation replied, "Sssssecurity?" Lex beamed at the lieutenant.

"Exactly, my young protégé," he cooed. "That is why you will guard our perimeter tonight."

"Me?" the Pescarian replied, exhaustion clearly etched across his face.

"No need to thank me," Lex went on. "I can think of no one better to entrust our safety to." And without waiting for a reply he turned the Pescarian towards the village entrance and pushed him that way. "Don't forget to ring the bell at the first sign of trouble," he said as he turned towards the largest barn that he had designated his private quarters. Dejectedly the young lieutenant floated towards his station.

When the ghosts arrived, they arrived in great numbers. They floated past the sleeping lieutenant and had massed themselves in the town square before anyone noticed them. It was a Pescarian child who spotted them first. She hadn't been able to sleep and being unable to rouse her sleeping parents had decided to look out of the window. At first she had thought that the green lights were pretty. They bobbed and weaved, leaving green trails behind them. She thought they looked like shooting stars and she watched them absolutely entranced until one of them turned to look at her, its face twisted and distorted in a rictus of agony and she screamed. A long, piercing scream that made all of the other ghosts turn to face her, which made her scream even louder. Her terror wiping out any instinct to run and hide, she stood at her window as if rooted to the spot and screamed and screamed and screamed. Fortunately her screams woke the rest of the village and from every doorway bleary-eyed Pescarians rushed out and froze in horror at what they saw.

Suddenly Lex's voice boomed across the square.

"BATTALION!" he yelled. "ADVANCE!"

Lex proudly watched as the Pescarians floated towards their spears. His pride quickly turned to dismay as his exhausted troops tripped over each other, dropped their spears and in some cases remained still, their eyes following the ghosts as they whipped around and around in ever faster spirals until descending as one force on the panicking Pescarians. In the confusion the Pescarians stabbed wildly with their spears, which passed harmlessly through the advancing ghosts and into their fellows.

Lex charged into the fray frantically bellowing commands but this just added to the confusion. Eventually the remaining Pescarians tried to retreat, floating as fast as they could towards the water. They never made it. The ghosts scooped them up and as one threw them with a force so strong that the terrified Pescarians didn't have time to float to safety into the floor, until only Lex was left. He dropped to his knees in the gory remains of what was once his private army.

"Now what?" he asked the ghosts, the usual brashness of his voice replaced with quiet acceptance. "Do you plan to kill me too?"

Silently the ghosts descended on him and with a mighty effort they lifted him up. Lex thought he should at least struggle but he was being held so tightly he couldn't budge, so he resigned himself to his fate, which to his surprise didn't come. Instead the ghosts carried him through the now silent village and into the darkness.

## CHAPTER FIFTEEN

# WHAT PRICE LOYALTY?

CRASIS WAS WORRIED. This was not a new sensation for him. Even as a hatchling he was worried about everything. His mother often remarked that he "carries the worries of the world on his wings". If he were capable of introspection Crasis might have realised that it was at that point that he began to really hate his parents and siblings. Crasis never considered his actions or his motivations. Actually it would be fairer to say that he only considered how his actions would affect him. Even at school he only concentrated in lessons that he felt would serve him later in life. He excelled in historical studies and writing but put no effort into any of the physical subjects. He learnt to fly although no crow would ever lower themselves to such an act because – as he said at the time – "You never know when you might need a quick exit," but refused point blank to take part in Egg-Toss, a barbaric sport wherein a petrified stone egg was thrown from crow to crow in an attempt to get it into the opposing side's nest and throw it down. The egg was heavy and had to be thrown over-wing. If it failed to clear at least two members of the opposing side before being picked up by a teammate then a penalty would be enforced. The guilty player would be buried under a pile of spare eggs and would be out of the game until they made their way out.

On one memorable occasion the young Crasis refused to make his way out of the pile, saying that he preferred it in there. The sports masters had then proceeded to pile more and more eggs on top, slowly suffocating him. Luckily a kind-hearted crow from the opposing side dug him out from underneath the pile shortly before Crasis ran out of air. The masters were furious and as punishment made both young crows scrub the locker rooms using only their wing feathers as mops. Crasis didn't show any gratitude to his saviour, claiming that he would have sorted himself out eventually and, besides, nobody asked him to interfere. The popularity of this pastime never failed to infuriate him. He could often be heard ranting about how "thick-skulled egg catchers" were "overpraised for a group of muscle-bound, half-witted bullies who couldn't be trusted to find their way out of their own nests in the morning never mind contribute anything meaningful to society". An assistant had once tried to explain that, "Sports stars entertain the people and a happy people are less likely to revolt." This assistant wasn't seen for four seasons until a body, plucked of all of its feathers, was found in a locked trunk buried way out in the desert surrounding Aridier.

Cragzac had succeeded to the level of Supreme following the suspicious death of his father, who had been out for his usual early morning ride when a sudden loud noise caused his mount to rear suddenly, throwing the previous Supreme to the ground. So spooked by the noise had the lizard been that he trampled his fallen rider in an attempt to get away. Guards had rushed to the scene but by the time they had subdued the lizard (subdued being an old crow army expression meaning stabbing the enemy through the heart and hacking away at it with swords until the screaming stopped) the Supreme was dead.

Cragzac made a big show of being distraught at the death of his father and said that he would reluctantly take over as Supreme, ruling over Aridier in the name of King Tyrell Mowser. Privately, however, he had been heard to joke that, "It would have been more appropriate to bury the remains of my father in a matchbox rather than the expensive coffin they had made the populace pay for."

Crasis had been dismayed to discover that his new boss was a huge fan of the Wingtown Warriors, a team famed for their violent style of play which was explained in no better fashion than by their own team nickname, "The Wing Breakers". Cragzac had thrown a huge party after his appointment to Supreme and amongst his guests he had invited the entire Wingtown Warriors squad. Crasis had smiled with smug self-satisfaction when he saw how uncomfortable they were in dinner suits surrounded by their betters. This smugness quickly turned to apprehension when he saw just how much sparkling WormFizz they drank (WormFizz is a highly alcoholic beverage made from fermented worm guts. It is usually served in a slim flute glass with two grass sprigs crossed over the top of the glass.) The Wingtown Warriors had dispensed with the flutes altogether and had produced from various pockets pint glasses and were pouring the WormFizz down in much the same way that a greedy Felixian might down milk. Eventually the very drunk Wingtown Warriors had started smashing their glasses over their teammates' heads. At least two of them had openly vomited over the ballroom floor (to much cheering and applause from their teammates). Crasis had his head in his wings fearing that Cragzac would blame him for this display.

Worse was to come, however, when the Captain (a huge crow with a beak so crooked it must have been broken and badly set multiple times) jumped into the musicians, who despite the chaos had been playing a very nice waltz, and wrestled a flute away from a terrified-looking, painfully thin crow who obviously decided that despite the cost of the instrument he had better just hand it over. In a moment of supreme irony, the Captain wiped the mouthpiece under one of his grubby wings and brought it to his beak. Much to Crasis' surprise the Captain played extremely well and his playing seemed to calm his teammates, who put down their drinks and proceeded to gather in a large half-circle. As one the team began to sing. At first it sounded quite melodious and although none of the team could sing in tune Crasis couldn't deny the passion with which they sang. By the second verse Crasis had picked up on the rhyming scheme and when he heard the team sing the line "Other teams may call us a farce but they can get down and now kiss…", he felt he should intervene, rushing into the middle of the half-circle flapping his wings urgently. Without thinking he jumped up and swiped the flute out of the beak of the Captain.

"That's quite enough!" he yelled.

Silence fell and Crasis began to slowly back away from the astonished-looking Captain. To his horror he soon realised that the half-circle had closed around him. The Captain towered over Crasis and in a loud voice squawked, "SCRUM!"

Crasis felt himself being lifted from the floor and with humiliating ease was tucked under the wing of the huge Captain. The Captain ran the full length of the ballroom (being sure to painfully jostle the squirming Crasis with every step). While shouting instructions to his teammates he hoisted Crasis high into the air and threw him across the now empty dancefloor. Crasis was too shocked to even scream and before he realised what had happened he was caught by another player who, without pausing, threw him to another player. There followed what felt to Crasis a long time of his being passed from player to player. Sometimes they threw him and sometimes they kicked him. On various occasions a player would throw him to the floor shouting, "GOAL!", every time they did it. More painful than any of that was the laughter from the assembled guests.

Eventually Cragzac stepped in and with much laughter slapped the Captain on the back saying, "I think that's enough for now, I would hate to train a new assistant."

With much laughter the team used Crasis to score one more goal and went to seek out the nearest waiter for more WormFizz. From that moment Crasis vowed revenge.

He wouldn't have to wait for long. Cragzac might have been a huge Warriors fan but he was also a very sore loser. It was the day of the Egg-Toss final and the Wingtown Warriors were playing against their rivals (and fan favourites),

Eagleton United. Cragzac had decided that as Supreme Leader he should introduce the game. If Cragzac had heard of impartiality he certainly wasn't in favour of it. His speech heaped praise on the "bravery and team spirit of the Warriors" and made numerous references to them "sweeping lesser teams out of their way as if they were dust on the streets".

The audience were shocked and appalled but it would have been a brave crow who dared not to applaud their Supreme Leader, especially as the Supreme Guard were positioned all round the stadium and were itching for the chance to break some beaks. As if incensed by the Supreme's speech, Eagleton came out fighting. They took the Warriors by surprise and by the end of the first half had opened up a commanding lead over them.

Cragzac sat in the special seating area he'd had built (at public expense). His mood had darkened considerably during the game. He had dismissed the first goal with a snort and jokingly said to his hangers-on that, "This will make victory taste all the sweeter." By the fourth goal, however, he couldn't make any more excuses. When the Eagleton captain (the dashingly handsome Brad Peckingburgh) ran past six Warrior defenders to score the fifth goal, Cragzac furiously ordered everyone except Crasis to "Get out of my sight." It was a furious Cragzac who had to award the Egg-Cup trophy to Eagleton. He put on a good face but everyone noticed that he stalked off the pitch, angrily muttering something to his assistant.

Later that night, after an evening spent drowning their sorrows in WormFizz in their private clubhouse, the

Warriors were surprised when the door flew off its hinges and several enormous and heavily armed crows stormed in, demanding they drop to the floor. Of course, a few of the drunker Warriors tried to make a fight of it but they were street fighters and as such were no match for the highly skilled Supreme Guard. The guard had tried to disguise themselves but considering the size of them it was bit like using a single curtain to hide a forest. In no time at all the Warriors had been pacified. From their prone angles they could only see a pair of boots slowly walk into the room and a scratchy voice quietly singing in mocking tones, "Other teams may call us a farce but they can get down and now kiss…" The Captain, in a furious rage, managed to rise to his feet and throw himself at Crasis, who stopped singing and leapt back. Before the Captain could reach Crasis one of the guards cracked him across the back of his head, dropping him to the floor once again. Before he lost consciousness he heard Crasis say, "I do hope you didn't hit him too hard, he won't want to miss what's coming."

It was some time later when the last of the Warriors regained their senses. They were in an unfamiliar stone room. The Captain tried to sit up but found that he was quite immobile. He struggled fruitlessly for a while in frustration, he squawked until his throat gave out. Rasping pathetically, he gave up struggling. Crasis' face then appeared over him, a smirk beaming across his beak.

"I thought Warriors never gave up?" he asked sardonically. The Captain glared at him. "You always were a crow of few words," Crasis sneered.

He moved away from his position standing over the

Captain. He snapped a few instructions to unseen minions and with the accompanying sound of pistons steaming and cogs turning the Captain felt the slab he was tied to move upwards. Within a few moments he had been positioned into a standing position. He found that he was able to move his head from side to side. As he did so he discovered the rest of the team likewise strapped to slabs. They had been positioned into a circle and in the middle, standing with his wings on his hips, was the diminutive form of Crasis.

"The Supreme is disappointed," he said eventually. "He doesn't like being disappointed," he said, fake concern battling with the clear enjoyment in his voice. "You were supposed to win. What happened?" he asked.

One of the Warriors started babbling excuses until Crasis nodded to someone in the shadows. The babbling was quickly drowned out by the sound of electricity ripping through his body. Blue sparks ran across his feathers and the smell of burning filled the air. Crasis nodded at the shadows and as quickly as it began the electricity stopped. The victim wasn't dead. Nasty burns ran across his body but he was breathing heavily.

"NO EXCUSES!" Crasis bellowed suddenly. (He had been determined to be cool and menacing but deep down he was a bully and knew that he was perfectly safe to do whatever he liked, and he liked shouting at these huge crows who reminded him so much of the sports masters of his childhood.) "Any more outbursts and the electricity stays on."

Crasis fondly imagined that he sounded tough and intimidating (he didn't). Silence followed, broken only by the ominous throb of the electric generator...

Crasis often considered that night the pinnacle of his career. He tortured that team all night, making sure to remind them of the fun that they had with him and just how badly they had let down their Supreme Leader. The events of that evening had led to Cragzac entrusting him with more information and letting him run the murkiest of his schemes, including one Cragzac had dubbed, "The Final Solution".

\* \* \*

"Wake up," he said, slapping Altheus across her face to rouse her.

The slap wasn't hard and Altheus was already coming around but Crasis felt that this would establish once and for all who was in control here. Her eyes flew open and took in her surroundings. They were deep in a forest (she would guess Silvestri but had no idea for how long they had been travelling). A fire was crackling in front of her and to her surprise she found that she could move freely. Crasis was still standing in front of her. He was flexing the wing he had struck her with in a futile attempt to relieve the pain it was in while the other was employed in pointing her own staff at her.

"Crasis!" she said sweetly. "What exactly do you think you're doing?"

"Sh… Shut up," he stammered back at her. (*Damn it*, he thought to himself, *don't let her intimidate you! You are in charge now*.) Drawing himself to his miniscule height he took a breath to steady his nerves and tried again. "You don't scare me," he said rather pathetically.

Altheus narrowed her eyes at him. She knew that she could easily attack him but she had to consider the staff. She didn't know how well he could use it and if she knocked the annoying little squirt to the floor there was no telling how the staff would react to being roughly handled. He spotted her looking at the staff.

"It's mine now," he sneered (sounding more and more like a petulant schoolboy). "I used it to carry you here and I will use it to resurrect my master."

"I thought I was your master," Altheus said in mock surprise. "It is so difficult to get reliable assistants these cycles."

As she spoke she attempted to slowly raise herself into a crouching position, the better to launch herself at Crasis. He spotted this at the last second.

"S... Stay back," he stammered, stepping backwards urgently.

As he stepped he tripped over the log he had previously been sitting on. To steady himself he rammed the staff handle roughly into the ground and used it keep himself upright. Altheus winced in alarm as the staff gave a sound of complaint and a single red spark erupted from the top.

"Yes," Crasis said in wonder, "I have the power now."

"You are a fool," Altheus said angrily, deciding to abandon the gentle approach. "You have no idea of the power you have there! You are more likely to destroy us and the entire world."

Crasis hissed at her, "I understand only too well! You are not the only mage, you know!"

Altheus was shocked. She had trained in secret, believing herself to be the very last magic-user left. She had travelled across the wastes of Aridier and beyond before finding her staff and now it was in the wings of another magic-user.

"It really is quite something," Crasis said in wonder, staring at the swirling colours in the orb. Altheus wasn't sure if he was talking to her any longer. "Such power," he whispered.

Suddenly a bright yellow bolt shot out of the orb, incinerating a nearby tree. Crasis laughed uproariously and turned to Altheus.

"It focuses your thoughts, doesn't it? I can make a fire but with this staff I could burn the whole jungle."

Her ears pricked up at the word "jungle". They couldn't possibly be in the Jungles of Lac! That would mean they must have travelled up across the entire eastern side of Venary. For how long had she been unconscious? She realised that Crasis was staring at her. Clearly he expected some sort of response.

"Is that how you will resurrect your master?" she asked. "By burning everything down?"

"Oh no," he replied airily, "I have other plans for that. Imagine what I could achieve with this staff AND the Collar of Honour."

Altheus suddenly felt very cold indeed.

## CHAPTER SIXTEEN

# SUNOLE

"I SPY WITH MY little eye something beginning with…" a cheery voice said in a sing-song fashion.

"In the name of the grass gods I will bite your nose off if you say S," came the weary reply.

"You're no fun," the first voice retorted.

"We need to do something to keep our spirits up."

"We are buried up to our necks in this blighted desert, miles away from anything even close to civilisation, with no hope of rescue and you have 'spied' 'sand' no less than twenty-seven times today! Why I let you talk me into this fool's errand in the first place I'll never know. Why did I leave the warren?"

"It's not my fault, Barnny. You are the one who promised the dogs a cut of the profit."

"Yes, but if you'll recall, Harnny, you told me that we'd be rich by now. What was it you said? 'Come with me, Barnny my boy! The desert is full of abandoned coaches ripe for the picking.' Well, that worked out well, didn't it?"

"I might have exaggerated somewhat but we did find that caravan train, didn't we?"

There followed a sound not unlike the noise made when a dirty pot is scrubbed vigorously with a wire brush as Barnny tried to turn to face his fellow. It was no good, the dogs had been thorough in the execution of their orders and had made sure that these two rabbits would not be escaping anytime soon. The sand had been packed in tight and all Barnny could manage was to wave his head around frantically. He howled in frustration and despite his throat being parched and his tongue as dry as tree bark he shouted at Harnny, "Yes, we also discovered that the dogs had already laid claim to it and weren't that keen on us carrying their stuff away, or had you forgotten?"

Harnny went to reply but the bickering rabbits were interrupted by the sound of a polite cough. They both looked up, instantly regretting this decision when the bright sunlight hit their eyes. Eventually a large, furry shape swam into view.

"Excuse me, gentlemen," Zakk asked, "might you know where the dog tribes are located?"

Harnny blinked. *Surely I'm hallucinating*, he thought.

"Excuse me," Zakk repeated a little louder.

"You are not there," Harnny replied. "You are merely a figment of my imagination."

At this he turned his eyes towards Barnny and was surprised to see him talking to a smaller shape. After a while his vision cleared and he could clearly see that Barnny was talking to a small Felixian with daggers tucked into his belt and a wide-brimmed hat (clearly two sizes too large for him) balanced on his head. The Felixian was barely older than a kitten and was clearly excited by something.

Harnny's investigations were cut short at this point by the sound of impatient foot-tapping and sighing from next to him. Painfully turning his head around once more he could see that far from being a hallucination another Felixian *had* been talking to him. This cat was clearly much older. He leaned unsteadily on a walking cane and was dressed in what once must have been a fine uniform but was now tattered and torn. Untidy clumps of ginger fur poked out of the many holes that adorned it. Looking up at the cat's face Harnny could see that the cat was starting to lose its patience.

"You're not a hallucination, are you?" was all Harnny could say.

"Not at all," Zakk said with a hint of irritation in his voice. "How long have you been in this predicament?" he enquired, pointing to the sand in which Harnny was buried. "Some sort of accident?" he asked.

"Yes," Harnny replied. "We accidentally stole from the dogs and in return they trapped and buried us out here to slowly cook to death," he said venomously.

"Thought as much," Zakk replied, totally ignoring the sarcasm. "It was the smell of slow-roasted rabbit that rather drew my young comrade and myself in your direction."

Harnny watched with horror as Zakk stopped to lick his lips.

"Bit surprised to find you so talkative to be honest but…" he leant towards the prone Harnny and took a big smell of the rabbit's face; he was so close that Harnny could feel hot breath on his cheeks and feel the rush of air as Zakk inhaled his scent, "I don't think that will last much longer, do you?" Zakk continued.

As he spoke he shook a battered backpack from his shoulders, letting it fall to the desert floor. With mounting horror Harnny noticed that Zakk was removing various items from the bag. First came a collapsible table that Zakk spent a lot of time setting up. Harnny noticed that Zakk wasn't very dexterous and that his paws shook slightly as he worked. After the table was set up Zakk produced an old cloth which had been tied up with string. Pausing only to lick his lips at him Zakk reached into his belt and after three attempts produced a knife with a hilt so shiny it reflected the sunlight. Harnny swallowed hard as Zakk admired the blade of his knife. Eventually he cut the string holding the cloth together and as it fell away Harnny could see it had been used to wrap up a selection of pearl-white plates and a set of cutlery which looked as though it might be made of silver.

Zakk busied himself setting the table for two, reached into the bag one last time and pulled out a dusty bottle which he blew at, barely dislodging any of the accumulated dust, and placed it with great care in the middle of the table. As he placed the bottle down, his younger companion bounded over with a look of concern on his young face. The conversation the two Felixians engaged in was conducted at a whisper and Harnny could only hear the occasional word. Whatever the young Felixian objected to was being dismissed by the other. After a short while the kitten returned to his position next to Barnny, who had gone a terrible shade of grey and was quietly sobbing into the sand.

"Rabbit," Zakk shouted towards him, "are you properly prepared yet? I can't stand overdone meat, ruins the taste of the wine."

He smiled, showing far too many teeth. Horrified realisation dawned on Harnny.

"No," he started to plead. "Please, dear sir, let us go, we have families. We have families," he repeated desperately, tears pouring down his face.

Through the blur of his tears he could see Zakk walk slowly around the table and head towards him, with his knife drawn. Slowly Zakk stalked the buried Harnny, arriving just as Harnny started to scream. His throat was worn and dried out by the heat so it came out as a hoarse rasp. Zakk raised the knife above his head and in one swift, yet unsteady movement he buried the knife in the sand made wet by the tears and carved a trench around the still sobbing Harnny. He could feel the sand start to lose its previously vice-like grip of him. Before he knew what was happening he felt himself pulled from the ground by his ears and placed gently onto a chair. Nervously he opened his eyes to see Zakk pouring water into a large goblet and passing it to him. Automatically Harnny took it but was too nervous to do anything more than stare blankly at it.

"Drink," Zakk instructed, "you've lost much water and you're not out of danger yet." Harnny gulped at the water but kept his eyes on Zakk. "Sorry if I scared you," Zakk said eventually, "I had to make sure the sand around you was moist before I pulled you out, and this…" he said, indicating the flask of water he was returning to his battered backpack, "is drinking water. My only choice was to make you cry. Young Scratch over there," he said, indicating the other far younger Felixian, "should be doing the same with your friend. Mind you he is taking his time."

As he said this a loud scream followed by the hiss of a

startled feline could be heard. Harnny jumped and Zakk just rolled his eyes as a startled-looking Scratch came into view followed by Barnny who was rubbing his ears and wincing slightly.

"You forgot to dig him up before pulling him out, didn't you?" Zakk asked Scratch, amusement in his voice.

Scratch looked very chagrined and muttered something about it working anyway. Zakk laughed loudly and clapped Scratch on the back.

"Yes, I suppose it did," he chuckled. "Let's get something to eat."

Zakk and Scratch sat down at the table, seating themselves directly opposite the rabbits. Harnny was starting to regain his colour but Barnny still glared at Scratch and continued to massage his long ears. Zakk returned once again to the large backpack and from the voluminous side packs removed a few parcels of wax paper. He spoke amiably as he unwrapped a selection of cured meats, raw vegetables, fruits and cheeses.

"You are a long way from home, gentlemen. Let me guess, you are attempting to seek your fortunes."

"Something like that," Barnny muttered, staring darkly at Harnny who was obliviously stuffing vegetable after vegetable into his mouth, his cheeks bulging. Barnny noticed that Zakk hadn't taken any food but had filled his glass with the deep red wine twice now. "We thought that we would have our pickings of abandoned caravans and when we got it home we would be heroes."

He blushed crimson as he recounted his story.

"Nothing wrong with questing," Zakk replied. "Why,

in my younger cycles I travelled from one end of Venary to the other."

Zakk paused and stared into the middle distance, absently bringing the glass of wine to his lips. It was more by sheer luck than skill that any of the wine made into his mouth. Barnny went to take the glass from his shaking paws but as he reached out he felt a small furry paw take his own and return it to the table. Scratch shook his head slowly at him.

"Where was I?" Zakk asked. "Oh yes, I saw some sights in those cycles…"

There followed a crashing noise as Zakk dropped the bottle he had been holding and fell from his seat onto the sand. Harnny and Barnny exchanged looks and then stared at Scratch, who had removed the cape from his shoulders and placed it around Zakk's unconscious form.

"That will be it until the morning," he said. "The pair of you had better get some sleep too, I'll stand guard."

With that he pulled a short sword out of his belt, walked towards a high sand dune and sat himself down. The two puzzled rabbits stared at each other for a while and having nothing to say dug out a small warren in the sand and settled in for the night.

"This is a needless delay," Tyrell said testily inside Scratch's head.

He had been quiet up until now. Even when Scratch and his unreliable mentor had been ransacking the unconscious forms of Mittens and Moglox he had contented himself with a few sighs of irritation. Now he was alone with Scratch he let his frustrations show.

"For how long do we have to wait for that old soak to sober up?"

"Don't call him that!" Scratch hissed back. "He's a hero."

"Don't give me that," Tyrell snapped back. "Don't forget I'm in your head! You're embarrassed by him."

"No I'm not!" Scratch replied unconvincingly.

"Is that why you haven't mentioned me to him yet?" Tyrell enquired. "Worried how the old fool will react?" Scratch said nothing. Tyrell pressed on. "I know that you have your own plans for the Collar of Honour but may I remind you that my father is most likely reasserting his control over Venary. It was bad enough before but Perix only knows what powers he has developed. He never had much regard for the other species. Imagine a world where you are hunted to the point of extinction, your lands turned into a playground for a mad king. Not much need for a knight with a pretty sword then, is there?"

Scratch tried not to listen but a small part of him understood that Tyrell might well be right. Tyrell laughed smugly at the thought.

"Remember," he said in a friendly tone, "a knight's first duty is to his king."

\* \* \*

Barnny didn't know for how long he'd been asleep before he was woken by a sudden and painful kick to his chest. His eyes flew open and before he could fully awaken he was pulled up by his still tender ears until he was face to face with the ugliest dog he had ever seen. For his part the dog seemed very pleased to see Barnny.

"'Ello, little bunny-wunny," he exclaimed around broken teeth.

The dog had clearly been in many fights over the spans, not all of them successful judging by the way his jaw hung loosely and a whistling sound from his broken nose punctuated every outward breath he made.

"Lord Sunole will be pleased to see you looking so well."

He giggled a horrible high-pitched laugh and dragged the still struggling Barnny towards a caravan of wagons emblazoned with a roughly drawn pile of gold surrounded by fire, the symbol of the dog tribes. The dog threw open the curtains at the back of the lead caravan and threw Barnny inside. Barnny looked around and saw that he wasn't alone. Harnny was curled up in a corner moaning softly to himself and Scratch was lying face down on the rough caravan floor, his four paws tied behind his back. Zakk was still sleeping soundly. The dogs clearly didn't regard him as a threat as he had been left untied. With no other option he made his way towards Scratch and with great effort turned him over onto his back.

"What sort of guard did you turn out…" Barnny began to chastise the prone cat but stopped as he looked at Scratch's face. His left eye was so swollen that it had closed and dried blood covered his face.

"Took me by surprise," was all Scratch managed to say before passing out.

Barnny turned towards the curtains at the back of the caravan. This was his only chance. If he could get outside he was confident that he could escape his captors, especially if he could find his way underground.

"Hey, Harnny," he whispered as loudly as he dared.

There was no response. He tried again. "Harnny, over here."

Harnny looked from his corner.

"Barnny?" he asked. "Barnny? Is that you? I thought those dog bastards had killed you." As he spoke he crawled towards the back of the caravan. "It is good to see you but I think this might be the end of our adventures, I don't think we can rely on…" as he spoke he motioned towards the prone figures of Scratch and Zakk. "Clearly not the heroes they think they are," he added. "One is barely a kitt and the other is an old drunk."

Barnny went to say that he felt this was a bit harsh but he was too scared to even agree.

"Never mind them," he said eventually, "I think that we can get away but we'll have to be quick."

With a quick look over his shoulder at Scratch and Zakk, Harnny made his way to the opening between the curtains at the back of the caravan, followed by Barnny. The two rabbits looked at each other and silently counted together.

"One," they began, "two…"

On "three" both rabbits stuck their heads out of the curtains and found themselves staring at the barrels of five flintlock muskets, each one being wielded by a smiling dog.

"Going somewhere, boys?" one of the guards asked. Barnny and Harnny just stared at them in stunned horror, unable to speak. "You wouldn't want to upset His Most Honourable Lordship, would you?"

At this all of the other guards laughed loudly. Without a word and feeling utterly defeated Harnny and Barnny withdrew back inside the caravan and sat dejectedly on the hard floor.

After what seemed like a very long time the caravan came to a halt. Zakk had regained consciousness during the journey and was trying his best to tend to Scratch's wounds. The younger Felixian had gone very pale but whether this was down to blood loss or fear neither Harnny nor Barnny could tell. They watched as Zakk tore strips off his already battered cape and fashioned them into makeshift bandages. After a while Scratch gently batted him away and slowly rose to his feet. He patted his belt with some confusion.

"They took your weapons," Barnny said eventually, "so whatever you're planning just forget it."

"Not that you've been much help to us so far," Harnny added bitterly.

"You ungrateful rodents," Scratch spat weakly. "If it wasn't for us you'd be nothing but a hot meal for the vultures by now."

"Oh and this is sooo much better, I suppose," Harnny shouted back. "What's the plan exactly?" he sneeringly enquired. "Perhaps you could let the entire dog tribe sneak up on you again while this sad old wineskin drinks himself insensible. That's worked well, hasn't it?"

"Come on, Harnny, let's not turn on each other," said Barnny soothingly.

Harnny spun to face him.

"Why are you defending them now? You were all for jumping out of the back and leaving them to it not so long ago as I recall."

"You cowardly lumps of gristle," Scratch growled. "We should have left you in the ground." As he spoke Scratch tore off his gloves and stretched out his paws, allowing razor-sharp claws to extend from each of his paw tips. "I don't need my daggers to deal with you!"

He went to jump at the now very scared Barnny, only to be held back by Zakk. He angrily spun round to voice his objection, only to be silenced by the angry look on Zakk's face.

"This is not our way," he said. "Remember the code of the knighthood, we protect the weak and accept our failures… and we've certainly failed today."

"Lovely words," came a sarcastic voice from the back of the caravan. As one everybody turned at once to see a massive dog with a large rifle pointed right at them. "His Lordship would be delighted to see you now," he added with a wicked grin on his face.


As they jumped down from the caravan the bright sunshine stung their eyes and beads of sweat formed instantly on their brows. Zakk used one of his large paws to shield himself from the bright light.

"Early afternoon," he muttered to himself.

Four heavily armed guard dogs surrounded them, their body language making it clear that while escape was clearly impossible they would dearly love someone to try. The dogs were all naked except for loin cloths and wide-brimmed hats. This lack of clothing served two functions: it kept them cool in the oppressive desert heat and displayed their muscles in very concerning ways.

The prisoners were already exhausted and desperate for water so allowed themselves to be led across the burning sands, past tents made of silk, until they reached the largest one in the centre of the camp. This tent was clearly more ornate than the others. It stood fifteen hands taller than the others and the silk it was made from was clearly expensive and of high quality. Two more burly dogs stood on either side of the entrance. Unlike the other dogs they had seen so far these guards were smarter and better-looking. They wore white silk gowns and held spears that looked like they had been forged from Pacidermian tusk.

One by one each of the prisoners was roughly thrown into the tent. Scratch collapsed to his knees and when he tried to stand he was clubbed across the back of his head by the handle of one of the spears so hard that he saw stars.

"Prisoners will remain on their knees," exclaimed one of the more refined voices of the silk-clad guards, "while His Imperial and Majestic Lordship Lord Sunole, protector of bones and very good boy, enters."

Once more the tent flaps opened and four dogs came in carrying an ornate golden throne on which sat a compact, muscular white dog. He glanced down at the assembled prisoners with barely disguised contempt. Walking in behind him was a far larger grey and white dog who was dressed in a military outfit. A row of shiny medals stood out across his barrel chest. Scratch guessed that the second dog had seen lots of battles and by the slightly vacant look on his face and lolling tongue most of these battles had taken place in areas where shade was non-existent. The throne bearers gently removed Sunole from his throne and carried him up a large pile of cushions and placed him on what was clearly the largest and most comfortable one. He yawned, opening his mouth as wide as it would go, showing off his viciously sharp teeth in the process.

"Colonel," he asked eventually, "why are those rabbits back in my presence?"

He either hadn't noticed the cats or was deliberately ignoring them. Scratch felt the anger burn inside of him at this insult. The grey and white dog excitedly jumped to his hind legs.

"Bad rabbits, sire! Very bad rabbits! Escaped, sire, yes they did, escaped they did, sire, yes, yes indeed they did."

As he spoke flecks of drool coated Zakk, who flinched only slightly.

"Escaped?" Sunole asked, looking down his stub nose at them. "And how did Flopsey and Mopsey manage this feat?" This question was greeted with silence. "COLONEL!" he shouted, looking over to his left.

He sighed as he realised why his question had gone unanswered. The Colonel had his head buried in his crotch and was noisily snuffling at his groin. Sunole cleared his throat and when this proved ineffectual he turned to Harnny and Barnny to address them himself.

"You are meant to be dead," he said simply. "You were caught raiding an abandoned caravan in my territory! MINE!" This last word came out as a howl and the rabbits huddled together terrified. "MINE! MINE! MINE!" Sunole continued to howl.

He reached such a volume that the Colonel eventually looked up. His eyes were crossed and he had a look of utter bliss across his face.

"YOURSSSSSS!" he joined in delightedly, clearly thinking this was a very fun game.

Sunole broke off from his howl and looked at the laughing Colonel.

"Back with us then, Colonel?" he enquired.

"Back, sire, yes, sire, we got them back, indeed we did, sire, got them back we did."

Sunole sighed again.

"I think our other…" as he struggled with the words he waved a paw in an idle fashion towards Zakk and Scratch, "guests had a paw in this." For the first time he directly addressed them. "You're a long way from Silvestri Forest," he said simply. "So what makes you think you can overrule my divine judgement?"

Scratch went to answer but Zakk silenced him with a glance.

"If I may be allowed to stand," Zakk asked.

Sunole made a big show of considering the request.

"We shall allow it," he stated eventually. "But be warned that the fearsome Colonel stands ready to tear you into the smallest chunks at my command."

Zakk looked over at the Colonel who was unfortunately trying to catch his own tail. Zakk wasn't sure but he could swear that the Colonel was laughing in between taking bites at his tail.

"I don't doubt that," he said, trying to keep his amusement out of his voice. "My lord?" Zakk continued, unsure of how to address this petulant dog. "My young apprentice and I are just travelling, trying to see a bit of the world. We chanced upon these rabbits purely by luck. Had we known they were your prisoners, then naturally we would have left them where we found them. However, as they are free and clearly sorry, I'm sure we can reach some sort of arrangement."

At this Sunole nodded slightly. Feeling relieved Zakk

turned back to his companions just in time to see the Colonel leap at the rabbits and with a speed which shouldn't be possible in a dog of that size he ripped the head off one of the rabbits. Scratch jumped back in horror and landed on all fours with his back arched. The Colonel rolled around in the blood and his jaws made a hideous crunching sound as he bit through the skull bones. Zakk couldn't tell which of the rabbits had been killed but before he could check he was distracted by the high-pitched laughter coming from Lord Sunole.

"The look on your face," Sunole said between bouts of hysterical laughter. "Who's next? Who's next?" he asked, clapping his paws together in delight.

"Tasty, tasty," muttered the Colonel, licking his lips.


"SCRATCH!" Tyrell shouted. "For once will you listen to me?"

"Be quiet," Scratch shouted back, too shocked to keep his voice low.

Every head in the tent turned to look his way. The only exception was Harnny who was sobbing into the remains of his now very dead friend. Sunole's face had turned a very dark shade of red and even the Colonel had managed to stay focused on him.

"I know the dog tribes," Tyrell hissed urgently. "I can get us out of this, just do what I say and follow my instructions to the letter and we might just get out of this in one piece."

Zakk watched in horrified fascination as Scratch, as if in a dream, rose slowly to his feet. Bowing his head in a court bow Scratch turned out his feet so they made a square and, stepping forward with his left foot, walked slowly towards

Sunole. He stopped with every third step and bowed deeply towards Sunole who had calmed considerably and was watching Scratch intently. For his part Scratch was clearly listening to something only he could hear. Reaching the bottom of the pile of cushions he placed his right paw as a shield over his eyes, clearly averting his gaze from Sunole. There followed a very long pause. Just as Sunole was about to grow annoyed once more Scratch spoke clearly but hesitantly.

"My Lord Sunole," he began, "permit your unworthy follower permission to address your wondrousness." Sunole nodded in ascent. "I, the humble creature who trembles before you, offer my obedience to your divine will as emissary to the Royal House of Mowser of which I am the fourteenth son…"

"LIAR!" Sunole screamed suddenly. "The fourteenth son is dead! You with your borrowed words dare to take his place…"

He trailed off suddenly as Scratch's head suddenly snapped up and fixed him with a stare. The kitten's eyes were glowing green and Sunole wasn't sure but it looked like Scratch was growing. Green light began to pour from Scratch's eyes and smoke appeared from nowhere, swirling around the Felixian as he began to float at least a handsbreadth from the floor. The smoke began to pool around the floating form of Scratch, taking on the shape of an adult Rodentian with a long nose and elegant whiskers.

"T… T… Tyrell," Sunole gasped in disbelief, "is that you, my king?"

The ghostly figure smiled and spread out his paws as if

to embrace the now cowering dog. Scratch's mouth opened but a stranger's voice came out.

"Yes, Lord Sunole, it is I. I have taken this Felixian's form, as my own is long since destroyed…"

"What happened, my king?" Sunole asked, all trace of his former arrogance absent as he stared at the form of his long-dead King.

"My expedition to the jungle was unsuccessful."

Everyone in the tent was now focusing entirely on the ghostly form of Tyrell. Even Harnny had looked up from the remains of Barnny. His cheeks were tear-stained but even he was transfixed by the spectacle in front of him. Tyrell didn't elaborate further on this expedition, instead opening his arms wide to encompass his travelling companions.

"Lord Sunole, I apologise for the lies told to you by my companions. They do not know you as I do, they never knew the great service you offered my family during the war."

At the mention of the war Zakk growled softly under his breath until one of the guards close by whacked him on the head hard with the butt of his spear. Tyrell continued as if he hadn't heard anything.

"I come to you now to beg a favour. These Felixians are on a royal quest to recover a prized artefact. If you assist us with supplies and a means of transport you will be handsomely rewarded."

At the word "rewarded" Sunole settled back into his cushion and grinned a wide smile, showing only the sharpest of his teeth.

"I'm sure we can come to some arrangement," he said eventually, as Scratch collapsed in a heap, the figure of Tyrell disappearing suddenly.

When Scratch regained consciousness some time later he was surprised to find himself lying in extreme comfort on many silk-lined cushions. Remembering where he was Scratch sat up with a start, dislodging the cold, wet flannel somebody had placed across his forehead. Feeling a sudden burst of pain behind his eyes he lowered himself back down again, suddenly grateful for the cloth as he returned it to his throbbing forehead. As he lay there, the room spinning around him in a sickening display, he whispered, "Tyrell." There was no response. "Tyrell, are you there?" he hissed louder. Again there was no response.

Clearly alerted by his calls for Tyrell Zakk raced into the tent. He was as worried as Scratch had ever seen him. Making his way to the head of the makeshift bed, Zakk sat down beside Scratch and placed a massive paw on Scratch's chest.

"You gave me quite a scare, young Scratch," he said eventually. "How long have you had a passenger?" he enquired gently.

"Since the palace," Scratch said eventually. "After that crow knocked me out I woke up with Tyrell inside my head."

Scratch had explained what had happened to the crows while Zakk was tied up with Mittens and Moglox but had neglected to tell him about Tyrell.

"I'm sorry, I should have told you," Scratch said, bursting into tears, "but I was afraid you'd think I was mad and not let me come."

Zakk shushed him gently.

"I can't understand what has happened to you. I wish Altheus was with us. This magic malarkey is more her thing than mine." He paused to sigh deeply. "But you have clearly been entrusted with a great purpose and now it is even more important that we find the Collar of Honour."

Scratch felt very tired.

"I can't, I can't," he said, his voice faltering with the effort of talking. "I can't hear Tyrell anymore," he said eventually.

"Sleep, young Scratch," Zakk said gently. "I'm sure he'll come back when we need him again."

It was several sunrises until Scratch had recovered sufficiently to leave his tent. He was still very pale and had heard nothing from Tyrell. As he slept he had terrible dreams. In one he saw a beautiful young Rodentian female, her face contorted by screams. In others he was being hunted by a giant Rodentian who kept shouting "DISAPPOINTMENT" at him until he collapsed into a huddled sobbing ball, rolled up on the floor. The worst one was that he was drowning slowly. He couldn't move his legs and they felt as heavy as lead weights dragging him slowly into a thick mucus-like liquid which entered his mouth and ears, filling him up from the inside. In all of them he heard the same high-pitched laughter.

While Scratch recovered Zakk made himself busy in the dog encampment. He felt a certain animosity towards the dog tribes. They had allied themselves with the Rodentian forces during the war. Zakk suspected that they didn't care about a land dispute, they just wanted to make trouble for the Felixians. Their interference had drawn out the length of the war and some of the bloodiest battles had been against the dog tribes. In a rare moment of gratitude King Faustus had granted them complete dominion over the desert wastes of Aridier. The crows weren't happy to have them so close to them but so far both factions had obeyed the boundary laws. Zakk had been in many meetings with their capricious leader, Sunole, and not all of them had been disastrous. He was grateful for the surprise intervention of a long-dead king but he wished he hadn't mentioned their quest. It had become an obsession with Sunole. The dog refused to discuss providing any supplies until Zakk had fully explained what he was looking for. Fruitlessly Zakk had tried to distract him with promises of gold and jewels but Sunole had proved smarter than their earlier interaction would have suggested. Zakk briefly toyed with the idea of lying to Sunole but he couldn't be sure that Tyrell wouldn't make a reappearance and tell Sunole everything. So, on the night before Scratch felt well enough to move, Zakk sat down with Sunole and told him everything he knew about the Collar of Honour.

"So, feline," Sunole said gruffly, clearly using the word "feline" as an insult.

Zakk bristled at this but decided he couldn't do anything about it now, especially with the erratic Colonel walking around him in a wobbly circle. At that moment the Colonel was attempting to whistle, however he kept sticking his tongue out before beginning. Zakk had been sprayed with a fine rain of spittle more than once and just wanted to get on his way. Sunole continued, clearly disappointed that the insult had been ignored.

"This collar thing…" He attempted to say it nonchalantly. He had splayed himself across his favourite pillow, his legs dangling in the open air. He waved his front paws in a dismissive fashion to imply that he wasn't really interested in a simple collar. Zakk would have laughed at such an obvious display but the bloody stain which was all that remained of the luckless Barnny reminded him just how dangerous this dog was. "… You say it grants wishes."

Zakk cleared his throat in embarrassment.

"I am informed that it grants the one greatest wish of its owner's heart before vanishing again."

As he said it out loud he realised how ridiculous it sounded but with all he had seen in his life he couldn't discount it.

"Interesting," Sunole said in languid fashion.

At this moment a deafening fart sounded throughout the tent. This was in turn followed by hysterical laughter from the Colonel.

"TOOT TOOT!" the Colonel shouted happily. "I TOOT TOOT!" he called again.

Throughout his life Zakk had been grateful for his strong Felixian senses. His sense of hearing had alerted him to nearby enemies and his sense of smell had allowed him to track prey when he was close to starvation. Now, however, he cursed his nose because the smell that assaulted it was beyond anything he had ever encountered before. The whole tent took on the aroma of rotted meat and stagnant water. It felt hotter than ever inside and Zakk just wanted to leave this camp and leave it quickly.

"Your Lordship," he said suddenly, "His Majesty King Hirax has been possessed by King Faustus and I'm sure you understand that if anybody will attempt to take your lands from you it will be him. We must use the Collar to send him back to where he came from. What will it take for you to honour King Tyrell's request?"

Sunole's grin grew larger.

"A castle?" Scratch said incredulously a little time later as he and Zakk were loading fresh supplies into their new caravan. "He wants a castle?" he enquired again when Zakk didn't answer.

Zakk strapped down a large case labelled "water" written in a shaky hand.

"Apparently all the other stewards have a castle in their domain and His Lordship wants one too."

"But who builds a castle in the desert?" Scratch asked, confused. "Surely it will sink in the sand?"

Zakk jumped down from the roof of the caravan and whispered into Scratch's ear, "He has supplied us with transport and supplies and in return he wants a castle. Compared to what he could have asked for I think we've done alright. I might give him our castle just to see the look on Oscar's face…" at this he paused, "assuming Oscar is still alive, that is." He seemed to gaze off into the distance momentarily. "Of course he's still alive," he said eventually. "His sort always manage to get out of trouble."

Scratch just shrugged at this and went to check on the ropes securing the cargo.

"You can't give him a castle," a voice said eventually.

Scratch was so surprised to hear Tyrell's voice that he let out a hiss of surprise and nearly cut himself on the edge of one of the large crates.

"I thought something terrible had happened to you," Scratch said eventually.

"Something terrible happened to both of us," Tyrell replied. "I wasn't expecting making my appearance to be so draining," he confessed. "Took me a while to get my strength back."

"I know what you mean," Scratch added.

"However, it does mean that if we can drag my father out of my son's body we should be able to weaken him long enough for your master to actually be of some use. In the meantime, promise Sunole whatever you like but I refused him a castle during my reign and he's not getting one now."

"But why not?" Scratch replied. "It's not like it means anything, it's just a building."

"Your master really has left giant gaps in your education, hasn't he?" Tyrell replied testily. "Buildings take on the soul of their inhabitants, castles even more so. The last thing Venary needs is another would-be king."

"I assume," Zakk said loudly, "that our former ruler is back with us?"

Scratch nodded solemnly.

"Well…" Zakk said, "I can't say I'm delighted. We have enough on our hands with the rest of his family but I suppose he might have his uses. Come on, young Scratch, we've been here quite long enough, the jungle beckons."

"Jungle?!" Scratch and Tyrell said simultaneously.

Zakk nodded and smiled.

"Call it an old knight's intuition."

Scratch gaped at him for a while.

"Have you seen that rabbit by the way?" Zakk asked, clearly hoping to change the subject. "I promised him a lift out of here."

And with that the old Felixian took up the reins and their adventure continued.

# CHAPTER SEVENTEEN

# WASTELANDS

"**D**AMN IT!"

Number One was furious. He paced around the wooden shack stamping his hoofed feet with each angry step. At one point he kicked through the floor, slicing his shin open on the jagged wood. Yani had rushed forward to treat the wound, her medical training overruling her hatred for this male. He had batted her away impatiently and resumed stomping back and forth across the wooden floor, although she noticed, with satisfaction, in a gentler fashion.

"An age we've been here," he snarled eventually, "and all we've found is this shed."

"It has sheltered us from the wind," she noted helpfully.

He glared at her, clearly searching for something hurtful to say.

"Shut up," he replied weakly and somewhat childishly.

Yani had noticed that recently Number One wasn't quite so calm and collected as he had been before. If she didn't know any better she would think he was scared of something.

To avoid his growing ire Yani returned to the map they had scratched into the wall furthest from the door. It was a fairly accurate map of the wastelands. She had suggested when they first arrived that every evening they sketch what they had found and if there were any clues as to the whereabouts of the Collar of Honour. That had been a while ago and the map remained as featureless as the landscape that surrounded them. All they had found was the shack they currently called home, and rocks, lots and lots of rocks.

Upon arrival Number One had fallen upon each freshly discovered rock pile, investigating each one in turn. He had shaken them, tapped them and at least once held them up to the sunlight as if he could see through them. However, the lack of progress was clearly starting to get to him. There had been a momentary glimmer of hope when Yani had discovered a small metal ring. It was too small and thin to be worn as jewellery but its colour distinguished it against the greyness of her surroundings. She had been fascinated by the light refracting off it, when she heard the dark mutterings which meant Number One was approaching. Yani absently pocketed the small ring and stood up to greet him.

"Another pointless day," he muttered darkly. "I don't suppose you've found anything?" he asked testily. Yani shook her head. This had been a few cycles ago and his mood had not improved. "I am convinced," he said between gritted teeth, "that those stones are breeding. Every daybreak we go out there and every daybreak there are more rocks." Yani knew better than to engage in conversation with him when he was in one of those moods. "Do we have any food left?" he asked eventually.

"There's some ground lizard left," Yani replied.

On their arrival at the wastelands they had been surprised to discover that they were not entirely alone. The only other occupants of the wastelands were multi-legged lizards – who like everything else in the area were grey-coloured. Due to the many legs they sported the lizards could move extremely quickly, however they were very trusting and would wander up to both Number One and Yani. It didn't seem to matter how many times Number One would kill them by bringing a rock down on their heads, more would appear and follow the Giraxians around.

Number One walked to the corner of the cabin they had designated the storeroom and picked up a recently cooked ground lizard by the now crispy tail and bit through the head.

"Overdone," he muttered to himself.

When they first decided to cook the now rapidly growing pile of ground lizard corpses Yani had suggested they build a fire far away from the shack in case the smell of cooking attracted predators. Number One had been very dismissive of this suggestion, reasoning that in a wasteland as flat as this they'd see any predator long in advance, and so they built a fire just by what they had decided was the back of the shack and roasted lizard after lizard each night.

Yani shuddered. She had eaten plenty of ground lizard herself but she rationalised it by telling herself it was this or death. It still horrified her to eat meat but Number One seemed to revel in it. She had to keep repressing dark thoughts that he might fancy a change in his diet. She had started to sleep with a large rock *very* nearby just in case.

"What made you think…" he said around a mouth full of overcooked lizard, "that the Collar would be here?"

She sighed inwardly and briefly debated with herself whether or not it would be a good idea to explain that she had suggested two possible locations and it was him who had chosen to come here. She decided against it. He had always been somewhat volatile whenever she tried to speak to him in the past but in his current agitated state he was likely to kill her. Annoyed at her lack of response he muttered darkly under his breath and stalked out of the cabin into the night.

He was gone for a long time. Hope wasn't something that Yani had felt for as long as she could remember but could something have happened to him? Could she finally be free? With these thoughts going around her head she fell into a deep sleep and dreamed of him…

Yaxil Greenleaf had been told all of his adult life that he was far too attractive to be a scientist. Tall even for a Giraxian he had deep green eyes and a mop of unruly hair which fell across his face no matter what he tried to do with it. It is a universal truth that when the fates give, they give generously. Not only was he devastatingly handsome he was also a brilliant scientist. He was one of the lucky few to be born outside of the labour camps and so was spared the terrible conditions that many of his fellows endured. He wasn't insensitive to them it was just that his head was so full of ideas and equations that it never occurred to him to think of others. Numbers he could handle, other Giraxians, however, were a boring mystery. He could often be found pacing the sterile corridors of the Science Corps building muttering formulae under his breath. He would breeze past the Pacidermian overseers as if they weren't there, only impatiently flashing his security pass at them should they ask. Most of the overseers didn't ask as they thought he was peculiar, not dangerous but very odd. If he was aware of their opinion it wouldn't have bothered him. He knew that the Pacidermians were oppressing his people and was vaguely aware that he should probably be angry about this, and once as an experiment he had tried to make himself mad about the whole thing, but to no avail. He knew that empires rose and fell and that science was the only constant. Science never picked sides so neither did he.

He had infuriated her at first. Yani was political, or as political as it was possible to be where their every move could be observed by the Pacidermian forces. Every Giraxian scientist knew someone (or had at least heard of someone) who had been arrested in the middle of the night for "salacious political views" and had never been seen again. Many of her fellows had actively started to avoid her for fear of being taken away when the authorities inevitably caught up with her.

Yani and Yaxil had been teamed together to find a more efficient way to harvest ivory, the Pacidermians having developed the paranoia that eventually runs through any organisation that rules through fear that its subjects might eventually develop courage and rise up against it. Yani felt slighted when Yaxil arrived, partly because she knew that she didn't require his help but mostly because she was working on her recipe for faux tusks and thought that if he found out he would turn her in to the nearest overseer. She needn't have worried because as soon as he realised what she was doing his scientific curiosity took over and he assisted her with her research. He was only annoyed that it had taken him so long to realise what she was doing. In fact, she had nearly completed the work but in all of her experiments she couldn't get the faux tusks to retain their shape longer than a day. If this breakthrough was to be a success they must last as long as genuine tusks.

It was Yaxil who solved the problem in the end. In what she considered an act of barbary he removed a vertebra from the neck of a deceased Giraxian worker who had recently arrived at the morgue and through his own cloning research merged the tensile strength of Giraxian bone with the toughness of Pacidermian tusk. The outcome of this discovery was bigger than even Yani had imagined. The value of real tusks plummeted and combined with Yani's earlier discovery of the non-existance of the Flying Drexes the Giraxians realised that they had been humiliated by the Pacidermians and their revenge had been bloody. Both Yani and Yaxil realised that they had to make amends and so they published their findings, which allowed the Pacidermians to support themselves. They had been naive. They thought that the Giraxians would rejoice in their freedom and that the Pacidermians now with no need for slave labour would leave them alone. Bitterness on both sides, however, made this impossible and the fighting continued. The Giraxians wanted revenge and the Pacidermians weren't prepared to set a whole slave class go free, especially after the attack on the farming plantation. Yani and Yaxil were hated by both sides and had to make their escape.

The couple had been in hiding for some time but their supplies were rapidly running out and they knew that sooner or later they would have to escape. But where could they go? They debated this for a long time. Yaxil thought they should go directly to King Hirax and plead their case. She disagreed. His Majesty had refused to intercede even when it was obvious that the Giraxians were being mistreated so she reasoned, *Why would he help now?* She wanted them to take their chances on the road, trust no one and find a peaceful part of Venary to settle down and let the world forget about them.

He eventually agreed to her plan and one night they packed up what was left of their meagre supplies and attempted their escape. Since declaring their independence, the Giraxians had taken what they believed to be their land back. Needless to say that the Pacidermians did not believe that the land belonged to them and proceeded to invade/ liberate (delete as per your own political opinion) these lands. In the resultant power struggle the Giraxians had established and lost no fewer than twelve capital cities. The latest capital, "Freedaxia 4", was little more than a shanty town of unstable wooden buildings. A sapling had been planted in what passed for the town square as a testament to new beginnings. A few cynical Giraxians had commented that this was the thirteenth new beginning but they had been largely ignored. There was no police force or schools. The theory put forward by the new "Government of Equals" had been that the Giraxians would "band together and rebuild their society on a more just and equal system". In reality, of course, no Giraxians would go out alone at night unless they wanted their few remaining possessions to disappear along with most of their teeth.

In a minor miracle they found a small sect of Girexian rebels who, whilst not exactly fond of the Greenleafs, offered to help them escape in return for their assistance on a mission deep in the centre of Freedaxia 4.

So, it was a deserted street that Yani and Yaxil found themselves and their "allies" on. They stayed close to buildings and moved quickly but quietly through Freedaxia 4. Yaxil was just thinking that they had made excellent progress and might just get away when a loud whistling sound pierced the silence of the night air.

"What's going on?" Yani hissed loudly.

As if in response to her question all of the doors of the nearby houses swung open and ginormous Girexians in black uniforms poured out and surrounded the group. Yani reached out for Yaxil's hoof but felt a sharp blow to the back of her head and fell into darkness.

She woke back in the shack screaming Yaxil's name. It took her a minute to remember where she was and a wave of despair engulfed her. Her lover was dead, she was a figure of hatred on both sides and she was stuck in this crappy hut with a male she despised who could kill her at any minute. At this thought she realised that he hadn't returned. She could have no idea for how long she had been asleep but when she looked through the one window the shack possessed it was pitch black outside – obviously the middle of the night. Even during the day, the view out of the window didn't offer much in the way of variety but at night you couldn't even see the stars. It was as if someone had placed a giant bowl over the wastelands.

Just as she was about to turn away from the window she was sure that something had caught her eye. It wasn't much but she was sure that she had seen a faint flashing light. She stared out of the window hoping to see it again. After a while of seeing nothing except darkness she muttered to herself, "Must have imagined it," and made to leave the window, except, there it was again, brighter this time. Yani had no idea what it could be but as a scientist (or at least at one brilliant moment in what felt like her distant past she had been a scientist) she couldn't leave something unexplained, uninvestigated.

The nights in the wastelands were bitterly cold and she was still wearing the ballgown she had been given before the jubilee. It was torn and dirty and wouldn't offer much in the way of protection. Vainly she looked around the shack for something to wear when she spotted the dinner jacket Number One had been wearing. *He must have left it behind when he stormed out*, she thought to herself and went to pick it up. Like her dress the dinner jacket was covered in dust and many tears from their time rummaging through rock piles but it was thick and would at least keep her warm. She shuddered with revulsion when she put it on, disgusted by the thought of wearing anything that had touched that vile male, but she had no choice. If she was going to investigate that light she would have to wear the jacket. Scanning the shack one last time for anything she could use, Yani closed the door behind her and walked out into the night.

The cold was shocking. Icy winds whipped around her and despite her discomfort at the idea she wrapped the dinner jacket around herself. She contemplated going back into the shack but at that moment she saw the light flashing again even brighter than before. Resolving to toughen up in the name of science she headed towards where she thought the light was coming from. Luckily the ground was even under her feet so she didn't have to worry about tripping over anything. Unluckily she was growing convinced that no matter how far she walked she got no closer to the source of the light. The intermittent flashes had continued to grow in intensity each time. The last one was nearly blinding but she was no closer to discovering their cause. She looked behind her and in the far distance she could make out the shack. By her calculations she had walked a great distance already so might as well keep going. She was so lost in her own thoughts that she failed to notice that she was no longer cold.

Much, much later, tired and thoroughly fed up, Yani was starting to wonder what had happened to the sunrise.

"Surely it must be morning by now," she muttered darkly to herself.

The last few light flashes had been brighter than any sunrise but when they faded they left the same darkness behind. The sky lit up again but this time it was different. The light seemed to come from below her this time. She stopped, shielding her eyes from the now almost burning light. When it passed she dropped to her knees and began tapping the ground. She wasn't surprised to find that it was solid rock but continued tapping in a circular pattern until eventually she felt something cold and metallic underneath her hooves. Frantically she began clearing the top level of dirt and uncovered... a large metal disk on which a rectangular pane of glass had been embedded.

"What in the..." Yani exclaimed, her voice cut off by a flash of light coming from below the glass rectangle.

Without the dirt covering the light nearly blinded her. She reeled backwards, stars exploding in front of her eyes. Utterly despondent by now she began to cry.

"Why are you crying?" a soft voice asked from nowhere.

Yani raised her head slowly. Everything around her was still fuzzy and lights still flickered in her peripheral vision. She could make out a blurry red shape somewhere to her left but couldn't see what it was.

"Why are you crying?" the red blur asked again.

If it was impatient or annoyed at her lack of response it made no show of it.

With what she thought was great dignity she replied, "I am crying because I have just dragged myself through this expanse of nothingness chasing a light which now serves no purpose other than to blind travellers too stupid to leave it alone."

She attempted to stand but was still very dizzy so collapsed to the ground again and resolved to just stay there.

"Hmm," the red blur said again. "You are crying because you found a light?"

It wasn't mocking her but she rounded on it anyway.

"Well, yes," she shouted, feeling very stupid and more than a little annoyed. A thought occurred to her. "Is this your light?" she asked.

The red blur made what she perceived to be a shrugging motion.

"My light?" he asked eventually. "No, it's not my light."

Yani sighed. Bad enough she was tired, exhausted and half blind, now she was in conversation with a simpleton. Why could she never meet anyone helpful?

"I built it of course," the blur said evenly. "Covered it with dirt and made sure it works but it's not mine."

"Whose. Is. It. Then?" Yani said with what she thought was remarkable restraint.

"Why?" the red blur replied with maddening calm.

"Because…" Yani said, "I want to…" Her voice trailed off. She knew that she wanted to find the source of the light but up until now she realised that she had no idea what she would do when she found it. "Because…" she began again, "I want to know what it is for."

"Ahhh," the blur replied, seemingly satisfied with this response. "It makes the darkness brighter," he said eventually. "What else would a light be for?"

Yani felt her head starting to swim. She was unsure whether it was from the light flashes or this maddening conversation but she did notice that it wasn't dark anymore and that whilst the light was no longer flashing, it remained on. (*A mystery for another time*, she thought, filing it to the back of her mind for now.)

"Then why," she said, realising that she had a question to stump him, "has it not been on at night until now?"

"Oh…" the shape said, clearly embarrassed, "I didn't know anyone was here except the lizards." There was a pause which it clearly felt needed to be filled. "Sorry about that. Hope you haven't been waiting long."

"Waiting?" Yani asked, feeling her moment of superiority slipping away.

"Well, you must be here to see me. I hope I haven't kept you waiting long?"

"Who are you?" Yani asked, realising that she must be talking to someone very important.

"Me?" the voice asked evenly. "I'm nobody."

Yani felt that one of them wasn't making any sense and she wondered briefly if it was her.

"Then why would I want to see you?" she asked.

"I don't know," the shape countered, "but you can't be here to see the lizards... Or perhaps you are," he added after a pause.

"We're looking for something," Yani said.

"Ah," the blur replied happily, "I haven't seen it."

"Haven't seen what?" Yani queried.

"Whatever you lost," he replied. "All lost things find their way here eventually," he sighed wistfully. "Let me show you," he said, suddenly brighter.

Yani heard him snap his fingers and felt very dizzy.

When the feeling of the world spinning around subsided, Yani was happy to discover that she had recovered much of her sight. There were spots still blooming at the corner of her eyes, however. She looked around, surprised to find herself indoors. Yani couldn't know where she was but wherever it was it was luxurious, even more so than Castle Mowser. Yani could feel a lush carpet under her hooves which was so deep she could feel herself sinking upto her ankles where they felt cushioned as if she were wearing expensive shoes. There were no windows but elaborate portraits showing beautiful landscapes hung from the walls. Yani couldn't trust her eyes fully yet but she was sure that the figures in the paintings were moving.

"We have arrived," a familiar voice said unnecessarily from behind her.

Yani turned as quickly as her sunken hooves would allow. Behind her stood a young-looking fox. He was dressed from head to paw in red and gold silk, from the ornate night cap that was perched on his head to the dressing gown he wore tightly wrapped around him, all the way down to his burgundy slippers. In his right paw he held a pipe which looked like it had been carved from the finest mahogany. Golden smoke flowed from the bowl despite it not being in the fox's mouth. Again she couldn't be sure but it looked like the smoke was forming itself into various shapes. She thought she saw a sailing galleon, then a castle, and finally the ginormous head of a Pacidermian scowling down at her. Reflexively she backed away from the image but it vanished as if it had never been there.

The fox grinned. Putting the pipe to his lips he inhaled and sighed.

"Felix," he said after taking his fill. Yani gaped at him open-mouthed. "My name," he said eventually, "is Felix."

"Y… Yani," she stammered in reply.

"I know," he replied in the same maddeningly calm voice he used outside.

"How do you know?" Yani asked, not bothering to keep the bewilderment out of her voice.

"I told you," he said, cocking his head to one side. "All lost things find their way here eventually."

Yani felt a cold chill run up her long neck.

"I'm not lost," she said eventually but privately she wondered if perhaps she was. Her husband dead, hated by her own kind, and no closer to finding the Collar of Honour.

As if reading her mind Felix nodded at her.

"Follow me," he instructed.

Felix popped the pipe back into his mouth and in a flurry of red and gold he turned around and headed off towards a small door set into the wall. As he approached it he lazily waved his hands and the door swung open soundlessly. Yani had to duck to fit under the door and found herself wedged inside a corridor. Felix had dropped to all fours and was scampering into the distance. Yani attempted to turn herself so that her stomach was on the floor and she could crawl along using her back legs to propel herself along. It didn't go well.

"Nurrggh," she grunted in pain as she kicked herself in her own head.

"Oh, sorry," Felix called out over his shoulder without looking back.

She didn't have a good vantage point from between her legs but she did see Felix flick both paws outwards. Immediately the walls began to move away and (not without a good deal of pain) she was able to unfold herself. Despite the corridor being wider she couldn't stand up but she could at least crawl after the retreating fox.

"How did you do that?" she asked when she had got close enough to him to be heard.

"I waved my hands," he said evenly. "Didn't you see me do it?"

Yani sighed. At the end of the corridor was another door. This one at least was tall enough for Yani to crawl through comfortably. What she didn't expect was for the room on the other side to be far lower than the door and she fell with a distinct lack of dignity onto another carpeted floor.

"When I made the corridor larger it changed the dimensions of the other rooms," a calm voice said from above her.

Yani groaned into the carpet.

"And I thought you were smart," said the familiar mocking voice of Number One from across the room.

Deep into the carpet Yani's groan became louder.

"Oh, you know each other," Felix said delightedly. "This will go so much smoother. Let us eat," he exclaimed, rubbing his paws together.

## CHAPTER EIGHTEEN

# REUNIONS

"WAKEY-WAKEY," A SINISTER-SOUNDING voice cooed into his ginormous ear. Lex felt his eyes flick open suddenly but when he tried to move he found to his horror that he couldn't. He struggled to raise his arms but they were pinned to his sides. He couldn't even trumpet in frustration, as when he tried he found that even his trunk had been tied down. He didn't let this stop him from trying, however. He shook and tried to throw himself around but eventually he stopped, panting with exhaustion, staring upwards. All at once he felt himself falling forwards. Instinctively he tried to put his hands out in front of him which just provoked joyless laughter from above him. When the expected fall didn't happen, Lex realised that he was tied to a table and that it was being lifted so that he was in a standing position. From his new vantage point he could see that he was back in the ruined hall of Castle Mowser, which could only mean…

"Welcome back." The ruined, grinning face of King Hirax filled his vision.

"King Hirax?" Lex questioned softly.

Hirax's face twitched in annoyance.

"An understandable mistake but not one you will be allowed to make twice."

Lex squinted slightly. Despite the blood and cuts it was definitely Hirax's face but there was something different about the voice. The face looked impatient.

"Come on!" it said testily. "Even you should be able to put this together."

Lex desperately thought back to the events at the jubilee. What was it Hirax had called the largest ghost? Suddenly he remembered, it had been "*Grandfather*".

"Faustus!" Lex exclaimed in wonder.

"You left so quickly that you missed my recrowning."

Faustus laughed at his own joke.

As he did Lex could see that the new King's face kept twitching violently and at times it looked as though Faustus had two heads – one cruel and mocking, the other screaming in pain.

"What do you want?" Lex asked eventually.

He tried to speak confidently but was more scared than he had ever been. Faustus grinned slowly and for a second he only had the one head, its mouth split into an ugly grin.

"Want? To talk of course."

As Faustus continued to grin the second head once again split off from its host and Lex could swear that tears were streaming down its insubstantial cheeks. Lex instinctively tried to back away but was too tightly tied down.

"I've been away for a while," Faustus said casually, walking around the bound Pacidermian. "Things have changed," he continued, one face smiling horribly, the other silently screaming. Faustus noticed Lex's eyes flicking between the two faces.

"Do excuse my grandson," Faustus sighed. "HE STILL HASN'T LEARNT HIS PLACE!" he screamed in a voice so high-pitched that Lex found himself wincing in pain.

The scream seemed to have the desired effect, however, as when Lex reopened his eyes he found that his captor only had the one face.

"Better," Faustus muttered hoarsely.

He seemed to forget about Lex as he distractedly rubbed his throat with his paw.

"Water," he croaked.

Within seconds a ghost floated up with a goblet held out to him. Lex felt a cold dread in his stomach as he noticed the ghost, remembering the massacre in the Pescar village. Faustus noisily slurped from the goblet and threw it casually back at the ghost. The ghost plucked it out of the air and disappeared with it.

"It's funny the feelings you forget," Faustus said, turning his attention back to Lex. "I haven't been thirsty in so long. I almost missed it." He chuckled darkly to himself. "Did you like the goblet?" he asked suddenly. "I noticed you staring at it." Lex went to shake his head but of course this was an impossible manoeuvre. "It's okay," Faustus cooed. "It's okay to like nice things. My grandson..." as he said the word grandson his voice took on an angry growl, "locked the goblets away, like he was ashamed of them." He shook his head. "I ask you, is that the actions of a king?" Without waiting for an answer he pressed on. "Does locking away a few trinkets make life any fairer?" He flinched suddenly as if distracted by something. "I TOLD YOU BEFORE!"

he boomed as if at some sort of adversary but Lex could swear they were the only two beings there. "WE ARE NOT AS OTHERS! WE RULE OVER THEM! WE ARE SUPERIOR, WE DESERVE EVERYTHING!" He tilted his head as if awaiting a response.

Lex cleared his throat and muttered non-committedly. Faustus looked at him.

"You understand, don't you, Pacidermian?"

"Err, it's Lex. Your Majesty," he added quickly.

"Lex," Faustus said softly, clearly mollified by the respect shown him. "My agents inform me that you had the largest dwelling in that little village."

Lex wanted to rage, he wanted to scream "MURDERER" at Faustus but he was too scared to do much more than gape.

"Dreadful business really," Faustus added to fill the silence. "Not great fighters the Pescarians but..." and at this he chuckled, "persistent."

Lex tried to fight it but a tear ran down his massive cheek. Faustus gently ran a claw down his cheek, following the track of the tear as it dropped noiselessly onto the table underneath Lex.

"A tear?" Faustus whispered in wonder. "But you are a general, are you not?" Faustus barked the word "general" and Lex was reminded of his own basic training.

"Those freaks attacked my forces," Faustus hissed, "but for a moment you were brave. It's a nice feeling, isn't it?" he asked conspiratorially. "Sending your forces in, watching as beings die just because you said so." Lex struggled again but it was half-hearted. Faustus moved so that his mouth was next to Lex's ear. "It's okay," he cooed, syrup dripping with each syllable, "I know you, Lex." Lex's eyes widened in terror. "Oh, don't get big-headed," Faustus snapped. "I don't know YOU specifically!" He broke off to laugh in his ear. "Why would I even care? No, I know your type."

Faustus rose and Lex couldn't see or hear anything for a while. Eventually he felt a soft thump as something landed on his chest.

"I have had a look around my castle." Faustus' voice was coming from the other side of the room. "YES! MY CASTLE!" he yelled suddenly. "And I found the invites to my grandson's jubilee. A celebration which in the circumstances would have been more appropriate as a wake…" he broke off again, "BECAUSE YOU OVERSAW THE DEATH OF US AS A RULING DYNASTY!" he boomed suddenly. "As I was saying," he continued with only a slight edge of annoyance in his voice, "I found invites to those flea carriages pretending to be knights. I found an invite to our warden in Aridier. Funny," he said thoughtfully, "I thought we'd appointed a male to the role not a girl spell-chucker, still…" he paused, lost in thought, "we might have a use for her but that's for another day. I found an invite to your old friends the Long Necks." At this he paused and made sure that he could see Lex's face again.

"Such hatred in those eyes," he said with satisfaction. "I even found an invite to those woodland pickpockets. What dreadful company my grandson kept. If it wasn't for the mess you made during your…" he paused, grinning at Lex, "tactical withdrawal through one of my walls I'd have this place scrubbed just to get rid of the stench of those lesser creatures. However, I also found an invite to the Pacidermian High Command and *that* is not *you*. Naughty naughty!" he scolded in mocking tones. "Let me tell you who you are," Faustus said, staring deeply into Lex's unblinking eyes. "Stop me if I'm incorrect. You're big, even for a Pacidermian and that is not muscle," he said, poking Lex's side. "So you're not involved in the fighting. Sooooo…" he exclaimed, drawing out the final syllable, "office staff, I would imagine. You saw the invite and decided this was your big chance. Very brave, or was it?"

Faustus made a big show of thinking about this.

"Nope," he decided eventually. "Bitter, I would guess. Your eyes are bloodshot and even tied down I notice a tremble in your arm. You have a weakness for tree bark gin, a ghastly concoction, but you don't rank highly enough for the sap brandy you crave." Despite himself Lex felt his mouth begin to water at the thought of that forbidden elixir. Faustus chuckled again. "So we have a fat old boozy desk warrior who wanted to pass himself off as a soldier."

Lex thought about struggling again but what would be the point? He felt his shoulders slump in despair but still Faustus continued.

"A failure who ran at the first sign of trouble. If that wasn't enough you took a village of peaceful freaks and tried to make them soldiers!"

Faustus had moved in even closer as he spoke. Now he was so close Lex could see every crease in his face.

"Tell me," Faustus spat at Lex, "how does it feel to be responsible for so many deaths? Does it feel good? Do you feel like the leader you always thought you were?"

Lex desperately wanted to look away but Faustus was so close he filled his field of vision completely. What Faustus said next surprised Lex.

"Feels good, doesn't it?" he asked simply. "To hold so many inferior lives in your hand, to know that you can snuff them out with a simple command. You see, it almost doesn't matter if you win or lose, it's the feeling of utter power." With this he stared at Lex, maintaining uncomfortable eye contact. "I can make it so that you have that feeling forever, would you like that?"

It was all Lex could do to nod.

Faustus grinned and began untying Lex from the table. It was so unexpected that Lex fell to the floor. He struggled back to his feet and dusted himself off. His uniform was torn and soaked in a green mucus. He scraped most of it off and held it under his trunk. In revulsion he smelt a fishy odour and realised he was splattered in the remains of his Pescarian army.

"No matter," Faustus said cheerfully, "you'll need a new uniform in any case, follow me."

He turned and headed towards the throne room door. As he walked Lex noted that there were far more ghosts than he had thought. They were everywhere. Some were repairing the hole in the wall (which Lex still felt ashamed of every time he thought of it), others were removing portraits of old rulers and carrying them outside where other ghosts had built a huge bonfire in the courtyard. One by one they threw the portraits onto it, causing flames to burn brighter and a smoke column to reach ever higher into the air.

"Out with the new and back in with the old," Faustus said, joining Lex who was staring at the pyre from an arched window.

"Aren't they your family?" Lex asked him.

"They were traitors," Faustus said bitterly. "SILENCE!" he yelled over his shoulder.

Lex dearly wanted to ask Faustus who he was continually shouting at but he realised that the King's moods were changeable and while he was on his good side he didn't want to risk it, especially as he had been promised power. Now he'd show his own people what they had missed out on and as for the Giraxians? His name would be whispered in fear and reverence by whatever remained of them gathered to hide.

Faustus was staring at him, clearly waiting for a reply.

"Yes, Your Majesty, traitors."

Faustus nodded at this.

"Trust nobody," he intoned. "Remember that," and with that he continued walking.

Lex trailed behind him. They passed by many rooms which all looked the same to Lex. Suddenly Faustus held up a paw and they stopped walking. Silently Faustus turned towards a closed door and pushed it open, beckoning Lex to follow him. It was a bit of squeeze but Lex managed to get his enormous frame through the opening into a massive room, which to his surprise was almost completely empty. The only furniture it possessed was a long wooden table. On the centre of the table was a glass bottle which had been chained to it. The bottle had a wide base which led up into a wide neck. The neck was blocked by a glass stopper in the shape of a sailing barge. Lex had never been on a sailing barge, his weight would surely sink such a delicate vessel, but he used to watch enviously as the Giraxian slaves would load ivory onto vessels like that and sail off to make deliveries. The bottle was full of what at first glance appeared to be a swirling green liquid but at closer inspection turned out to be green smoke.

"Good evening," Faustus said gravely and for a moment Lex thought he was being addressed. He went to answer but before he could open his mouth the green smoke stopped its slow swirl in the bottle and an ancient and sad face of a Rodentian started to take shape.

"Sire," the face said.

It sounded tired and in pain and it was then that Lex realised he had met this Rodentian before.

"The butler?" he said in wonder.

"You've met then?" Faustus asked, surprised for the first time.

"He greeted me when I arrived for the jubilee," Lex explained. He leaned towards the bottle. "Not quite so pompous now are you, Mr Butler?"

"Brabbinger," the face replied.

"What?" Lex responded, stunned.

"My name is Brabbinger. I'm afraid I can't show you to your room right now."

Lex looked from Brabbinger's floating form to Faustus who had begun twitching again. The second face had reappeared but was more solid this time, once again creating the appearance that Faustus had two heads on one body. Now that it was clearer Lex could see that it was the face of Hirax as he remembered him – no cuts or wounds but clearly in some sort of pain. Lex took advantage of Faustus' distracted state to look closely at him. Clearly Faustus had somehow taken over the body of Hirax and somehow Hirax – being a practical sort Lex struggled with terms like "spirit" but what else could he call it? – was trying (and failing) to reassert control. Lex obviously had a choice. Did he stick with Faustus? Or try to help

Hirax? Lex did what he did whenever faced with difficult decisions. He did nothing.

"ENOUGH!" Faustus cried out, slamming his paws down upon the table.

As the bottle was securely chained down it didn't move but Brabbinger's face did slowly turn to face the raging King.

"Be strong, my young King," he said simply.

"NOOOOOOOOOOOOOOOOOOOOOOOO!" screamed Faustus, so loudly that Lex had to cover his ears. "You don't speak to him! I'm the King! I will always be the King! That young wimp isn't worthy of this frame, he gave it up so easily."

"Be strong," Brabbinger said again.

Faustus went to hit the bottle but pulled his fist back at the last moment. He went to shout at the remains of Brabbinger but instead looked up sharply towards Lex who was awkwardly standing across from him.

"This is what I was talking about," he said quietly. "Traitors are everywhere." Pointing at Brabbinger he carried on. "Even this! 'The Royal Butler'." He used his claws to mime the quotation marks in Royal Butler. "Sworn to serve the rightful ruler, WHICH IS ME!" he roared at the bottle. "And if you remembered this you could be free to stand at my side."

Brabbinger's face didn't even flicker.

"Be strong," he said once again.

Lex looked at Faustus, fully expecting another explosion. Instead Faustus stuck his paws into the pockets of his flowing gown and went to leave the room.

"Lex!" he called as he left.

Lex paused for a second to look back at the table. He found Brabbinger regarding him with an impassive expression. Lex wanted to look away but he couldn't draw his eyes away and ended up backing out of the room, banging his head on the door frame as he left. Lex had to trot slightly to catch up with Faustus. They walked in silence for a while, passing ghosts who were enlarging doorways to accommodate Lex. If they expected his thanks they would be disappointed.

"His father was butler before him," Faustus said suddenly. "Shame I couldn't find his ghost, he'd be loyal."

He stopped and stared at Lex. After an uncomfortable moment, Lex realised Faustus expected some sort of response.

"Where… where could it be?" he stammered.

Faustus sighed.

"Tell me, Lex, where do you think we go when we die?"

"Go, Your Majesty?"

Lex was stunned by the question, he had never really thought too much about his own death, he mostly thought about the death of Giraxians who as a slave class wouldn't go anywhere.

Faustus was staring at him now and Lex could feel his impatience grow. Desperately Lex thought back to the church services his mother used to take him to. He was never that interested in what the priest was saying but he loved watching the lights coming through the stained-glass windows. Faustus let out a sigh and Lex knew that he had better come up with something quickly. Then it came to him, a memory of the ancient priest pointing directly at him.

"The Long Plains," he spluttered out.

Faustus raised an eyebrow.

"And what are they?" he enquired.

Lex was struggling now. Desperately he racked his memory.

"The Long Plains," he repeated, playing for time, "are plains that…"

"Are long?" Faustus completed sarcastically.

"Well, yes," Lex replied, "but we are reunited with our loved ones."

"And where does the long plain lead to?" Faustus asked.

"I don't know," Lex admitted, lowering his head in shame.

"Oh, that doesn't matter," Faustus said cheerfully.

"It doesn't?" said Lex hopefully.

"No, no, no," Faustus cooed cheerfully.

Lex felt such relief. He knew he'd be safe now.

"Because that's a load of childish rubbish," Faustus snapped back, any trace of his former warmth now gone. "Let me tell you what death is really like," he added sinisterly.

## Faustus' Tale

At first Faustus thought he was underwater. Everything was black and he could feel pressure from all sides. A muffled sound came from above him. Suddenly a bright light assaulted his vision. After a while his vision cleared and he was staring at a canvas sky.

"Oh, Father, what have you done?"

Faustus recognised his son's voice but when he tried to turn towards it he found that he was unable to move.

"What is happening?" he growled weakly, grateful that he could still speak but angry that his voice was so reedy.

"Sit him up," Tyrell instructed and Faustus felt strong paws underneath him lifting him into a seated position.

He was furious to be manhandled in this way and insulted, snarled and spat at anyone he could see. He knew that he could do nothing but he was angry. Why was he still here? Had the Collar betrayed him?

"How dare you touch your King?" he spat. "I'll have your paws cut off for this insolence." Tyrell nodded and Faustus heard the staff leaving the room. "I haven't dismissed you!" he rasped after them.

He was then struck with a coughing fit. He was surprised when he found that he was coughing up blood.

Tyrell moved in closer and wiped his father's mouth with a silk handkerchief.

"No, you won't, Father." Faustus scowled at Tyrell in confusion. "Cut their paws off, I mean," Tyrell explained. "I am the King."

Faustus wheezed, "No."

Tyrell said firmly, "We looked through the remains of your laboratory…" Tyrell cut off, unable to finish, haunted by the horrors he had seen. "You are no longer King. For the sake of the kingdom we have decided that you won't face judgment for what you did. As far as we can tell none of your creatures exist anymore so everybody's safe…"

Faustus interrupted him at this point.

"Who are 'we', boy? Can't you make these decisions for yourself?"

Tyrell shook his head.

"Brabbinger," he said eventually.

Faustus was so horrified that he coughed up more blood and bile.

"The butler?" he questioned in anger and disbelief. "You are taking advice from the servants?"

Tyrell shook his head again.

"I'm taking advice from Brabbinger, he has been more of a father to me than you ever were." Faustus snorted in derision. "It was him who persuaded me not to throw you in the dungeons. You will stay here in comfort until you die but you are no longer King."

"What about your boy?" Faustus asked, not bothering to disguise the disgust in his voice.

"Hirax?" Tyrell asked, confused. "He'll inherit the throne from me as always. Why do you ask? You've never liked him. Are you hoping to see him before you die?"

Tyrell felt a small surge of hope. Perhaps if Faustus developed a bond with his grandson he could find out exactly what he had been doing.

"Yes," Faustus replied, "I would like him to see me, give the little wimp nightmares!"

He started laughing but was cut short by another coughing fit.

Tyrell went to the door.

"Get some sleep," he said. "I'll come back and see you again soon."

Faustus was alone and as he drifted off to sleep he wondered why he had been spared when all of his disciples had been taken, and if there was any way he could start again.

As sunlight streamed through a gap in the room's curtains Faustus woke from a dreamless sleep to find Tyrell placing a tray in front of him. His breakfast consisted of a single egg and some buttered bread. He looked up into the face of his son and sneered.

"So, this is the duty of a king?" he sneered. "Serving a broken-down old mouse! What's next? Can I expect a royal bed bath?"

Tyrell ignored his jibes.

"What were you doing in that laboratory?" he asked simply.

"I told you," Faustus said, tapping his egg on the table. When he had cracked the shell to his satisfaction he began peeling it with a long claw. "I was improving upon my citizens, making them more appropriate for their glorious purpose."

"What purpose?" Tyrell asked in horrified bewilderment.

"What other purpose could be more glorious than serving me?" Faustus asked casually, as if this was the most natural thing in the world. He bit into the egg and chewed slowly.

"You butchered them," Tyrell said aghast.

To this accusation Faustus pushed the remains of the egg around his dry mouth and swallowed painfully.

"Water," he choked.

Tyrell blinked in surprise but quickly moved to the bedside table and poured water from the glass flask thereon. Passing the water to Faustus he noticed that the pillow slips were covered in flecks of blood. Clearly his father didn't have long left.

Faustus sipped at the cold water, which soothed his parched throat.

"It must have been that academy," he said after finishing the water.

"What must have been the academy?" Tyrell asked, growing annoyed that his father showed no guilt or remorse over his actions.

"The reason you are so soft." Faustus thought for a second. "I suppose the boy is already signed up? I'm sure he'll blend in well."

"FATHER!" Tyrell shouted. He wanted to shout some more, so great was his anger, but he was silenced by the sinister grin on Faustus' face.

"As King," Faustus said, "you must make use of all of your resources."

"Does that include magic?" Tyrell asked.

Faustus waved a dismissive paw.

"The Collar of Honour is a tool like any other. Besides which, it didn't work as I'm still here."

Tyrell scratched his chin thoughtfully.

"Perhaps not," he said thoughtfully. "You did wish to survive."

As he spoke Tyrell couldn't believe what he was saying. A magic collar that granted wishes! It sounded so absurd, but he knew there were magical beings in Venary so perhaps it wasn't totally ridiculous.

"Not for much longer though, I'm sure," Faustus said, suddenly very tired.

Tyrell decided that sympathy wouldn't be appreciated or for that matter deserved so he ignored that.

"We searched through your laboratory," he said eventually, feeling his insides go cold as he remembered the various horrors they discovered. "There was no sign of the Collar. Could it have been destroyed?" he asked hopefully.

"No," croaked Faustus, struggling to remain awake.

"Disappears when wish made… could be… could be anywhere," and with that he fell asleep.

Time passed. He couldn't tell how long as he would alternately fall asleep and then be up for what felt like cycles as painful coughing fits attacked his body. Tyrell would visit him once more. Faustus knew it was the end. He'd had a terrible night. His entire body felt like it was on fire and his sight was failing. He sent for Tyrell and Hirax. He claimed that he didn't know why he requested them but in reality, he didn't want to die alone. It hadn't gone well. The second he saw Hirax trying to hide between the traitor Brabbinger's legs he exploded in rage.

"Well, here they are," he croaked, "the heir and the spare."

Ever the peacekeeper Tyrell tried to silence him and this angered him further. He screamed as loudly as his ruined throat would allow, raging about the Collar, his heart's desire and the various betrayals he felt. Eventually the traitor and the child retreated. Red-eyed and in agony he looked up at Tyrell who was leaning over him.

"You are a hateful old rat and you deserve this, and because I left it too late to stop you I deserve my fate. When the kingdom is settled I will leave on an errand to find the Collar of Honour. It's the only way to undo the horrible things you did!"

Faustus stared up at him, furious that everything he had tried to do could be undone. He tried to shout again but all he could was croak. That was the last thing he did as the exertion had been too much for him and he died in the same way he had lived, in furious rage.!

Mauve, that was what he saw, mauve in every direction he looked. He expected that the colour would fade in certain areas but it remained the exact same shade of dark mauve as far as he could see, which to his surprise was a lot further than he could see before. He looked down at his paws. He wasn't sure what he expected to see but the fact that they were glowing green and slightly see-through seemed oddly fitting.

"HELLO!" he called into the mauve, delighted to find that he no longer rasped but spoke as loudly and clearly as he had in his youth.

He was mildly annoyed that there was nobody there to shout at. Suddenly in the far distance he spotted it. It was so faint that, at first, he wasn't sure that he had seen anything at all but it was definitely there, on the horizon a green glow that he hoped meant that there were others.

With nothing else to do he started walking towards it. As he stepped off, the mauve underneath him started to shake as a black path came into view under his feet, stretching all the way into the distance. He had a sudden thought: if his voice was strong again perhaps… He started to run. It was easy. He found that he could run faster and further for longer than he could remember running. As a pup he would run on all fours when he wanted to run faster. His parents considered it unseemly for one of his stature to run at all, never mind on all fours, and he been on the receiving end of many a clipped ear. Now here alone he thought, *To hell with it*, and dropped to the ground. He was right, he could run even faster. He hadn't felt such joy in so long. He had enjoyed his work, his glorious purpose, but this was freedom and for a while he was tempted to just spend eternity running, but then he saw him. Standing in the path in front of him, glowing green like he was and larger than he had ever been in life.

"Brockstein?" he said in bewilderment.

"You were expecting somebody else, Your Majesty?" the badger replied.

"Where are we?" he asked uncertainly.

"You know exactly where you are, Your Majesty," Brockstein said evenly. "Your followers have been waiting for you."

With this he bowed deeply and with an outstretched paw directed him towards a gathering of green shapes. As he got nearer he could decipher many different beings, all of whom turned as he approached. There were rows and rows of them, mostly Rodentians, but dotted here and there were cats, crows, squirrels and many more. When he reached the front row, every creature snapped to attention and as one called out, "Awaiting orders, Your Majesty."

He grinned, perhaps the Collar hadn't betrayed him after all.

* * *

"Where were you?" Lex asked, equally amazed and horrified at the same time.

"The afterlife, of course," Faustus replied.

Lex gaped at him.

"B... But the Long Plains," he stammered.

"CHILDISH RUBBISH LIKE I ALREADY SAID!" Faustus screamed, his head shaking again. Clearly Hirax was trying break through once more, seemingly with more success this time as his face was the more solid while Faustus' had turned almost transparent, its mouth still silently screaming in rage.

Hirax looked at Lex as if seeing him for the first time.

"Run," he said simply. "I don't know what my grandfather has planned for you but don't be fooled, he… he… he…"

Hirax broke off his conversation with an agonised scream. For a moment both faces were solid and their screams blended together. Their faces turned towards each other and a look of disgust crossed Faustus' while a look of fear crossed Hirax's. For a moment Lex thought both personalities would exist. He wasn't sure he wanted to be around to see that! Panic started to overwhelm him and he just wanted to get away but before he could make his exit the two-headed Faustus-Hirax being threw itself into his path and was thrashing around violently. Lex, by now almost blinded by panic, let out an involuntary trumpet from his massive trunk. It was LOUD, even Lex was surprised. It echoed through the halls, and what birds had settled in the courtyard outside flew away in droves. Even some of the ghosts looked up from their dedicated tasks. Lex continued trumpeting. Beads of sweat stood out on his forehead and his skin had turned pale in terror. He remained rooted to the spot until a voice called out, "STOP!" Lex didn't know if it was the commanding voice that made him stop or if he was simply out of breath but stop he did.

"That is better," the voice said, and it sounded oddly familiar to Lex. "We haven't got much time," the voice continued, and Lex realised that it was coming from behind him. He turned to see who was talking to him. "We haven't got much time," the voice repeated. "Pick up His Majesty and follow me."

As if in a dream Lex scooped up the struggling figure at his feet. He didn't want to look at it but couldn't prevent his eyes from travelling downwards. He was so shocked that he nearly dropped the squirming figure. It was a horrifying sight, arms and legs splayed in all directions. They would switch between being solid and see-through and looked like they were attacking each other. The faces were screaming in a mixture of pain and rage which would increase when one face got a clearer view of the other. Lex hadn't noticed that Faustus didn't have the green glow of his followers but now his body was glowing so brightly that Lex feared he might start running hot at any minute. Summoning up what was left of his courage he turned and found himself looking into the face of Brabbinger.

"Come with me," the butler instructed.

"H… How?" Lex said, although Brabbinger's tone must have got through to him as he found himself following him back along the corridor.

"I cannot sit around in a bottle while my king needs me," he said briskly.

"But you were trapped," Lex said eventually.

"Really?" Brabbinger said imperiously. "And who told you that? Faustus brought that bottle back from wherever he has spent the last few spans."

"He said it was the afterlife," Lex cut in.

"Hmm, King Faustus was always prone to the dramatics, something I'm relieved to say wasn't inherited by his offspring."

"Then where?" Lex cut in again.

"I'm sure I don't know, sir," Brabbinger answered in that tone which so infuriated Lex.

"Will you explain what is going on?" Lex asked, slightly panicked by the increased thrashing in his arms.

Brabbinger continued floating ahead of him but Lex was sure he heard a "tut" of annoyance.

"You are holding the rightful King of Venary in your sizeable arms. He is currently possessed by the ghost of his grandfather. I'm dead but still can't get any peace and there is an army of ghosts outside. If there is anything else, sir, I'm afraid it will have to wait."

With that Brabbinger turned into a side room. Once again Lex found himself having to squeeze into a room which, while large, wasn't built with him in mind.

"Put him on the bed if you would, sir," Brabbinger requested, grateful for the chance to offload his increasingly erratic cargo.

Lex lowered it onto the bed. It had been a handful but he hadn't noticed any real weight. He thought it had been down to him being a strong Pacidermian but as he placed the King onto his bed he noticed that he made no impact on the sheets, which still looked as smooth as they had when they first entered the room. There wasn't even a dent in the duvet where the King lay. Brabbinger noticed this and for the first time Lex noticed a flicker of panic across his normally superior face.

"What's happening?" he asked as Brabbinger floated over to the head of the bed.

Brabbinger didn't even look his way, preferring to stare stony-faced at the thrashing body on the bed.

"Something awful," was all he could say.

## CHAPTER NINETEEN

# SAVIOUR

HAPPINESS IS A *strange thing*, Greeta thought to herself. When she joined the Thieves' Guild she told them that possessions made her happy but that was a lie. What she really wanted was companionship. She had been the youngest of a litter of five. Her parents had tried for spans to produce a litter with no success, so when her mother finally went into labour it was greeted with a huge celebration throughout the hedgerow. Her four brothers had been delivered with no issues but she came in breach. The nurses did what they could and for a while it looked like she and her mother wouldn't make it. After much screaming she was finally delivered to rapturous applause. Applause which turned to screams of horror as the roof started to cave in. Panic spread throughout the assembled hedgehogs as dirt rained down upon them. Hedgehogs were climbing over each other in an attempt to get away, smaller hedgehogs found themselves being trampled underfoot.

This was nothing compared to what happened next. Suddenly the reason for the cave-in became horrifyingly clear as many sharp claws reached through the earth and began blindly and wildly thrashing about, scooping up and slashing any hedgehog unlucky enough to be within their terrible grasp. Even rolling up into spiky balls didn't help, as it made it easier for the claws to scoop them up. Greeta's father positioned himself in front of his partner and children when the last of the roof gave way and moonlight flooded into the ruination of what was once his home. His vision was suddenly filled with the horrible flat face of an owl, its beak open as it screeched in victory.

It would be the last thing he would ever see.

By early morning the parliament of owls had totally devastated the hedgerows. They had been very thorough. Piles of bloodstained earth were dotted in lines showing that the owls knew where the hedgehogs had been.

"This isn't random," Hestor said to her followers. "They knew where our people were."

A larger hedgehog snorted loudly.

"They should have moved in with the guild the second they joined. This is their own fault."

His head snapped back violently as Hestor quickly drove her fist under his chin with such force that he momentarily left the ground.

Without wasting any more time on him she turned back to the devastation where, to her surprise, she discovered Greeta sleeping peacefully underneath the bodies of her family. Hestor didn't know why she took Greeta back with her. She had never wanted children and certainly had no desire to groom her own replacement, but as she held the now waking newborn in her claws she knew that she was taking her home. Especially after she noticed Greeta's sneaking claws dip into her inside pocket and close around the sovereign Hestor kept there for luck.

*She's one of us*, Hestor thought to herself as she turned away from the devastation that surrounded her.

Greeta had never admitted to anyone, not even herself, but she had never been happy there. She was a dreadful thief and had never really got on with anyone in the guild. However, here with the moles things were different. She had traded in her skin-tight thieves' outfit for a simple yet roughly hewn smock and trousers. Her cycles were spent tilling the fields which produced the vegetables which made up their bland but sufficient meals. Her nights were spent in bed with the High Priestess and now she realised exactly what she needed to be really happy.

It was late night. Greeta didn't know what the time was as the order felt that categorising time was "a foolish conceit". There were only three epochs of time: "The Time Before He Who Hops", "The Time of He Who Hops" and "The Time After He Who Hops", also known as "The Dark Times" or "The Time of Great Patience: He is Coming Back, Honestly, No I Can't Give You an Exact Time But Trust Me On This". It was a still night with only a slight breeze coming through the bedroom's large windows. Sleepily she reached out for the High Priestess but her claw found only bed sheets. They were cold. She had been in bed alone for a while. This realisation brought her fully awake. Sitting up suddenly Greeta turned so that she sat on the edge of the mattress and prepped herself for the drop to the floor. To Greeta's mind the High Priestess was perfect in every way but she did insist that their bed was elevated from the ground so that she "was closer to the heavens". Every night they would be lifted to the bed by her followers who would create a mole pyramid for them to climb up every night and then recreate the pyramid each morning to lower them back down. This was all very well and Greeta did enjoy being served in such splendour but in situations like this when she wanted to get out of bed she had to drop to the floor. Part of her training in the guild had involved being pushed out of trees and learning to roll up into a ball before hitting the ground. The first time she had done it she was so frozen with fear that she fell all the way to the ground without rolling up. She hit the ground with a solid thump, knocking all of the air out of her lungs and badly spraining her wrist. She had got better at it but still felt the pang of fear as she fell through the air and her wrist still throbbed on very cold cycles.

Taking a deep breath, she launched herself into the air and landed gently on the wooden floor tucked up tightly into a ball. She bounced once and carefully unfurled herself. Wiping the panic sweat from her forehead she made her way to where she had thrown her clothes last night and pulled the smock over her head. Until they were summoned no male was allowed in the corridors but Greeta still refused to leave the bedroom without making sure that she was covered. Stepping out into the darkness of the corridor Greeta cursed the reliance she had placed on the night-vision goggles provided by the Thieves' Guild. Like all hedgehogs she had been born with exceptional night vision but the goggles made things even clearer so it was like walking around in the daytime. Occasionally she worried that using these goggles would damage her natural ability but dismissed these fears with the logic that she'd never leave the guild so wouldn't be without the goggles. Now in a pitch-dark corridor she cursed her former foolishness. She had learnt from the time spent in the cell into which she fell when she first came to the order that her eyes would adjust in time but until then she was literally in the dark.

She reached out a claw in the direction she vaguely recalled as the location of a torch. She felt emptiness so stretched out a little further until she felt it brush against the wooden shaft of a long-extinguished torch. Shuffling forwards, her claw still touching the torch, she was eventually close enough to wrap her long fingers around it and pull it free of its wall hanging. Reaching into the pouch on the front of her smock she rummaged about a bit and pulled out a box of Goose safety matches. Removing one from the pack she struck it. It sparked slightly but didn't catch. Swearing softly under her breath she tried again. Success! The tip of the match blossomed into life. Gently, for fear of it going out, Greeta touched the flame to the dry torch and the twigs caught light with a satisfying "WOOF". Greeta was so pleased with her work that she failed to notice that the match had burnt its way down to her fingers.

"Bloody ouch!" she cried out into the corridor, shaking the still lit match frantically so that it would go out.

Nobody had reacted to her shout so she realised that the High Priestess must be further away than she had originally thought. Still flexing her singed claws slightly, she held the torch out in front of her and made her way along the long corridor.

The torch threw unnerving shadows on the walls as Greeta made her way carefully towards the great hall. When she eventually found her way there she was surprised to find it empty. She was sure this is where she would have found the High Priestess. Greeta often found her here, she had become almost obsessed with studying the engraved columns. Greeta knew that she was looking for any clue to bringing back the Saviour. Search parties had been sent out to find the Collar of Honour but so far none had been successful. When the parties had been put together Greeta reluctantly volunteered to lead one. She didn't want to be away from her love but also wanted to do everything she could to please her. She was relieved when the High Priestess refused her offer, saying that she'd rather keep her close. However, as time moved on and the Collar had not been found Greeta noticed that the patience of the High Priestess was wearing thin.

Leaving the empty hall behind her Greeta continued to make her way through the corridor. The only place left to check was the outside. It was dangerous out there, especially at night, but she had to find her. As she approached the front door of the church she saw that it was open so with excitement building in her heart she stepped through and found herself outside.

Greeta looked around and her heart leapt when she spotted the High Priestess. She was sitting on a rock next to the stream they collected their drinking water from. The moonlight was shining directly on her and Greeta thought (as she always did) that this was the most beautiful sight she had ever seen. The High Priestess looked up. A flash of annoyance crossed her face at the disturbance, which quickly changed to a warm smile when she realised who had disturbed her.

"Were you worried about me, my love?" she asked softly.

"I'm always worried about you," Greeta replied. "You work so hard."

The High Priestess sighed deeply.

"Is it work if you love it?" she asked.

Greeta shrugged so the High Priestess moved on.

"The fourth search party returned today," she said.

Greeta looked up hopefully.

"And?" she asked, barely hoping to believe that they had been successful.

The High Priestess shook her head sadly.

"We are running out of time," she said to Greeta. "Think, is it likely that anyone else at the jubilee could have found it?"

Greeta scratched her chin.

"Altheus," she said eventually.

"The crow?" the High Priestess asked with contempt. "Cowards, so scared of magic that they banned it."

Greeta cleared her throat.

"Not her," she said softly. "She has magic, she is very powerful. If anyone could find the Collar of Honour it would be her."

"Could she be persuaded to help us?" the High Priestess asked.

"I don't know," was the only reply Greeta could come up with.

"Not worth the risk then," the High Priestess replied sadly. "I do have another idea though," she said and brought Greeta in for an embrace.

The next morning the High Priestess called a meeting of her acolytes. Greeta positioned herself out of the way on top of her favourite column and watched as the High Priestess laid out her new plan.

"Yes, most amusing, Your Holiness," the Key Master chuckled. "Let it never be said that you lost your sense of humour, even in the direst situations. Oh yes," he continued chortling. The High Priestess narrowed her eyes at him. He abruptly stopped laughing. "Your Holiness," he exclaimed in horror, "you can't be serious?"

She raised herself to her full height and towered over the now terrified Key Master. Even the Key Keeper managed to marshal his limited faculties and was paying full attention. He still had a slightly vacant grin on his face, Greeta noticed, but he was more aware of what was happening than usual, but that wasn't saying much.

"When it comes to The One Who Hops," she said imperiously, "have you ever known me to be anything other than serious?"

For a moment it looked like the Key Master might just burst into flames. Temporarily abandoning his instincts for survival he swallowed hard and tried another tack.

"What you're proposing though," he stammered, "it's blasphemy." He whispered the word "blasphemy" as if terrified that saying the word out loud might bring demons into the world.

The High Priestess rolled her eyes and the Key Keeper fell off the high chair he was sitting on. To Greeta the sound of him hitting the floor reminded her of the sound dry leaves made when you walked across them. It did, however, have the advantage of breaking the tension between the

High Priestess and her Key Master as they both turned to see what had happened. Seeing his opportunity, the Key Master immediately rushed to the side of his young assistant.

"See, Your Holiness," he said, pressing his perceived advantage, "this poor young believer has become so overwhelmed by what you are proposing that his love for the order overpowered his senses, plunging him..." At this point the Key Master was running out of things to say. The High Priestess considered stepping in at this point but was finally becoming so entertained by the ridiculous creature that she wanted to see where he was going with this so let him continue. Sweat started to form on his brow as he struggled to marshal his thoughts. "Plunging him... plunging him..." he stammered for a while, "plunging him both mentally and physically..." at "physically" he waved his paws theatrically at the prone figure of the Key Keeper, who was still face down on the floor and looked for all the world that he had fallen asleep, "to the very pit of despair. For his sake I beg you to reconsider."

Greeta couldn't help herself, she had to give this a round of applause. Standing up on the pillar she frantically clapped her paws together. Surprised, the Key Master looked up and seeing the hedgehog, scowled at her. The High Priestess pretended not to hear anything but Greeta could see that she was smiling slightly.

"This is not what your sainted mother would have wanted, Your Holiness," he implored, and for good measure pointed to the Key Keeper who still hadn't moved and in fact appeared to be dribbling.

"I don't know," the High Priestess replied, her voice so cold that the Key Master later checked himself for frostbite.

"My mother was very keen that young moles get lots of sleep."

The Key Master gaped at her. He knew that one of them was losing this discussion and the sinking feeling in his stomach suggested that it might well be him.

"Sleep, Your Holiness?" he asked eventually.

In a moment of timing that he would never be consciously capable of the Key Keeper started snoring, loudly. At this the Key Master's face turned as crimson as his tunic and he gave the slumbering Key Keeper a subtle kick.

"If Brother Key Master has finished," a distinguished and even voice exclaimed from the other side of the room.

Greeta turned in surprise. This was a voice she hadn't heard before. She saw a mole lounging in his wooden chair. Unlike the others who sat with their backs rigid against their seats, their legs placed alternately underneath the chair or with both knees locked together, his long legs were sprawled out in front of him and he was casually throwing a small rock into the air and lazily catching it. Every eye turned to him but instead of speaking he plucked the rock out of the air, lazily waved with a free paw at the now apoplectic Key Master and made a big show of using the rock to sharpen his claws. Like everyone else Greeta stared at him. She noticed that unlike the others his robes looked brand new. The crimson was bright and the golden symbol of an open book across his chest almost glowed.

"Brother Librarian," the Key Master hissed, not bothering to hide his annoyance.

The Librarian grinned at him, showing perfectly white incisors. The Key Master instinctively closed his mouth, embarrassed by his own brown chipped teeth and, realising (too late) that he had lost any authority, sat back down, folding his arms and settling in for a good sulk. The Librarian stood up slowly, straightening his immaculate tunic as he rose. He was the tallest mole Greeta had ever seen. He pushed his long hair off his forehead and stroked his neat beard which had only just started to develop a few strands of grey, which if anything made him look even more distinguished.

"Your Holiness…" he said, not bothering to look at the High Priestess. Instead he focused his attention on one of her handmaidens, a small plump young thing who blushed furiously at the attention. The High Priestess narrowed her eyes at him and Greeta realised with interest that the High Priestess and the Librarian clearly had some history together. "… As the Collar of Honour remains ever elusive, are we to assume that this new plan of yours is an admission of defeat?"

The room collectively held their breath. The High Priestess smiled but there was no warmth behind it. She remained seated. It was a calculated move. If she stood she could appear more regal but by remaining seated she could better look like she was in full control. She waited in silence for a few seconds, letting the tension build around her before replying calmly.

"Our new agent informs us that there are many seeking the Collar and as it appears that nobody has found it, I believe that we should look into other possibilities."

"Pillow talk?" the Librarian asked slyly.

The High Priestess visibly bristled and the Key Master looked on hopefully. *Could this be the moment he finally gets what he has had coming to him for so long?* he wished. He even crossed his claws for good luck.

"At least my 'pillow talk' is productive rather than vacuous," the High Priestess replied, looking at the Librarian and the plump handmaiden in turn.

The Librarian grinned lasciviously at her and replied, "Perhaps we could work out an exchange, Your Holiness."

*This must be it*, thought the Key Master. *Surely he has gone too far this time.* He leaned forward in his seat, eager to see how this played out. To his immense disappointment the Librarian merely chuckled at his own joke and carried on.

"… But enough about pleasure," he cooed, "let me see if I understand your plan. The Collar of Honour remains undiscovered despite the numerous teams trying to find it. So, you plan to use the power of the Elemental Spirits to resurrect our Saviour? This is despite the fact that there is no evidence that these spirits even exist?"

He was correct of course. The High Priestess had admitted as much to Greeta as they spoke by the lake outside earlier that morning.

"If we cannot find the Collar soon," she had said to Greeta, "then it's possible that someone else will. If Faustus gets his disgusting claws on it then that could be ruinous for everyone. We've both heard enough stories about his reign after all. He'll most likely have the entire world in shackles for the rest of time. We also can't let the Giraxians or the Pacidermians get their warring hands on it either. I'm sure I speak for the rest of Venary when I say that I wouldn't lose any sleep if they wiped each other out, but if either army got the Collar there's no telling where they would stop. The crows have been very quiet since the mage purge but if as you say the magic is returning to their realm they could threaten the natural order of things. It's important that we have it! The Saviour must be brought back. It's best for everyone. You do see that, don't you?" she asked softly, holding Greeta in a tighter embrace.

Greeta nodded but at the back of her mind she really couldn't see how this helped. She knew that nobody else should get hold of the Collar or even who else was looking for it. From the devastation she had fled from in the great hall it looked like the cat knights hadn't survived but word must surely have reached their citadel by now. Like all carnivores Greeta thought they would want the Collar for bloody revenge. Hestor hadn't known anything about the Collar's powers. Had she discovered Greeta's betrayal? If she had, did she care? She had threatened to expel her on numerous occasions.

"Perhaps," the tiny voice at the back of her head said, "it might be better if YOU had the Collar. You could wish all of this away and be with the Priestess forever, make her forget about this 'Saviour' nonsense."

Greeta tried to ignore the voice. She wouldn't do anything to hurt the High Priestess but perhaps she would be helping her, she wondered. The High Priestess hadn't noticed any sign of this inner turmoil. She let go of Greeta and indicated that they should both sit down.

"Have I ever told you about the Elemental Spirits?":

## The Spirits' Tale

Long before Perix the First (or Perix the Bloody if you got in his way) unified the disparate species of Venary, even before the Collar of Honour had been forged, there was nobody to record history as it unfolded around them. This has led to many legends and stories springing up about life in the early cycles of Venary. Most of these legends have been discounted and are regarded as mere fairy stories in the modern world but among the moles one legend has remained persistent and is still believed by many. The Elemental Spirits are (or were) five spirits who embodied the elements of Venary, namely: Fire, Earth, Water, Wind and Magic.

The Fire Spirit (named Incandescentina) was said to have taken the form of a giant red bird who flew around the world spreading warmth and light wherever she went. The Earth Spirit (whose name was Macrocosm) was a huge yet delicate bull who moved slowly across the world creating different lands for the eventual species to live on. He was slow and deliberate, and the stories said that he had so enraged the other Elemental Spirits that they would often leave him behind. The Water Spirit (the impatient Aquarias) created the lakes and great seas. She was still used as a tale told to young Brundians about the dangers of water. The Wind Spirit (Zephyr) was the cruellest of the five. He delighted in destruction and chaos. Finally, there was Majeka, the Magic Elemental Spirit. He was far more powerful than the others but (and for one of the only times in history) he hadn't been corrupted by it. Individually they were powerful. The story went that they had split up the creation of Venary but when the work was finished they found that life had failed to rise up. They had created a lifeless rock. For eons they waited and while Venary spun merrily away life stubbornly refused to develop.

To the surprise of nobody Zephyr cracked first. He charged across the surface of Venary getting faster and faster with each rotation. He went so fast that he caused the planet to slip slightly from its axis but after an eon of circling the globe still no life came forward. Seeing Zephyr's failure Aquarias decided to try summoning all of her power. She made the seas and rivers rise, bursting their banks and coating the planet in a never-ending sea; she brought down dark clouds which battered the mountain ranges that poked out of the deep and unending sea. For eons the rains fell and for eons after the waters slowly receded, but all she had achieved was to create a huge wilderness (to this day many moles refuse to travel to the wastelands as they were the site of a holy tragedy).

Eventually Macrocosm was persuaded to try. Over a painfully slow age (called the 'Eternal Stone Age' by the old mole clerics before they died out from celibacy-related complications) he built animals out of stone, pebble by pebble. Eventually he had a menagerie of stone animals but no matter how much he nudged them they refused to come to life. Much to the concern of the others Incandescentina announced that where the others had failed she would burn away their mistakes in a "cleansing fire". Before anyone could stop her she took off at top speed. Flying faster than she ever had before she spread her wings wide and scorched the planet.

After the eons it took for the fire to burn out the Elemental Spirits walked across the devastation, cinders cracking underfoot. Macrocosm was surprised to see that even his statues had melted such had been the heat (nobody could tell quite how surprised he was because it took a decade for it to register on his face).

"Arrggh," Zephyr cried out in frustration. "Nothing has worked."

He exhaled so powerfully that the soot, which is all that remained of the forest they were standing in, blew up into the sky and blanketed the planet for two more centuries.

"Perhaps we are too powerful," Aquarias bubbled sadly.

"Or perhaps," Majeka added softly, "we are not powerful enough."

The other four spirits stared at him. He hadn't spoken for as long as they could remember. They continued to wait but after an ice age it became apparent that Majeka had nothing to add. Unsurprisingly Zephyr broke the silence.

"Brilliant!" he exclaimed. "Just brilli…"

He broke off suddenly as with the slightest gesture Majeka plucked his voice straight from his mouth and held it as a glowing ball in between his fingers. Zephyr stared in horrified silence as Majeka idly threw the still glowing ball from hand to hand.

"Err," Aquarias said eventually, panicking that her voice might at any minute be taken from her. When it wasn't she continued, "What did you mean?"

At this he smiled and took her hand. Instinctively she knew what to do. She reached with her free hand and took Incandescentina's, who did the same. In a short time they were standing in a circle.

"All at once NOW!" Majeka shouted and as one they released their powers until they met in the middle.

On and on they poured their collective powers until a red glow began to erupt. The glow began to slowly spread outwards and with painstaking slowness spread across the whole planet. It was impossible to say how long this took but even Macrocosm began to tire. Just as the spirits felt that they couldn't go on any further the entire planet was bathed in a red glow which shone so brilliantly that it stood out to other planets. It was a shame there was no one on the other planets to see it. Eventually the spirits collapsed, exhausted, as all around them the first life forms sprang up. The spirits all lay spread out on the soft grass that had risen up, breathing heavily (which was an impressive feat as being incorporeal beings they had no lungs). Trees were the next to sprout, reaching higher and higher into the sky. Strange furred creatures with many legs and wide, staring eyes scuttled between the exhausted spirits. Smiling with satisfaction each spirit started to fade away, leaving only five coloured gems which were eventually covered over by the slowly healing land.

The High Priestess stood up and stared into the arrogant and unblinking eyes of the Librarian.

"I still lead," she said firmly.

He grinned at her and bowed low.

"I live to serve."

And with that she waved her hand and the meeting broke up. Greeta scuttled down from her perch and approached the High Priestess, who was removing her ceremonial bonnet. Her blonde hair cascading down her back.

"Who was that?" she asked in a worried tone.

To her surprise the High Priestess started to laugh softly.

"Him?" she answered eventually. "That is just my chief rival."

"A rival?" Greeta exclaimed, horrified. *How could anybody want to hurt the High Priestess?* she wondered.

Seeing the look of horror on her face the High Priestess took her paws and said softly, "Don't worry about him," a trace of laughter in her voice. "We'll either have the Collar of Honour or the Elemental Spirits and it won't matter anymore."

"But what good are the spirits if they died?" she asked.

The High Priestess smiled at her and no matter how many times she saw it her legs still went weak.

"The second part of the story says that if the gems can be found and brought back together the spirits will return and with their combined powers we can bring back our Saviour."

"But they could be anywhere," Greeta said, concerned. "If we continue to look for the Collar of Honour it might take a long time but we only have to find one thing not five."

The High Priestess smiled again and simply said, "One."

She then started walking towards the still open front door and beckoned for Greeta to follow her.

They walked in silence through the corridors, Greeta still puzzled by what the High Priestess had said. They reached their quarters and the guards immediately leapt to attention, opening the big doors so Greeta and the High Priestess could walk through without stopping. Greeta watched as the High Priestess hurried towards the opposite wall. She felt her way along the smooth surface and with a "click" she found a hidden switch, and a small tray silently slid out of the wall. Greeta noticed that as she brought the tray over to her she walked carefully. The tray was covered by what looked like a satin cloth and as she placed the tray on the table built into the wall she pulled back the satin cover and beckoned her over.

Greeta looked first at the expectant face of the High Priestess and then into the tray. She gasped at what she saw.

Nestled inside in their own indented section were four shiny gems, one red, one blue, one green and one clear.

"We are only missing one," the High Priestess whispered, looking around as if to check they were alone but Greeta could hear the excitement in her voice. "My mother handed these on to me. Her mother had found three of them." She pointed at the red, blue and green gems in turn. "A few spans ago I found this one." She picked up the clear gem and held it up to her eye, which magnified it in comical fashion. "There is only one left to find. I think it's Majeka. It doesn't help that we don't know the colour of his gem."

"Purple," Greeta breathed quietly, excitement building inside her.

The High Priestess cocked her head quizzically.

"Do you know something?" she hissed urgently.

Greeta beamed in excitement at the thought of pleasing her. Without saying a word she dashed to the drawer she had been given when she moved into the room and pulled out her Thieves' Guild uniform. The High Priestess watched with growing excitement as she threw the trousers over her head, quickly followed by the soft-soled shoes. When Greeta headed back to her she was clutching her leather pouch.

"I was a very bad thief," Greeta exclaimed, reaching into the pouch. "I never managed to break in anywhere." As she spoke she laid out the bag's meagre contents. "As a pickpocket I didn't have the reach to get to the larger animals." A few bronze coins clinked together as they were thrown onto the bed. "I was starting to question my purpose, even my purpose here," she admitted. The High Priestess moved to speak but Greeta cut her off (her excitement overwriting her usual shyness around her). "But I think I know why we were brought together."

At this she triumphantly produced the foul-smelling purple gem that had been thrown at her all that time ago.

Almost instantly the High Priestess summoned everyone to meet at the Saviour's quarters, pausing only to put her ceremonial bonnet back on and pull Greeta into a passionate embrace of gratitude. The High Priestess picked up the tray of now complete gems and made her way to her destiny.

She desperately wanted to run. This was it, the conclusion of so many generations' hopes. With the Saviour back, even Faustus couldn't stand against her. Soon she would rule and the long persecution of her people would be at an end, her church would rule over everyone and peace would reign forever. She made herself walk. As High Priestess she knew that she must make them wait for her and that she must appear calm and in full control. This was her birthright after all and she should act like it was expected, but her stomach was spinning in anticipation. She wasn't the last to arrive, however, that was the Librarian who arrived with a dishevelled handmaiden and a lazy grin on his face. As furious as she was at this, the High Priestess decided that wiping that smirk off his face would be punishment enough.

"Gentlemen," she addressed them all, "our moment of triumph approaches."

With this she opened the doors in front of her and strode into the Saviour's quarters.

Greeta followed all of the moles in and was nearly beaten back by the smell. It was a horrible combination of incense and rotten meat, which made her gag as the taste of bile forced its way up her throat. She swallowed hard and, breathing through her mouth, continued her way into the room.

The room was empty except for a huge bed. So big was it in fact that Greeta noticed that many rooms must have been knocked together just to get it in. Lying in the bed was the source of the foul smell: a ginormous and almost totally rotted rabbit corpse. Arcane symbols had been painted onto its rotted flesh and onto the wall behind it. Greeta was surprised to see that the head looked perfectly preserved. If anything the rabbit didn't look much like a saviour with the head lolloped comically to one side, the glassy eyes staring vacantly at a wall. Greeta had to stifle a giggle she felt rising up inside her.

Standing at the head of the bed the High Priestess made a show of taking each gem out one at a time and placing them in a circle. As she positioned the last one she said, "Gentlemen, may I introduce the Elemental Spirits." At this she threw her arms out and…

… Nothing happened. The High Priestess continued to stand with her arms outstretched until a voice called out, "Very quiet, aren't they?"

It could only have been the Librarian, nobody else would have dared. Slowly, and feeling her dignity and authority ebbing away, the High Priestess began to lower her arms when from behind her and with no visible source flames leapt up. In the stunned silence that followed wind whipped her hair out in a myriad of directions. The ground beneath her split into cracks which quickly filled with fast-running water. As the wind picked up, getting stronger and stronger, the High Priestess was gently lifted from the ground, the tips of her paws brushing the ground. The other moles who had already started backing away towards the door started climbing over each other as from behind the High Priestess five figures emerged.

"It can't be," the Librarian said in wonder.

"WOOOOOO," Incandescentina shouted as she flew around the high ceiling.

"Where are we?" a loud voice which filled the entire room asked.

As every figure cowered underneath the still floating High Priestess the purple, glowing face of Majeka floated ominously up to each mole in turn. The Key Master pointed a shaking claw up at the High Priestess. Majeka gave him a contemptuous stare and turned away.

"Brothers and sisters," he announced, "it appears we owe our rebirth to her."

The winds dropped and the High Priestess was gently returned to the ground, the winds gradually died out completely and the pinched face of Zephyr bobbed gently over her left shoulder. Incandescentina flapped down from the ceiling and perched on her right shoulder. The High Priestess felt a gentle pressure behind her knees as the giant bull form of Macrocosm eased her on his back, while Aquarias created a slowly flowing moat around her. The floating head of Majeka flew down so he was eye to eye with the High Priestess. For the first time the High Priestess was genuinely scared as Majeka studied her in silence, narrowing his eyes suspiciously.

"Why?" he asked eventually.

The High Priestess smiled.

"Oh, Great Spirits," she said loudly, "it was indeed I who awoke you from your millennia-long slumber and I…"

"Don't do that," Majeka said evenly. "We are immortal, you are not. So before you waste any more of your very limited time just tell us what you want."

The High Priestess nodded, feeling more than a little silly.

"Do you see the body in the bed?" she asked. Incandescentina snorted in response to this obvious question and even Majeka rolled his eyes. "Yes, silly question," she admitted weakly. "He is our Saviour and I have summoned you here to bring him back to life."

"If you wouldn't mind," Greeta piped up.

She loved the High Priestess but in this situation felt that manners might just keep everyone alive. She had scampered through the crowd as they attempted their escape and was sitting at the edge of the moat created by Aquarias. She had attempted to cross it but every time she did a wall of water rose up, blocking her way. She had tried to jump over it but the water took the shape of a big paw and slapped her back to the ground. Greeta was grateful that everyone had been too engrossed in what was going on to witness that.

Majeka nodded magnanimously down at the little hedgehog and at his command the spirits made their way to the head of the Saviour's bed. Majeka floated up to the face of the half-rotted rabbit and with wordless commands positioned each of his siblings so one was stationed at each corner of the bed. When he was satisfied that they were positioned correctly he floated down so that he was equidistant between each spirit.

"Begin," he intoned.

At this command each spirit poured their unique power at Majeka who grew larger and larger, his natural purple glow becoming brighter and brighter until he opened his mouth and poured a stream of red light directly between the eyes of the giant rabbit sitting up in his bed. On and on he poured power into the still unmoving body until, exhausted, he floated back down to the ground. All of the other spirits had become see-through, flickering between their solid life forms and their crystals. The High Priestess rushed to the side of the Saviour, fearing that it hadn't worked. Then everything seemed to happen at once.

His eyelids flicked open and the High Priestess got a terrifying glimpse at his mad, unfocused eyes as they rolled around wildly in his head. With a deafening roar he leapt out of his bed, his fur rapidly growing back across his body as it healed. He stared wildly around the room and with an evil grin on his face locked his vision on the crowd of spectators as for the third time they all rushed towards the exit. Leaning his enormous face down towards the huddled moles he took a long, deep sniff, which was so powerful that two moles at the front were lifted from their paws. The Saviour threw his head back and bellowed at the sky. Without a second thought he lifted one of his powerful legs up and with startling force brought it down with a sickening squelch on the huddled moles.

"SAVIOUR!" the High Priestess yelled out in horror. "What are you doing? You're meant to be our protector."

As if in answer to this panicked question the Saviour brought his foot up but this time he brought it up to his face and to the High Priestess's disgust flipped his ginormous tongue out and licked the blood and matted fur from it. He grinned wickedly, manoeuvred himself into a squat and leapt through the roof, causing dirt and roots to rain down. The High Priestess dashed to the devastated scene of what until recently had been her acolytes, finding only the Librarian still breathing. He was coated in blood and his once handsome face had been reduced to almost unrecognisable pulp. He was muttering something and the High Priestess had to lean in so that she could hear what he was saying. As she leaned in he grabbed at her with his ruined paws and spat blood into her face.

"Doomed us all," he croaked and then his eyes rolled back into his head and he went limp.

CHAPTER TWENTY

# INTO THE GREEN

THE JOURNEY TO the warren was a long one and Harnny had only spoken once during the entire length of it, having spent three cycles curled up at the back of the caravan, his knees tucked under his chin and ears flopped over his eyes. On a few occasions Scratch tried to engage him in conversation but each time he did Harnny would turn away from him and curl up even tighter in a furry ball. It was only when the desert land of Aridier gave way to rolling green hills did he poke his head up. Scratch was shocked to see how pale and gaunt the rabbit looked.

"What will I tell his mother?" he said eventually from the back of the cart. His voice cracked through emotion and lack of use.

Scratch stammered slightly until Zakk handed him the reins and somewhat unsteadily sat himself next to Harnny.

"Why did you leave the warren?" he asked the distraught rabbit.

"You know why," Harnny said dejectedly. "We thought we could get some salvage from the abandoned caravans."

Zakk pulled off his large hat and scratched at the thinning fur atop his head. He seemed to consider the hat's wide brim for a few seconds before putting it back on. "And what plans did you have for it?" he asked eventually.

Harnny flushed red with embarrassment.

"Any quest comes with risks…" Zakk said, staring directly into Harnny's red eyes. Zakk exhaled heavily and to Harnny he looked so much older. "You had images of fame and fortune."

At this Harnny hopped to his feet.

"What do you know about anything, you old drunk? Barnny and I… we… we…" Suddenly Harnny crumpled back to the ground. "I told him we'd be rich," he admitted quietly. "He didn't want to come." The confession came thick and fast now, as if a plug had been pulled deep inside him. Tears streamed from his eyes as he continued, "He wanted to stay at the warren but I told him it would be easy. I said the dogs were too stupid to catch us." The rest of the confession was drowned out by a wail.

Zakk waited until this sudden noise died down.

"Then that is what you must tell her," Zakk replied evenly. Harnny just gaped at him. "Perhaps…" Zakk said, returning to his feet, "that should be your quest. Make amends for your former arrogance. Then you may be ready for the responsibility next time you decide to go questing."

Harnny sighed and nodded.

While Zakk was talking to Harnny Scratch stayed up front steering the caravan. In addition to the supplies, Sunole had provided a fleet of pack rats to pull the wooden caravan. Surviving in the desert had made them large and strong enough to pull caravans with little effort but unlike their distant cousins, the Rodentians, they were completely unintelligent and mute, suited only for physical labour. Scratch found himself wondering what they tasted like.

"You're a savage, you are aware of that?" Tyrell asked from inside Scratch's head.

"I'm not going to eat them," he said, pouting. "I was just curious is all."

"I don't understand how your species ever progressed from the Dark Ages. Bloodstained savages," he spat contemptuously.

"Remind me," Scratch said cheerily, "whose father are we trying to stop from taking over the whole planet?"

There followed a long silence.

"Regardless of that," Tyrell muttered darkly, "we shouldn't be going to the jungle, the Collar isn't there."

"How do you know that?" Scratch asked, becoming irritated.

"That's where I looked…" Tyrell replied quietly.

## Tyrell's Tale

"Sire, I must insist you reconsider," Brabbinger pleaded. "You're still grieving and what of the Prince? What should I tell him?"

"Tell him the truth," Tyrell replied. As he spoke he moved around his quarters, taking things out of various drawers and putting them one by one into the saddlebag he had placed onto his bed. Brabbinger watched in stunned silence as Tyrell held two almost identical pairs of riding boots up to the light. "What do you think?" he asked, showing Brabbinger the boots. "I can only take the one pair if we travel light."

"Dark brown, sire," Brabbinger answered automatically. "They won't show the dirt." Realising what he had done Brabbinger slapped his forehead. "You can't leave, sire. You are the King now, you have duties."

Tyrell paused at this and gave it some thought. He turned his back on Brabbinger and put the dark brown riding boots into the saddlebag. "Retrieving the Collar of Honour IS my duty." He spun back on Brabbinger. "We could have stopped him earlier," he said quietly. "We both knew he was up to no good."

"But, sire, we couldn't have known…" Brabbinger tried to counter.

At this Tyrell scoffed darkly, "Oh come on," he sneered, "it's your job and favourite pastime to know what's going on in every part of this mausoleum and as heir I was the only one who could remove him. How many of our citizens did he torture while we ignored it out of duty and cowardice?" Brabbinger looked to the floor in disgrace. "No, we didn't do our duty then but by the grass gods we'll do it now!" Tyrell said urgently.

Even in this tense moment Brabbinger felt a surge of pride that the King wasn't shouting, despite obviously wanting to. Clearly his etiquette training hadn't been entirely in vain.

"But, sire," he tried again, "Venary needs its ruler and you must stay here to do that."

"Enough!" Tyrell said, his voice getting slightly louder. In his frustration he slammed the covers of the saddlebag closed and in one movement threw the large bag over his shoulder. "I have established social changes to overturn the punishments of my father, I have lowered taxes on the overburdened population and I know that Hirax will be safe in your hands. Everything else can wait. I'm going to find this dratted Collar and undo the horrors we allowed my father to get away with. And you…" Brabbinger went to speak but was silenced by the steely look Tyrell shot him. "And you…" Tyrell continued once he was sure Brabbinger was listening, "will advise my son in his role as Regent…" Brabbinger went to speak again but Tyrell held up a paw. "He'll have to grow up a bit, another victim we'll have to make it up to. You can also get rid of the portraits of my father. We'll have my coronation when I've managed to undo this mess."

Leaving Brabbinger speechless Tyrell briskly walked out of his quarters and headed towards the courtyard.

The Royal Guard were waiting for him when he arrived. They were all wearing their dress uniforms and were next to fully laden horses.

"Can I help you, gentlerodents?" Tyrell enquired, heading towards his own grey mount.

"We, err, await your command, Your Majesty."

"Well, I commend you for remembering your training but why are you here?" he asked sarcastically.

The guardsmouse looked a bit flustered but as none of his fellows looked like they were going to assist him at any point in the immediate future he had to carry on.

"You are leaving the palace and as your Royal Guard we must accomp…" He trailed off when he realised that Tyrell wasn't listening to him.

Instead Tyrell had attached the saddle and mounted his horse.

"I am leaving the palace," he admitted, shooting an accusing glance at Brabbinger who was trying to look everywhere but at the King. "I need to find something and bring it back. I cannot risk anyone outside of the palace finding out. So, I don't need a full escort wearing…" He turned around and looked at the assembled guards properly for the first time. They were all wearing the same uniform of tabard, jodhpurs, knee-high boots and cape, all of which were coloured bright yellow. "By the grass gods my father had terrible taste!" he exclaimed.

The guards murmured in embarrassment and Brabbinger stepped forward.

"Your royal father thought that his guards should stand out so that the public would always see them coming."

Tyrell looked alternately at his butler and his guards.

"Perhaps I should just abdicate," he muttered to himself. Before Brabbinger could object he turned to the only guard who had spoken. "You and only you will accompany me." The guard nodded and went to mount his own horse. Tyrell put his paw on the guard's shoulder to stop him. "Change first."

"So…" Tyrell said eventually, "you are not the captain of my personal guard?"

The two of them had been on the road for a few hours now. Castle Mowser was no longer visible behind them.

"No, Your Majesty, I'm actually the newest member." At this admission Tyrell drew up his reins and halted his mount. He stared directly at his companion, taking him in properly for the first time. "By the gods, you're young," he said sadly.

"I'm only a span younger than you... Your Majesty," he added quickly.

Tyrell snorted humourlessly.

"I guess some of us age better than others. What is your name, soldier?" he asked.

"Faustus," the young soldier admitted quietly.

"Of course it is," Tyrell exclaimed. "Did you ever meet my father?"

"Once, Your Majesty..."

Before he could continue Tyrell cut across him.

"We're trying to go unnoticed so stop calling me 'Your Majesty', it's a big giveaway."

"Sorry, Your... What should I call you?"

"There's only two of us here so you don't need to call me anything, just speak and I'll assume you're talking to me. Anyway, you were telling me about meeting my father."

"It was a very brief meeting," Faustus admitted. "He saw me subduing the Cottage Street uprising." Tyrell nodded slowly. "He said that he admired my form," Faustus added with pride.

"I should have known," Tyrell said sadly. "You're another one of my father's butchers."

Faustus felt his face flush red.

"I wouldn't say that," he countered.

"Tell me," Tyrell asked hotly, "do you know why the citizens of Cottage Street were rebelling?" he asked quietly.

Automatically Faustus replied, "They were rebelling against the King's divine rule and had to be brought back under control..."

He got no further as with sudden fury Tyrell leapt from his horse and with a strength fuelled by anger dragged Faustus from his own horse and punched him squarely in the face. Faustus responded automatically by sweeping out a massive leg, knocking the still furious Tyrell to the ground. Tyrell was strong but Faustus was a trained soldier and before Tyrell could get back to his feet he felt the air being knocked out of him as Faustus jumped on top of him, pushing his full weight into the King's chest.

Even with his vision blurring in and out Tyrell was surprised to see a look of fear on the face of Faustus. Before he passed out he felt the weight lift from his chest and suddenly he felt himself being lifted back to his feet. Standing unsteadily on his feet he gulped down mouthfuls of air. When he recovered he was further surprised to find that he was holding his sword and that Faustus was on his knees before him.

"What?" Tyrell said stupidly.

"My king," Faustus' voice sounded muffled as his head was facing the ground, "I have betrayed you by placing paws upon you. I welcome my punishment."

To his surprise Tyrell started laughing, quietly at first but once he started he found that he couldn't stop. Louder and louder he laughed; he laughed until he couldn't breathe. Once again he felt himself collapse to the ground wheezing and coughing with tears streaming down his face.

Feeling angry Faustus snapped his head up.

"I know that I betrayed you but please don't laugh at me."

Wiping the tears from his eyes Tyrell struggled to bring his breathing under control.

"Don't you get it?" he asked between ragged breaths.

"Even after his death my father controls me. When I was fighting you, I could only see my father. Oh, for cheese' sake look up! I'm not executing you." Faustus looked up, confusion across his face. Tyrell patted the ground next him. "Sit down," he instructed.

After a little while Faustus sat next to Tyrell. Neither spoke for a while.

Tyrell reached into his tunic and removed a metal canister. He fiddled with the stopper for a bit. Eventually he removed it. Putting the canister to his lips he took a long slug at the liquid it contained. Sighing with pleasure he offered it to the other mouse.

"No thank you, Your Majesty," he replied.

"Why not?" Tyrell enquired. "I'm sure you've worked up a thirst."

"Orders, Your Majesty," was the stoic reply.

"Whose orders?" Tyrell asked.

Faustus looked awkwardly back at him.

"Your father's," he said quietly.

"I can see why he liked you so much," Tyrell stated, rolling his eyes. "Do you ever question orders?"

"Why would I do that? I'm a soldier."

Tyrell put the flask back inside his tunic.

"No you're not," he said sadly. "You're another victim of my father's cruelty. Another life I need to pay for."

"I don't understand," Faustus admitted.

"I know," Tyrell said, patting him on his enormous shoulder. "But we have a long way to travel."

As night began to fall Tyrell and Faustus set up camp and in a short while they were sitting around a fire. Tyrell took a bite from the lump of cheese he had roasted over the fire. He had finished telling Faustus everything on their journey and the soldier was staring at him in horror.

"I killed innocents?" he asked eventually.

"You did what you were told to do," Tyrell said evenly. "Brabbinger would say that you did your duty."

"What would your father say?" Faustus asked.

"I doubt he even knew your name, which when you think about it is an insult he would have enjoyed." Tyrell chuckled darkly at his comment but Faustus continued to stare at him.

"And what do you think?"

Tyrell sighed.

"I suspected my father was abusing his power and I ignored it. He chased my wife away and all I could do was feel sorry for myself." He felt tears well up in his eyes for the first time in as long as he could remember. Angrily he threw the remaining cheese into the fire where it melted quickly. "This is why we must find the Collar of Honour."

It was silent for a while except for the occasional crackle from the campfire.

"I should probably change my name," Faustus said eventually.

Tyrell made sure that as they travelled they avoided all major settlements, so by the time they arrived at the jungle lands quite some time had passed. The tropical lands in which the jungle spread was the only area in Venary to reach high temperatures and both Rodentians were quickly covered in sweat. Even the horses had begun to struggle. They had tied their tunics around their waists and were leading the horses when they saw it.

"The River Lac," Tyrell exhaled. He wouldn't admit it but the heat was getting to him.

"I thought it was only a legend to scare the cats," Faustus said in wonder.

"No, it's real enough," Tyrell exclaimed, pausing only to wipe the sweat from his fur. *Damn it*, he thought bitterly to himself. *I'm slowly melting here and this young upstart isn't struggling at all.* He chastised himself for letting the trappings of luxury make him go soft. He resolved at this point to make sure Hirax was toughened up. This thought pulled him up sharply. Was he more like his father than he realised?

His thoughts were interrupted by Faustus exclaiming in wonder, "But a river of milk, it shouldn't be possible."

Ever the pragmatist Tyrell rolled his eyes at this.

"Well, it is obviously possible," he spat testily. "It's here… Be careful," he said suddenly as Faustus was reaching into the lake. "Don't be fooled by the slow current, there are subcurrents which will drag you under. Our ancestors believed it was a righteous trap for the greedy Felixian who would be unable to resist a lake of pure milk and stick his head in and…" he made a fast sweeping gesture with a paw, "never be seen again."

It did look inviting though. He was close enough to feel the chill coming off it and the scent of milk made even his mouth water. Maybe his ancestors were right. The Felixians were a very greedy people and legendarily stupid! He could see those furry idiots lining up to throw themselves to their doom. Gods, that river looked so inviting. Realising that he himself was starting to drift closer and closer to the riverbank he pulled back.

"What's that?" He heard a distant voice echoing.

Forcing himself to concentrate on something other than the flowing milk he saw Faustus pointing at something on the other side of the river. Tyrell looked in the direction the younger Rodentian was pointing towards and couldn't see anything unusual. He squinted. *Gods!* he thought. *Even my eyes are starting to fail me.*

He raised a paw to his forehead, hoping that shading his eyes would help him see better. As much as it pained him to say it, he would have to admit that he couldn't see anything. This would be embarrassing after the fuss he made back at the castle about going on his own. Then he saw it. At first it looked like an ordinary stack of rocks but there, perched on top of the pile, was something shiny. It reflected the bright sunlight so perfectly that it was impossible to identify.

"I'm not sure what that is," he admitted to Faustus, "but I do remember how shiny that Collar was when I last saw it, so we need to investigate."

Faustus snapped immediately into action.

"We need to scout the length of this river," he announced, his voice full of confidence for the first time since the trip began.

Tyrell was momentarily impressed before he remembered whose orders had been pumped into his head during his basic training.

"We are principally looking for a bridge..." Faustus announced.

Secretly he had no idea what "principally" actually meant but it felt like the right thing to say. He was in his element; his favourite part of basic training had been the overnight survival course. He had made a shelter which was a damn sight more comfortable than the draughty barracks he shared with his squadron.

"Failing that…" he continued, puffing out his chest. He would give anything for an officer's swagger stick right now. To compensate he snapped a branch off a nearby tree and tucked it under his arm, mimicking every commanding officer he had even seen, "we should see if this river becomes narrow enough for us to build our own. We should use this opportunity to reconnaissance the local area for vines and logs…" He lost confidence in the word "reconnaissance" as soon as it left his lips but he was committed to it by now. "I will set up a base of operations here and you can…"

His voice trailed off as he realised that His Royal Highness was nowhere to be seen. Panic gripped his chest. Bad enough he had fought with him earlier (the King hadn't mentioned it since but Faustus was convinced that a court martial awaited him) but to lose the King? Obviously it wasn't his fault. Bloody royalty think they can wander off as they please, but he'd be held responsible.

"Are you finished?" a pompous voice asked from directly above him. Looking up Faustus was surprised to see Tyrell sitting on a long thick tree branch. He was tying vines together with a grim determination. "Only if you have," Tyrell continued, now that he was sure that he had Faustus' full attention, "perhaps you could join me up here. I need a strong arm and you might as well be some use to me."

Automatically Faustus followed the given order and in a very short time he found himself holding a lasso made up of vines.

"You want me…" he asked slowly, "to throw this rope into the tree on the other side of the river?"

"Yes," Tyrell replied wearily.

Taking his life into his own paws a bit, Faustus swallowed nervously and replied, "Are you sure that's a good idea… sir." He added the "sir" hastily after Tyrell scowled at him.

"Why would it not be?" Tyrell asked.

By now sweat was visibly running along his long nose. Faustus had been desperately trying to recall the training he received for the treatment of heat stroke but army medical training under the old King boiled down to "Leave them where they drop", not really a viable option in this case.

"Well, we don't really know how strong the vines are. We don't know if that other tree can hold our weight and… and…"

His voice trailed off as Tyrell forcibly turned him in the direction of the river.

"Throw, in the name of every grass, sky and river god in this blighted kingdom," Tyrell shouted hoarsely. "Just throw the bloody vine, man!"

Faustus shuffled slightly further down the branch. If he was going to do this he was going to get it right. He swung the vine over his head a few times, building up a head of steam, and released. To his relief his shot was good. The vine found its mark, wrapping itself around the branch of the intended tree first time. He pulled the vine back and, following Tyrell's instructions, lashed his end to the branch he was sitting on. A strong line was now crossing the River Lac.

"I must insist that I go first," he said to Tyrell, and without waiting for confirmation he kicked off his boots and tied them around his neck.

His nimble Rodentian claws now free of the cumbersome boots he reached out to the vine and, hanging upside down like the sloths he had once seen in the royal menagerie, travelled along the vine slowly, one paw at a time. By the time he reached the halfway mark he had opened his eyes and was feeling positive that he was going to make it. What happened next happened so fast that Faustus couldn't even be shocked or horrified.

"I grew impatient," Tyrell admitted. "I was so desperate to see what was on the other side that I climbed up onto the vine. I barely made it a few steps before the vine snapped, plunging us both into the River Lac. It was a quick but stupid death," he added sadly.

"And that's why you don't want to go back to the jungle?" Scratch asked. When he got no reply he tried a different tack. "But what if that shiny object was the Collar of Honour?"

"Then we must go to the jungle."

Zakk's voice was so sudden that Scratch nearly jumped out of his seat. As it was he only just maintained hold of the reins. He did take a bit of pleasure that Zakk's sudden pronouncement had startled Tyrell so much that he was still shouting many unkingly words in his head.

"Did you hear him too?" Scratch asked Zakk, his breathing still coming in sharp gasps.

"Hmm," Zakk replied. "No, no, of course not, he's still a stowaway in your head but I heard you mention a shiny object in the jungle."

"He… He doesn't want to go," Scratch said sadly. "It's where he died." The last part was whispered.

"Fortunately," Zakk said cheerfully, "he doesn't get a vote. He is going where we are going. And what have I told you about being so squeamish about death, young Scratch? It comes to us all eventually. Just some animals…" Scratch wasn't sure but he felt that this last part wasn't being directed at him, "have the common courtesy to remain deceased."

Scratch winced slightly as Tyrell began shouting in his head once more.

"He says…"

Zakk didn't let him finish.

"I can imagine only too well what our former ruler is saying," he said, chuckling. "But to the jungle post haste, my young squire, the game is afoot." As if noticing him for the first time Zakk remembered they had another job to take care of first time. "After we drop Mr Harnny off first," he added.

As the caravan drove slowly through the warren Scratch noticed that the street cleared quickly for them, but rather than go about their usual business the rabbits started following the caravan. By the time they reached what could only be the town square they had amassed quite a following. They pulled up in front of the largest hill in which were set two enormous glass doors on which were carved various woodland scenes.

Without a word Zakk jumped down from the caravan.

"Ooooof," he said on landing. "I'm getting too old for that."

To Scratch's amazement a cheer went up from the assembled rabbits and Zakk was soon mobbed by happy, cheering rabbits. Before he could do anything to assist, the glass doors burst open to reveal a rabbit in a purple three-piece suit, complete with pocket watch and a ridiculous top hat which had to be twice as high as its wearer and kept slipping over his face.

"Sir Scratch," the hat seemed to say, "you have returned to us."

Zakk reached down and gently lifted the hat to see who was underneath.

"Is that you, Farnaby?" he asked incredulously. "They haven't made you Mayor surely? Or did you just steal his hat?" The assembled crowd and the Mayor all roared with laughter at this rather weak joke. Letting the laughter die down Zakk pulled himself up to his full height. "Sadly I bring bad tidings," he intoned ominously.

"Drunken old ham," Tyrell muttered sourly to himself.

"I have one of your missing citizens," Zakk continued, banging on the side of the caravan with a clenched paw.

Slowly, very slowly the pathetic figure of Harnny emerged. He dropped to the ground, refusing to look up.

"Harnny! Harnny!" A shrill female voice rang out from the crowd and an elderly rabbit with grey fur and thinning whiskers made her way through the ground towards the small huddled rabbit. "My boy," she shouted in clear relief, "you are safe, I was so scared, well, we both were."

As she spoke another female rabbit came forward. Far from relieved she looked on the verge of tears.

"Harnny?" she asked softly. "Where's Barnny? Where's my Barnny?"

Harnny looked over to Zakk who nodded at him encouragingly. Harnny stood up straight and wiped the tears forming in his eyes with the back of his paw. The entire courtyard stood silently as Harnny took her paws in his and in a voice barely above a whisper said, "I'm sorry, I'm so sorry."

The female collapsed into his arms wailing loudly. Without looking back or asking for permission Harnny guided her into the closest building which just happened to be the Mayor's office. The loud wailing died down a bit as they moved further into the building. Awkwardly the Mayor removed his hat in a sign of respect, only slightly ruined when the weight of it nearly pitched him forwards. Managing to right himself at the last moment the Mayor looked back at Zakk and said, "Thank you for bringing at least one of us back."

Zakk nodded.

"We have a code, you and I. You would do the same."

They nodded at each other.

To fill the awkward silence the Mayor clapped his paws together.

"A feast," he announced. "Sir Zakk has returned and we must have a feast."

Scratch jumped down when he heard this, feeling smug that his landing was far more graceful than his mentor's but not as well received, he noted.

"We can't stay," he blurted out, "for we are on a noble quest."

To his embarrassment the assembled rabbits all laughed loudly at this. In Scratch's opinion it went on for longer than necessary.

"Of course," the Mayor said grinning. "We know about you knights and your quests. I'm sure it's mighty and noble, like you say, but I'm likewais sure it can wait for now."

Scratch, red-faced with embarrassment, opened his mouth to speak but Zakk spoke for them both.

"Absolutely! Always time for a feast."

"Splendid," the Mayor replied, "and you both must stay with me."

With no further ado the Mayor turned to his aides (in reality two young males with clipboards) and proceeded to bark rapid instructions at them.

Feeling humiliated Scratch squared up to Zakk and hissed at him, "What was all that about? First the dogs and now this? We'll never get anywhere at this rate! And what was all that laughter about?"

Zakk smiled at his young apprentice.

"Dear boy," he said gently, "rabbits don't see any merit in questing. They think it ridiculous to leave a place they know just to go somewhere they don't to get something they haven't needed and probably never will. There's an old rabbit saying, 'There's no place to roam better than my home'."

"That's nonsense," Scratch said in disbelief. "Then why did we find Harnny and Barnny (at the mention of Barnny Scratch crossed himself) so far from home?"

"Occasionally," Zakk admitted, "some young males will convince themselves that there is a fortune to be had outside of the warren."

"Well, there is," Scratch countered hotly. "There's action and profit and wondrous adventure all over Venary."

"And how many famous rabbit explorers can you name?" Zakk asked gently.

Scratch thought to himself but none came to mind. Occasionally, when he thought he could get away with it, Scratch would sneak down to the massive library in the knights' castle and read the collected stories of former knights as they quested through Venary. Occasionally other species would be mentioned but Scratch realised now, that none of these had been rabbits.

Zakk smiled again.

"Rabbits don't make good adventurers," he said with a shrug. "However, they do make an excellent carrot wine I haven't had in so long that I've almost forgotten the taste."

Before Scratch could reply Zakk bounded off into the crowd that followed his every move. Scratch sighed deeply and went to look after the pack rats.

"Oh good, another drink," Tyrell said snarkily. "I'm sure that won't cause us any problems."

Scratch ignored him and led the pack rats to a barn he had spotted on the way into the warren.

The feast was a brightly coloured event. Several long wooden tables had been set up in rows across the courtyard and someone had strung brightly coloured bunting which ran from building to building, criss-crossing over the tables in a confusing pattern. Scratch walked along the tables until he came across two place settings. In a scrawl someone had written, "Sir Zakk: honoured guest" and on the other "Noble Quester: companion of Sir Zakk".

*Trust me to get a village of comedic bunnies*, Scratch thought to himself. He hadn't seen Zakk in a long while despite Tyrell's continued insistence that they keep an eye on him "to avoid a diplomatic incident at the very least. I wouldn't put it past that old soak to get drunk and start eating his hosts." Scratch didn't feel it was his place to check up on his master and had continually assured Tyrell that "Zakk is a knight and he won't do anything to break the code."

Taking his allotted seat Scratch watched the other guests arrive. It appeared as if the entire village had been invited. Still no sign of Zakk, however, or the Mayor now he came to think of it. His thoughts were interrupted by a fat rabbit in grubby chef's whites ladling steaming vegetables into a plain wooden bowl in front of him. Scratch was used to bad food. As a serf he would often be served nothing more than a thin meat paste but at least that was meat. He hoped they weren't staying here for an extended period.

"I fear that may be a forlorn hope," a familiar voice said mockingly.

"What do you mean?" Scratch asked, feeling both bored and annoyed by Tyrell's continual presence.

"Looks like our merry leader has fully embraced his diplomatic responsibilities." Scratch had no idea what he was talking about but had come to realise that Tyrell would eventually answer his own questions before too long. "Take a look to our right."

Reluctantly Scratch turned to the right. At first he couldn't see anything but then he spotted them: Zakk and his friend the Mayor were sitting on a bench at the far end of the town square. Zakk was waving his arms around as if conducting an invisible orchestra; the Mayor was trying to follow the movements with his eyes but eventually fell off the bench. The two friends laughed uproariously at this. Scratch noticed that placed at their feet were several metal bottles with a thick orange crust around the neck of each one, the same orange crust which Scratch noticed had stained the fur of both Zakk and the Mayor.

"I'm no expert…" Tyrell began and Scratch knew that he

was grinning, "but the knights' code has changed somewhat since my day."

Without saying a word Scratch threw down his wooden cutlery and, not caring if it was rude, he pushed away his uneaten bowl of vegetables and stalked furiously back to the caravan.

Scratch was still in a foul mood when he woke up the next morning. His journey back to the caravan had done nothing to improve his evening. Every rabbit he encountered had grinned at him and bowed low, calling him "Bold Adventurer", so muttering darkly under his breath a hungry and fed-up Scratch tried to get some sleep. He was refilling the pack rats' water trough when two rabbits approached him. Between them they were carrying the unconscious form of Zakk and were clearly struggling under the weight.

"Arrgh…" the one on the left with blue fur and an unfortunate patch of white shaped like a heart just above his nose exclaimed with feeling. "Where can we put Sir Zakk?"

His partner, a smaller rabbit with bright red fur, was struggling on the other side so was unable to say anything. He was, however, breathing hard.

"The water trough would be my suggestion, preferably with as much soap as can be found," Tyrell suggested.

Despite himself Scratch smiled but decided better of it.

"Prop him up against the caravan, in the shade," he instructed.

Grunting with the effort the rabbits dragged Zakk to the caravan and dropped him as delicately as they could (that is to say not very) in the shade. After the rabbits had limped off, both rubbing the small of their backs, Scratch got a cup of fresh water and went to see what sort of state Zakk was in. The smell was incredible. Perhaps Tyrell had been right when he suggested dunking Zakk in the trough. He hadn't smelt that badly since the first time they met and then Zakk had been sitting drinking in quarters for a long time. This was the result of one night.

"What on Venary is in that carrot wine?" he muttered to himself.

"Apart from carrots you mean?" Tyrell asked unhelpfully.

Zakk's face was almost completely stained orange. It took Scratch five cups of water and a lot of scrubbing to get Zakk's fur back to normal. Zakk didn't wake up once during this and Scratch was starting to worry that he never would. As he worked he noticed that Zakk had seemingly got much older since their first meeting. Guilt washed over Scratch. *I shouldn't have let him talk me into this quest*, he reflected.

"He wouldn't have appreciated that," Tyrell said softly.

"Can't you just for once stay out of my head?"

Scratch was embarrassed but for the first time Tyrell chose not to mock him.

"He's a knight. Questing is the life he chose and it's clear to see that he thinks the world of you. You could learn from him…" Scratch was momentarily taken aback by this sudden kindness. "Both good and bad things," Tyrell added.

Scratch rolled his eyes and turned his attention to the condition of Zakk's tunic. *It might be easier to burn it*, he reflected. *I think there's another tunic packed away somewhere*, he thought to himself.

"How well did you know your father, Scratch?" Tyrell asked out of nowhere.

Shocked, Scratch froze.

"I'm an orphan," he said quietly. "I was left outside of the Felix Regalis compound and they took me in."

"So it was the kindness they showed you that made you want to be a knight?"

Tyrell was surprised at the response this provoked. Scratch laughed, quietly at first but it got louder and louder, stopping abruptly with a snort.

"Not kindness then?" Tyrell asked.

"Why are you asking?" Scratch asked, confused. "You have access to my memories, don't you?"

"Not all of them," Tyrell admitted. "I know your name and your desire to be a knight is so strong it covers almost everything else. I tried digging deeper," he admitted, and Scratch wasn't sure what he thought of that, "but I couldn't get past the knight stuff. It's like your desire is guarding everything else."

"What does that even mean?" Scratch asked, uncomfortable that Tyrell had tried so hard to see his memories.

"I mean," Tyrell admitted quietly, "that I would like to start our relationship over again. It hasn't been easy for me, you know. My father was and is responsible for a lot of suffering and if I'm being honest every time I have tried to fix the mess I have only made it worse. I don't even know why I'm here." Once he started his confession Tyrell found that he was unable to stop. "I don't think for one moment that my father's wish to return involved me. The last thing I remember was falling into the River Lac and then I was floating above what used to be a very nice throne room."

"But why did you pick me?" Scratch asked.

He had been wondering about that for a while. Secretly he feared that it was because he was so weak and easy to beat. Even that greasy crow Crasis managed to knock him out.

"I found two unconscious bodies when I looked into the mind of a female crow but it was like a maze in there, so many plans. If you ever see her again be very wary of her. There was a sense of power but you only had noble beliefs and I thought…" Tyrell sounded embarrassed; he took a deep yet entirely unnecessary deep breath, "I thought I could trust you," he admitted.

"But you've been so nasty to us," Scratch said. "Why didn't you just ask for our help?"

"I was a king albeit briefly. I'm not used to asking for things. I'm asking now though. Will you help me?"

He sounded so genuine that Scratch felt guilty about some of the thoughts he'd had about him.

"Of course we will help you," he replied.

The moment was broken by a sudden grunt from the slumbering Zakk.

"Snnrk… A knight must always offer help whenever able."

Scratch waited for more but it must have been a reflex as Zakk was sound asleep.

Zakk didn't wake until the next morning. If he felt any ill effects from the carrot wine he didn't show it, apart from a slight tremble in his paws as he took the reins.

"Next stop the jungle," he announced jovially. He looked over at Scratch who had been practising with his sword, much to the amusement of the onlooking rabbits. "That is," Zakk added with a smile, "if our royal guest approves, obviously."

Scratch performed a final parry and deftly slipped the sword back into his belt.

"Leave him alone," he snapped back. "We need somebody to take this mission seriously."

Zakk raised an eyebrow in surprise but before he could respond Scratch hopped into the back of the cart and busied himself with checking the supplies.

They travelled in an uncomfortable silence. For a while Zakk called out facts about the scenery they were passing but apart from the occasional grunt Scratch refused to engage. They felt the jungle before they saw it. It was like a wall of heat.

"It's like the air is trying to kill me," Scratch spluttered.

"Make sure you have plenty of water when we disembark," Zakk advised.

"Really?" Scratch replied. "I didn't think you had much use for the stuff."

"Now, listen here…" Zakk growled but before he got further Scratch grabbed a canteen of fresh water and jumped off the still moving caravan.

He landed on all fours in a foul-smelling puddle. Letting out a hiss of frustration he jumped so high he nearly became tangled in the overhanging canopy of vines. Landing for a second time, thankfully on a dry patch of the jungle floor, Scratch shook out his sopping wet paws.

"Tyrell," he enquired, "do you remember where that rock pile was?"

Before Tyrell could answer Scratch felt something slap the back of his head. Furious, he spun around and grabbed at his sword. Sadly, he fumbled the grab and took hold of his belt with such force that he pulled himself off the ground, landing painfully on his shoulder. Before he could rectify himself again he felt a pair of rough hands pull him to his feet. Scratch then found himself face to face with a scowling Zakk.

"I cannot begin to fathom what has possessed you today, Scratch, but you do not leave my side," he shouted.

Scratch was momentarily stunned. Zakk had never before raised his voice but he was angry too.

"But you can leave mine?" he shouted back. "If you hadn't insisted on getting that bag back we could still be travelling with Altheus but no! You had to get your wine back. If you hadn't drunk so much in Aridier the dogs would never have captured us." He knew he should stop this but once he started he found that he couldn't. "We didn't have to stay at the rabbit village but you had to get your fill of carrot wine, never mind how long it took you to recover. Tyrell was right about you! You are just an old soak! No wonder Oscar gave me to you, he was probably hoping that I'd be poisoned by the constant stench of alcohol on your breath!"

This last bit had been delivered at top volume and Scratch was breathing heavily. Zakk just stood there frozen by shock. He hadn't even put Scratch back on the ground. This shock turned to horror when he heard a familiar whiny voice.

"Well, well, well, thunder in paradise?" This question was punctuated by a nasal snigger.

Both Scratch and Zakk turned their heads towards the voice. Scratch felt his blood run cold when he saw who was there. His fur was badly burnt and his tail broken but despite this Scratch would always recognise Mittens.

"Surprised to see me?" Mittens asked, the remains of his tail clicking audibly with each swish it made. "We came round just before the fires totally consumed us but not without injury, as you can see." Mittens was angry now. "LOOK AT ME!" he yelled, running up to the still shocked Zakk and Scratch who recoiled in horror at the condition Mittens was in. "Do you know what happened to the rest of the order?" Mittens asked, suddenly calm.

"Be careful, Scratch," Tyrell cautioned. "I don't know your history with this Felixian but I fear that more than just his tail has snapped."

"Mittens," Zakk said jovially. If he was trying to defuse the tension it didn't work.

"I have no interest in you," Mittens sneered, "I'm here for the wimp."

He pointed a scorched paw at Scratch who tried to stare him down but in his current predicament, the tips of his paws just brushing the floor, felt that it didn't inspire the fear he hoped it would.

"Dead," Mittens spat at Scratch's feet, "the Knights of Felix Regalis are dead!"

"Then we should work together," Zakk said, realising that he was still holding up Scratch, and returned him to the ground.

"NO!" Mittens screamed. "I have something quite different planned for you." Looking behind himself Mittens simply said, "Now." At this command a huge fearsome figure emerged from behind a big tree. The figure was almost completely hairless and hideous burns pitted its flesh. It raised its paws high in the air, revealing dirty but incredibly sharp claws. "You remember Moglox?" Mittens asked triumphantly. "He certainly remembers you."

Before Zakk could react Moglox charged into him, knocking him cleanly off his feet. So powerful was the charge that Zakk and Moglox disappeared from view entirely, but the horrible sounds of a vicious fight echoed throughout the jungle.

Scratch dropped to all fours and leapt in the direction he thought the fight was coming from.

"DUCK!" Tyrell yelled.

Scratch was surprised but his instincts took over and he threw himself to the ground just as Mittens flew overhead, snarling and shouting threats at him as he went. Scratch jumped back to his feet just in time to see M

ittens land on all four paws and charge back towards him. Scratch only had enough time to raise his paws in defence as Mittens laid into him. Scratch howled in pain as Mittens bit into his cheek, pulling back with a spurt of blood as he tore a chunk of skin from Scratch's face. Scratch barely had time to scream in pain as Mittens slashed at him with razor-sharp claws. Luckily Scratch was wearing a thick tunic so Mittens only just grazed his chest.

"Roll to your right," Tyrell screamed and Scratch, grateful for the distraction from the pain, rolled to the right just as Mittens slammed a rock into the space which until just that moment had been occupied by Scratch's head. Howling in frustration Mittens once again leapt at the retreating Scratch.

"Draw your weapon!" Tyrell instructed urgently. "Come on, Scratch, it can't end here."

Scratch was suffering now. The combination of the oppressive heat and the blood loss he had suffered was making him woozy but luck was on his side as his paw found the hilt of his sword, and in one fluid movement he drew it. Breathing heavily, he held the blade out in front of him, staring down the charging Mittens who by now was foaming at the mouth.

"I'm going to rip you apart, Sniffsunn!" he cried out as he closed the gap between them. Scratch said nothing, planting his paws firmly in the ground. "You've always been a coward, Sniffsunn," Mittens taunted as with surprising speed he kicked Scratch square in the stomach. It was incredibly painful but Scratch didn't drop, instead he slashed at Mittens' leg, taking pleasure in the howl of pain that elicited.

Mittens was just snarling now, his eyes bulging with ill-concealed hatred as he launched at Scratch again, nimbly dodging the blade Scratch thrust at him, catching his opponent under the chin. Scratch felt his head snap back, adrenaline coursing through him so fast that he felt no pain despite hearing something crack in his jaw. He jabbed wildly with the sword but it passed harmlessly through empty space. It was then that Mittens appeared to be everywhere at once as he filled Scratch's vision, completely knocking him once more to the ground. Scratch grunted in pain as he hit the ground loudly. Before he could right himself he felt Mittens leap on top of him, his paws wrapping themselves tightly around Scratch's throat, claws piercing his throat. In shock Scratch dropped his sword, which clattered to the ground and rolled out of reach. Scratch forced himself to focus on what was happening but all he could see was the maniacally grinning face of Mittens directly above him. He tried fruitlessly to raise himself, which just made Mittens grip his throat even tighter and with an evil grin he spat in Scratch's pale face. His vision was fading now. This was it.

"SCRATCH!" Tyrell yelled as loud as he could. "Just tighten your right paw, COME ON!"

"Be quiet," Scratch tried to yell back but he had no breath to speak. It would be so simple to just give up.

"SCRATCH, I ORDER YOU TO JUST GRAB WITH YOUR RIGHT PAW."

With annoyance Scratch tightened his paw and discovered that he was now gripping a rock. Automatically and with the last vestige of his strength Scratch slammed the rock into Mittens' head. The effect was immediate. The pressure on his neck lessened and as Scratch greedily sucked mouthfuls of air into his burned ruined and very painful throat he noticed that there was a dead weight on top of him. Pushing the unmoving body of Mittens off himself Scratch unsteadily returned to his feet. He could feel blood trickling from the puncture wounds on his throat but he had been beaten up enough times to know that they weren't serious. Still breathing heavily, he scrabbled about on the jungle floor until he found his sword. He was very disorientated and his body was screaming at him to rest. Well, not all of his body, a familiar voice was shouting inside his head, "Scratch! Stay upright, it isn't safe, you must keep moving."

Scratch couldn't focus, he just wanted to rest. His breath slowly returned to normal and he became aware of his surroundings. He had rolled quite some distance and had lost his bearings. Looking at Mittens he saw a nasty wound on the side of his head. Moving to check for a pulse Scratch jumped as he heard a loud roar from very nearby.

"Zakk!" he called out suddenly, and drawing on reserves of energy he ran off in the direction of that terrifying roar.

It wasn't difficult to find Zakk and Moglox, there was a path of destruction leading the way. Bursting through a canopy of vines Scratch came upon a horrifying sight. He was in a clearing and rolling around in bloodstained sand were Zakk and Moglox. Scratch was frozen in shock as he watched Zakk move at a speed a Felixian of that age and size shouldn't have been capable of. He kept jabbing at Moglox's side with a small dagger, causing blood to spurt out of the giant cat's side with every jab, but it seemed to be having no effect as Moglox used his teeth and claws to tear great wounds in Zakk's old body. Over and over they rolled.

"Do something!" Tyrell insisted.

"I can't get close enough," Scratch wailed.

"Do something!" Tyrell repeated with more urgency. "Can't you see what they're rolling towards?"

Scratch hadn't paid much attention to where they were, his attention had been distracted by the horrifying fight taking place in front of him, but as he looked around he saw it. He was surprised that he hadn't noticed it before. Running through the clearing, making a deafening roar, was the powerful white foam of the River Lac. As soon as Scratch realised what that meant he noticed that Zakk and Moglox were rolling straight towards it. His body was screaming in agony as he leapt towards the bloodied forms of Zakk and Moglox but his legs gave way underneath him and once again he felt himself slam into the ground face first. He raised his head, spitting out dust and vine leaves just in time to see both combatants roll into the river with a mighty splash and almost immediately be sucked underneath the mighty currents and disappear immediately. Scratch tried to scream but the combination of shock and the pain from his wound overwhelmed him, and all he could do was silently mouth his horror as he finally gave in and passed out. The last thing he heard was Tyrell and he was surprised to hear that the old King was crying.

\* \* \*

At the other side of the jungle Crasis leapt suddenly at the sound of an almighty roar.

"What was that?" he shouted, unable to keep the fear out of his voice.

Altheus noticed that the bubble he had created to keep her trapped shimmered slightly at the reaction, disappearing but reappearing before she could do anything.

*Interesting*, she thought to herself. Out loud she said, "Could be anything, these jungles are vast and largely unexplored."

"Sh… Shut up," he replied, his old stammer coming back. Once again the bubble shimmered along with it.

"Surely with your great power you have nothing to fear?" Altheus cooed sweetly.

"Th… That's correct," Crasis spluttered. "With my powers and my staff I fear nothing."

Once again the bubble shimmered out of existence, longer this time, but maddeningly it returned before Altheus could react.

"Well," she goaded, "why don't you deal with it? If you can." She knew it was dangerous to goad him but she realised this could be her only chance.

"You think I… I can't," he screeched at her.

At this Altheus merely shrugged.

"R… Right." Crasis pointed the staff to an area of the foliage that had started to rustle violently. "I Crasis the all powerful…" Altheus rolled her eyes at this, "servant to the mighty Cragzac order you to…"

Whatever he intended this order to be Altheus would never know, as at that very moment a tangle of fur and claws came rolling out and knocked the stammering crow off his claws. Altheus was sure that she recognised part of the tangle but it rolled past her before she could react. She did notice the dropped staff, however. It lay on the jungle floor, furiously spitting red sparks. She reached out for it, the red sparks painfully burning her wings. As she went to lift it she found a weight on the other end.

"NOOO," Crasis screamed, clutching hold of the other end of the staff. "It's not fair," he shouted petulantly. "It's mine."

Altheus was surprised at the strength of the deranged Crasis. This coupled with the spitting and burning sparks meant that she was losing her grip. With a scream of triumph he pulled even harder.

Altheus could only gape in horror as the staff slipped out of her wings. This horror turned to shock as the victorious Crasis fell back with a mighty thump on the jungle floor, slamming the end of the staff he had been holding into his own face. Either through annoyance or just because it had been mishandled the staff fired a bright yellow light into Crasis' injured face with such force that he left the ground and was catapulted into the far distance, leaving the now calm staff behind him.

Altheus returned to her feet and using the staff as a crutch followed the path of destruction left by the tangle of fur and claws that had been the method of her salvation.

Staggering and wincing in pain as her burns continued to annoy her Altheus came upon a clearing. There was no sign of the violent tangle but when she spotted a familiar furry shape lying unconscious next to a flowing river of milk she rushed forwards, forgetting her pain. But was she too late?

# EPILOGUE

"HALT," THE BIZARRELY cheerful voice barked into the night. "Yes, halting now, halting is what you must do."

It was pitch black but the stranger could tell without a doubt who she was talking to.

"Colonel…" she said with trepidation, knowing how quickly he could turn, "I must see His Excellency."

"Sleeping," the Colonel snapped back. "Excellency sleeping, no wake, must not wake. Orders."

"Colonel!" the voice pressed a little harder. "I must speak with him."

"Morning time," the Colonel sang back. "Come back in the morning, nobody sees His Excellency when sleeping."

The figure stepped into the light seeping out of Sunole's tent so the Colonel could get a better view as she lowered the hood on her robe.

"Not even his daughter?" she asked.

"Little Lollie?" the Colonel asked, squinting to see her better. "LITTLE LOLLIE!" he shouted with delight. "It's you! It's you! Little Lollie come home!"

"Yes, Colonel," she said happily, "I have come home, I must speak to my father."

"Yes, yes, of course you must," the Colonel agreed. "I will wake him."

"You already have." Sunole sounded sleepy but if he was annoyed at being woken or happy at the return of his daughter he didn't show it. "Daughter!" he announced formally. "Do you have a report for me?"

"Father," she answered equally formally, "I do."

He said nothing, turning around and re-entering his tent. Stopping only to favour the Colonel with a smile Lollie followed him in.

He clambered up atop his throne of pillows, making a show of getting himself comfortable while she stood, her arms folded, waiting to see what he would do to show her who was boss.

"You're late," he said simply.

"My brief was somewhat vast, Father, you wanted details about a lot of beings."

"And yet I find myself still waiting. I will be most displeased if you have woken me for no good reason."

His eyes flashed at this and Lollie thought to herself, *There it is, my father's temper, always just under the surface.*

"Well?" he questioned. "Am I going to be disappointed?"

Lollie cleared her throat. "I got in touch with my contacts following your orders."

Sunole interrupted her with a long and loud yawn, stretching his stubby arms out as far as they would go.

"I know this," he sang out in boredom. He rolled onto his back and took a few rapid bites at the air. "I was the one who sent you, after all."

Lollie had a sudden image of herself tearing out his throat. Stifling a smile at the thought she tried once more to explain.

"I found my agents and collected some of the information you wanted."

"Get on with it," Sunole snapped. "I am aware that you consort with rats in all the major cities so do stop dressing it up."

"Fair enough," Lollie replied through gritted teeth. "His Majesty King Hirax is possessed by the ghost of his grandfather King Faustus... ow!" She growled with a mixture of pain and annoyance as a stone thrown by her father bounced off her chest.

"I KNOW THAT!" Sunole screamed at her.

"But what you don't know," she spat back at him, no longer trying to remain calm, "is that the Pacidermian Lex is in league with them."

For the first time Sunole seemed vaguely interested.

"The Pacidermians have been looking for allies to fight their silly little war for ages now. I wouldn't have thought that even Faustus would involve himself in that."

"That's not all," Lollie continued. "My sources..." when she said "sources" Sunole started making squeaking noises much to his own amusement, "my sources tell me that the King has taken ill."

"Interesting," Sunole said, stroking his chin. "But he is not the only one seeking the Collar of Honour. What else did you find out?"

Lollie reached into her pocket and delicately brought out a grinning shrew.

"The hedgehog Greeta is in a relationship with the

High Priestess of the moles." Lollie sneered as she saw the rapacious grin spread across her father's face. "With her help the moles have resurrected that oversized rabbit creature they call their Saviour."

Sunole leapt up.

"That thing is back?" he asked suddenly.

"Well," Lollie answered, "back in body, not in mind. It was last seen running through the forest wailing."

Sunole chuckled at this.

"You understand now why I never let you join the church?" he asked. "Your mother…" Lollie detected a slight twitch under his eye when he said "mother" but wisely chose not to pursue it, "was insistent that you join. That was before the divorce though," he added nastily. "So, we have a brainless giant rabbit in Venary?" he asked. "With any luck it will run into the sea. In any case it doesn't concern us, yet. What else?"

"The Giraxians have been spotted in the wastelands."

"Well," Sunole mused, "with any luck Felix will keep them occupied. Is there any news of my champions?"

He tried to sound casual but Lollie saw through this.

"Bad news, Father."

He growled deeply and Lollie took an involuntary step backwards.

"The old knight Zakk has fallen into the River Lac and is believed dead. His young apprentice has been reunited with the crow Altheus but they are no closer to finding the Collar of Honour."

Sunole leapt down from his cushions and began to pace back and forth.

"Looks like we'll have to get creative," he said eventually.

THE ADVENTURE CONTINUES IN:

THE COLLAR OF HONOUR 2
THE SINS OF THE FATHER